CW01499192

EIN

I

THEY PASSED HWITEBI at dusk.

Not that there was much point in hiding their arrival: this visit was intended not so much as a raid, more as an encouragement to the grateful locals to remember they owed their allegiance to Thorfinn Sigurdarson, Earl of Caithness and Orkney. So far from Orkney, they had a tendency to forgetfulness, which even the stones of the abbey on the cliff, ruined conclusively by the Danes two hundred years ago, could not wipe out. Now there was talk of building a new abbey. Ketil offered up a prayer for their success, as he pulled his oar on the longship, slipping quiet up the deep river inlet with the others. On either side, the steep dark green of the hillside was pricked with points of light: the few households left here from that proud settlement around the monastery were bedding in for the night. Soon they themselves would be in camp, too, longships cooped on a beach, oars shipped, fires lit, tents up against the persistent rain. Ketil sighed. His cloak was twice its normal weight and dripping, and his boots felt as though he had waded from Trondheim. A cup of hot wine would have gone down very well. It was a shame they had forgotten to restock as they travelled down the Scottish coast.

As it turned out, it was just as well they were not fuddled with wine. The attack came at the darkest hour of the night, just when they were sinking into sleep and the sentries were relaxing. Heavy treads, clunk of metal on wood, breathless whispers: Ketil was awake instantly, hand on his sword, out of the tent before he knew what he was doing. Three shiploads of mixed Scots and Norse, tired from long journeying, were still ready for action. How many there were in the attacking band it was hard to tell.

Helpfully, someone tried to torch one of the tents, but the linen was too wet to take and a plume of choking smoke swirled through the rain. Figures ran in confusion between the tents and the ships. Blades collided more by chance than by design. Grunts and oaths pattered the air. The cooking fires had been damped down – not quite enough, it turned out. One man screamed as he stepped back into hot ashes.

Then there was a flare of sparks and someone did manage to light a torch. For a moment everyone was dazzled, the bright light scouring patterns on their eyes. But another was lit from it, and soon they could see the attackers, big, angry-looking men with heavy weapons. Not many of them, though: perhaps twenty. What had they been thinking of?

The skirmish lasted less than an hour, before the attackers, realising their error, scrambled off into the night to lick their wounds. Ketil and the other two captains calmed everyone down, sorted out their own injured men, considered the damaged tents and rearranged the camp. There were no bodies, their own men or the attackers'. Ketil was just rubbing a weary hand over his short-cropped head when one of his men shouted,

'Bastards! They've nicked my good silver cup! It was sitting on my bed roll!'

'Not the brightest of places to leave it, though,' Ketil remarked. The man shrugged.

'In case I was thirsty in the night.'

'Trust you, Skorri. Anyone else would make do with wood.'

'Aye, it's your own fault, Skorri.' Lambi, a big easy man, joined in. 'Your standards are just too high for a fighting man, eh?'

The rest of the men laughed, used to teasing Skorri and his fine ways.

'Lambi, you were in the tent that was torched, weren't you?' said Ketil. 'Have you somewhere else to sleep?'

'Aye, but my bags are still in there.'

'Let's give you a hand, then. Come on, Skorri, stop moaning and help.'

Ketil held the smouldering linen up while the others ducked under and started retrieving Lambi's scattered belongings. Lambi

A Wolf at the Gate

The Second
in the
Orkneyinga Murders series

Lexie Conyngham

First published in 2019 by The Kellas Cat Press, Aberdeen.

ISBN: 978-1-910926-53-6

Cover design by Helen Braid at www.ellieallatsea.co.uk

With so many thanks to Bryony, Jill, Kath and Nanisa, and greetings to Indra and Zorro, the real wolves at the gate.

Cast of characters:

The Household and Men of Earl Thorfinn Sigurdarson:
Ingibjorg, his wife
Asgerdr, his daughter
Tosti, a priest
Ketil Gunnarson
          His man Lambi
Hakon Hakonson
Aud
Skafti

Thorfinn's visitors:
Abbot Konrad of Colonia
Otto, his manservant

The household of Asmund, boat counter:
Olvor, his wife
Sigrid, a visitor

The household of Ubbi, farmer:
Steinar Valison, his brother-in-law
Svanhild, his sister
Thorgunna, his wife
Freya, Steinar's dog

On Einar's lands:
Oddr, Einar's man
Helga, not Einar's woman
Gnup, servant to Sigrid

Sorli, on his own by choice, a combmaker

leaned forward to direct them, something clunked dully, and Skorri gave a cry.

'My cup!'

'Where?'

'It fell out of Lambi's cloak!'

'What?'

Somehow, all the men were on their feet. Lambi looked around them, laughing.

'What, do you think I stole it? Don't be daft!' There was no response. The men had circled him, not too close, but certainly close enough to prevent him from running. He laughed again, less sure of himself now. 'Whoever took it must have been the one who torched the tent, and it fell down there with my stuff. Why would I take it?'

The silence was wordy. The men were woven tight together, like any fighting band: theft amongst them would not be tolerated. And for some reason, they were ready not to trust Lambi.

'Right, it's the middle of the night, and we're tired. We'll deal with this in the morning,' said Ketil. 'Lambi, you're in my tent. The rest of you, find your spaces and get to sleep. Skorri, sentry. Put your cup somewhere safe.'

Lambi, his shoulders defiant, marched off to Ketil's tent. When Ketil followed, he drew breath to say something, but Ketil raised a hand for silence, and went to bed.

Next morning, though, there was little time to deal with such matters. The sentry who was on duty at dawn cried out at the sight of a small ship approaching up the river. Wary after last night's attack, they slipped, armed, from their tents, wiping sleep from their eyes as they peered into the morning mist. The little ship, quick and light, was easily beached and a young man leapt from the prow, showed he had no hands on his weapons, and walked up to the men in the camp.

'Are you Thorfinn Sigurdarson's men?' he asked.

'That's right,' said one of the other captains. 'What do you seek?'

'I seek Ketil Gunnarson,' said the man.

'I'm Ketil.' He raised his hand, but did not step forward. That was the kind of move that could result in too close an acquaintance with an arrow, particularly here under high banks. Not that he could think of anyone who would specifically like him dead, but a life raiding made you cautious.

'I have a message from Thorfinn,' said the man. Ketil glanced at the messenger's companions at the boat, who looked merely bored. He walked over to the man.

'What is it?'

'He says,' and the young man half-closed his eyes, calling to mind Thorfinn's words. 'He says he has two men come from Colonia to help him with – er, laws and things, and he wants you to come and assist, as you're acquainted with one of the men.'

'I am?' asked Ketil. 'I don't know anyone from Colonia. Who are they?'

'An abbot called Konrad, very grand, very important!' The young man's eyes widened at the memory. 'And his servant and a kind of bodyguard.'

'I certainly do not have the honour of knowing any abbots,' said Ketil thoughtfully. 'Nor indeed their servants. How soon does he need me? I take it he's in Caithness, is he?'

'He says to come straightaway – I'm to take you back. It's a good ship, fast, though it's small,' said the young man, eager to help. 'But no, he's not in Caithness. He's back at Birsay. In Orkney, you know.'

'Oh, I know,' said Ketil. He sighed. Orkney again. But at least this time he had a friend there. He thought so, anyway.

He turned back to the camp and his men, surveying them. Most of them had heard the exchange.

'Right,' he said. 'Skorri, you're in charge of our lot, and don't let yourself be distracted by finery. First job is to look over that burned tent and see if it can be mended. I'm off to Orkney.'

'What about Lambi?' asked Skorri, hopeful. Would the putative thief be left to his mercies? Ketil turned a cold blue gaze on Lambi's hapless bulk.

'Lambi,' he said, 'is coming to Orkney too.'

The journey to Orkney was going to take several days. For the first day, Ketil took his turn at the oars and made sure Lambi was working while he was resting. The rounded Icelander was new to his band, collected somewhere in Caithness after a couple of

well-lubricated nights playing King's Table in someone's hall.
Ketil watched surreptitiously as the man threw himself into rowing
with apparent content. His hair was contained, mostly, by a tight
woolly cap, though the random directions of the locks that escaped,
like eels desperate to leave a basket, seemed likely to push it off.
His beard was equally ebullient: Ketil had seen Lambi comb both
hair and beard without any obvious improvement. Light blue eyes
slid easily away from meeting anyone else's gaze, and his wide
mouth was always ready to laugh. Ketil had thought him popular
enough, but that morning by Hwitebi the others had been very
ready to condemn him. If he had had time, he would have made
closer enquiries, sorted the matter out properly to his own
satisfaction, at least. He preferred his men to be happy in their
work and in each other's company.

The coast was busy, lively with fishing boats and trading
kvarrs taking advantage of the summer weather to make their
journeys. The boats skimmed south on the current or laboured
north, like them, keeping the land in sight. They made good time,
browning in the sunshine, dipping in to land at night and camp
near the ship, still warm from their work and the sun. When low
islands appeared in the distance, the helmsman directed them to the
sea side of them instead of skipping in between them and the land:
Ketil knew this was the usual course, and knew as well that just
beyond they would see Holy Island, where the Danes had wreaked
such destruction so long ago. He lifted a hand from the oar to touch
the cross at his throat. Such things would not happen under
Thorfinn's rule, anyway, tentative though it might be, this far
south. Thorfinn was powerful, and now, at least, actively Christian.

They made good progress: the days were long, the rowers
fit, and the good light allowed them to keep well out from the coast
and catch steadier winds, when they were lucky enough to have
them blow in the right direction. The Scottish coast appeared, and
the mouths of the great firths, Forth, Tay, Moray. They skipped
from headland to headland at the outlets of each, camped on a
beach in Fife, on another somewhere north of the Dee, guards alert
though there was no trouble. Then they rounded the topknot of
Caithness, tucked themselves between the land and the bump that
was the Isle of Stroma, skirted the tumbling rocks of the Men of
Mey, passed ancient cairns and stone huts on the cliffs and rested

at last on an east-facing beach where they lit fires and cooked a good meal. Before they retired for the night, the men considered the wind and tides, compared notes, and examined the clouds at sunset, stripes of blended purple, turquoise, aquamarine, butter yellow. The islands they were making for bulged dark on the horizon, and the men nodded their satisfaction. Next morning, with the tide just past the slack, they slid the ship back into the waters where it belonged, and took the plunge across the Pentland Firth. The wind was next to useless, coming as it did at this time of year from the south west, but the oarsmen had had a rest and were strong still. They were up to any oddities of current or leftover curls of wind, and had done this many times before. They were in safe hands.

They slid around the south of Hoy around midday, close enough almost to smell the cooking fire smoke from the longhouses at Rackvig. Half a dozen arrow-winged terns angled over the ship, indecisive, then away. The high-peaked north of the island was behind them even as Caithness was still in sight, and Ketil bade goodbye to anything like a mountain for the rest of his stay. Ahead they could see the low sprawl of the mainland, the cluster of boats around the comfortable harbour at Hamnavoe, curled into its bay. But they passed it by, and were able for a little to take respite with the sail. Lambi, eyes darting sideways, came to sit by Ketil and stare at the green land they were passing, the sea dark and glittering around the churn of their racing prow.

'Been here before?' Ketil asked.

Lambi shook his head, clearly relieved that Ketil was talking to him.

'Never. Looks good land.'

Ketil nodded briefly.

'So all this is Thorfinn's?'

'Yes.' For the moment. The phrase came unbidden to his mind. The land was all Thorfinn's, hard fought over and hard won. Ketil thought about the band that had attacked them in the night by Hwitebi. If Thorfinn weakened, how long would his lands stay together?

'But Thorfinn's not biding at that nice wee harbour?'

'No, he's probably at Birsay, at his hall. Up the coast here, on a headland sticking out into the sea. There's a harbour there.'

'And that's where he bides? With his family and all?'

'Yes.'

'I hear his daughter's a bit that's worth looking at!'

Ketil gave him a look that subdued him a little. Asgerdr was definitely worth looking at, but Ketil had not given her more than a passing thought since he had last seen her. He had had other things on his mind.

'She's a handsome woman. No doubt Thorfinn has a good match in mind for her.'

'You've no a wife yourself, then?' Lambi persisted.

'No.'

'Aye, well, it's best to be footloose, eh? See me, I think roots are over-rated. Have a bit of fun with this one, move on to the next one before it gets boring, eh? That's the thing, in my view.'

'You're from Iceland, yes?'

'Aye, that's right. Moved on from there, too!'

Ketil looked away from the unsteady eyes, back to the land they were passing. Skaill, he thought – more longhouses, a nice little harbour. Had Lambi moved on of his own accord from Iceland? Or had he, perhaps, been exiled for some crime?

'Aye, too many laws in Iceland,' Lambi said, almost as if he had heard Ketil's thoughts. 'No freedom. Used to be the Thing passing sentences on you, now the church is taking control. Gets to be a man can't do anything without looking over his shoulder to see who's watching and clyping on him.'

Ketil gave a little nod, as if agreeing, though he was really agreeing with his own assessment. Exile, probably for theft. Lambi would need an eye kept on him here, too.

The whole crew and passengers hauled the ship on rollers up on to the beach under the headland of the Brough, the tongue of land, high by Orkney standards, poking out into the eastern sea. The messenger, brushing salt from his fair face, gathered them under his wing, and guided them towards the broad path that led up to the buildings on the Brough. Ketil, giving the gunwale of the ship a grateful pat, squinted upwards to see how Thorfinn's settlement looked from here: the building work seemed to be unfinished. He could just see what seemed to be frames of new longhouses, lined up towards the grazing land at the top of the Brough. Ketil had been away for over a year, but Thorfinn's building plans were ambitious.

They stepped out of the shelter of the gateway, and the wind caught them briskly, shaking out their cloaks and slapping their faces into alertness. Lambi's helpless hair flapped back and forth under his woollen cap. From here Ketil could see more clearly that the monastic buildings, a hole in the ground when he had last been here, were roofed now, with smoke coming from the hole under the turf ridge. He was not expecting such progress, with building no doubt having been halted for the winter. He shivered, looking up at the site past the church. That had not been a good night.

He turned his attention to the more commonplace arrangements around him: bath houses, smithy, brewery, kitchens, sitting a little apart from the hall and longhouses to lessen the risk of fire. All seemed complete, now: slabs of the local flat stone covered neat lines of drains, and he could feel warmth coming from the bath house and hear lazy conversation mumbled inside, even though it was not Saturday bath day.

Thorfinn's hall, however, was much as he remembered it. The messenger who had brought him from Hwitebi bustled in importantly in front of him, making sure that Thorfinn knew Ketil had not arrived by chance, that he had done his job as directed. Ketil allowed him his moment of justification, taking in the others in the hall.

Thorfinn Sigurdarson, stocky, dark, the focus of attention without even trying, had been standing at a table, talking with the little priest Tosti and with a tall man in monk's robes, a man somehow imposing even from behind. Tosti, his face anxious, seemed to be acting as interpreter, to judge by the sway of the conversation and the tilt of the other men's heads towards him. Beyond them, in the dim corner of the hall behind the high chair, Ketil caught a flash of almost white fair hair – Thorfinn's daughter Asgerdr, hips jutting, hands behind her slim back, elaborately-braided head attentively on one side, listening to the man standing a little too close to her, his back to the door and to Ketil. He was not immediately familiar. Were these Thorfinn's visitors, the new advisors? Advice could take a while, filtered through even the cleverest of translators. But if they had come from Colonia, they would hardly speak much Norse. Perhaps Asgerdr was helping.

The messenger bravely interrupted Thorfinn's conversation, standing politely but obviously by Thorfinn's elbow. Tosti finished a sentence, saw Ketil, and grinned. Thorfinn turned, and muttered an excuse to Tosti and the monk.

'Ketil! You've arrived, good. This your man?'

Standing lumpy just behind him, Lambi nodded eagerly.

'Lambi, my lord. One of my soldiers.' Ketil kept his voice expressionless, not wishing to appear to recommend someone over whom he had doubts.

'Better fated than the last to come to these shores, I hope. Welcome, Lambi. Ketil, I'll present you to our visitors. Father Tosti, can you help?'

The little priest came round the table with both hands held out to take Ketil's own.

'It's good to see you, my friend! God must have blessed you while you were away – you seem whole and healthy!'

'Healthier than when I last left these shores, certainly,' said Ketil, unable to help smiling at the man. 'But I'm pleased to see you well preserved, too.'

'Oh, no time to be ill or injured!' said Tosti cheerfully, though a brief crease about his eyes hinted that perhaps he was kept a little too busy at present.

'When you're quite ready,' said Thorfinn pointedly. Ketil straightened, and allowed himself to be led over to the table. There was a lamp over it, and a quantity of papers on it with writing scattered like woodshavings over them. It meant nothing to Ketil, so he ignored it, and concentrated on the tall monk next to him.

Round black eyebrows arched over sharp, glittering eyes, questioning, glancing from Ketil to Thorfinn to Tosti, the one who would be able to answer the question. Tosti obliged, in what Ketil assumed was Latin – it had a flavour of the Mass about it.

'*Hic Ketil est, quem dominus Thorfinn advocavit ut nos adiuvet.* I'm saying Thorfinn's called you here to help us,' Tosti threw back to Ketil, half-including Thorfinn in the explanation.

'Only speaks Latin and German,' Thorfinn explained, with a tut, though he seemed in some awe of his guest.

'*Hic Konrad est* – oh, sorry,' said Tosti, blushing. 'This is Abbot Konrad, Ketil, from the court of the Archbishop of Colonia.'

'They have some interesting ideas about land taxation,' Thorfinn explained, though Ketil blinked in surprise. 'And coinage, too. I stayed there a little while on my way to Rome. Impressive.'

Ketil blinked again. Land taxation? Coinage? Truly, Thorfinn was abandoning the old ways. He bowed to Abbot Konrad, nevertheless. The monk inclined his head, a beatific smile on his lips – if perhaps not quite in his eyes – then turned back to the table.

'How can I be of assistance, my lord?' Ketil asked Thorfinn, trying not to show that he was genuinely baffled.

'Well, they'll need to go about a bit,' said Thorfinn, 'and I daresay you can show them the mainland, at least.'

'My lord ...'

Thorfinn shuffled his feet, in a most un-Thorfinn-like manner.

'And that man over there, making sheep's eyes at Asgerdr – my daughter, if you remember? He said he knew you well, and I thought, perhaps ... if you were here ...'

'He would find more useful things to do with his time, my lord?'

'Well, yes.' Thorfinn cleared his throat noisily.

The German gentleman must not be considered an appropriate match for Asgerdr – well, not by Thorfinn, anyway. Asgerdr seemed to approve, to judge by the way she was now fiddling with the end of one of her braids, a little smile teasing the edge of her mouth, her long lashes dark on the pale skin of her cheeks. Ketil suppressed a smile of his own. Asgerdr was an awful flirt.

'It can't be easy, though, with him speaking German,' he remarked, trying to comfort Thorfinn.

'Oh, he's not German. Hakon!' Thorfinn turned and bellowed the length of the hall, making the others jump. There was just a trace of rage in that shout, enough to make everyone turn and make sure they were not the ones transgressing. Hakon, though, finished what he was saying to Asgerdr, and turned to look back at Thorfinn. Smiling genially, he let his blue gaze pass over Thorfinn's head, dance briefly at Lambi, then land on Ketil.

'Ah, Ketil!' he said. 'At last – good to see you again!'

Ketil's blood, he found, had frozen in his veins.

'Hakon,' he managed, though his lips were wooden. 'It's you.'

TVEIR

II

HEAVENS, THOUGHT SIGRID: if she had to stay here another week with Olvor and her husband she would have to put an axe through both their heads, and then go and explain herself to Thorfinn. And she was fairly sure Thorfinn would understand.

'Look,' she said, then started again trying harder to keep the impatience from her voice. 'Look, these are the working loops here. That's where you have to put the nail through.'

She sat on her hand to stop herself snatching the wooden nail as Olvor, breathing heavily, hesitantly pushed it through the right loops, both of them, and for once, for a wonder, in the right direction. The top of her thumb was almost blue with the tight wool around the base of her nail.

'Now, pinch the nail in place, and swivel it back through this last tight loop, just where it twists ...' It was painful to watch. She had long ago – well, three days ago, just after she had arrived – given up wondering if Olvor was determined or just someone so unimaginative she could not think of doing anything other than what she was told. When Sigrid had asked Olvor if she had not been taught nailbinding and card-weaving by her own mother, Olvor just looked at her in silence, and Sigrid could have kicked herself. Olvor's mother, now dead, had been above all that kind of thing, and regarded her daughters only as quite well-dressed slaves. Woolwork was something you paid someone else to do – in her case, she had often paid Sigrid.

How Olvor had got through her first marriage without such skills was uncertain, but, widowed, she had recently married Asmund, who had no other women in his household and who needed someone who could run up hats and straps with ease. Olvor, to Sigrid's surprise, had come to her longhouse one morning and asked, very politely, if Sigrid would mind coming home with her to teach her. Olvor would give her her keep and a little over, Sigrid would be able to carry on with her own work at the same time, and she had a lad who helped her with her little farm and would delight in managing on his own for a few days. Sigrid had accepted.

No doubt the good Lord had intended Olvor for some useful purpose, but that purpose did not seem to be working with wool. Sigrid was nearing the stage where she would keep her own work well away from Olvor, just in case by her mere presence Olvor caused the whole thing to knot itself into an irredeemable tangle. She thought longingly of her own quiet longhouse, but she was not quite ready to give up yet. Well, not while Asmund was out, anyway.

Asmund, in Sigrid's admittedly uncharitable opinion, was a complete coal-eater, lazy as a cat and without any of the decorative qualities of one. He was not even good conversation. She heard his footstep at the door now and her heart sank. Olvor ripped the twists of wool from her fingers and abandoned them, hurrying over to the fire.

'Hello, Asmund!' Sigrid said cheerily, trying to sort out Olvor's work so that she could resume it later, or at least save the wool.

He grunted.

'You're still here?'

She forced herself to smile. She had decided yesterday that Asmund was not really hostile, just too lazy to bother with being polite. Asmund slapped water over his face at a barrel, and sat by the fire, staring at it. He said nothing to his wife.

'Have you had a good day?' Sigrid persisted. There was something about his silence that drove her to this over-bright chatter – stupid of her, she thought. She would be happy enough never to have a conversation with him. But Olvor's tension was infectious, and Sigrid had to talk her way past it.

'I went to the harbour,' said Asmund, the information positively flooding out.

'Oh, that must have been nice. Were there many boats in?'

He looked at her as if she had made some baffling connexion.

'There were fourteen boats, six big ones and eight small ones, and a kvarr on the water. One of the small boats belonged to the kvarr.'

'Busy, then! Did you go to look at the boats?'

'I went to buy a barrel.'

'Oh, good! Did you find one you liked?'

'No.'

'Was there any news?'

He seemed to think for a moment, poking the fire where Olvor was trying to arrange the cooking pots.

'What kind of news?' he asked at last.

'Just anything. Gossip. Word of new arrivals. Interesting things for sale from the kvarr. Anything.' She could hear desperation creeping into her voice. He considered.

'No.'

Sigrid gave up, and silence fell. She worked on on her own nailbinding, fine work for stockings for Thorfinn's wife, and out of the corner of her eye studied Asmund. He sat by the fire as though there were no life in him, mouth shut, eyelids heavy. He would have been a handsome enough man if he had ever smiled, she supposed. Olvor was pretty, with pale skin and dark hair and eyes, a delicate version of her striking mother, but the worried expression that had lived on her face all the time Sigrid had known her had not lessened since her marriage. Sigrid thought that Olvor's prettiness was probably irrelevant, unappreciated by Asmund. She and her young children had needed a protector, and Asmund, long unmarried and older by ten years at least, had needed a cook and woolworker. Thanks to Thorfinn, there had even been a bit of a dowry. Well, Olvor could cook, certainly, and she was safe here, if not obviously happy. More might come.

Olvor brought the meal to something quite near perfection, and handed dishes to her husband and Sigrid. When she had helped herself too, and sat back, she announced nervously,

'Ubbi and his family are coming this evening.' Her gaze lifted briefly to Asmund's face, then dropped again. Asmund sighed, reminding Sigrid of nothing so much as a spoiled child being asked to do something he didn't fancy.

'Why?'

'Because they're our neighbours, I suppose. He just said, or Thorgunna did. I'm not sure. It just happened!' There was a hint of tears in her words, but Asmund neither admonished her nor comforted her. Sigrid was not even sure he was angry. The trouble was, Olvor had been brought up to be defensive, to assume she was about to be told off. Sigrid, though she was not even family, felt like taking both of them and giving them a good talking to. Well, that might come, too.

They had hardly finished clearing up after their meal when there came a patter of knocks on the doorpost, and a friendly shout.

'Anybody at home?'

Olvor scrambled to her feet and went to fetch ale cups. Asmund stayed by the fire, and it was left to Sigrid, a guest herself, to stand and usher in two men and a large and initially ferocious-looking dog. She waved them towards Olvor to be greeted and given drinks. The dog began a snuffling tour of inspection. The first man, short and blond with a thick beard, inserted his slim form into a space at the fire, raising his cup to Asmund and grinning. Then he turned to Sigrid.

'Hallo,' he said comfortably, 'I'm Ubbi, from the next house. You're from up the hill, past Einar's place, aren't you? I've seen you around.'

'Sigrid,' she said, liking him at once – though it could have been the contrast with Olvor and Asmund. 'Yes, I'm down to stay for a few days to give Olvor a hand.'

'This is my sister's husband.' Ubbi waved the other man forward. 'Steinar, this is Sigrid from up the hill. Steinar's the clever one in the family!'

Steinar had a respectable, solid look about him, and smiled, too, as he greeted Sigrid. He seemed a little more reserved than his wife's brother, but pleasing, too, and the dog, inspection complete, kept close to him. The evening was beginning to look promising.

'The women are following,' Ubbi explained. 'One of the bairns was greeting. Teeth, Svanhild said,' he added knowledgeably.

'How are you, Asmund?' Steinar asked, settling himself between Sigrid and his host. 'Have you been to the harbour today?' Steinar was careful in his speech, and though both visitors were a good deal younger than Asmund, Sigrid had the impression that Steinar was in some way looking after Asmund, going gently with him, out of kindness rather than wariness. Asmund, casting an anxious eye at the dog, began to tell him about the boats he had counted, no more excited by them than he had been earlier. Steinar nodded with him.

'So what do you think of life down here?' Ubbi asked Sigrid. 'A bit less draughty?'

'Depends on the wind direction,' said Sigrid, unable to help smiling at his friendly face. 'Olvor and Asmund would be protected from the northerly winds, but just now it's all south westerlies. Straight in to the bay here!'

'I suppose you farm? Is your husband at home at the moment, or off on Thorfinn's business?'

Sigrid cleared her throat.

'My husband died last year. I've a boy looking after the farm. He's a good worker, very sensible. And I make braid and weaving, you know.' There was no harm in advertising her services, just in case he or his wife might fancy something new.

'Nice.' Ubbi nodded, and took a sip of ale. His right hand, Sigrid noticed, had only two fingers, yet it did not look like the result of a battle wound, or any kind of injury. She tried not to stare. Plenty of men here lacked fingers or ears, or even limbs. That was life.

There was more bustle at the door and this time Olvor was quicker to react, jumping up to greet two women, each carrying a small child bundled on her hip. The dog followed, quickly circling the women before settling again at Steinar's feet. The first woman was tall, stately almost, with a face that was handsome rather than pretty, serene in her expression. Sigrid noted her three strings of beads, currently being clutched by the baby. There were some particularly fine decorated glass beads, and some lovely amber, and her overdress was in a fine wool that was rarely seen around Birsay. And her figure set it off perfectly. Even the baby was clean, pink and delightful.

'My sister, Svanhild,' Ubbi explained, nodding to her. Sigrid was prepared to hate the woman from the start. 'And my wife, Thorgunna,' he added. Sigrid took her eyes from Svanhild and saw the woman behind her. Thorgunna immediately took more of her sympathy. The child on her hip, red-faced and smear-eyed, had rucked up her overdress and dribbled over her shoulder, then completed its work by tugging on her headcloth until it came half over her face, freeing a mop of unbrushed brown hair. Thorgunna plumped herself down with a sigh next to Ubbi, who gave her a hug. 'Has he stopped crying, then?'

The child turned to look at his father. His little red lips turned down, and he drew breath.

'Oh!' cried Thorgunna, looking as if she could have benefitted from several more hours' sleep at night. She spun the child expertly on to her lap, still bundled up, and slipped her little finger into that threatening mouth. The child, after a moment's consideration, decided to take what was offered, and sucked ferociously on the finger. Ubbi and Thorgunna exchanged relieved looks.

'Sorry,' said Thorgunna, leaning to look past her husband, 'he seems to have been greeting for a month! Teeth,' she added, sure Sigrid would know exactly what she meant. Sigrid nodded. 'How many do you have?'

'I had one,' said Sigrid, knowing that she did not mean teeth, 'but he died.'

'Oh.' Thorgunna gave her boy a little hug. 'I'm sorry.' She gave it a moment. 'I didn't catch your name?'

'I'm Sigrid, from up on the hill, past Einar's place at Buckquoy,' she explained. 'Staying with Olvor, giving her a hand.' She nodded at Olvor, who had come with a cup of ale for Thorgunna, and was puzzled to work out how to hand it to her since both Thorgunna's hands were busy. She set it down beside Thorgunna, but Ubbi reached around his wife to pick it up and hold it ready for her.

'Where are your own boys, Olvor?' Thorgunna asked.

'Staying with my sister at Tingwall,' Olvor said. Out of the way to allow Olvor to concentrate on learning how to make caps and belts, Sigrid had realised. It might not have been worth the trouble.

'Well, we have news!' said Svanhild. Her voice was low and sweet, just as annoying as the rest of her. Sigrid could have listened to her for an hour without a break.

'Have you?' asked her husband Steinar in surprise. 'We

only just left you!'

'Gossip, then!' she smiled at him. 'And it's news that will interest you, too, husband. We just heard as we came here.'

Ubbi laughed.

'We only left you for a minute! It's about three steps between the two longhouses, Svanni. Did you go the long way round?'

Svanhild glared at him, and Sigrid liked her better. There was nothing like a younger brother for bringing perfection back to reality. Svanhild deliberately turned back to Steinar and Asmund.

'There's a party visiting the Brough – they came from Kirkuvagr, leaving their ship there, so that's why we didn't see them here.'

'There are always parties visiting the Brough,' said Ubbi, unbothered. 'People wanting Thorfinn's opinion on this, that and the other. People wanting him to go and sort stuff out in Caithness or the Western Isles or wherever…'

'Yes, little brother,' said Svanhild, 'you're very clever.' Her grin made it an old sibling taunt. 'But as I said, Steinar will be interested in this party. They've come from Colonia.'

'From Colonia?' Steinar did indeed sit up straight. Sigrid tried to remember where Colonia was (she would never ask if she could help it), and wondered what Steinar's connexion was with it.

'Yes, an abbot and his servant and his bodyguard, they say. And today two more people arrived to see them, too, two of Thorfinn's men from somewhere south of Scotland. Busy times up on the Brough, eh?' Her face was alight with delight. Svanhild certainly liked her gossip. Olvor hurried about, pouring more ale, readjusting the contents of shelves, straightening the clean pots by the fire. Her mother's strictness had left a legacy of anxiety.

'I wonder who the Colonia people are. An abbot, you say?'

'Sent by Archbishop Herman,' said Thorgunna, surprising Sigrid. Thorgunna had appeared to be concentrating on her son. 'That's what they said. To advise Thorfinn on something – coinage, they thought.'

'Coinage?' Ubbi, her husband, laughed. 'I wonder what he wants that for? Or maybe he thinks there's some fake stuff around? Silver painted with gold, something like that?'

'No doubt he wants coins so we can pay taxes the more

easily.' Asmund made an unexpected contribution to the conversation, his voice somehow heavier than the others. Steinar turned to him and nodded.

'I believe you may be right, my friend. You can't eat coins, but when you're paid in hens and grain, it's not always easy to use it all in time before it goes bad.'

'I wonder if we'll be able to afford new taxes?' Thorgunna said softly, possibly hoping only her husband would hear.

'Thorfinn won't want to starve us,' Ubbi replied, reassuringly. He slipped an arm around her, helping her to support the head of their son, who now seemed to be asleep. He touched his son's forehead with one of the two fingers on his right hand, tucking back a lock of pale hair, a tender gesture Sigrid could never remember her own husband doing with their son.

'What were you doing in Colonia?' she asked Steinar, not wanting to think about raised taxes. She could barely meet what was asked for now, doing as much woolwork as she could fit into decent daylight. 'It's in Saxony, isn't it?'

'That's right,' said Steinar, nodding in a friendly way. 'I went with Thorfinn to Rome, and we travelled south through Colonia. I made some friends at the Archbishop's court – he's a great man, very holy, but a good administrator, too. He has made sure that the people are guided by good new laws based on the new faith, not on any old beliefs: everyone knows where they stand, and they know why. I came back here with Thorfinn but he asked me to return last spring to find out a bit more about how the place was run. Archbishop Herman was very helpful, and it's a beautiful city. I half thought of taking Svanhild there with me.' He exchanged a smile with his beautiful wife. Thorgunna and Ubbi, Sigrid noted out of the corner of her eye, were also exchanging glances. Not smiles, though: something had given them cause for concern. She wondered what. The child seemed peaceful enough now.

'I like Orkney too much!' Svanhild was saying, following her husband's conversation. 'But maybe one day I'll go to Colonia. Steinar makes it sound wonderful!'

'I'm not long back, in fact, only a few weeks. I suppose what I was able to tell Thorfinn made him ask for more help from the same place.' He frowned just a little. Sigrid wondered if he were feeling left out. If he had returned only a few weeks ago, Thorfinn might well have summoned help before Steinar had had the chance to report, making Steinar's work a little pointless. But Steinar brightened. 'I wonder who it is that has come here? And who is the bodyguard? Chances are I know at least one or other of them. They might well be friends. I'll go up to the Brough tomorrow and see who it is. Would you like to come too, Asmund? They can tell you all about Colonia, much more than I did.'

'Colonia sounds interesting,' said Asmund, more eager than Sigrid had yet heard him. 'I like to hear you talk of Colonia.'

The neighbours stayed late, easy in Olvor and Asmund's house, but they eventually tucked in their heels and stood to go. Thorgunna helped to tidy up the cups. Ubbi, holding their baby, stumbled – too much wine, perhaps – and both Svanhild and Steinar seized him and the child to steady them. Steinar, Sigrid noticed, had an odd look on his face as he hande his nephew back: did he disapprove of Ubbi's wobble?

Outside it was summer-dark – the sun, only dipping below the sea, cast a warm pink light over everything, like a river trout freshly baked and split. It was a deceptive light, Sigrid thought: you believed you could see much more than you really could. Pale things loomed near, colours muddled, and details blurred. Full winter darkness was more honest.

'I like it when Steinar comes on his own,' Asmund was saying. 'I don't understand the others.'

Olvor said nothing.

'They'll hear you, Asmund: your voice carries,' said Sigrid, feeling she'd lived in the longhouse long enough to give her opinion. But Asmund only looked puzzled, and said no more about it than his wife.

'I'll just go and take a look at the boats in the harbour,' he said. 'Some might have gone, on a long night like this.'

Sigrid drew breath to offer to go with him. She loved to watch late ships go out on nights like this, the glow of a lamp or two close to the prow, the murmur of voices across calm waters. But she knew Asmund liked to be by himself for a last walk in the evenings, so with a sigh she left him to his own devices, and followed Olvor into the longhouse, to pull the curtains around her own bedspace and close her eyes against that midnight light. She did not hear Asmund return before she slipped into sleep.

Olvor was her usual self the next morning, sweeping the details of the flag floor as breakfast cooked over the fire, wiping cups clean even though she had washed them before she went to bed. Sigrid stretched and pulled a shawl over her shift to go out to the privy, nodding a mumbled good morning to Olvor. Asmund was not apparent, but the curtains were still drawn around his and Olvor's bedspace. It was unusual for him to sleep late: he liked to be out and about when it was quiet.

Once out of the privy, Sigrid rubbed her forehead and eyes and gave the day a brief, assessing glance. There was a little haar, but it would burn off quickly, she thought - no end yet to this spell of hot weather. The grass about the longhouse, nibbled short, was yellowish. Absently she pulled a tuft of dun-coloured wool off a bush, then saw another, larger and cleaner, on the next bush. The grass prickled her bare feet as she worked the wool off the tangled twigs. There was something else pale further along the back of the longhouse, up at the far end. Already cleaning out the rubbish from the wool she was holding, feeling the oils soften her fingers, she walked along the field edge towards the corner of the gently curving building. She was only halfway when she heard the scream.

She ran the rest of the way, sure it had come from that direction. At the corner of the longhouse she stopped, grabbing the sharp angles of the sandstone slabs to steady herself. It took a long moment to take in what she saw.

Up the hill, not quite in line with Olvor's longhouse, was the home of their neighbours, Ubbi and Steinar. To this, the lower end, was their own privy, its woven door swinging. Thorgunna stood beside it, shift rumpled, shawl askew, mouth agape. Ubbi was emerging from the longhouse door – he must have heard the scream. Sigrid felt that she was examining the scene in a spiral, from the most distant details sweeping round slowly, reluctantly, to the focus. Asmund stood to Sigrid's right, as if he had come up from his own door, maybe going to look for his friend Steinar. His face was blank. Sigrid's eyes swivelled a little further, a little closer to where she was standing. Halfway between the two houses, Svanhild lay like a great white bird flung across a low wall. Sigrid could hear her gasping breaths. In her arms, Steinar lay, his face grey, his arm flung down on Asmund's side of the dike. And Steinar's head ... Sigrid's empty stomach lurched, though her mind would hardly take it in.

Steinar's head had taken on a strange, inhuman shape. The cause was clear: there was an axe, embedded far into his skull.

THRIR

III

'HOW LONG HAVE they been here?' Ketil asked quietly, nodding just past Abbot Konrad and Hakon. Lambi had gone off somewhere – probably, Ketil thought ruefully, on his own private raid. He rubbed his eyes. He had not slept well, his dreams full of half-buried memories.

Tosti shrugged

'About ten days? They'd only just arrived when Thorfinn thought to send for you. Hakon being a friend of yours, and all.'

'Yes, we've worked together before.' And would, now, have to work together again. Ketil was not sure how he was going to manage it. Thorfinn's realm extended from Shetland to England, from Fife to the Western Isles – how could he have had the bad luck to meet Hakon again? Why could he not have avoided him?

'What's he like to work with?' Tosti asked. 'I've hardly exchanged two words with him since he came.'

'I saw he was with Asgerdr, Thorfinn's daughter.'

Tosti eyed him sideways, perhaps trying to judge if Ketil thought Hakon was stepping on Ketil's toes there.

'She's an attentive hostess. Or hostess' daughter. You know Ingibjorg's expecting a child?'

A child? Ketil remembered one or two things a friend of his had said about Ingibjorg, and grinned at the thought of what that friend might now be saying. She might, for example, expect Ingibjorg to give birth not to a human child, but to a lamb or two.

'I didn't know. Thorfinn must be pleased.'

'If it comes healthy, yes. You know she lost one or two, and then there was a boy born … not quite right.'

'Really?' It was news to Ketil.

'Yes … you know, not quite fit for baptism. And he died, soon after.'

'Poor Ingibjorg,' said Ketil, moved despite himself. To bear a deformed child, that the church would not accept, was harsh.

'Indeed.' Tosti blinked, clearly upset too even though the story was familiar to him. He was a kindly priest: the idea of barring from baptism a child, any child, would come hard to him. He took a deep breath. 'Anyway, what's this Hakon like?'

Ketil paused.

'Popular,' he said. Tosti waited, but Ketil said nothing more.

'Well, I'm sure we'll all work together very well,' said Tosti, awkwardly, glancing at Ketil's face and not sounding remotely sure. 'Abbot Konrad is a man greatly respected in the church, so Thorfinn tells us.'

'Does he speak only Latin?'

'Latin and Saxon, of course,' said Tosti. 'But not Norse.'

'And I take it your Latin is pretty fluent?'

Tosti nodded modestly.

'It goes with the job, really.'

Ketil was impressed. He knew churchmen had to know the Latin of the mass and, he supposed, a few extra prayers, some of which he himself could probably recite even if he was not entirely clear which bit meant what. But to pass a conversation in another language, that was something. He had travelled to lands where Norse was scarcely spoken, but rarely in any capacity where he had had to converse with the natives. Norse was such a common language it was hardly worth the average person knowing anything else.

'So what is Abbot Konrad like, then?'

'Oh,' Tosti shrugged, 'he's clever, anyway. He should have all Thorfinn's lands organised for him by about … well, supper, I should think.'

'I'm to take him out on a tour this morning, apparently,' said Ketil.

'Yes, I'm coming too, in case there's anything he doesn't

understand. And Hakon and Abbot Konrad's servant will be there. What about your man? Lambi, is it?'

'It is. Look, Father Tosti, just a word of warning about Lambi. Don't leave any valuables unsecured, just in case. I don't say he's definitely a thief, but I think it wise to be careful.'

Tosti's eyes opened wide.

'And he's in your band of soldiers?'

'Well ... we recently acquired him. Origin unspecified. We might soon lose him again. We'll see.'

Tosti reflected, concern on his face. He probably owned little of value himself, but the church had a few nice pieces brought by Thorfinn to adorn his new place of worship. Tosti was probably skipping through a quick mental inventory.

'But is he going to come with us today? Lambi, I mean.'

'Not unless he turns up in the next few minutes. I think Abbot Konrad is ready to go.'

'Well, when Abbot Konrad is ready to go, it behoves the rest of us to shift ourselves,' said Tosti, his grin just a little nervous. 'I think my mule is ready. Are you?'

'Feel free,' said Ketil quietly to Tosti, 'to add any details I leave out. I did remind Thorfinn that I don't know his lands here particularly well, but – you know what Thorfinn is like.'

'That's true,' said Tosti. 'If Thorfinn thinks you can do something, you just somehow have to get on with it.' He grinned. 'And by the grace of God, it usually works out. Or at least, no one actually dies.'

'All well?'

Hakon was riding ahead of them, but hung back at the sound of their voices. His smile was helpful.

'All well, yes,' Ketil agreed. 'We were just discussing the route. Today we'll just cover the lands governed by Einar Einarson, whose longhouse and hall are just along there. See?'

'Will we call on him first?'

Ketil shook his head.

'Einar's elderly. We don't want to tire him out. We'll call in later, when he won't feel obliged to come with us. Can you tell Abbot Konrad what's happening?'

'I could,' said Hakon, 'but it wouldn't be much use. I don't speak Latin or Saxon.'

Ketil bit his lip.

'Good thing we have Father Tosti with us, then.' He nodded down to Tosti. 'We'd better catch up with the Abbot, I suppose, and tell him we'll go along the north coast first.'

Abbot Konrad, with his surly, silent servant Otto, rode ahead of all of them. The Abbot sat stately on his horse, while Otto, like Tosti, was on a mule, three paces behind. He had his hood up and a shawl wrapped tightly about it to hold it in place against the frivolous wind, and another shawl about his shoulders, flapping dismally. Ketil and Tosti guided their mounts alongside the Abbot, and Tosti, while Ketil nodded encouragement, outlined Ketil's plans in Latin. It sounded much more important that way, even if Ketil did not understand a word. Abbot Konrad followed Tosti's pointing finger, sharp eyes on the coast to the north, the longhouses in the middle distance, and Einar's hall down to the right, above the bay where the harbour stood. He asked some question, apparently about Einar, to judge by his and Tosti's gestures to the hall. Ketil looked, too, not having seen the place since his last visit. It seemed shabbier than it had done, with weeds around the walls and in the turf roofs. He wondered how the family was.

But he still guided his little party towards the left, the north coast of the spit of land, where two longhouses lay some distance apart. Both had doorways facing their direction, both tilted a little to the left, following the slope, so that the animal end of the house lay below the end designated for human habitation – life was much more fragrant that way. Ketil squinted against the morning light that glittered through the haar. As far as he could see, the doorway of the further house was open, but that of the nearer house was closed. He had not asked after Sigrid at Thorfinn's hall last night. Had something happened to her?

It was not long before they were much closer to Sigrid's neat longhouse, and the door was still closed. It had a faint air of neglect, nothing obvious, just a hint that no one was living here just now. A cow grazed outside, elderly and unconcerned at their arrival. Hens pecked with precision, and further from the house sheep of varying shades focussed on steady grazing. No one seemed to care that they were there.

Abbot Konrad waved at the house, his black eyebrows arched in a question.

'A widow lives here – lived here,' Ketil said, not liking the feel of the words on his tongue. 'Tosti, do you know anything about Sigrid?'

'I hadn't heard anything,' said Tosti, looking concerned. At that, a lad of about nine appeared round the side of the house, clearly drawn by the sound of voices and hooves. A dog followed him, and a cat appeared from somewhere to wind about his legs.

'Gnup!' Ketil breathed a silent sigh of relief. 'You're still here. Where is Sigrid?'

'Oh, Ketil!' Gnup smiled and nodded as if he had seen Ketil only yesterday. 'She's away off. I'm looking after the place.'

'Very well too, I'm sure,' said Ketil. 'But where has she gone?'

Gnup frowned.

'She's off to stay with Auntie Olvor. I don't know why.'

Ketil frowned. Should he know who Auntie Olvor was? He had planned never to come back to Orkney, so he had not troubled to remember many names of the people he had met.

'But she'll be back?'

'That's the plan – I don't think she'd abandon this place completely,' said Gnup happily, bending to placate the cat with a few strokes along its arched back. 'There's still wool in the house.'

Abbot Konrad, speaking slowly and clearly as if Ketil might then understand, interrupted with a string of Latin.

'The Abbot says,' began Tosti, as Gnup gaped at him, 'who lives here, and where are they? Shall I just tell him?'

'Yes, please, Tosti.'

Tosti began to explain. Gnup looked up anxiously at Ketil.

'Is it Mass? Should I kneel down?'

'No, no. The same language, but not a service.'

Gnup found this perplexing, but Tosti had turned back to Ketil.

'He wants to know what her condition is. What should I say?'

'Say she is poor and dependent on this boy and her woolwork for survival.'

Tosti met his eye, nodded, and began again in Latin.

'Well, if she comes back,' said Ketil to Gnup, 'tell her I sent my greetings.' He felt Hakon's gaze on him. 'I'll bring her some food if I get the chance,' he added. He glanced around. Tosti had finished his conversation with the Abbot, and Hakon was still mounted, unwilling to waste time somewhere so unpromising. Ketil swung himself back on to his horse, and nodded to Gnup.

'What's your obligation to the old woman?' Hakon asked him as they rode on. Ketil contained a smile.

'She did me some favours on my last visit. She's an excellent braid weaver.'

He said no more, and Hakon seemed satisfied.

At the next house, three children were playing outside the door and stopped in awe at the approaching procession.

'Mother!' yelled the eldest. 'There's people! And the priest!' he added, as though priests were not strictly people at all. He pulled his little brother and sister aside out of the way, lined against the house wall. Good defensive position, Ketil thought in passing, and then the mistress of the house appeared. In the visiting party, even the surly Otto straightened up.

'Ketil!' Helga, pretty in a dark red overdress with plenty of beads, went pale at the sight of him. Ketil dismounted slowly, not sure of his reception.

'Helga, this is Abbot Konrad from Colonia, and Hakon who has brought him here to advise Thorfinn. He doesn't speak Norse, so Father Tosti is translating. Is Hrolf about?'

Helga swallowed hard, swept an appreciative glance over Hakon, and almost met Ketil's eye.

'Hrolf's down at Einar's place,' she said. 'But I'm sure I can answer any questions. I suppose.' Her extraordinary dark blue eyes slipped back to Hakon again. They had once done something similar to Ketil, but he had burned that boat.

'Tosti, would you mind translating the Abbot's questions?'

'Of course.' Tosti and the Abbot set to, and the children grew bored and began to play again. Hakon drew Ketil aside.

'She's married?'

'Yes, to one of Einar's men.'

'What's your history here, then? Pretty girl like that?'

'She's married,' Ketil repeated.

'The look she just gave me says she doesn't think so.'

'I know.' Ketil sighed. 'Look, all right, she's perhaps wandered a little in the past. But just to warn you, bad things happen to her lovers. I'd advise against it.'

'You speaking from experience?'

'I've seen the results,' Ketil replied drily. Hakon looked thoughtful. Helga was certainly a temptation, Ketil knew. He had done his best: let Hakon make up his own mind.

Tosti finished questioning Helga, and Abbot Konrad, whose long fingers never left the reins, absorbed the information gleaned like a cloth taking in water, nodding at each answer. Ketil thanked Helga formally, and they bade her goodbye. The children stopped their play to watch them go, three serious little faces taking in even more detail than the Abbot himself.

The day wore on. Ketil had planned a broad sweep of Einar's lands, taking in all his followers right down to the elderly couple who lived behind the hall, supported directly by Einar's household. Still avoiding the hall itself and its longhouse, Ketil indicated that they should take the road down to the settlement by the harbour where Einar's lands extended a little around the coast: he had not yet seen his old friend Afi, a boat builder. He was less certain of his way down here, where he had rarely been even during his last visit, but there were several longhouses clustered fairly close together on the easy slopes that turned into beach and harbour by the sea. It was surprisingly sheltered down here, and he felt the warmth of the midday sun on his face as he went to the door of the first longhouse. The door was open, but no one was at home.

Surprised, he turned to Tosti, who knew a little about the household and gave Abbot Konrad some preliminary information.

'Odd, at this time of the day,' said Hakon, and Ketil nodded. He peered into the house, seeing a pot of food pulled back from the fire, a shawl on the flagged floor.

'Something's wrong,' he said to Hakon, though Tosti caught the words, too, eyes wide. 'Let's try the next house. Maybe they'll know something.'

But the next house was deserted, too.

'I don't like this,' said Ketil softly, noting here that someone had been chopping onions on a stone, and left the job half finished. Tosti, off his mule and holding its reins at arm's length to squint at the empty room, said suddenly,

'I hear voices. Up that way?' He looked away from the sea, up the hill. There was a third longhouse along the bay from them, and another uphill from it and a little further away. Ketil shielded his eyes to stare at what seemed to be a bustle of figures around a low stone wall, women and men. And could he hear … sobbing? A chill ran down his spine. Something bad had happened here.

'Tell the Abbot he'd better stay here for the moment,' he said, handing Tosti his horse's reins.

'I'll come with you,' said Hakon, solemn. Ketil nodded, and set off, Hakon following.

A cry came from the group ahead of them.

'I want to take him home!' A woman's voice, anguished. Ketil and Hakon exchanged glances. They knew nothing about what had happened, but the words were heartbreaking. Murmuring followed her cry, perhaps remonstrating, perhaps comforting, it was hard to tell. And then they were there, just outside the crowd, and Ketil could see a booted foot limp on the ground, the hem of a woman's pale shift, grubby in the grass. The man in front of him, conscious of someone else arriving, shifted out of the way to let him see, and he had a full view of the axe, the split head, the black blood dried over the weathered skin around the ear and chin and neck. How long had the corpse been there?

'What's going on?' asked Hakon, straining to see. 'Oh, that's not good. Who is it?'

At the unfamiliar voice, the others in the crowd began to look around. The woman kneeling by the body, shawl wrapped about her shoulders, did not at once look up: she glanced across at the other woman, the one clutching the dead man's hand, the one with the curtain of pale hair veiling her face, the one whose shoulders were unsteady with sobbing.

'It'll be Einar's man, now, you see, and then we'll get this sorted out,' said the first woman, and only then did she glance up to look at the newcomers. Ketil, ready for her, had his face set with a quizzical look, and fully appreciated the shock on Sigrid's face as she recognised him. She jumped to her feet, pulling her shawl around her shift in apparent embarrassment. He raised an eyebrow, but did not look away, and she scowled at him.

'Ketil Gunnarson! Are you come from Einar's place?'

'Not at his direction, if that's what you mean,' he said. 'I haven't seen him.'

'Oh, for Heaven's sake!' Cross now, she seized him by the elbow and propelled him a little away from the others. Hakon watched curiously, but they were out of his hearing by the time Sigrid stopped.

'What are you doing here?'

'I'm beginning to wonder,' he said lightly. 'Do you wait for me to arrive on Orkney before you find a dead man, or do I just happen upon you at the right moments?'

'Don't be ridiculous. Svanhild found him, anyway,' she added, as if that made a difference. 'That's the utterly beautiful and probably thoroughly talented and undoubtedly nice woman who's clutching his hand. She's his wife – his widow. He's Steinar. Did Thorfinn send you?'

'How long has he been dead?'

'We found him this morning, at first light. He hadn't been dead long by that point. Since then they've just been arguing about what to do. I said Einar should be told and someone should come and see him as he was found. Svanhild wants to take him home – that's their longhouse just up there. I think her brother Ubbi's gone to see Einar, but he seems to have taken a while. You didn't see him on the way? Fair haired, slim, cheerful looking when he hasn't just seen his sister's man with an axe in his head … I want to get dressed, really. I only came out to use the privy, and I've been stuck here ever since.'

'Does anyone know who did it?'

'Well, it's his own axe, but I think we can probably rule out accident or self-killing. Beyond that, everyone seems bewildered. What are you doing here, anyway? Do you just wait until there's a puzzling corpse before coming to Orkney?'

He smiled, and turned to look back down the hill.

'I have with me a Saxon abbot and his servant, his Norse bodyguard, and Tosti translating into Latin.'

She blinked.

'Even if you're not allowed out on your own, that seems excessive.'

'I don't think they were expecting a murder.'

'I suspect Steinar wasn't, either.'

'Who was he?'

'I only met him last night. I'm staying down here – just there, in that house, with Olvor – remember Ragna's daughter?'

'No.'

'Well, nobody does, usually. Anyway, Steinar and Svanhild, and Ubbi and his wife – that's her, holding the babies – all came round for a newsan evening, and that was the first I'd seen any of them. He's not long back from Colonia, apparently – oh, is that your Saxon abbot? The one from Colonia?'

'The very man. What was Steinar doing in Colonia?'

'Finding out about taxes and coinage for Thorfinn.'

'That's what the abbot is here for. Thorfinn seems keen on the idea.'

'He wants to run his lands like a foreign king, that's the thing.' She sighed. 'Look, if you're going to be here for a bit, can you just look frightening and stop them moving him before Ubbi comes back with Einar's man? I need to get dressed.'

'Yes, probably best,' said Ketil solemnly. Sigrid glared at him, but took her chance and fled to the lower longhouse. Ketil looked over at the crowd surrounding Steinar's body, but there seemed little inclination in them to hurry the corpse off to his own house as soon as Sigrid had turned her back. A couple of the neighbours had even sat down, biding their time, waiting for Einar's representative to appear. Ketil wondered who it would be.

'Who was your friend in her nightclothes?' Hakon was smiling, but sensitive enough to the circumstances to keep his back to the crowd while he did so.

'Someone I met when I was here before. She says she's been here since first light when the body was found. They're waiting for someone from Einar's place to come down and see the body in place.'

'Oh, of course. I suppose that's more useful than just a description. Or several descriptions.' Hakon nodded. 'We'd better tell the abbot what's going on. I take it that's not Einar's man coming now? He looks familiar.'

Ketil turned. Hakon was looking down the road towards the south, not up towards Einar's hall, so it seemed unlikely. But as soon as he saw the approaching figure, he knew he had nothing to do with Einar. It was Lambi, sauntering up the road as though he had lived there all his life and this was his usual midday stroll.

'Where have you been?' Ketil snapped as he approached, trying not to sound peevish.

'Oh! Sorry,' said Lambi at once, apparently contrite. 'I didn't realise you needed me for anything.'

'Need might be a strong word,' Ketil conceded, 'but you should have checked with me first, before disappearing. Where have you been?' he repeated.

'Oh … just finding my way about. You know, here and there.' Lambi was cheerfully unconvincing. If the essence of a lie was the intention to deceive, it did not look as if Lambi held out much hope of lying.

'Well, you can make yourself useful now. Get down over there and tell Father Tosti what's happening so that he can tell the Abbot. Then the Abbot had better decide what he wants to do in the circumstances.'

'Right,' said Lambi, looking important. 'And what is happening?'

'A man has been murdered,' said Ketil, keeping it simple. Lambi looked over at the crowd. At that moment, a few people happened to move, and Svanhild sat back on her heels, tossing her thick hair back out of her face. Lambi gasped.

'That's …' He seemed to have lost the power of breathing. He struggled for a moment. 'She's *beautiful*!'

FJÓRIR

IV

SIGRID SCURRIED DOWN the hill in her bare feet to the door of Olvor's longhouse. The house was deserted, of course: Olvor and Asmund were both among the bystanders outside, watching over Steinar's cold corpse. They could not stand out there all day. Poor Svanhild was quite right in wanting to take her husband home, but someone in authority really should be able to see him first. Where on earth was Ubbi, with Einar's representative? Sigrid was quite sure Einar himself would not slink down the hill to look at a dead man, not this time. Einar was too old, too vague, too caught up in learning to be a scholar, in forgetting all that he had done in his violent, raiding past. He would send one or more of his men.

She splashed water over herself at the barrel, half-heartedly snatched the curtain about her bed space for some privacy, and slipped into a clean shift. Then she pulled her overdress on, sliding the cloth loops into her old oval brooches on each side. Two strings of beads - nothing special, the ones she had not been able to sell when she was really poor - linked the brooches, and she hooked the metal ring holding her scissors, keys, and knife on to the left brooch. Finally she slung on a plain leather belt with two pouches on it, one containing her nailbinding: if she were to be stuck perhaps at Svanhild's house helping her to watch the corpse, it would be hours wasted with no work done. She could not afford that, even now.

From the other pouch she pulled out her comb, and tried to make some kind of sense of her hair. It had not benefitted from being tumbled about in the wind outside for the last few hours. Ketil must have been laughing at the mess of it, as he often had as a boy. Well, she could laugh at how close-cropped he kept his own blond hair. Was he trying to look more Christian than a priest, or was it lice? As if she deserved some kind of punishment for the thought, she felt a crack between her fingers. Her comb had snapped. She threw it on the floor in disgust, and tried using her fingers, mouth twisted in annoyance.

Ketil again. She sighed, not knowing whether to be pleased to see him back or not. Her childhood neighbour, so far away in Heithabyr, of whom she had barely thought in years, until he turned up unexpectedly in Orkney last year. He had not, at the time, seemed much impressed by the islands where she had settled with her late husband – indeed, when he had left she was fairly sure he could not wait to go back to Norway and do – whatever it was he did – for Thorfinn there. Thorfinn must have hauled him back for some reason: what had Ketil said? He had an abbot with him? An abbot from Colonia, too, where Steinar had just been.

Hm, she thought, abandoning all hope of her hair and forcibly twisting it into a clean headcloth. An abbot arrives from Colonia, and a man just back from Colonia is murdered. Was that a coincidence?

Hose and boots. It was a bit warm for hose and boots, but if there was a murderer about she felt, in some way, that she had to be prepared for anything. Or was it Ketil's arrival? Things had certainly not been peaceful the last time he was here. She tied her boot laces firmly.

She wanted to see this abbot. She patted down her overdress, making sure it was straight, poked at her headcloth, and headed back outside.

Something was already happening up where Steinar's body lay. There were three horses and a couple of mules, not near the corpse, it was true: a man she had not seen before, almost smothered in shawls, was standing with five sets of reins looped about his right arm, at the back of Olvor and Asmund's longhouse. He had a general look on his face that would bring the rain on from a cloudless sky. The locals were dispersing, mumbling, from the crowd, sombre at the death of a neighbour but some clearly irked to be sent back to their daily work when they might be missing something interesting here. There were more women than men, of course, even now with Einar and Thorfinn not leading summer raids themselves. Some of the men still found reasons to go travelling while the women did the work – though the women were generally quite content to let them go while they ran things on their own terms for a couple of months. And the men often brought back some rather nice placatory gifts from foreign lands.

Left around the body were Olvor and Asmund, together but not touching, too stunned to move; Svanhild, still on her knees, her beautiful face setting into an empty shell; Thorgunna, her brother's wife, still standing with a child on each hip, as if she had forgotten them; and now Father Tosti, also on his knees, head bent in prayer. The huge dog, solid as a cairn, lay with his nose to his master's hand, chin on the ground, silent now. Sigrid noticed that Tosti had a hand on the dog's collar. Ketil stood to one side, with a couple of men she did not know, but both rather better dressed than the miserable man holding the horses. And standing at the foot of the corpse, regarding it as if it were a particularly difficult passage in the Bible, was a tall, slim man, hands folded calmly into long robes that were – not ostentatious, but quietly very fine indeed. Steel-grey hair, neatly clipped, receded from a tonsure which looked almost like a natural loss. What she could see of his face from this angle was sharp, precise, controlled. He appeared to have delegated the praying to Tosti, for his erect posture had nothing prayerful about it at all. As she watched him, he turned his head slightly, taking in all the details of the longhouses above and below him, the condition of the roofs, walls, animal enclosures, grazing, the proximity of the sea and the harbour – nothing, she would have sworn, escaped his keen attention.

Sigrid, not anxious to be subjected to that examination, moved back over to where Ketil was standing, left hand absently on his sword hilt, his gaze too thoughtfully moving between the body, the two women, and the longhouse from which they had come.

'That'll be the abbot, then?' she asked.

Ketil nodded. Hakon, beside him, pushed forward.

'I'm Hakon, from Trondheim. Ketil will never remember to introduce us!' He had a friendly face, and Sigrid smiled a little, taking in the woven band on his cloak, the well-made, well-fitted kirtle that covered his shirt, and the fineness of his linen sleeves.

'Sigrid,' she said, 'from up on the hill. Are you one of Ketil's men?'

'No!' Ketil said at once, then quickly clarified his denial. 'Hakon's far too important to be one of my men. He's here with the Abbot.'

Hakon grinned.

'You're not – forgive me, Sigrid – but you're not by any chance a widow, with a young lad looking after your farm while you're away?'

Sigrid glanced at Ketil. The expression on his face was very odd, she thought.

'I am, yes. What has he been saying?'

'Oh, nothing! We've been taking the Abbot on a tour of – it's Einar, isn't it? – of Einar's lands, while he works out how to advise Thorfinn on – coinage, and such. We called at your door this morning, but of course you were away. The boy greeted us.'

'Gnup seems to be fine,' Ketil put in.

'Good – well, I thought he would be.' Not quite sure of the relationship between the two men, she felt awkward. She was about to turn away when there was a rumble of throat-clearing from behind Hakon.

'I'm Lambi,' said a large man in a woolly cap, shambling forward. He reminded Sigrid of a bundle of uncarded wool, rounded and unkempt, but his smile was pleasant enough. 'I am one of Ketil's men!'

'Ah, well,' said Sigrid, 'I suppose, until you find something better. Good to meet you, Lambi.'

'Who's she? Do you know her?' Lambi seemed disposed to chat. Sigrid looked to see who he was pointing to.

'Oh, that's Svanhild. She's Steinar's widow now – Steinar's the man with the axe,' she explained bleakly. It had seemed so horrible at first, yet now, after a few hours, Steinar's split head almost seemed normal. She had sent Olvor for a cloth and laid it over Steinar's face, but it would have taken a small sail to cover face and head and axe. 'It's her brother Ubbi who went for Einar. I can't think what's happened to him – oh! At last!'

Ubbi had appeared, on foot, around the corner of Olvor's

longhouse, turning back to urge someone else up the hill behind him. It seemed to take a while. Ubbi glanced behind him at the waiting people around Steinar's body. His fair hair stood on end, and his movements were agitated, tapping the stone wall beside him as though he could speed up someone else's footsteps with his rhythm. At last, another man emerged around the corner, at a pace so steady he looked as if he were measuring a field. Sigrid recognised him: Oddr, one of Einar's oldest and least excitable followers. The most interesting thing about him, she had often thought, was his luxuriant moustache, thick and long and golden, for which the hair on the top of his head appeared to have sacrificed itself. Oddr barely looked towards the corpse, concentrating on his stately progress towards it. At last he fetched up almost too close, glanced suddenly at Abbot Konrad, and backed off slightly. The great dog shifted itself and went to sniff him. Oddr flinched.

'I am come from Einar,' he said, his voice surprisingly soft. 'I hear there has been a death?'

Sigrid resisted the urge to clap her hand to her eyes in despair. Yes, you pompous fool, there's the body in front of you!

Abbot Konrad stared at him, saying nothing. Svanhild, however, struggled to her feet to greet him.

'My husband has been killed, as you see.'

'His name?'

'Steinar Valison. Thorfinn's man.'

'Thorfinn's man,' Oddr repeated, nodding. Sigrid guessed he would be working out how to pass any responsibilities for this up to the Brough. 'And who claims the blame? Who did this?'

'We don't know.' Svanhild's low voice cracked. 'I found him lying here, not long after dawn.'

'And no one knows anything about this?' He looked about, blinking a little at the Abbot. 'But that would make it murder! But look!' he interrupted himself. 'There are strangers here! Who are you?' he asked in surprise, catching sight of Otto lurking with the horses, then of Ketil's companions. 'You I recall – you're one of Thorfinn's men too, aren't you?' he asked Ketil, as though that alone made a suspicious connexion between Ketil and the victim.

'I am – I think we played a game of ball together last spring,' said Ketil mildly. He had trained a little with Einar's men when he first came to Orkney. Sigrid remembered that he had not been much impressed by them. To judge by Oddr's sniff, the feeling was mutual.

'Who are you?' he carried on to Hakon.

'Hakon Hakonson, from Trondheim. It's a pleasure to meet you. I'm travelling with Abbot Konrad there, who is here to help Thorfinn.'

'Thorfinn again,' Oddr muttered. 'And you?'

'I'm his man,' said Lambi amiably, nodding at Ketil. Ketil, Sigrid thought, did not look that delighted with Lambi's loyal declarations. Oddr, too, studied him closely, the magnificent moustache undulating slightly.

'What do any of you know about this?'

'We happened upon the scene,' said Ketil. 'We're taking the Abbot around Einar's lands, for the purpose of advising Thorfinn.'

'I wasn't told.'

'We haven't been to see Einar yet,' said Ketil. 'We wanted to go to him last, as the principal man in the place.'

Oddr frowned.

'So he was dead before you got here?'

'By several hours, yes.'

Sigrid looked at Hakon. Why had she asked if he was one of Ketil's men? It was clear from his face that he was used to being the one answering for the party, the one in charge, but he was easy enough, she thought, to let Ketil assuming command. Ketil did not work for him, then, it seemed, but he was in some way junior. And Hakon, she thought, would be a good commander, calm, friendly, with an air of knowing what he was doing. He inspired confidence.

Oddr did not. He considered, then spun slowly on one heel to look back at the body again. The cloth over the face seemed to confuse him, and he stepped over and plucked it away, studying Steinar's shocked expression, then peering down at the axe. His whiskers swung in the wind.

'If we find whose axe it is,' he announced after a moment's thought, 'we'll have the killer. Who recognises the axe?'

'It's his axe,' said Thorgunna, at last shifting the children a little. One was asleep, the other sucking its thumb intently.

'Whose?' snapped Oddr.

'His own. Steinar's own axe,' said Ubbi, going to stand beside his wife. He took the nearer child from her, the sleeping one. 'We should settle these two indoors, eh?'

'His own axe? He killed himself?'

This time Sigrid sighed sharply, but he did not appear to hear.

'Don't be stupid,' said Ubbi, his exasperation clear. If he had had to trail back from Einar's place with Oddr it was not surprising. 'How could he have driven the axe into his own head like that? Have you never wielded an axe?'

Oddr stiffened, cross. Sigrid lost patience, and strode over.

'Well, if you've said anything useful you can think of to say, Oddr, Svanhild would like to take her husband's body home. Who will help carry Steinar home?' She looked about. Ubbi and Asmund stepped forward, followed by Hakon and, after a moment, Ketil. Ubbi handed the sleeping child back again to his wife, then leaned forward and eased the axe out of Steinar's head, with an unpleasant sound. He handed it gently to his sister, then gestured to the other men. They managed to lift Steinar's stiff corpse, and Tosti rose, taking Svanhild's arm, to lead her and them back to the longhouse. Thorgunna followed, a sob breaking out at last from her sturdy frame.

Sigrid nodded at the abbot, left alone by the low wall, and went to join Olvor who waited where Asmund had left her, like a cloth left out to dry.

'If they need us, they'll no doubt let us know,' she murmured. 'Come on, Asmund will need his dinner.'

'Oh, yes!' Olvor seemed pleased to have something straightforward to do. She allowed Sigrid to guide her back down to her own longhouse, and set to straight away with carrots and onions. Sigrid drew out her nailbinding and sat in the doorway, thinking. Oddr was not inspiring. If Thorfinn found out about the murder and considered the matter, he would probably ask Ketil to help again, as he had before. And that probably meant that Ketil would need to be helped himself. Hakon might look competent, but he certainly would not have the local knowledge that would doubtless be required. Nor would the affable Lambi, though in his case Sigrid was not so confident of his competence.

'What do you know about what Steinar was doing in

Colonia?' she called across to Olvor.

'Not much more than what he said last night, I think,' said Olvor. Asmund appeared at the doorway, came in and settled near the fire, watching his wife's busy hands. He must not have stayed long with Svanhild. 'He liked the place, from all he said.'

'Who liked what?' asked Asmund.

'Steinar liked Colonia.'

'He told me a good deal about Colonia,' Asmund said. 'He said there were seven churches, St. Andreas, St. Apostein, St. Georg, St. Gereon, St. Maria, St. Pantaleon, and St. Severin. Seven churches!' He waved seven fingers, as if to prove it.

'I don't think I've heard of any of those saints,' said Sigrid.

'It's a different country,' said Asmund, nodding wisely. 'And there's another place where they go for St. Ursula. It's where she was killed, with a thousand virgins, and you can see all the bones. The Romans killed her,' he added, as if it were only reasonable that the Romans should behave in such a way. Steinar said that St. Georg's church was like a cave, the walls were so thick. And St. Gereon's had curving walls, like a longhouse!' He gave a rare smile, pleased to have such knowledge.

'It's funny that Steinar should die just after some more people arrive from Colonia.'

'It's not funny that Steinar's dead,' said Asmund, solemn again.

'No, I mean it seems a bit peculiar. A coincidence, don't you think?'

'I didn't like that abbot,' said Olvor suddenly, without looking up from her cooking. 'He was like stone. Father Tosti was very kind to Svanhild, and he prayed, but that abbot just stood there looking around him. I don't think he liked us very much.'

'I don't think he spoke any Norse,' Sigrid said, just realising that. 'He couldn't give Svanhild any words of comfort if all he speaks is – what, Saxon?'

'Steinar could speak Saxon. I heard him once,' said Asmund.

'Oh? Who was he talking to?'

'Oh, just to me. He thought I might like to hear what it sounded like. I did.'

'And what did it sound like?'

49

'Like Norse, but with corners,' was Asmund's rather obscure reply. Sigrid smiled to herself, and went back to considering how she could help Ketil, when he came to ask her.

After their meal, Sigrid set Olvor some weaving to do and, acknowledging that it might be easier for her without Sigrid watching over her shoulder, she offered to take some food up the hill to Svanhild's household. Olvor agreed readily: Asmund had already gone out to do whatever it was Asmund did in the course of the day. Sigrid was often puzzled by it.

Thorgunna came to the door to welcome Sigrid, her eyes red, but for once she was without a child on either hip. She ushered Sigrid in and took the bundle of bread with quiet thanks. Inside, a few of the other neighbours were keeping Svanhild company, and Ketil and the other men had gone. Steinar had already been laid straight, a bandage holding his head in some reasonable shape, clothes changed, and skin washed of the black trail of cold blood. The great dog lay on the floor beside him, emitting the occasional sighing whine. Sigrid paid her respects, nervously patted the dog, and retreated to a seat near the door. Thorgunna came to sit beside her.

'It was good of you to come,' she said in a low voice. 'I know it can be difficult for both Olvor and Asmund: neither of them is easy in company.'

'Asmund liked Steinar very much, in his own way. The bread is of Olvor's making, not mine,' she added. 'It'll be good.'

Thorgunna gave a little smile, acknowledging the humour.

'I'm sure it will be. Svanhild makes our bread, usually, so we'll be glad to have it.'

'She's taking it hard.'

'He was only just back. They were still so pleased to be together again.' Thorgunna's mouth snapped shut, holding back tears. 'Ubbi's so sad, too. He really admired Steinar, looked up to him like a big brother.'

'Is this Steinar's farm?' The question struck Sigrid and was out before she could consider it.

'No!' Thorgunna seemed happy enough to answer. 'The farm belongs to Ubbi. Steinar has no land, though he had hopes that Einar or Thorfinn might grant him some soon, in reward for all his work on Thorfinn's behalf. Not going to happen now, though,' she added sadly. 'Not that we couldn't all manage here. This low land is good, and it's easy to keep a boat, too: when Steinar was home he helped Ubbi, and we all got on well here together. He'll be badly missed.'

'Asmund was telling me some of the things Steinar told him about Colonia,' Sigrid pushed on while she could. 'Steinar really seems to have enjoyed his travels there.'

'Oh, he did! He talked a good deal about it. And it gave him pleasure to bring information that would appeal to Asmund. He always liked to go and talk to Asmund. But I think he would happily have lived in Colonia, if Svanhild had agreed to go with him. He said it was a town full of faith, with leaders who had a true Christian vision. He would be sorry to have missed the Abbot's visit. He had such great admiration for the churchmen of Colonia.'

'It's a shame, isn't it? But I hear the Abbot doesn't speak Norse.'

'Maybe not, but Steinar spoke good Saxon – or so we believed,' she said with a little smile. 'No one else here could understand it, of course, so we don't really know. But it sounded convincing!'

'He seemed like a thoroughly good and kind man,' said Sigrid, entirely truthfully. 'Why on earth would anyone kill him?'

Thorgunna looked at her.

'There were bangles missing. And a ring,' she said. 'The bangles were just for paying for things, but the ring was a gift from Svanhild. He wouldn't have let it go easily.'

'A thief? Attacking a man so near his own doorstep? Einar won't like to hear that – assuming that dolt Oddr manages to tell him anything useful.' She sat back, thinking. 'So when was he attacked? Last night?' The body had been almost cold when she touched it, the blood already stiff.

'This morning. Svanhild said he had gone out early, something to do with going to see the Abbot on the Brough.'

'Before dawn? Well, what passes for before dawn at this time of year.'

'Yes, I think so, very early. I vaguely remember hearing something, but I was more than half asleep. I wish ... I wish I'd at least called out to him.'

Sigrid laid a hand on Thorgunna's own hand, pressing it gently. But the gesture was a little absent. Who would be around before dawn to attack a man for his bangles and rings, just by chance, so near the longhouses? Or had someone, quick enough to get his hands on Steinar's own axe, thought to prevent Steinar from meeting the Abbot?

FIMM

V

'IT FEELS A bit odd,' said Hakon, 'to leave the lady's longhouse so soon after taking her husband's body inside. We should at least have stayed for a second cup of wine.'

Ketil shrugged. He had ushered Hakon and Lambi out as quickly as courtesy would allow, and he was not going back. He could sense that the Abbot, interested though he might be in local customs of death and murder, was eager to be on his way. There was little point in surveying the rest of the settlement today, with everyone already sneaking back to Svanhild's house as soon as the Abbot's back was turned: there would be no one to interrogate. The Abbot took a good look about him, nevertheless, noting the narrow flat land by the river, the steep sheltering slope up to the south, the clear view of the Brough across the bay, the convenience of beach and harbour. There was a small chapel, Thorfinn's construction, no doubt, for the benefit of the locals, and the Abbot gave it particular scrutiny, casting open the door with authority, tossing questions back at Tosti who fielded them neatly. The others waited politely, Lambi whistling through moist, thick lips. Coming from Heithabyr, Ketil found the houses too close together here: he had left Heithabyr to escape that kind of overcrowding. But here the sea breezes and the open grazing inland made it much healthier than Heithabyr had been for many a long year.

Otto handed them back their reins and they led the horses back down to the path that wound through the settlement, the one that led south to Hamnavoe. Doubtless he would have to take

Abbot Konrad down there, too, and perhaps around the other islands. He scarcely knew them. If Thorfinn insisted he oversaw this, he would have to enlist more local help. Perhaps Sigrid had some useful contacts. He had heard her talk of a farmer on Rousay who sold her wool, so that might be a start. His mouth twitched a little as he remembered the look on Sigrid's face when she had seen him. It had almost been worth the trip.

Tosti's voice came to him from up in front, the Latin steady, loud enough to be heard even though the Abbot was so high on his horse and Tosti so low on his mule. The Abbot was nodding, taking note: Ketil was sure he was memorising every detail that he saw and heard.

At last they were clear of the settlement, and Ketil decided to lead the party back up on to the landspit, not try to have the horses pick their way past the harbour. Progress was slow enough, with Lambi on foot. At the top of the upward path, not far from Einar's hall, they overtook Oddr. The man stopped, rearranging his moustache, and caught his breath as he allowed them to pass.

'You will be reporting this to Einar, won't you?' Ketil called down.

'Of course, of course!' said Oddr with what was presumably intended to be a reassuring smile. 'He'll be very interested to hear what happens.'

But not keen to make anything happen, Ketil thought.

'How is he?' he asked. Oddr's face became bland.

'He's well enough,' he said. Ketil nodded. Never admit your leader's weakness, not even to an apparent ally. You never knew where the next leader might be coming from.

'Should I ask Abbot Konrad to visit him?' he suggested.

Oddr considered, then shook his head.

'Maybe tomorrow?'

'I'll send word ahead, see if it suits Einar,' said Ketil. He suspected that what he meant was 'see if Einar is capable of hosting a visit'. If he was not strong enough to meet an abbot, with all his newfound Christian devotion and scholarship, he was ailing indeed. Oddr nodded agreement, and waved them off as they turned left to head for the Brough.

The wind beat them steadily as they rode the length of the landspit to the gates of the Brough, and it was a relief to reach the shelter of Thorfinn's settlement, to smell the smoke and the oils at the bathhouse, and wonder if there might be any food left from the midday meal. Otto led the mounts away, and the others made for Thorfinn's hall to report on their day. Ketil saw Tosti look with longing at the church as they passed: he had probably not joined the Church simply to be a translator.

The hall had a chilled, greasy smell to it, as if dinner was long gone and not that easy on the stomach. Ketil's eyes adjusted to the dimmer light, and his heart sank. Arranged on one high chair at the head of the hall, a luxuriant fur over her lap, was a woman with a long pale face and a pleased expression, a few attendants at her feet. She gave a little cry of delight, and ushered Ketil forward to come close. Reluctantly he complied – this was Ingibjorg, Thorfinn's wife, of course.

'Ketil Gunnarson! Thorfinn said he'd asked you to come and help. I'm so glad you were able to join us!'

She gazed up at him from under her lashes, confident of her appeal, and held out a hand for the privilege of her touch. Her confidence, as far as Ketil was concerned, was misplaced, and he bowed, pretending not to see the hand.

'My lady,' he said. 'I am honoured to do Lord Thorfinn's bidding, of course.'

The hand, ignored, twitched back to touch a curl of white-yellow hair that had been teased from her headcloth. Ingibjorg bestowed a toothy smile, then looked past him.

'And Hakon, I hope you've all had a successful day! Have you eaten, all of you? Tosti, do ask the Abbot if he wants anything. Asgerdr.' She did not look around, but waved her daughter forward imperiously. 'Asgerdr, fetch wine for the gentlemen.'

Asgerdr beamed at Hakon, and flicked a look of disgust at her mother. She vanished into the dimness behind Ingibjorg's chair.

'Is Lord Thorfinn about?' Ketil asked.

'Oh, he's around somewhere, Ketil. No doubt he'll be back soon. You've heard that we have a child on the way?' Her expression fell somewhere between smugness and warning, as if she wanted to tell him she was not currently available. It was faintly nauseating.

'I wish you both every blessing on it,' said Ketil, not

meeting her eye. To one side of him he thought he heard a very slight chuckle: Hakon seemed to find the exchange amusing, anyway. Asgerdr returned and gave the two cups in her hands to the Abbot and to Hakon, and disappeared again with the least sideways glance at Ketil. Asgerdr was a beautiful girl, but she was just as flirtatious as her mother. Returning with his cup, she pressed it into Ketil's hands and looked up confidently into his eyes. He smiled, but stopped the instant she turned away. He was firm in his belief that toying with Thorfinn's daughter was not the way to a successful career.

Abbot Konrad bowed graciously to Ingibjorg as his hostess, and seated himself on a high seat which seemed to have been brought into the hall for his specific use. Tosti, with a weary smile, sat on a low stool beside him and thanked Asgerdr for the cup of wine that eventually reached him. Hakon and Ketil settled on a bench, backs against the long table, prepared to wait for Thorfinn to arrive. Hakon passed the occasional remark, his gaze mostly on Asgerdr. Ketil did not respond. He was trying to focus his mind on Steinar's death, but it was not altogether successful. He was relieved when Thorfinn finally appeared.

Thorfinn strode into the hall with the confidence that recognised that everyone would notice he was there. His dark face widened into a smile when he saw Ingibjorg waiting for him, and he paid no attention to anyone else around him until he had walked straight to her, and kissed her forehead gently, exchanging a few murmured words. Ingibjorg purred, and Thorfinn for a moment looked almost handsome. Then he patted her hand, and turned to survey his hall.

'Well, Ketil? How did the day go?'

Ketil stood politely.

'A little unexpectedly, my lord. We surveyed most of Einar's lands, but he was not … available to see us, and we encountered a difficulty down at the harbour settlement. We will probably have to go back at a more appropriate time.'

'A difficulty?' Thorfinn shot Ketil a sharp look.

'A man had been killed. Steinar Valison was the name.'

'Steinar Valison? But he was here only last week. I was going to speak to him soon about Colonia – he was only just back, and I wanted him to meet Abbot Konrad.' He stopped, hands behind his back, and stared at the flag floor for a second or two, a moment of regret. 'What happened to him?'

'Someone split his head with an axe. His own axe,' Ketil added. He heard Hakon, on his feet beside him, murmuring agreement. Thorfinn looked shocked.

'Who would have done such a thing? He was well-liked, I thought.'

'They think it might have been a robbery.' He had heard the first tricklings of the rumour when they had carried Steinar into the longhouse, and his widow had for the first time looked properly at her husband's hands. A ring, apparently, was missing. He had seen himself the skin rubbed where it had been pulled roughly free. 'No one has come forward.'

'Does Einar know?'

'A man called Oddr came down to see what had happened. He was heading back to Einar's hall when we saw him later.'

'Oddr? Moustache?'

'Oh yes.'

'Ha.' Thorfinn took a few steps up the hall, thinking, then turned back, looking for the messenger who had gone to Hwitebi to fetch Ketil. 'Go and give Einar my respects and ask him if he knows what's happening.'

The messenger bowed and left. Thorfinn said nothing, still apparently lost in thought, and everyone jumped when Abbot Konrad rose smoothly from his seat and addressed Thorfinn with grace and dignity. Tosti sprang up beside him, frowning with concentration.

'My lord Abbot says,' he began, hesitated, then plunged in, 'that it behoves him at this sad, not to say tragic, moment, at a time of apparent and comparative peace and tranquillity in the realm of Orkney previously so unfortunately accustomed to the vagaries of warring parties of one persuasion or another to offer his deepest condolences to my lord the Earl Thorfinn on the loss of one so dedicated to his work, so loyal to his lord, and so skilful in negotiations, as the man Steinar Valison, whom he – that is my lord Abbot – delighted in the privilege of being acquainted with when he – that is Steinar Valison – visited the court of his Grace the Archbishop Herman of Colonia, on many occasions.'

Thorfinn stared at Tosti, then at the Abbot. He breathed out sharply upwards, jutting his jaw.

'Tell the Abbot he's very kind,' he said. Tosti murmured something that sounded slightly longer than that, and both clerics sat once again.

'Was that the man with that tall, skinny wife?' Ingibjorg's words interrupted all their thoughts.

'Svanhild, his wife's name,' said Thorfinn. Ketil felt Lambi move beside him, and kicked him unobtrusively. 'Rather a lovely woman, I thought.' He spoke absently, unaware of Ingibjorg's scowl. 'And Steinar was a good man, a hard worker. I shall miss him. Well, we'll know nothing more until we hear from Einar. Is supper nearly ready?'

His daughter Asgerdr skimmed forward, bringing him a cup of wine.

'The food is nearly ready,' she said. 'Please, Father, have the tables set out and we'll bring it through in a moment.'

She swept away, back into the recesses of the hall, with a little half-smile and a glance that could have been directed at Ketil or Hakon. It was hard to say.

A few of Thorfinn's men helped to rearrange the tables and benches in the accustomed manner, and the great fire was lit in the centre of the hall though there was little need of it for warmth this evening. Other men of Thorfinn's hird, freshly washed and combed, appeared for their meal, finding their places on the benches, exchanging news about their day. There was as yet little talk of Steinar: Ketil assumed that the local gossip had not quite reached this far yet. Asgerdr, deputising for her mother, directed the bringing in of cooking pots and dishes of meat, cheese and fish. Everyone brought out their bowls, knives and spoons, some giving them an attentive wipe, some already holding them out for a dollop of soup from the largest pot by the fire. Ingibjorg smiled in satisfaction as her women went about pouring ale from large jugs, as if she herself had made the fragrant brew rather than hiring the best brewers to do it for her. The thought made Ketil look about the hall, a new building since his last visit. There were hangings on some parts of the walls, rich with gold thread and striking colours, some of the finest he had seen in his travels. He wondered how many of them Sigrid had made: he knew Ingibjorg had been angling to employ her for the job.

He had a fancy to sit with Tosti and catch up with more of the claik from Buckquoy and Birsay than he had already picked up from the day's travels, but looking over he saw that Tosti was inevitably bound to the Abbot, seated up near Thorfinn and Ingibjorg. Ketil stayed where he was, hoping instead that Hakon would find someone more congenial to talk to somewhere else. But Hakon seemed keen to stay with him, and gestured one of the women over to pour them both more ale. Ketil helped himself to roast pork and onions, taking another piece of flatbread to wipe the last traces of the soup from his dish, trying to look as if the last thing on his mind was conversation with Hakon. It worked for a few minutes: Hakon assessed the charms of the woman who had brought the ale, compared notes with his other neighbour, picked a chicken wing clean with delicate teeth, drank two more cups of ale. Then he turned his attention back to Ketil.

'So, how's life treating you?'

'Fine, thank you,' said Ketil. 'I keep busy.'

'I'm sure. I hear you're running round the world seeing to problems for Thorfinn. Interesting work, no doubt.'

'Very interesting.' He did enjoy much of his work for Thorfinn, but he did not feel easy talking about it. And it was Thorfinn's business, not his, and not Hakon's, even if Hakon was also Thorfinn's man. 'What were you doing in Colonia?'

'Oh, Colonia!' Hakon laughed, leaning back, at his ease. 'What a place! The church runs it, you know, there's no earl or king that has any power around there. Archbishop Herman is all-powerful.'

'And does that work well?'

Hakon pondered.

'Well enough, I suppose. He has no need to take anyone raiding: it's a whole system based on taxes and they have coins with fixed weights and values, you know, like off to the East.'

'So that's what Thorfinn wants to introduce here?'

'Something like that,' said Hakon comfortably. 'The old Abbot has done a lot of land valuation around Colonia, you know, so it's fair, or so it sort of looks fair. You know, a small piece of good grazing is worth more than a big piece of bad grazing, that kind of thing. But surely you have more interesting things to talk about than land valuation, Ketil! Come on: tell me what else you've been up to. What about that fine young widow of yours, Sigrid? You didn't tell us what she looked like when you were saying what a poor thing she was!'

'She's not well off. She had compensation to pay on her late husband's behalf.'

'He killed someone?'

'Yes.' More than one person, probably, but he was not going to tell Hakon that.

'She should marry again. That's a nice bit of land, and she'd easily find someone.'

'It's early days.'

'It's over a year, isn't it? I thought you said she was a widow when you were here before.'

He had forgotten how Hakon remembered details. He needed to be more careful.

'I suppose so.'

'You hoping she'll wait till you're ready to settle down?' Hakon leaned forward to give Ketil a heavy nudge with his elbow. 'Or do you have your eye on young Asgerdr? Now, she's a pretty bit – and you'd have a very influential father-in-law.'

'Never a good idea to marry into a great family like that,' said Ketil firmly. 'Not unless you're from one yourself.'

'She's ripe for marrying, though,' said Hakon thoughtfully, watching Asgerdr directing Ingibjorg's women. 'Thorfinn should be looking to it, not relying on whatever the next bairn is going to be, or leaving it till she starts looking like her mother.'

'Heavens, no,' Ketil found himself muttering. He glanced at Asgerdr. That white-blond hair, and the long face, still delicate in the daughter … there was a high chance she would turn into her mother, though he would not wish it on anyone. 'What about you, then, Hakon? Married yet?'

Hakon grinned.

'Well, I needed someone to stay behind and keep an eye on the land. And she's a pretty thing, too, as well as being tough with the slaves. Hopes of a son before the autumn …'

'Congratulations.'

'You remember my mother? She was there when you came to stay that winter, remember? She's still going, still working away on weaving, and teaching the wife the ways of dairying, though she's slowing down now, of course. They get on well enough, thank goodness. The land is in good hands.'

'That's good to hear. It's fine land.'

'And no taxes on it yet!' Hakon laughed. 'But your little widow with her nice bit of grazing and those fields of bygg – she might find herself needing another source of income soon. Think about it, Ketil: married life, somewhere to come home to, a warm bed on a cold evening. Can she cook?'

'Not noticeably.' Ketil prayed Hakon would never report those words to Sigrid.

'Oh. Oh, well, there's always something, isn't there?'

Talk moved on to other shared times, other women, with Hakon doing most of the talking. Ketil let him tell his stories, pretending he was someone else, somewhere else.

At last the tables were drawn back, and Thorfinn's men, the ones with no homes of their own to go to, made their beds on the floor with the ease of custom. Ketil wrapped himself in his cloak, then flicked the top of it away from his arms. It was warm, and he doubted he would get much sleep tonight. Hakon had brought back too many memories, more tonight than before. Hakon's mother, that farm cleared from the forest, the snow thick on the frozen ground, the animals' breath steaming at one end of the broad wooden longhouse. It was, he told himself, a long time ago. He should let it go. But sleep would not come for hours, and when it did, it was filled with dreams of a girl neither of them had mentioned that evening.

When the dawn light began to strengthen, Ketil shook the last of his uneasy night from his head, and slipped out of the hall. The sun was already appearing over the low hills to the east, and someone, by the scraping sounds, was preparing the fires in the bath house for lighting. He shivered, not so much from the cold as from sleepiness, and rubbed his arms hard to warm and waken himself.

He turned and strolled around Thorfinn's new buildings, walking back up the gentle hillside to the church. Its door was at the far end, and he carried on towards it, intending to take a closer look at the new monastic buildings. They rose unimposingly, not feeling any need to impress, only to shelter on this exposed headland. Abbot Konrad had apparently taken up residence there, for lack of monks, and Ketil had no wish to go inside and disturb him. He was still standing by the corner of the church, unobtrusive, when Otto, the Abbot's servant, appeared from the other direction, embedded in shawls, and let himself in to the monastic quarters. He must be an early riser, too, Ketil thought, pushing his shoulder away from the wall and walking forward. Otto had closed the door behind him. The door to the church was open, though, and Ketil slipped in there instead.

Two figures already knelt separately in prayer. One was Father Tosti, taking a well-earned break from his translation duties. The other, to Ketil's surprise, was Lambi, almost unrecognisable without his woolly cap. Ketil crossed himself and knelt, too, a distance away from both of them, offering up a litany of requests and thanks as he often did, even when the opportunity of a church did not present itself. When he opened his eyes, he had already sensed that someone was standing close by, and was faintly annoyed to find that it was Lambi, grinning like an over-persistent dog.

'Good morning, Lambi,' he said, rising and bowing his head once more in the direction of the altar. Tosti remained motionless. 'Did you need to speak to me?'

'No, no, not really,' said Lambi. 'Just saying good morning. That Thorfinn keeps a fine table, doesn't he? I've a thick head this morning!'

'You don't seem any worse than usual,' said Ketil drily.

'Oh, I wanted to get up early and go and buy a new comb. I've broken mine,' he said, fishing in his pouch to produce the remnants of what had been a greyish object, much worn by the strain of trying to keep Lambi's hair in order. 'See? I don't think that wee bar across the top was strong enough. They rarely are. I go through a lot of combs. They don't make them the way they used to, I think.'

'Do you know where you'll find a combmaker, then?'

'Oh, aye. I just thought I'd tell you. You don't need me with you today, do you?'

Ketil sighed.

'No, no. Go on and get yourself a new comb.'

SEX

VI

SIGRID WISHED SHE had not bothered with her back cloak and a short dress that morning. It was far too hot, at least down here by the harbour where the wind only teased. But it had not seemed quite right to make for Thorfinn's hall underdressed, and the short dress, that covered the most worn part of her overdress, was the finest piece of clothing she owned. She had been able to make it from oddments cut from elsewhere, and the colour was a pleasing dark red that she had more often seen on expensive sealskins. A little fancy braiding covered the bit where the material had run out a little too short. No one had ever seemed to notice.

She stopped to rest briefly before climbing the path from the harbour to the gate of the Brough. She still felt sweaty when she reached the hall. She paused at the door. Voices were raised inside: she had no wish to walk in on Thorfinn taking his temper out on one of his men. At first she did not understand the words and stood in confusion: then light dawned, and she went in quietly.

The Abbot, that tall figure with the exceptional clothing, was seated very upright in a high chair, speaking what Sigrid assumed must be Latin. Thorfinn had a conciliatory look on his face, a look so unusual for him that he seemed to have snatched it from someone else and stretched it to fit. Ketil was standing opposite the Abbot, hands behind his back, an expression of thoughtful repose on his still face. Hakon, on the other hand, dark hair gleaming even in the shadows, seemed to sense that someone else had entered the hall. He glanced around and immediately saw Sigrid in the shadows, nodded, and winked. Sigrid raised her eyebrows, and Hakon, with a glance back at the conversation in the middle of the hall, strolled over to join her.

'What's happening?' she asked, not giving him a chance to ask what she was doing there.

'Oh, Abbot Konrad wants to carry on his survey of Thorfinn's lands, and Thorfinn is anxious for his safety after Steinar's death. The fellow there – you know him, maybe?' Sigrid looked where he was nodding, and saw an abundance of moustache. Oddr, of course.

'Yes, Einar's man.'

'He came to tell us the latest. It looks like a robbery that turned violent.'

'It certainly did.' Sigrid tutted. 'But if that's true, then presumably it was an opportunist, if they attacked at that hour of the morning using the man's own axe. Why should Thorfinn think that the Abbot, escorted in broad daylight by three armed men – I assume that miserable-looking manservant is armed - and Father Tosti, would come to any harm?'

'I'm sure he's just being careful,' said Hakon, soothing. 'Are you still staying down there? Next to Steinar's house?'

'Yes.'

'So is that the gossip? That it was an opportunist thief?'

Sigrid hesitated. She had worked the opportunist bit out for herself – wasn't the idea obvious, if you didn't know anything more than that? – but some men, in her experience, did not listen to arguments that women came up with. Better just to say that everyone thought so, then the idea would begin to circulate and the investigation would make some progress.

'Yes, that's what everyone is saying,' she agreed meekly. 'But I'd still like a word with Thorfinn, because there's something that might help him with the Abbot.'

Hakon did not try to stop her, smiling as she moved past him and into the centre of the hall. She nodded to Ketil when he saw her. Thorfinn, mid-sentence, stopped and waited as he watched her approach, a hint of resignation in his eyes.

'Sigrid. Welcome,' he said when she was close enough. 'What can we do for you today? Ingibjorg is still abed, if you've come to discuss hangings … but I think I can tell from your face that it's not women's work you've come to talk about.'

'Quite right, my lord,' she said, confident enough that Thorfinn, at least, would listen to her. 'It's about Steinar Valison.'

'How did I guess?' Thorfinn smiled, though, and turned to take a seat on one of the benches, waving her to continue. Father Tosti, she noticed, murmured something to the Abbot, who raised his perfect eyebrows in astonishment.

'Well, I've been staying down at the harbour settlement with one of Ragna's daughters,' - now it was Thorfinn's turn to raise his eyebrows - 'just to help her learn to weave, and Steinar's longhouse, or rather his wife's brother's longhouse, is nearby. In fact, Steinar and his family visited us the night before last. You know that Steinar was not long back from Colonia.' She felt she had pronounced the odd placename awkwardly, but it must have been accurate enough, for she noted Abbot Konrad's sudden attention. 'He only found out that evening that Abbot Konrad and his party had arrived. And according to his sister-in-law, Steinar was setting out early yesterday morning particularly to come up here and speak with Abbot Konrad, if he could.'

'With Abbot Konrad?'

'Now, I don't know,' Sigrid went on, determined to lay out the possibilities. 'He might indeed have been killed by someone who just wanted to steal his ring and a couple of ordinary bangles. But it just seems to me a bit of a coincidence, all this Colonia business. And Steinar could speak Saxon, too.'

'What does that have to do with it?' Thorfinn frowned.

'I have no idea, but it does mean that he and Abbot Konrad could have spoken together without using an interpreter. I know Father Tosti is completely trustworthy,' she added, with a reassuring smile flung at Tosti, 'but there might have been something that needed to be said in the strictest secrecy. I'm guessing,' she admitted. 'Or it could have been something more general, some reason why someone did not want Steinar and the Abbot to meet.' She looked about her, struck by the quiet of the hall. 'Well,' she said, 'I thought it was worth mentioning. I know – I know Einar's not in quite so much control as he used to be,' she nodded at Oddr, whose moustache was agitating. 'It's true, Oddr, you know it is. But I don't think things have become so bad that a man leaving his house a little early on a summer's morning is in danger of having his head split open for a bit of silver. You know that, too, my lord,' she added, risking a direct appeal to Thorfinn himself. She tried to ignore a soft chuckle from behind her, telling herself that Hakon was not laughing at her. Father Tosti's susurration of Latin continued to her left. She wondered what Abbot Konrad was thinking.

'Have you discussed all this with Ketil?' Thorfinn asked at last. Ketil met Sigrid's eye, but there seemed to be no message there, the blue eyes shaded.

'Well, I saw Ketil yesterday, but that was before I knew where Steinar was going, of course.'

Thorfinn tapped his fingers on the edge of the bench, leaning forward and staring at the flag floor. Then he stood, shoving himself up as if his legs had stiffened. He pointed to Oddr.

'You, go back to Einar and say I'm taking this out of his hands. I intend no insult, he knows: there are other matters to which I believe he would much prefer to attend.' He rubbed a hand over his face, weary and, Sigrid thought, regretful. Thorfinn had once had great respect for Einar, and to admit that the older man was not capable of fulfilling his obligations would be hard. Oddr bowed, though his moustache looked furious, and left the hall with just the least stamping of his feet. Thorfinn watched him go, shrugging a little. By overlooking Einar, Thorfinn had diminished Oddr's own standing.

'Right,' said Thorfinn, fists on hips. 'Ketil, I want this business of Steinar's death sorted out. Sigrid, give him whatever information you have, and – whatever else you can do to help.' He looked her straight in the eye, then his gaze wandered, as if he was not quite sure that he wanted to know how much help that might be. 'I don't feel happy about Abbot Konrad surveying the islands if there is someone murdering people for their rings, and equally I do not want him wandering abroad if there is some question of a direct connexion between him and a dead man – he might be intended to be next. The sooner you sort this out, Ketil, the better. I imagine Abbot Konrad wants to be on his way home before the onset of winter.'

'My lord ...' Ketil seemed to be struggling to find an excuse. In a moment he would be pleading a lack of local knowledge, Sigrid thought. There was another slight chuckle from somewhere behind her, and Hakon stepped forward, any laughter controlled on his face.

'My lord, if I can be of any assistance to Ketil I should be delighted. We have worked together before, though it was a number of years ago. Two heads will no doubt be better than one!'

Have I suddenly become headless? Sigrid wondered, crossly.

'And I was a little acquainted with Steinar, of course: he was still in Colonia when I arrived there.'

That made Sigrid pay more attention. Perhaps he would be useful after all. There was a muttering to her left, and Abbot Konrad raised one graceful hand, enunciating what sounded to Sigrid like a blessing. Tosti took a deep breath and began in Norse.

'My lord Abbot says that my lord Thorfinn might wish to bear in mind that he himself was to some extent, though not, of course, due chiefly to a lack of time but also to an undeniable distinction in station and function, intimately, acquainted with the late and much lamented Steinar Valison, and would willingly provide any assistance in the matter of the investigation of the man's death that it is in his modest powers, modest, that is, specifically in this land which though it has much to recommend it is not his home country, to afford.' He stopped to breathe again, and Thorfinn, who had been watching his lips in fascination, nodded.

'Tell him it's much appreciated,' he said. 'Well, Ketil –'

'And my lord Abbot adds, with all due respect to my lord Thorfinn, which it is his privilege and pleasure always to accord, that if, as he understands it from the account of the woman who has approached Lord Thorfinn with the information this morning,' Tosti cast a swift apologetic glance at Sigrid but did not pause in his speech, 'and who, if my lord Abbot remembers correctly, was present at the scene of death yesterday in a state of regrettable undress perhaps occasioned by her womanly emotion at the events which had come to pass in that place, but who through her direct involvement in those same events may indeed have reliable information relating to the tragedy, tempered, of course, with the possibility that that same womanly emotion which led to her excessive distress at the scene might also distort the strict accuracy of that information ...' Tosti stopped, as if trying to find his thread again, 'if, as my lord Abbot says, the man Steinar was indeed on his way to approach my lord Abbot with questions, greetings or a message of any kind, he, that is, my lord Abbot, was completely unaware of it.'

'Yes,' said Thorfinn after a moment. 'I daresay he was.' He bowed a brief acknowledgement to the Abbot, no doubt hoping he would not contribute further. Sigrid was almost too busy disentangling the casual insults from the Abbot's speech to see Thorfinn turn again to Ketil. 'Ketil, you see you have several sources of information on Steinar Valison. You have the family, and you have those who knew him in Colonia. You also have the possibility of finding the bangles and the ring that were stolen from the dead man. No doubt somewhere in there will be the answer to the question of who killed him and why, and thereafter the Abbot can proceed with his work in peace and safety.'

'Come on, then, Ketil,' said Hakon, taking his arm, 'let's go and find a cup of ale somewhere and discuss what we'll do.' He guided Ketil towards the back of the hall, where the side door to the kitchens was, and no doubt, Sigrid thought acidly, Asgerdr with a ready barrel of ale and a sideways smile. She glanced around the hall. Thorfinn had gone back to looking at some papers on a table, and Father Tosti was deep in discussion in that impenetrable Latin – though, she thought, it could not be much worse than when it was translated into Norse – with the revered Abbot. She bit her lips hard, turned on her heel, and left the hall, furious.

The wind outside, tumbled by having to skip through the close-packed buildings on the Brough, caught her playfully and tossed her backcloak up to catch her headcloth. She slapped them down, folded her arms and stood for a moment, considering the benefits of setting fire to the hall then and there, in traditional fashion. Regrettably, she would probably have to burn the kitchens as well if she wanted to catch Ketil and Hakon – which she did. She decided to postpone her slaughter, and taking a few very deep breaths, until the blue sky fizzed when she looked at it, she loosened her arms deliberately and stalked off. She might as well make some practical use of her walk up to the Brough.

Sorli the combmaker lived and worked up to the north of the Brough, near the blacksmith but not so near as to risk random fires. Burning horn gave off the kind of smell that people preferred to go to some lengths to avoid. Sorli himself was not the sociable type, but his combs lasted well and no one had to visit him too often, or at least that was how Sigrid saw it. She was surprised, when she approached the workshop beside his small longhouse, to find another customer seated comfortably on a rock seat by the open hatch and work table, apparently gossiping easily with the combmaker. Well, the customer was gossiping easily: Sorli, as usual, was completely focussed on the detailed work in his hands, and Sigrid hurried over as unobtrusively as she could, hoping to watch another new comb take shape.

It was clearly one of Sorli's standard combs. He had antler brought in, as people did, sometimes red deer from Caithness and sometimes reindeer from Norway, and spent his evenings, as far as Sigrid could ever judge, filing the dark outer layers off to find the smooth creamy material beneath, slicing the most suitable portions into long, flat laths, selecting stronger, thicker sections to make the braces that held the teeth in place. It was a question, then, of assembling these components to suit the customer's requirements, or occasionally (as Sorli did not ask many questions) what Sorli thought the customer ought to require. The laths for this customer's comb were already cut into oblongs and laid side by side, and had then been braced together with two of the thick, curved brackets, their edges filed beautifully smooth to sit comfortably in the hand. Now Sorli, with a drill and a saw, mere toys in his large hands, was preparing the decorative band that would hold the nails to secure the whole thing. He sketched zigzag lines delicately with the saw, and used the drill to add little circles with dots in the centre, the balance and proportion coming easily to someone who made that pattern maybe three or four times in any week. Once the comb was in one piece, he weighted it at the very edge of the table, and began the tricky task of sawing into each of the oblong slices of lath, to make the comb's teeth. The customer, clearly aware that at any point a slip of the saw would destroy all the work before him, watched with his mouth open, his woolly cap pushed back on to his thick hair in case he would miss the least move. Sigrid looked at him more closely. Had he been at Olvor's house yesterday? She thought he looked familiar, but she had been a little distracted at the time. She turned back to the comb, hoping that Sorli was cutting the teeth to be as strong as possible. The man's hair looked like a challenge.

As Sorli cut down between the last two teeth, both Sigrid and the customer breathed a sigh of relief. The comb was complete, and perfect.

The customer turned, and grinned at Sigrid.

'Hello! How are you this morning?'

'Well, thank you. And you?' Lambi, that was his name. Affable, but perhaps a little unreliable, she remembered thinking. He made a job out of sorting out some pieces of hacksilver in payment, and waved the comb delightedly at her.

'Nice, eh? You getting one?'

'I always buy my combs from Sorli.' If she had thought this would earn her anything like a smile of acknowledgement from Sorli, she would have been disappointed. 'The usual, please, Sorli.'

'Break it?' Sorli demanded.

'Yes.' She produced the pieces, hoping some could be reused. Sorli prodded them, unimpressed.

'You need something stronger. Thick antler. Maybe iron.'

'No, no, the usual is fine. It was an accident.'

Sorli made grumpy noises, and fiddled round with his supplies of antler pieces to find what would do, casting pieces down and picking fresh ones up, peering at them and tossing them back on the table in disgust. Sigrid met Lambi's eye and raised her eyebrows. Lambi laughed.

'They're great combs,' he said, trying his new one out on his fringe, without taking off his cap. 'I might order another one, if I could. More decorative, though. Maybe with some runes on it?'

'Runes?' Sorli eyed him suspiciously, though he often, Sigrid knew, carved runes on to his combs. The letters would spell out anything from 'To My Mother' to 'Sorli made this'.

'Yes,' said Lambi, fiddling with the comb now. 'I thought maybe I could put someone's name on it? And some nice little crosshatched panels, or something? Or can you do pictures?'

'I can do straight lines, and I can do dots,' said Sorli uncompromisingly. 'Make what you can of that. How many runes?'

Lambi counted on his fingers, muttering to himself.

'Eight, I think. I'm not sure.'

'Find out. Women don't like it if you get their names

wrong.'

'I never said it was for a woman ...' said Lambi, his shoulders sagging. Sorli snorted, and laid out the pieces for Sigrid's comb. 'No, I think I'm right,' he said, knowing when he was beaten. 'But I'll check.'

'This must be a new love!' Sigrid said lightly, trying to make up for Sorli's unwelcoming manner. 'Someone local?'

'Mphm,' said Lambi, indistinctly. 'I'll, um, I'll show you what I want.' The path in front of the stall was slabbed, and he found a piece of charcoal and began to draw runes. 'Something like that?'

Sorli glanced down, and grunted.

'Come back at midday,' he said.

'Thanks. I'll see you at midday. Good to see you, Sigrid,' he added, and shambled off towards the hall, or the baths, or the gate, or almost anywhere – not a direction that gave a half-curious observer any clue as to where this new love might be. She grinned. It did not matter to her.

Following him down the hill with her eyes, for want of other distraction while Sorli was pessimistically filing a piece of antler to fit, she saw him disappear round the corner and almost immediately Ketil and Hakon emerged from the direction of the hall's kitchens. They must have had their private conversation about the investigation, she thought, remembered anger surging up again. But no, she told herself, looking away from them deliberately: if they wanted to waste their time running around looking for a killer, let them: she had other things to do, woolwork and farming and preparing for the bygg harvest and all those much more important ways of spending her days. If they felt they didn't need her help, then it was their loss. But she could not help just looking back, to see if they were heading her way.

She was just in time to see Hakon, handsome and confident, slap Ketil lightly on the shoulder, and go on his way with a cheerful wave. Ketil stopped to watch him go. They were a little distance away, but Sigrid was shocked to see the look of – what was it, disgust? – that passed over Ketil's face as Hakon headed towards the bath house to groom his shiny brown hair and beard. Then just as quickly, the expression vanished, and Ketil was once more bland-faced, looking about him as if he could not quite remember why he had come out this way. Then he caught sight of Sigrid watching him, and started across to the comb maker's stall.

'All organised?' she asked brightly, a little too soon for him to hear clearly without straining.

'We've made some progress, yes,' said Ketil. 'Was Lambi here? Awkward looking man, woollen cap?'

'Yes, he bought a comb.'

'What else?' Ketil shrugged, as though he had asked a stupid question. 'Is that one yours?'

'Yes.'

He sat down on the rocks that Lambi had vacated, propping his elbows on his knees.

'Not sure this is the best place to talk.'

'I don't know why not,' said Sigrid briskly. 'I can't imagine what you have to say that a combmaker couldn't hear.'

Sorli, sensibly, ignored them. Ketil looked at her.

'Will you be staying down there for long?'

'It depends,' she said. 'I'm there to teach Olvor tablet-weaving and nailbinding. It was not made clear whether or not I could leave before she's competent. If I wait until she is, I'll be buried down there.'

Ketil smiled slightly.

'They can't have lived there long.'

'She can't, no. But the house has belonged to her husband's family for years.'

'And the neighbours?'

Sigrid glanced at Sorli. The matter would be common knowledge, soon enough, anyway.

'Steinar is married to Svanhild, the beautiful woman you saw. Svanhild's brother is Ubbi, the fair-haired man who went for Einar's help. It's Ubbi's house. He's married to Thorgunna, the other woman, the one who was holding the children.'

'Whose are the children?'

'One for each couple. They seem to be of an age.'

'And what age is that?'

'Seven or eight months, I thought, when I saw them the night before.'

Sorli began sawing the teeth on the comb.

'Anything strike you as strange about any of them?' Ketil

asked. Sorli swore.

'Be quiet till I finish this, or go and talk somewhere else,' he said. Ketil's eyebrows shot up, but he shut his mouth and remained almost motionless until finally Sorli said,

'There! Done.'

Another comb finished.

SJAU

VII

KETIL WATCHED AS Sigrid paid carefully for the comb and slipped it into one of the pouches on her belt. The combmaker charged her a fair price, he thought, and seemed to accord her some respect. He was pleased to see it. Anyone who had grown up in the markets of Heithabyr knew what they were doing buying and selling – well, perhaps not him, he admitted to himself, smiling. He had not made much of a trader.

'I'll walk with you back to the harbour,' he said, when she had finished her transaction.

'Whether I like it or not? Is that your part of the work, then? What's Hakon up to?'

'He's gone for a bath,' said Ketil, quite bland. 'I'm going to see if I can find out anything more about Steinar from his family.' He wanted to ask them if they had any idea what Steinar had been going to say to Abbot Konrad, and who else might have known about it, but no doubt Sigrid would have thought of all that already. It would not take long to walk down to Steinar's house, but it would be more than enough time for Sigrid to instruct him on what he should be looking for and how he should go about it. He found himself almost looking forward to it. And anyway, anything was better than working with Hakon. For just a moment he contemplated the possibility that Hakon might drown in the bath house – accidentally, of course. Then, reluctantly, he reminded himself that it was sinful to want such a thing – however tempting it might be.

They had begun walking towards the bath house and the gate as he was thinking, and he had not noticed that Sigrid was silent, walking a pace or two ahead of him. He lengthened his stride to catch up.

'How have things been here in the last year, then?' he asked, not used to having to make conversation with her.

'Fine. We manage quite well.'

'Thorfinn been all right?'

'As you saw.'

'And Einar?'

'As you heard.'

There had to be more than that. They both knew that Einar's year would have been out of the ordinary, at the very least. She edged ahead of him again, as if trying to create the impression that they were just two people who happened to be heading in the same direction. He let her.

They reached the settlement by the harbour without another word spoken between them. At the longhouse she had said belonged to Olvor's husband – Ketil thought but could not remember having heard his name – she stalked to the door and disappeared inside. Ketil walked past, turning up the hill to go to the house where they had taken Steinar's body. He would rather work with Sigrid than with Hakon, but just at the moment he would rather not work with either of them.

He was about to knock at the longhouse door when a movement caught his eye, and he saw a woman come round the top corner of the longhouse, walking slowly, carrying a bundle in her arms. She did not seem surprised to see him, and he thought he recognised her as the woman who had held the two children yesterday. Who had Sigrid said she was? Steinar's sister? No, Steinar's wife's brother's wife, that was it. Thor-something, but it could be anything. He paused at the doorway, and waited for her to come closer.

'Hallo. You were with the Abbot yesterday, weren't you?' Her voice was pleasant, though she was not as beautiful as her husband's sister. On the other hand, few were, Ketil thought.

'That's right. I'm Ketil, Ketil Gunnarson. I work for Thorfinn.'

'Oh! You're not from Colonia, then?'

'No, from Trondheim. From Heithabyr, originally, but that was a long time ago. You're …' he hesitated, still not quite sure, 'you're Steinar's … Steinar's wife is your husband's sister?'

'Yes.' She smiled. 'Well done for remembering! Everyone remembers Svanhild,' she added, without rancour. The bundle in her arms shifted, and he saw it was one of the children, a pink face and a mat of fair hair, pursed lips making faint sucking noises, eyes firmly closed. She shifted her grip, and hummed a little.

'I suppose so. That's not always a good thing though, is it?' he asked, speaking more quietly in case he woke the child.

'No, not always. Svanhild would like to look quite ordinary, like me,' she said. 'But I'm forgetting my manners. Come in – are you here to pay your respects?'

'Yes, in the first place.'

'I had to take the baby out for a bit. He sleeps much better if he's had a bit of fresh air. Svanhild's child would sleep on a roof ridge. Ours needs attention before he'll nod off!' She led the way into the longhouse, and announced, 'I think he's settled now. Here's someone come from Thorfinn's hall to pay his respects – Ketil, yes?'

Ketil stepped forward as the woman went to lay the child down in a bedspace by the side of the house. The dog rose at once and came to inspect him: Ketil rubbed its ears. Svanhild, pale as a ghost, stood and brought Ketil a cup of wine.

'Welcome,' she said. 'Please take a seat. Thank you for coming.' She glanced up into his face. 'Oh! I think I know you – you helped to bring – to bring my husband's body home yesterday.'

'I was happy to be of help.' He bowed his head a little awkwardly. It was difficult to know what to say to someone quite so beautiful. Ordinary conversation seemed wrong. He looked away to find somewhere to sit. Steinar's body lay much as he had seen it yesterday, bandaged and prone, the great dog already lying by his side again. Ketil sat nearer to the fire, next to the fair-haired man there.

'I'm Ubbi,' said the man at once. 'Svanhild's my sister. We met yesterday, too.'

'You went for Einar.'

Ubbi's face, already heavy with sorrow, twisted a little.

'Much good that did us,' he said. 'It looks as if Steinar was robbed, but I don't know that anyone up at Buckquoy is going to be out looking for the killer or what was stolen. Oh, this is my wife, Thorgunna.' The woman Ketil had met outside had returned to the fire and was stirring a pot there. She nodded and smiled at Ketil.

'Well, Steinar was Thorfinn's man, wasn't he?' Ketil asked generally. 'Thorfinn has sent me to ask some questions, to see if we can find Steinar's murderer.'

'Really? Thorfinn has?' Ubbi seemed very surprised. He and Thorgunna exchanged glances. Ketil wondered if Thorfinn was beginning to seem as ineffectual as Einar.

'He's sad to hear of your loss,' Ketil tried, 'and he has no wish to have robbers wandering his lands so freely. And he valued Steinar's work.'

'Did he?' asked Ubbi, even more doubtful. 'He sent Steinar to Colonia but had already summoned this Abbot from there before Steinar had the chance to tell him whether or not it was worth his while.'

'Really? That's a bit strange. He told us all this morning how useful Steinar's report had been. Perhaps he just wanted to have the Abbot here and most of his work done before the winter. Would Steinar have recommended the Abbot to Thorfinn? Was there, perhaps,' he tried to think fast, 'someone else Steinar would have preferred, if he had been able to tell Thorfinn in time?'

The three of them looked at each other, not sure. Ketil gave them a minute, then tried,

'Do you know why he was going up to the Brough yesterday morning?'

'Oh, he wanted to see the Abbot,' said Ubbi at once. 'He admired the Abbot, and the Archbishop – he was always going on about the Archbishop. I don't think, like you said, he'd have recommended anyone else. He was very enthusiastic about the way the Archbishop had everything organised to run on Christian law. I mean, if the Archbishop had recommended the Abbot, Steinar would have thought that was enough for anyone, but I had the impression he liked the Abbot personally, anyway.'

'So he was just going up to say hello to the Abbot?'

'Yes, I think so,' said Ubbi, frowning. He was a good-looking man, Ketil thought, but nothing to his sister. He seemed to have lost a finger or two at some point, but he had no scars to mar his handsome features.

'I'm not so sure,' said Thorgunna, glancing across at Steinar's still face. 'I had the notion – I mean, he went out gey early. I thought he was in a hurry to see the Abbot. As if he had something important to tell him.' She raised her eyebrows significantly. The others seemed surprised, but not against the idea.

'That's likely enough,' said Ubbi. 'Otherwise why go out so early?'

'He didn't say anything about it to me,' said Svanhild. Ketil looked at her, but she did not seem put out at all. 'But when a man has been away a lot, he forgets to confide in his wife, I daresay.'

'I imagine that's right,' Ketil said. 'It's a habit, I suppose.' He was not even sure she had been addressing him, but he felt the need to respond. He cleared his throat. 'When is the funeral?'

'Tomorrow,' said Ubbi. 'I don't know if Einar – or Thorfinn – needs us to delay, but the weather's warm, so if you hear anything then you'll need to get word to us fast if you want us to hold back.'

Svanhild's eyes surged with tears. Ketil rose, and said,

'With your permission, Svanhild.'

He stepped across to Steinar's body, and took another look at the still face, the bandages around the wound that barely disguised it. Though of course he had now been washed clean, there had been enough blood around him and on his skin and clothes to convince Ketil that Steinar had been killed where he had been found, and the body had not been moved afterwards. The dog shifted. Svanhild put out a hand to her, but the dog edged away from her.

'Steinar's dog,' she said, a crack in her voice. 'Always Steinar's dog. Who will you allow to tend to you now, poor thing?'

'She's fond of Thorgunna,' said Ubbi loyally. The dog settled again.

'Were there any other wounds?' Ketil asked, without looking round.

'No,' said Thorgunna, 'nothing that I saw.'

Ketil gently lifted Steinar's hands and looked at his nails, then at his palms. An unarmed man, faced with a raised axe, will often use even his bare hands to try to defend himself. But there was no sign of injury, no blade strokes, no bruising, no ripped nails nor anything under them.

'He did not run,' he murmured, half to himself. 'He must have been taken completely by surprise. And yet … his own axe … He wore it in his belt, I assume?'

'He did,' said Ubbi, with a look towards Svanhild. 'On his right hip, though: he liked to pull it out and swing it up straight.'

'His right hip,' Ketil repeated. 'So someone following him could have reached it, without being tangled in his cloak.'

'That's right,' said Ubbi.

'And he carried it all the time?'

'It was his preferred weapon, if he was to carry one,' Ubbi confirmed. 'Like me.' He indicated the head of an axe at his own waist. Ketil looked down at it as Ubbi sat, then caught a movement at the door. Sigrid was there, propped against the doorpost, watching the proceedings grimly.

'And he was in all respects ready to go up to the Brough? Cloak on, I remember, armed, booted, hair combed, and everything?'

'Yes, yes,' Svanhild replied, wiping her face impatiently. 'I think I remember him going out before that to the privy, so he'll have washed and combed his hair and everything then, and come back in to dress.'

'Did he wear his ring all the time?'

'Yes, he did. He never took it off,' she said.

'What was it like?'

'It was a simple twist,' she said, 'but it had two lines engraved along it. Steinar … Steinar said it was our paths, running side by side always.' She ended on another sob.

Ketil looked across at Sigrid.

'I wonder why they waited until he was armed before they robbed him, then? They could have caught him earlier, when he went to the privy.'

'Maybe they weren't there then. Maybe they only arrived after he came back inside.' Ubbi was frowning, not sure that this mattered in the least. Ketil nodded.

'You could be right, indeed. I see you have a guest, though,' he said.

Thorgunna jumped, and turned to the doorway.

'Oh, Sigrid!' She went to greet her, taking a cup of wine. 'Sigrid, this is Ketil, one of Thorfinn's men.'

'We've met,' said Sigrid shortly, and accepted the wine. 'Thank you.' She sat down near the fire. 'Olvor wants to know if there's anything we can do for tomorrow. We'll be here, of course.'

'That's all we need,' said Svanhild softly. 'Our neighbours with us. Thank you, Sigrid. But is Asmund all right?'

Sigrid made a face, though there was sympathy in it.

'I think so. He hasn't been in much. He knows he has to come and help with the bier, though.'

'It would have meant so much to Steinar,' Svanhild assured her.

'He will miss Steinar's company,' Sigrid said. 'Steinar was very kind to him.'

No one spoke for a moment. Ketil watched Sigrid. He would have to remember to ask her about Asmund.

'I'll leave you in peace now,' he said at last. 'I hope all goes well tomorrow.'

'You are most welcome to be here,' said Svanhild. 'I hope we shall see you again.'

'He'll need to ask more questions, no doubt,' said Ubbi to his sister. 'You're welcome, indeed. If you can find who killed Steinar, we'll all be very grateful.'

Ketil bowed his head, and made his way to the door, not looking at Sigrid.

Outside, he glanced about. He had no intention of going far just yet, and he wanted a better impression of the way the longhouses here fitted together in the settlement. The longhouse he had just left – Ubbi's, he reminded himself, though Svanhild seemed more like the hostess than Thorgunna did – was set inland from the one where Sigrid was staying, and a little forward of it. Ubbi's house was the furthest inland in the settlement, and beyond it, to the south, was a river, narrow and deep. Those who could ford it could make their way down towards Hamnavoe without cutting further inland, but carts and more nervous horses had to take a longer way around. Ketil glanced that way, remembering a ride he had taken down that direction himself. No doubt he would have to escort the Abbot south soon, when Thorfinn deemed it safe again, or ran out of patience.

Between the path that led through the settlement and the flat shore, three or four further houses were tucked as if huddled against the sea breezes. Beyond them, the loop of sea that formed Thorfinn's safest harbour was caught within the wall of the Brough, lying suspiciously calm and green against a blue sky. If you believed that Thorfinn had keen eyesight, he could be watching Ketil's progress down here. Ketil jumped as a crow on the longhouse ridge rasped a sudden cry. Hugin or Munin? he wondered. Maybe Thorfinn did not need sharp eyesight: he could send his ravens out, like Odin, to see what was going on in his realm.

He walked back to the end of Ubbi's longhouse, and propped himself comfortably against the wall, considering. When Sigrid emerged from the longhouse a few minutes later, she found him there, and jumped. The look on her face was very gratifying.

'You still here?' she asked.

'Yes, as you see.' She had probably hoped that he was long gone. 'I was considering where this opportunist thief might have come from.'

She gave a snort, and folded her arms, but she did not walk off.

'I was wondering if he came from Hamnavoe direction,' he went on. 'A stranger. We should ask around the settlement here, see if anyone has seen a stranger passing through.'

'A stranger sprayed with blood? First thing in the morning?' She tutted, then added, 'and you needn't think I'm helping you. Who's this 'we'?'

'Hakon and I will do it,' he found himself saying. He had no wish at all to work with Hakon, but the very thought of it would annoy Sigrid nicely. 'We've worked together before.'

'So he said. Very nice for you. He's clearly a patient man.'

To that, he could not bring himself to respond, but his silence proved useful. She could not resist breaking it.

'And anyway, do you really think it was an opportunist thief? Aren't you even tempted to look at all the connexions with Colonia and Abbot Konrad? Surely the coincidences are big enough that even you can spot them?'

'Nevertheless,' he said calmly, 'there is a clear motive for the opportunist thief. While I'm happy to admit that there are indeed plenty of connexions with Colonia, can you tell me why anyone connected with Colonia might have come here first thing in the morning to put an axe through the head of someone else connected with Colonia? I think both ideas need to be looked at seriously.'

She stared at him for a moment.

'You know,' she said at last, 'you're just as annoying now as you were when you were ten. Did that take a lot of effort, or does it just come naturally?'

'As naturally to me as it does to you,' he said, then smiled. 'Come on, Sigrid, you know I need your help. And value your help. And will be very grateful for your help.'

'Oh …' she looked away, and he could see her toes twitching with irritation. 'I was wrong. You're more annoying now than you were when you were ten. But you'll never get anywhere unless I do help you, and if I don't then Thorfinn will be cross with me and with these new taxes coming in I can't afford Thorfinn's anger, so I suppose I'd better do what I can for you.'

'Thank you.' He bowed his head politely, partly to hide another smile. There was a limit to what he could get away with, he knew. But there was some progress: the nine-year-old Sigrid in Heithabyr would have poked him with a spindle by now.

'Come and meet Olvor and Asmund,' she said, 'if Asmund is about. He's an odd character. And you've sort of met Olvor before, though you probably didn't notice. No one really did, while her mother was still alive.'

He followed her to the nearby longhouse, trying to catch her words as she continued over her shoulder,

'They'll know the family there much better than I do. I only met them the day before yesterday. Olvor,' she said, stopping in the doorway, 'do you remember Ketil?'

Ketil caught up with her. Olvor, her face white, had stumbled to her feet by the fire, mouth agape.

'Hello, Olvor,' said Ketil politely. 'I'm glad to see you again.'

Olvor seemed to try to pull herself together.

'Ketil, yes … I remember. Last year …'

'I've come to ask for your help, if that's all right,' said Ketil. He thought it might be best not to refer to last year's events: he had been there when Olvor's mother had died, but strictly speaking it had not been his fault – had it? He had mentioned it at confession, not happy with the circumstances, but Father Tosti had been very reasonable, in the end. But now, would it stop Olvor from talking to him? She had never talked much anyway.

Olvor stood motionless for a moment, only her eyes flicking back and forth between Ketil and Sigrid. Then she seemed to make a decision. She stooped to pour a cup of ale from a jug, and brought it forward to where Ketil still stood by the door.

'Welcome,' she said, though she did not quite meet his eye. He bowed, sipped, and thanked her, and she gestured him to take a seat by the fire. She sat opposite, elbows tucked into her waist, hands crunched together on her knees, waiting to see what they wanted of her.

'We just want to ask about Steinar – well, about the family over there generally,' Sigrid began, her voice surprisingly gentle. 'I hardly know them. And Ketil has to try to work out, for Thorfinn, why Steinar might have been killed.'

'He was killed for his ring and bangles, wasn't he?' Olvor looked up at Sigrid in astonishment. 'Someone stole them.'

'Yes … it's a shame, though, isn't it? Steinar was a very nice man.' Sigrid watched Olvor, though she cast a quick sideways glance at Ketil. Ketil nodded. Olvor clearly needed careful handling. Her fingers threatened to pull each other off her hands, wriggling and writhing on her lap.

'He was a very nice man,' she agreed at last. 'Asmund liked him. He was very kind to Asmund.'

'He was. Was he always nice to everyone?'

Olvor frowned, considering.

'I think so. He hasn't been here very much since I came to live here, but everyone was pleased to see him come home. Especially Svanhild, of course. And Asmund. And Ubbi really liked him, and Thorgunna, too. I can't think of anyone who didn't like him, truly.'

'Lucky man,' murmured Sigrid.

'Till now,' Ketil added, though only loudly enough for

Sigrid to hear.

'It must have been a stranger, for no one else would have done it,' said Olvor, happy now she had decided that.

'Have you heard of any strangers around?'

Olvor shook her head.

'But that's what it will be, a stranger.'

'What else do you know about the family?' Sigrid tried another angle, shrugging at Ketil. She was not too bad at this, he admitted to himself. He knew he came across as stern, even when he was trying to be friendly. Sigrid was cleverer at hiding her opinions, when she wanted to, anyway. He watched her out of the corner of his eye as Olvor again turned over her thoughts.

'It's Ubbi's house,' Olvor said at last. 'He and Thorgunna married two years ago, I think. The little boy was born around Yule, the same time as Svanhild and Steinar's boy, near enough. There was a big celebration for the two christenings. Svanhild is older than Ubbi, by a few years, and Steinar was older again. Ubbi has the land, but he looked up to Steinar as a big brother always. I think Steinar and Svanhild had another child once, but it died – or there may have been more than one. I'm not sure. This one is their only one now, anyway. They were such a happy family!' Olvor caught her breath on this thought, and there was something wistful in her eyes – not just grief for that happy family broken, Ketil realised, but regret that she herself had never managed quite that happiness for herself.

ÁTTA

VIII

SIGRID SIGHED, SEEING the sorrow on Olvor's pretty face. Some people just seemed to be born to be unhappy, she thought: when one bad situation came to an end and you thought they were free, they managed, somehow, to find themselves another place to be miserable. Yet she had seen no sign that Olvor and Asmund disliked each other, or were actively unhappy: there was not enough feeling on either side for that kind of thing.

She caught Ketil's eye.

'Shall we walk a little?' she asked.

'You've had nothing to eat!' Olvor was suddenly concerned.

'Some bread and cheese will do,' said Sigrid, anxious to leave this hearth before the empty misery spread. She had enough melancholy of her own to deal with in life without catching anyone else's, too. As a longterm guest she helped herself to a couple of large flatbreads from a hanging shelf, and a smallish, flat cheese, soft and fresh, before chivvying Ketil outside into the sunshine. Once out, she led the way down to the path through the village, and along to the river that cut it off at the south end. There was a perch where she could dangle her feet over the cool water, her back against a comfortable stone. She settled down, and Ketil, after a moment, slid down to sit against the stone but to one side, his long legs stretched parallel to the river, his sword laid carefully beside them. She passed him one of the flatbreads and broke the cheese in half, handing one half to him and licking her fingers.

'That's the bigger half. Want to see and make sure?'

Ketil often brought her back to feeling she was nine years old again.

'I trust you.'

She grinned. There was silence for a moment as they ate, enjoying the warmth of the day. The bread was tasty and the cheese cool, and it was quiet there with few passersby. A damselfly hovered above the grass, catching the light, and a cloud of midges contented themselves in the damp air of the stream, not bothering them, until they were scattered by the mighty wings of a yellow dragonfly. A few gulls cried above them, but most were busy streaking from place to place on some mysterious errands of their own. Sigrid felt unobserved, and hoped it was true.

'What's wrong with Asmund?' Ketil asked at last, wiping his fingers on the grass.

'Oh, nothing really. He's just a bit odd. Doesn't seem to know how to talk to people. Likes boats.'

'There's nothing wrong with liking boats,' said Ketil, a little too quickly. Sigrid smiled.

'I meant that he likes counting boats. He goes to the harbour and counts how many boats are there each day, and what kind. It's just hard to connect with him. I don't think Olvor has, yet, though she seems content. But Steinar was very patient with him. They really seemed to enjoy each other's company.'

'Steinar could do no wrong.'

'It sounds like that, doesn't it?'

'What was your impression of him?'

'He spent most of the evening talking with Asmund. I liked him, I think: I thought he seemed kind, and good to his wife. Keen on the church, and on Colonia, and on the way the two worked together there. He would have liked to live there, if Svanhild would have gone with him.'

'She never travelled there with him?'

'She said not.'

Ketil sighed, but said lightly,

'A shame. I had hoped for some jealous lover following them from Colonia to murder him.'

'She is beautiful, isn't she?' Sigrid tried not to sound too wistful.

'She is,' said Ketil. He was thoughtful. 'Though I'd have said most men would not dare approach her. Beautiful in an inaccessible way. I suspect Steinar was safe, in that direction.'

'Interesting,' said Sigrid, feeling slightly smug. Poor Svanhild, she thought. Too beautiful to be loved. But she had found her man, and her brother loved her, and even Thorgunna seemed to like her too, though she might be expected to be jealous … perhaps Thorgunna realised, being so close, being ordinary, how such beauty set a woman too far apart from the world. Sigrid told herself that she was glad she herself was not beautiful. An awful burden, surely. She smiled.

'So you favour the connexion with Colonia?' Ketil interrupted her thoughts.

'I think I do. It seems too much of a coincidence, that someone should be passing at the moment he left the house so early, right at the end of the settlement, that it should happen just when someone else had arrived at the Brough from where he had just been. Yes, all right, perhaps someone decided to take his ring and a couple of bangles for the look of it, or because they could not resist, but they could have taken more, and need not, maybe, even have killed him.'

'Perhaps they were interrupted.'

'By whom? No one said anything.'

'Or thought they were about to be interrupted. They heard a noise, thought someone was coming. You wouldn't stop to see whether or not you were right, in that situation.'

Sigrid ran the idea through in her head, trying to picture Steinar leaving the house, smartly dressed, his axe in his belt by his right arm; someone seeing him, quick to sense the possibilities, following behind him so close and silent that they were able to seize his axe before he could resist; striking him down; snatching his ring. Wait: something was wrong … what was it? Something just not right in that picture …

'Hello!'

The greeting made her jump, and she craned round her rock, past Ketil, to see Thorgunna on the path below them. As usual, she had the look of someone who had dressed in a hurry, and perhaps in the dark if there had been such a thing at this time of the summer. For once, she had no child on her hip: instead,

Steinar's dog had stopped too and leaned against her, head hanging low.

'Hello!' said Ketil.

'I had to take the dog out,' Thorgunna explained, pushing her headcloth back from her eyes. 'Though she was aback of going, without Steinar.'

'What's her name?' Ketil asked.

'Freya,' said Thorgunna. 'Steinar always said she was as near to a Christian as one could meet, but if she couldn't be baptised she might as well have a name from the old faith as she was clean faithful to him all his days.'

'That's a nice thought,' said Sigrid. 'Had he had her a while?'

'Oh, yes, since she was a pup, before he and Svanhild were married, even. She must be eight years old, I should think, from what he's said. I don't know what she's going to do without him.'

Sigrid opened her mouth to ask, then realised Thorgunna meant the dog, and not Svanhild. Freya sat without stirring, not even twitching a nose in the direction of the many scents there must have been in the grass around the path.

'She does look unhappy,' Ketil agreed. 'Poor girl.' He clicked his fingers, and the dog half-raised an eyebrow at him, then slumped again.

'Come on, Freya,' said Thorgunna encouragingly. 'Maybe if you go for a good walk you'll want to eat something. I'll see you again,' she waved a hand at them, and led the dog by her collar over the stream southwards.

'Some people treat their dogs better than other people treat their slaves,' said Ketil, absently watching them go.

'True. That's a well-loved dog, anyway. No reason, though, for some people to treat their dogs even worse than they treat their slaves.'

Ketil shifted his head.

'Slaves are people, too.'

'Hm,' said Sigrid, 'they are, but you're not supposed to have feelings for them, are you? Or that's what they say: it's hard not to, when you get to know them. Not that I can afford to have any. But it's the same with animals. My old cow, now, Kari: she has served me better than many a slave, and I'm very fond of her.'

'What if a slave becomes a Christian?'

'That's a difficult one,' Sigrid admitted. 'Can a slave become a Christian? Can a priest baptise a slave? You'd better ask Father Tosti, if you're going to come out with questions like that. And anyway, like Freya the dog, I can't have Kari baptised, however fond I am of her.'

'And do you think she does more for you because you treat her well, or would you beat her to make her work harder?'

'Beating her wouldn't make her give more milk, or produce healthier calves,' said Sigrid, a little surprised at the turn the conversation was taking. From his tone of voice she thought that Ketil was taking this seriously, not just talking at random.

'A dog, then. Some say the more you beat them, the more obedient they'll be.'

'I've never thought so. Well, maybe, in some cases, if they're scared of you … but it doesn't make them inclined to help, either slave or animal. Don't you think?'

Ketil was still watching Thorgunna and the dog Freya climb the hill on the other side of the stream. Sigrid's eyes followed, too, and she saw Thorgunna raise a hand above the dog's head. Was she going to strike her? But no, the hand must have held some treat. The dog reached up and took it, Thorgunna rubbed her head and ears fondly, and the dog's tail made the least swish of pleasure.

'Oh,' said Sigrid, even as she smiled. The hand above the head had triggered something.

'What?'

'Why,' she said, watching it again in her mind, 'why would the attacker, if he wheeked the axe away from behind, why would he strike from the front?'

'What?'

'You saw the body,' she reminded him patiently. 'The axe handle was pointing upward as he lay on his back. He was attacked from the front.'

'Of course he was,' Ketil said, gratifyingly surprised. 'You're quite right.'

'I often am,' she told him.

'Well, in your own head,' he agreed kindly. 'But just this once you seem to have made a good point.'

'Oh, choke on your cheese,' she muttered. But she was pleased to have distracted him from his thoughts of slaves and cruelty.

'Too late: finished it ages ago.'

'Anyway.' She brought the conversation back. 'He was attacked from the front. Now surely, if you were lit on by a stranger who had just stolen your weapon and had not, for whatever reason, hit you on the back of your head – in your case because he would need a ladder to reach, if he was a normal size of a man – what would you do?'

'If I were in time to spin around and see what was happening? I'd try to defend myself, of course,' said Ketil, ignoring the taunt about his height.

'But there were no wounds to his hands, were there? You did look, I assume?'

'I did,' he said, 'and no, his hands were completely unscarred. If he had been quick enough to turn, then why did he not put his hands up, at least? And if he had not been quick enough to turn, then how was it that he was hit from the front?'

'I think it was someone he knew,' said Sigrid firmly. 'He feels the axe taken, of course, turns in surprise, and sees it's someone he knows. So he's puzzled, and asks what's going on? Or maybe he thinks at once that it's a friend teasing him, and so he jokes a bit with him. Does that sound right?'

Ketil considered, his left hand toying with the hilt of his sword as if the very thought of a fight made his blood run faster, his fingers tense to join in. Well, she supposed, feeling charitable, she suffered much the same thing when she saw a nice bit of tablet-weaving, her hands twitching to work out on their own how the pattern had been made.

'It would fit,' he said, his hand returning to his lap, 'or perhaps if the attacker immediately made some kind of connexion with him, explained why he had taken the axe in some way that at the very least caught Steinar's attention. It would need to be quick and good, though, if it was a stranger. No man is going to want anyone stealing his weapon like that. Not even someone as kindly as Steinar seems to have been.'

'Well, then,' she said, 'there was a connexion of some sort, whether he knew his attacker or whether his attacker was quick to explain what he was doing before he killed him.'

'I can just imagine it,' said Ketil. '"No, wait a moment," says the attacker, "before you say anything, Steinar, I'm just here to kill you." That would certainly stop anyone in their tracks.'

Sigrid sighed sharply.

'It was your idea that the attacker explained what he was doing. I still think it was someone he knew. Anyway, what's the next stage? Why was Steinar going to see the Abbot? Did he have news for him? Did he want to ask him something? Warn him about something? Or even give him something, and we don't know what it was because it's been stolen too?'

Ketil tutted.

'You think of too many possibilities all at once. He might just have been going to say hello.'

'You just don't have enough imagination.'

'You have too much. Let me think.'

'That might take too long. Did someone want to stop him from seeing the Abbot? If so, how on earth did they know he might come out of his house at that hour of the morning to try to make his way up to the Brough?'

'That's a very good question. How did they know Steinar would be there? When did Steinar decide to go? In fact, when did Steinar find out that the Abbot was in Orkney?'

'The previous night,' Sigrid remembered. 'I was there. Olvor said the neighbours were coming over after supper. The men arrived first, Steinar and Ubbi, and sat chatting, and then the women arrived a little later.'

'Why did they come separately?'

'One of the babies had been greeting. Teething. They wanted to get – whichever one it was – settled before they came.'

'They left the babies at home?'

'No, they brought them with them. But no one wants to bring a howling bairn into someone else's house.'

'Fair enough.'

'And in the short time between the men arriving and the women arriving, the women had apparently bumped into someone who had told them of the arrivals at the Brough, not only the Abbot and I suppose Hakon but also you, coming later.'

'In that short distance between their longhouse and

Olvor's?'

'They probably saw someone down on the path, heading south.'

'Late in the evening to be heading south.'

'But if they were heading north, how had they heard news from the Brough before the rest of the settlement?'

'You don't know who it was they spoke to?'

'No idea. We could probably find out, though.'

Ketil drew in his knees and tapped them thoughtfully.

'Are you sure that was the first that Steinar heard about the Abbot's arrival?'

Sigrid reflected. The sun was high and her head was growing hot: it would be time to find shade soon. She hoped her nose was not burning. Ketil seemed unbothered by the heat, despite his fair skin and short-cropped hair.

'It looked that way. He was surprised, and I think a little disappointed – it would be too much to say annoyed – that Thorfinn had sent for the Abbot so quickly. I mean, for the Abbot to have arrived already would mean that Thorfinn had pre-empted Steinar's report on what he had found at Colonia, and although Steinar thought that everything in Colonia was good, it meant that Thorfinn had not waited to hear about it and had just gone ahead as if anything Steinar would say was unimportant.'

'I see. Yes, that would be complicated to pretend.'

'I think so.'

'And Ubbi? Was it news to him?'

'It seemed to be news to everyone. They were all quite excited – excited, I think, mostly for Steinar's sake, as there might be people come that he knew and admired. And for themselves, to think they might hear more about the place that Steinar had come to love so much.' She sighed. 'They seemed a very close family. It was a pleasure to spend the evening with them: all so easy together, no bickering, no jealousies – except perhaps the dog, who was devoted to Steinar alone, I think. The children looked loved, the couples loving. Maybe they were all still in the first happiness of having Steinar back safely, but it looked accustomed, somehow.'

'So much the worse now, then.'

'Yes.' She pulled her feet up to try to stand, but thought

better of it. It was comfortable there, despite the heat. 'So he was trying to communicate with the Abbot, we're fairly sure of that, even if we don't know what he was trying to communicate. The Abbot said he had no idea, if I followed Father Tosti correctly.'

'The strength of Heaven be with Father Tosti,' said Ketil. 'I should not like to have to translate all that he has to translate.'

'No ... You think the Abbot was being truthful?'

'The Abbot? Why?'

'Well, he's an abbot, yes, but he's a powerful man, isn't he? And powerful men ... well, power can go to one's head. What if he did know about Steinar? It would not take much: if he had met Steinar in Colonia he would know he was from Orkney: he might well have known he was coming straight back here. He very well might have expected to see him here. Why not? And what if there was some reason why he did not wish to see him? Or some reason why he needed Steinar dead?'

'Abbot Konrad?' Ketil seemed to be trying to clarify her words, but she could tell he was thinking about the idea. 'Surely not.'

'But it's a possibility,' she persisted.

'Do you think,' he went on after a moment, 'I mean, assuming this was indeed a possibility - do you think he would come here himself to do it, or would he send someone?'

'Oh, he'd send someone, don't you think?'

'Whoever killed Steinar must have been splashed with blood,' said Ketil.

'I can't see Abbot Konrad letting that fine robe of his be splashed with anything, not even holy water. What about that miserable bundle of rags that was holding the horses? Could he have been sent to do it?'

'Now, wait: you've no proof. Abbot Konrad is a powerful man and, as far as I've seen, a holy man. And he's also intelligent,' he added, with emphasis. 'If he has really killed Steinar – or indeed had him killed, then he's not going to make it easy to prove it. So go steady, and let's keep our options open. It's not going to be a matter of anyone flinging themselves on Thorfinn's mercy and confessing all, just like that.'

'All right.' Sigrid did not really mind: Ketil was being sensible, and anyway, she had nothing against Abbot Konrad.

Well, nothing except that he had made remarks about her state of undress on the morning of Steinar's death. Oh, and some comments about her unreliable emotions … Well, she thought, pursing her lips, she had no proof he was a murderer, anyway. Or not yet.

'I have to say I favour the idea of someone else wanting to stop Steinar communicating with the Abbot,' Ketil was saying. 'It seems to me much more likely. But I think we'll need to find out a bit more, don't you?'

'Oh, yes!' Sigrid had thought that was obvious. 'We need to find out properly what Steinar was doing in Colonia and who he knew there, how he came across the Abbot, what the Abbot thought of him, what he might perhaps have found out or brought that someone else would not have liked … could he have found out something that would be damaging to Thorfinn, even?'

'If he did, I don't think Thorfinn knew about it,' Ketil said at once. 'Thorfinn was keen to have the murder sorted out and solved. His main concern seemed to be the Abbot's safety, not anything connected with himself.'

'Well, Thorfinn didn't become the man he is today without being able to hide his feelings sometimes,' said Sigrid sharply.

'I thought you liked him?'

'I do,' she said. 'I just don't have any illusions about him. I trust him more than I would trust many another leader in his position, I suppose, but still.'

Ketil nodded slowly. Sigrid knew it was true: even leaders who had taken to heart the new faith were still leaders, still had to kill and deceive and bully and control. And even if Thorfinn were laying down new Christian laws, well, leaders could impose laws, but it did not always mean they had to obey the laws themselves. Such power was not necessarily to be envied: Sigrid would not want to make the choices a leader had to make, to keep others down so the leader could look tall, never to be able to rest or trust or lay down the sword and shield … give her wool and her weaving tablets any day, and a quiet hearth of an evening. Any other way madness lay.

'Well,' said Ketil at last, 'we're agreed, I think. We need to find out more about Steinar's work in Colonia, and his connexion with Abbot Konrad.'

'And with anyone else who was in Colonia at the same time, of course. The bundle of sulky rags.'

'Otto, I think his name is. I don't think I've heard him speak, but Tosti says he only speaks Saxon.'

'That's not going to help us move forward. Unless you happen to speak Saxon?'

He smiled.

'No, do you?'

'No. Is Otto the only man in Abbot Konrad's train? He didn't bring a trained sausage cook, or something?'

'I don't believe so, but perhaps Otto is a man of unexpected talents.'

It was her turn to smile, as she scrambled up to stand by the rock.

'Any talent would be unexpected in that bundle,' she remarked. 'So, no one else?'

'Just Otto with Abbot Konrad.'

'But it wasn't just Otto, was it? The Abbot would not travel all this way with just one servant. Not in those expensive robes.'

Ketil looked up at her, then slowly pushed himself to his feet.

'Hakon,' he said. And suddenly she shivered. His eyes had gone the blue-grey of a sword blade, and his face was grim.

NÍU

IX

WHY HAD HE not thought of it before? Obviously it was Hakon.

'What's happening?' Sigrid demanded. 'What is it about Hakon?'

'It has to be Hakon,' was all Ketil said, as thoughts and memories poured through his mind.

'But why? Ketil, explain yourself!'

He turned towards her, only half seeing her. In his mind she had another face, a frightened, thin face, lovely and loved. And Hakon there too.

But now Sigrid had grabbed his arm and was shaking it, hard.

'I'm running out of patience, Ketil! Come on, tell me what it is!'

'We need to find evidence for Hakon killing Steinar. I can't just accuse him without something. He'll wriggle out of it.' He was talking partly to Sigrid, partly to himself. 'So we need to see if anyone remembers seeing him around here before yesterday. When did he and the Abbot arrive, again?'

'I don't know. I don't think I heard.'

'Friday, that was it. Last Friday. They've been here over a week, just. He could easily have found Steinar down here.' He found his feet were tapping, eager to go, but he knew he needed to plan first, to sort out and rein in his galloping thoughts.

'I remember now,' said Sigrid, though she was giving him a wary look, 'that Steinar said the night before he died that he would go up to the Brough in the morning to see the Colonia party. No sense of urgency, just a social call that he was looking forward to, I thought. But Ketil, the only people there were his family, and Olvor and Asmund, and me. None of us, I'm sure, had any reason to tell anyone he was intending a visit.'

'Hakon could have been watching the place,' Ketil said at once.

Sigrid blinked.

'All the time? On his own?'

'Maybe.'

'That would certainly attract attention, a stranger lingering in a small place like this and watching someone's longhouse.' Her tone was sharp, between annoyance and sarcasm. 'I think you'd find someone round here who had seen him. And how could he be looking after the Abbot if he spent all his time down here?'

'You don't understand,' he snapped.

'No, not really. It's hard to understand when you're not explaining anything.'

'Hakon is very capable. And intelligent.'

'And able to be in two places at once? And perhaps hover invisibly over Steinar's house?' Arms folded now, she was trying to catch his eye, convince him he was wrong.

'Well, if you won't listen ...' He had no time for this. He needed to find out how Hakon had killed Steinar.

'Oh, look, there's Asmund! Olvor's husband, remember?'

'Where?' A potential witness whom he had not yet seen – maybe Asmund was the man who could tell him he had seen Hakon. He looked to the path. A big man, not fat but bulky, paced along steadily towards them and the river, looking about him with a serious face. Sigrid called a greeting, but the expression did not change as the man looked over at them both.

'Asmund, this is my friend Ketil who works for Thorfinn,' Sigrid said, seeming to reassure the man before he quite reached them. To Ketil she hissed, 'Go gently with him, all right?'

Ketil frowned. Why should she think she needed to say that?

'Asmund,' he nodded as the man approached. 'I'm trying to find out about Steinar's death. He was your friend, wasn't he?'

'I liked Steinar,' Asmund conceded. 'He told me interesting

things about Colonia and sometimes other places and things.'

'Then you'll want to help find his killer, no doubt. Have you seen any strangers around here lately? Or anyone from the Brough who seems to be spending more time than usual here?'

Asmund regarded him.

'Did a stranger kill Steinar?'

'I think I know who killed Steinar, but I need to find someone who saw the killer.'

'A man from the Brough?'

'A man visiting the Brough.'

'A man from Colonia?'

'Not – quite.'

'Steinar said Colonia was full of good men, under Christian law. Steinar liked that. He said it was very orderly. I think I would like that, too.'

'Well, this man might have visited Colonia, but he did not belong there.'

'No, he wouldn't. Because killing someone the way Steinar was killed is against Christian law, the way I understand it.'

'Yes, I think you're right.' Odin's beard, but this was slow. 'Do you think you might have seen anyone like that, here? In the last week, perhaps.'

Asmund seemed to think back, from the look of him going over each day and hour one by one. Ketil made himself stay still, pulling himself back, concentrating on his breathing. He was always a patient man, controlled by nature and by training, but this – this was hard to bear.

'I have seen,' said Asmund at last, 'three strangers here in the last week, whom I have not seen before.' He produced two large hands, and laid one flat in front of him, pressing the index fingers together. 'The first was a man at the harbour. He came in a kvarr from Lervig and I knew the others on the boat but I did not know him. He had come for the first time and he wanted to go for a walk and see more of the land before they sailed on. His name was Ingvarr and he was the son of the kvarr's owner who has been coming here for twenty-three years. Ingvarr is fair haired and blue eyed and he is seventeen years old.'

'All right, that is not the man I was thinking of. Who was the next one?' Ketil asked, trying to stay calm. Asmund pressed his index finger into the middle finger of his flat hand.

'The second one was a woman. She came from Skaill over the river here to visit her sister who is married to Afi the boat builder. I have known Afi and his wife for many years but I had never seen her sister before. Her sister is called Groa and she is a widow. She has grey hair and blue eyes and I did not ask her age.'

'Probably best,' murmured Sigrid. Ketil had the brief impression she was laughing at him, but he could not be bothered to react. He had more important things to think about.

'Thank you, Asmund,' he said. 'And the third stranger?'

Asmund paused to reflect.

'The third stranger was a man. He came down from the Brough,' – Ketil felt his heart beat faster – 'but he had not been there for long. He had arrived there from Sanday on a boat with otter skins to sell. Ingibjorg who is Thorfinn's wife did not like the skins and so no one on the Brough would buy them, so he was trying to sell them at Einar's place up at Buckquoy and down here. He had thirty-two skins when he came and he had eight when he left. He was a very short man with red hair and blue eyes and he told me he had passed his fortieth birthday. His name is Egil. He went back to Sanday on his boat on Wednesday.'

'That's it?'

'Every one,' said Asmund. 'The man from Lervig, the woman from Skaill, and the man from Sanday.'

Ketil let out a long breath.

'And that's all the strangers you have seen this week?'

'That is all of them.'

'And no one else from the Brough?'

Asmund considered again. No one could accuse him, Ketil thought, of making hasty answers.

'I saw four men from the Brough yesterday. That was the Abbot, the man with the horses – I don't know anything about him because I didn't have the chance to ask him any questions – the man Hakon, and you.'

'And you saw us only after Steinar had been killed?' Ketil felt he was clutching at straws.

'Yes, only then. That's why I didn't have the chance to ask them any questions.'

'I understand. Thank you very much, Asmund.'

'If you are trying to find out who killed Steinar, I should help you. But if something could bring Steinar back to life, I would do that.'

'I know,' said Sigrid. 'Lots of us would. He was a good man, wasn't he?'

Asmund nodded, still serious.

'I have to go and find the sheep,' he announced.

'Of course – thank you for your time,' she added, as if she did not trust Ketil to be polite to the man. They waited, motionless, until Asmund was well up the hill and out of hearing, then Ketil slapped the rock beside them, hard enough to make his palm smart.

'Could he be lying?'

Sigrid watched the departing figure.

'I don't think it would occur to Asmund to lie. But if you're determined that your friend Hakon was down here, remember Asmund doesn't see everything or everyone.'

'True. Yes, true.' He bit his lip. 'Do you think Thorgunna will be back?'

'She might have gone round in a circle.'

'I want to ask the others, anyway. Maybe they saw him.'

He secured his scabbard in his belt and turned back towards the longhouses.

'Maybe you should leave it for a little,' Sigrid suggested, tentatively. 'You were in there earlier, asking questions.'

'I'm trying to find out who killed their kin. That should be enough for them.' Even as he said it he regretted it. Ideally he would leave them in peace to mourn, to grow gradually used to the emptiness, to say in the silence around Steinar's corpse the things they needed to say before he was buried and gone for good. But if his questions helped him to find evidence against Hakon, then surely they would welcome a solution, the killer identified and brought to answer to Thorfinn – he would have to go back. He pushed his cloak back over his left shoulder, feeling the heat of the day heavy on him. His head was teeming with thoughts, and before he had even made a final decision, he found he was heading for Ubbi's longhouse door once again. He was just about aware of Sigrid resolutely following him.

Thorgunna was not yet back: the dog Freya was not in her usual place. Svanhild was, though, sitting with her elbows on her knees by the head of Steinar's bier, within touching distance of his face. Ubbi sat beside her, an arm around her slumped shoulders. The only sound in the place was a contented murmuring coming from one of the bed spaces, where Ketil could just see the two babies of the household crawling about, playing with a wooden toy boat. They looked almost out of place in the weight of the sorrow around them. Ubbi looked up as they came in, a puzzled frown on his face.

'You're back,' he said, automatically waving them to sit down. 'I'm sorry, Thorgunna is out and my sister is – not well.'

'I just have a few more questions,' said Ketil. 'Then I'll be away.'

Ubbi nodded, but his frown did not change. Svanhild barely moved, only a flicker of her eyelashes showing that she was even aware of their arrival.

'I'm trying to find out if a particular stranger was seen around here in the last week. Perhaps you'd seen him a few times and no longer thought of him as a stranger, or perhaps you saw him only once.'

'What did he look like?' Ubbi asked, ready enough to help.

'He's a little shorter than me, with dark-fair hair, curling and thick. He wears a short beard, redder than his hair. Does that sound familiar?'

Ubbi looked blank for a second, then shook his head.

'I don't remember anyone that looked like that round here. In the last week, you say? Not just yesterday?'

'I believe he may have been here during the last week to see where Steinar lived, to work out how, perhaps, to catch him. I may be wrong.'

Ubbi shook his head more definitely this time.

'I don't remember seeing anyone like that. But then I'm often off round the farm during the day. Svanhild, does that sound like someone you've seen?'

Svanhild lifted her head a little, and shook it.

'No,' she managed.

Ketil sighed, casting about for anything else he should perhaps ask them now, rather than disturb them again. Svanhild moved her arm slightly, and the lightest chink of bangles made him think of something, vague though it was.

'The ring and the bangles that were missing. They say the ring was a gift from you, Svanhild, so presumably you would know it again.'

She nodded, and cleared her throat, her voice hoarse.

'I'd know one of the bangles, too,' she said. 'It belonged to his father, and it had a stamped ring pattern on it.' She coughed again. 'He wore it always, but once he was stuck somewhere with nothing else and he had to pay for food and shelter. So the bangle has two little hacks out of it, just nips. It wasn't comfortable to wear, he always said, but it was his father's. The other –'

She broke off, as skittering claws on the flags at the door drew their attention. Freya the dog had returned, with Thorgunna. Thorgunna raised her eyebrows to see Ketil and Sigrid back, but let the dog go to sniff them. Freya looked livelier, but after a brief moment of inspection she returned to her post by Steinar's body, lying full length, and licking her paws before settling flat again. Thorgunna shrugged at her, but looked pleased.

'She even ran after a bird or two,' she told the others, settling down near Ubbi. She looked up at Ketil. 'Was there something else you needed?'

'He was asking about a stranger. Curly hair, red beard … wasn't that what you said?'

'The man who was here with you yesterday?' Thorgunna asked.

'That's right.' She was observant, anyway.

'He looked familiar … I thought at the time I'd seen him before. Why?'

'I wondered if he had been around here in the last week, maybe looking for the house Steinar lived in, or asking questions.'

'He wasn't asking questions,' Thorgunna said slowly. 'Not when I saw him. Let me think … Oh, yes: it would have been the day I went to the dyeshop with some wool from our sheep. That's over near the harbour, where they throw the rotten fish. He was there – or someone like him was. I couldn't be sure.' She smiled at Ketil, and he nodded back, trying not to seem too happy with the information.

'Nowhere else?' he asked.

'No, no, I don't think so. Ubbi, had you seen him anywhere?'

'No, nor had Svanhild. We already said. You don't really think that that was the killer, was it?' he asked Ketil, his voice a little shaky. 'Standing there looking down at what he had done?' The arm around his sister's shoulders tightened as she slumped down again.

'That would be terrible,' Thorgunna agreed, touching her husband's knee. She moved a little closer to him, and all three looked up at Ketil, appalled, but firm together. Svanhild would be well looked after as a widow, he could see. He could no longer trespass here.

'Thank you for your help,' he said, the words sounding light and hollow. He gestured to Sigrid, and she skipped quickly to the door, eager to be away.

'I'd have thought it would be better,' she said as soon as they were clear, 'not to tell them what the person you're looking for looks like. You know what people are like. They'll think they remember something when half the time they weren't even there.'

'She saw him. Thorgunna saw him down here, earlier in the week. It's Hakon.'

'Why do you suddenly think so? You hadn't even considered him! And now you're determined it was him. Why?'

'I need to speak to someone at the dyeshop,' he said, ignoring her. 'Do you know where it is?'

'The smelliest part of the harbour,' she said, wrinkling her nose. 'That's why I make my own. I can keep the pots small and the smell under control. Nasty.'

'Show me.' He caught her glare, but paid no attention. Had Hakon been asking questions at the harbour before coming here? Getting directions? It made sense: there would be other strangers at the harbour, and he would be less obvious. 'Come on.'

He marched off, not even looking round when he heard her muttering along behind him. The harbour was not that far, and there were plenty of people about: not wishing to be caught up into a conversation with the amiable giant Afi, he avoided the boat builders and picked his way to the dyeshop, turning now and again to see if Sigrid agreed with the direction. She had been right: the place stank, as you would expect from a trade that relied so heavily on piss. A man with a cap pulled over his dark hair appeared to be directing operations inside, helped by two or three others who by their dress were probably slaves. When he saw Ketil in the doorway, he came outside rather than draw him in further to the reek.

'Looking for a man,' said Ketil without much preamble, 'a stranger, brown hair, curling, reddish beard. Have you seen him around here?'

The man looked at Ketil's plain cloak and fine shirt. Ketil knew his value was being assessed, and drew out a few silver coins from his pouch.

'Does that make it easier?' he said. The man took the coins and examined them.

'Aye, Eastern,' he murmured. 'I hear tell we're getting Saxon coinage here soon, did you ken?'

'Did you see the stranger?' Ketil felt his own voice growing narrow and sharp. The man weighed the coins in his hand.

'Brown hair, do you say? And a reddish beard? Aye, aye, I saw him.'

'Did he speak with you?'

'No,' said the man. 'He was just passing.'

'In which direction?'

'Oh,' said the man, 'now there's a question. South, I believe, though I could be wrong.'

'South, right.' Ketil was happy enough with that answer. 'Right.'

'Glad to be a help,' said the man with a grin. Sigrid let out some kind of sigh, but Ketil was already heading on round the harbour, making for the path up to the Brough's gate.

'Wait!' she cried. 'What are you doing now?'

'Going to take a look at his pack, if I can find it,' said Ketil. 'Who knows what I might find in there?'

'You've no proof!'

'I can't sit around waiting for proof,' he told her. 'He did it, that's all I need to know.'

'It might be all you need to know, but I can tell you it won't be nearly enough for Thorfinn,' Sigrid bit back. 'What do you think you're doing? I think the sun's gone to your thick head.'

'Go home, Sigrid, or go back to Olvor. Leave me in peace to get on with this.'

'I will not,' she said. 'Leave you to make a fool of

yourself? If I can't stop you, I can at least be there to watch so I can say I told you so.'

'Very well, it's up to you.' He turned and strode on to the path and up as quickly as he could. Sigrid's panting followed him surprisingly steadily. If he had been in the mood he might have been amused.

It was the middle of the afternoon and things were busy on the Brough, but no one much was around Thorfinn's hall. Ketil strode in, half-expecting to have to explain himself to Ingibjorg and her ladies, but only Lambi was there, lying back against the table with his feet up on a bench, taking his ease. He struggled to his feet when he saw Ketil, but not with great urgency.

'Glad to see you're making yourself useful,' Ketil remarked, barely glancing at him as he made for the row of packs tucked against the wall, the belongings of those staying in the hall. Lambi darted across.

'Can I help?' he said with unexpected eagerness. 'What are you looking for? Are you looking through the packs for something? Is this to do with that man's death? Nothing's happened to his widow, has it?'

Ketil stopped and looked round at Lambi, taking in his sheepish look and shiftless hands.

'Which is your pack?' he asked. Lambi skipped to one side, fumbled with a half-open pack, and brought it over, holding it out as if offering it as a gift. Ketil shook his head sharply. 'I don't need to see it. Now, which is Hakon's pack, do you know?'

'Hakon's? Oh ...' Lambi surveyed the row of packs, then leaned in and tugged one out, rearranging it slightly to hold together. 'I think it's this one.'

'I don't think this is a good idea, Ketil,' Sigrid muttered, one eye on Lambi. 'What if he comes in?'

'I have every right,' said Ketil. 'Didn't Thorfinn tell me to investigate?' He was unfolding the top of the pack, methodically taking back the layers of cloth. Something rolled out and clinked as it hit the flag floor. 'What was that?'

He stood, careful not to step on whatever it was. Lambi stepped back out of the way. It was Sigrid who spotted it, leaned forward, scooped it up to hold out on the palm of her hand.

It was a bangle. He could see quite clearly that it was

decorated with a punched ring pattern, and that two neat clips had been taken from one edge. He plucked it from Sigrid's hand between his finger and thumb, holding it high to examine it closely. Steinar's missing bangle.

They heard voices at the door. Sigrid and Lambi spun guiltily, backing as if to try to hide the open pack. Ketil stood his ground. He knew who was there.

'Ketil? Is that you?'

Thorfinn's voice.

'Yes, my lord.'

'Any progress with finding Steinar's killer?'

'Yes, my lord,' said Ketil, hearing the words come from somewhere very deep inside himself, somewhere finally satisfying. 'That's the killer there. Hakon did it.'

'Hakon?' Thorfinn asked.

'Me?' said Hakon. 'Oh, no, Ketil: that's not right at all!'

TÍU

X

'HAKON?' THORFINN LOOKED from one of them to the other. Sigrid, staying in the shadows behind Ketil, felt slightly sick. What on earth was Ketil going to say? As far as she could see, he had no proof whatsoever, and unless there was something he had not told her, he had no idea why Hakon might even have known Steinar. Although, come to think of it, there was probably plenty that Ketil had not told her. She wound her hands into her skirts behind her back, praying for something to interrupt them, allow her to get him away before he made a complete fool of himself in front of Thorfinn. And in front of Hakon, who seemed a perfectly reasonable man even if he had assumed that he and Ketil would not need her help to investigate Steinar's death. An almost perfectly reasonable man.

'I haven't finished yet,' Ketil was saying. His voice was ice-cold, his face looked as calm as ever, and perhaps only Sigrid could see the way the knuckles of his right hand clenched bone white on his belt. 'There is more to investigate.'

'So you have nothing?' Thorfinn asked – not angry, just making sure he knew exactly what was happening.

'Of course he has nothing.' Hakon was still half-smiling, still, it seemed, prepared to treat this as a joke, or an amusing error. 'Why would I kill Steinar, of all people? I barely knew him! I knew him less well, in fact, Ketil, than you know me!'

'Do you have anything?' Thorfinn repeated. One of the reasons men followed him was that he had faith in them – sometimes more than they felt was realistic, but it made them work hard for him. Now he was giving Ketil his chance to explain this strange aberration. He waited, but he would not wait forever.

Ketil opened his mouth to reply, but Hakon interrupted.

'Is that my pack? Have you been going through my pack?'

'I –' Ketil began, but this time Thorfinn spoke.

'He has my authority, if he is suspicious of someone, to do whatever is required to look for evidence.'

'Thank you, my lord,' said Ketil, at the same time as Hakon said,

'Oh, oh yes, of course. I understand. And of course I have nothing to hide. Carry on, Ketil – just leave it tidy, eh?' From somewhere, some unfathomable source of amiability, Hakon again summoned a grin. He was really taking this very well, Sigrid thought. If only Ketil did not have this blood on his tooth, this outlandish determination that Hakon had killed Steinar - if he would only back down now …

'In his pack,' Ketil was saying, 'I found this.'

He held out his hand, long and flat. Thorfinn came closer. Sigrid could see the bangle glint against the palm worn from sword work.

'A bangle … Steinar had two bangles stolen, did he not?'

'And from the description given by his wife, this is one of them. It belonged to Steinar's father.'

'This was in Hakon's pack?'

'It was?' Hakon asked. 'Whereabouts?' He seemed genuinely interested.

'Near the top,' said Ketil. 'Presumably in much the same place as you left it.'

'I don't believe I've ever seen it before. Of course, if Steinar wore it a lot I might have seen it on him in Colonia, but I don't make a habit of examining men's jewellery.' He shrugged, an edge to his voice now. It was only natural: anybody would be annoyed, innocent or guilty.

'I suppose,' said Thorfinn carefully, 'that someone else could have put it there. What's your name? Lambi?'

Sigrid had almost forgotten that Lambi was still there. The Icelander shuffled forward, an anxious grin on his face. She thought in passing that his new comb had made little impression on his hair.

'Aye, my lord?' he said.

'You were in here earlier, weren't you?'

'Aye, my lord. I was waiting for Ketil, to find out what he wanted me to do today.'

Or dodging him so that you could take your ease, Sigrid suddenly thought. He looked the type.

'Have you seen anyone near the packs? Since this morning, that is, when everyone tidied them away.'

'No! No, I've seen no one near them. Mind, my lord, I was out for a bit earlier – I went to buy a comb.'

Thorfinn drew breath to reply, then seemed to notice Lambi's hair.

'I hope it works,' he said, almost kindly. Then he turned back to Hakon. 'You deny seeing this bangle before?'

'As I said, my lord, I may have seen it. But I certainly deny taking it from Steinar, alive or dead, and putting it in my pack.'

'And where were you yesterday morning? It was yesterday morning, wasn't it, Ketil?'

'Yes, my lord.' Ketil's eyes were fastened on Hakon, as if daring him to confess all. 'Very early.'

'Very early?' Hakon repeated with care. 'I rose early, it's true. I washed, and I tidied my things here in the hall, then went straight to the church, where I joined the Abbot in prayer before breakfast. I went with him and with Father Tosti to his quarters to break the fast there. In fact, I don't believe I was out of the Abbot's company until well after we met you again later to take our tour. Didn't you see me leaving the hall, Ketil? You used to be an early riser, too.'

Thorfinn looked from Hakon to Ketil. Neither spoke. Sigrid thought she heard a buzzing in the air, as though the hall itself were as tense as she was, then realised it was the blood in her own ears she could hear. She held her breath. She wanted to tug Ketil's sleeve, draw him away, at least remind him he needed more information before he pursued this further – if he was even right, if Hakon had anything to do with Steinar's death at all. As regards that, she would take some convincing herself. But if she were the one to break this silence and urge him to leave, Hakon would certainly laugh at him for having a woman tell him what to do. Her fingers itched. She stared at Ketil, willing him to turn and leave, willing him to admit he might be wrong, or at least premature. But

Ketil did not speak. At last, though, Thorfinn did.

'Well, Ketil, it looks as if you have some more work to do. It's early days yet, surely?' He glanced at Sigrid. 'The problem may be a local one. I suggest you listen to some more local people, see what they have to say about the family, perhaps? Now, I'd better see how Ingibjorg is doing. Hakon, will you go and see if the Abbot is content or in need of anything?' He waited until Hakon had bowed and left the hall, then turned to Ketil again. 'Next time make sure you have all the proof before you accuse someone, Ketil.' He nodded to reinforce his words, then headed off to the back of the hall in search of his wife. At last Sigrid could poke Ketil's arm as she had been longing to do.

'Come on,' she said. 'I can't guarantee there'll be a fire, or food, but at least at my longhouse there'll be peace and quiet away from this place. Back to sleep, there, Lambi,' she added, and chivvied Ketil out through the main doorway, then walked beside him, not letting him fall behind, all the way off the Brough, along the headland, and up the gentle slope to her own home. There was no smoke, as she had predicted, and no sign of Gnup, as she had hoped. The cat emerged from some secret place and curled about their legs, and she let herself in to find a bit of salt fish for it. Then she came back outside, and sat beside Ketil with their backs against the warm stone wall. He had not spoken since Thorfinn had dismissed him. She let the silence run on, looking about her, comfortable at being back by her own door. The ground around them was busy with flowers and she noted what might be useful: lamb's toes, yellow and red, made good dye though only in that bright yellow. The meadow pinks had no use that she knew of, but she liked their ragged purply heads. Low down on the ground, sneaking amongst other plants, the tiny buttercup-like smero was a handy thing to have, though harvesting something so small would try her patience: she hoped she would not need its particular charms, but a dose of worms was no pleasure, either. She put that thought out of her head and stared up into the blue sky, glittering with birds as busy as the ships at the harbour. The sun was still hot, but here in the shade it was pleasant to look out at the dazzling green of the pasture where her sheep grazed. If she were Thorfinn, she would take one look at this land and think it was worth a heavy tax. But he might not look at it quite the same way as she did.

She jumped when Ketil finally spoke.

'He must have had someone else do it.'

'Why?'

'Because he would not tell me he was with the Abbot if he wasn't. It would be too easy to prove wrong.'

'No,' she said, making the effort not to sound as if he were trying her patience, 'I mean why would he have done it? Why would he have wanted Steinar dead?'

Ketil breathed out heavily.

'I don't know.'

'Then what makes you think –'

'I don't know yet. I'll find out.'

'But what made you even consider him as the murderer in the first place? Sorry, Ketil,' she said, gritting her teeth, 'but you just shot off as if you'd had some kind of vision – Hakon as killer. Why?'

'Because he is one,' Ketil replied.

'But ...' Most men had killed, at some point.

He seemed to understand, flashing a look round at her.

'Not in battle, not on a raid. I mean he has killed in cold blood.'

'Murdered?'

He sighed, a long sigh, one that sounded as if it had been held in for a very long time.

'Not in law, no.'

She considered. Even outside battles and raids, men killed, men died.

'You'd better tell me, if you can.'

He hesitated, and she thought he might refuse. Instead he shifted slightly, easing his shoulders against the stone wall, and lifted his hands to his face, rubbing his eyes with the heels of his thumbs as if he had been asleep. Then he dropped his arms on to his knees, and stared out across the pastures below them, towards the Brough, the blue sea clasping it on either side. But his eyes were not really looking at the view. His voice was low, but clear.

'It was – it was a long time ago. I suppose. It was, really, but when I saw Hakon the other day, when we came here – suddenly it seemed like yesterday again.'

'You'd put it to the back of your mind, I suppose.'

He flashed a look at her from those blue eyes, but they were less certain now, less like cold metal. She was sorry she had spoken. She bit her lip, dropped her gaze.

'I suppose I had. Deliberately.'

This time she let the silence fall between them, like the sunlight falling from smoke holes, peppered with dust motes.

'My first winter in Trondheim, working for Thorfinn. It was a slow time, I can hardly remember why. Was the King ill? Something like that. It didn't look as if the winter was going to be full of feasting and gossip and intrigue. It looked dull. Hakon had been around longer than me, and he said he'd never seen it so dull. He said he would rather go home to his farm, see his old mother, catch up with friends there.

'Thorfinn likes to have a few Norsemen working for him at Trondheim. You remember what it was like then: one month he'd be friends and allies with the Norwegian king, the next he was rowing in for a fight, or taking lands the king said he had no right to, or squabbling with Rognvald, as the king put it. And kings change, too: old Magnus died, and Harald took the throne: it's to Thorfinn's advantage to know which way the wind is blowing. But that winter,' Ketil's pale hands spread wide, 'there was no wind at all.'

'So Hakon made his preparations to travel home, and at the last minute he asked me to go too. I think it was for company for the journey. And I had nowhere else to go, except the court: any family I had were left in Heithabyr, so I thought it was a kindness. An honour, too, perhaps. Hakon was popular, friendly, a good leader, a reliable comrade, and he chose me to go home with him.

'Three days' journey it was, in heavy snow, on horseback, and two more on skis, leaving the horses at someone's house to be collected on the way back. The forests dark and still, the skies grey as stone, and the farm, when we came to it, as warm and welcoming as any great hall. I felt I had come home. Hakon's mother was good to me, his sisters treated me like a little brother, spoiling me with all the farm's best produce, and the other longhouses round about were friendly and sociable. It had every hope of being a wonderful winter and Christmas. I can still remember the smell of spiced cakes cooked on that fire.'

He fell silent again, his eyes now fixed on somewhere –

112

some time – far away. Sigrid held her peace, almost smelling the spiced cakes herself.

'Hakon comes from a prosperous family,' Ketil went on at last. 'I realised it was a large farm, with good grazing down by the fjord, plenty of fields for barley, cows and sheep, and a dozen or so slaves to help with all the work. The longhouse was large and the end where the animals and slaves slept was nearly the size of a hall. My bed space was nearly at that end of the family space: a bit ripe, but very warm. And one of the slaves caught my eye.'

The words were light, almost flippant, but his tone was bitter. Sigrid blinked, wondering what was to come. Ketil swallowed.

'Her name was Mara. She was Irish, of course, brought to Norway as a child. She worked in the house, cleaning, washing the clothes, and cooking the slaves' food. Heavy work – not as heavy as the farmwork, of course, but she was so fragile-looking. Delicate, you know, and so pale, as if she had never been allowed out of doors, but her hair was black as soot, her lashes and eyebrows so dark they were like coal.' He took a heavy breath, almost shuddering. 'It was a busy household. We had odd chances to talk, out of sight of the family, away from the other slaves, without being missed. I had never in my life ... I know she was a slave,' he snapped, as if she had said something, 'but she was a woman, too. How can people treat them as animals? As worse than animals?'

She had never seen him like this. His words came out stiff and knotted, like wet rope, his whole body tense. Part of her wanted to touch him, to give him the comfort of a human touch, but part of her was afraid, in case ... in case what, she was not sure. In case he struck her? In case he shattered?

He seemed to gather himself together again, slowing his breathing, eyes closed. When he opened them again he was ready to go on.

'I had a little money. I was going to offer to buy her from Hakon or from his mother, and give her her freedom. And then ... well, I would have taken her back to Trondheim, if she had wanted to go with me. And she told me that she did.

'And then, before I could talk to Hakon about her, I came back from visiting the neighbours one day with Hakon's sisters, and Mara was gone. No one mentioned her, and another slave was doing her work. I didn't want to ask, so I took a look about, out on the farm, around the area, thinking she might have been sent as a messenger somewhere. By chance my route took me past the farm midden, with all the rubbish, bones, rotten leaves, a chicken carcase. I saw something black, and glanced over the wall. And there she lay, thrown there with as much ceremony as the chicken carcase.

'I stayed there until I had calmed down. I couldn't go rushing into the longhouse demanding to know what had happened. When I was ready, I went back to the longhouse for supper, and asked casually why the new slavegirl was doing Mara's work. Hakon's mother told me Mara had broken her leg, slipping on the ice, so Hakon had got rid of her. She could have been a broken cup, for all they cared. Killed, because she had broken her leg, because they could not be bothered to let her rest and heal. Because she was only a slave.'

Sigrid found she was blinking back tears, and now she did put out a hand and cover Ketil's own hand with it. He did not move, but she stayed there for a long moment, unable to let go until she had found words to say.

'Some people are like that,' she said, 'thoughtless, I suppose.' Even to her own ears, it sounded a completely useless response.

'Hm,' he said, as if he did not quite trust himself to speak again.

'Poor Mara,' she whispered. She could picture her, picture her black hair and pale skin, imagine her hopes of freedom with this young warrior. Would Mara have gone to Trondheim with him? Almost certainly. Why on earth would she not? Ketil would have treated her well, even if he had not loved her, as he clearly, obviously had. She swallowed hard. Lucky Mara, if even for a short while. Lucky to be so loved.

'So that's the kind of man he is,' Ketil said at last, clearing his throat. 'He's a killer. And someone has been killed. The connexion seems sound.'

'Look, Ketil,' she began, but he had pushed himself to his feet. She scrambled up, too. 'You know that isn't sound at all. Yes, Hakon seems cold-hearted, but ... well, you know the law. If Mara was a slave she was his to dispose of. Maybe if he had known how you felt …'

'Don't you think I haven't wondered that?' he spat. 'If I had only mentioned it in time, wouldn't he have spared her? Allowed me to buy her?'

'You can't go back and change what has happened. But listen, Ketil, killing a slave and killing a free man are different, you know that. Whether that's how it should be or not, it is. And when you don't even know why Hakon might have wanted to kill Steinar, it's not a good idea to go around saying that he did. Is it?'

Ketil strode off, and she thought he was leaving. But he stopped abruptly, ten paces away, and stared out across to the Brough, his back to her. How on earth could she convince him this was a bad idea? Enough damage had been done already: Thorfinn clearly thought he was on the wrong track completely.

'Look,' she called. Look, listen, look: she needed him to pay attention to her. 'Look, I'll help you.' Now that, she thought, was also a bad idea. 'If there was any reason Hakon would want to kill Steinar, I'll help you find it. But you have to tell me that you understand that there might not be a reason. He's right, someone else might have dropped that bangle into his pack, accidentally or on purpose. Even if he did come by it himself, there might be an explanation other than that he tore it from Steinar's corpse. He might, however many other people he has killed, be entirely innocent of this death. And yes, maybe you'll say that he deserves to be punished. But if he is punished for this, and he didn't do it, then the real killer will go free and unpunished, and will maybe even kill again. Will you tell me you know this is true?'

He was motionless, still with his back to her, the wind catching his cloak as he stood with his arms folded. Stubborn, she thought. Just plain stubborn. He doesn't like someone else to be right. A bit like me, some small voice added in her head.

'Well, stay there if you want to. Stay in the house tonight if you want a bit of peace. Gnup might have some food he could share with you. I have to go back to Olvor's, heaven help me, and disentangle whatever guddle she's made of her wool today, to have it tidy for Sunday. Remember the funeral's on Monday,' she added, still inclined to treat him like a little brother. She straightened her short dress and cloak, brushing off the decent cloth which she would have to wear again in the morning for church. Hands on hips, she gave his back a final, assessing glare, then strode past him to follow the path down to Buckquoy and on to Olvor's place. But as she passed him, his hand flashed out and caught her elbow, stopping her.

'You'll help me,' he said, staring into her eyes.

'I will, if you'll admit he might be innocent of this.'

He took a deep breath.

'Very well. Yes, I admit he might be innocent. I – I might have been wrong.'

She nodded.

'If you were, you might have to apologise to him. But if you weren't, then he deserves whatever punishment Thorfinn wants to give him. And I'll help you.'

ELLIFU

XI

'VERY WELL.' KETIL straightened his shoulders. He was more relieved than he had thought possible. Sigrid was on his side. 'I need to find out more about what Steinar did in Colonia. If Hakon killed him, that's likely to be where the reason lies. And if he did not,' he added, the words sticky in his craw, 'then there is still a good chance that the reason lies there, since, as you say, he was killed when Abbot Konrad appeared here. I can't go back to his household. Not yet.'

'No,' Sigrid agreed. 'I think you've outstayed your welcome there at least until after the funeral. But I might find out something more, either from them or from Olvor and Asmund. Asmund was very keen on hearing about Colonia. All I have to do is to find the right questions, and he'll answer.'

'Yes, you might get something useful. But what can I do? I can't question Hakon.'

'Not yet, no. You've had a grand day burning your boats, haven't you?' But when he looked, her smile was more kind than cross. Should he have told her all he had told her? He had never told anyone about Mara before, not allowed her name to pass his lips since she had died. Part of him feared he had raised her ghost, brought her back to haunt him as she had for so long after he left that prosperous farm, that warm and welcoming Christmas that had so scarred him. But if he had not told his story, Sigrid would never have understood about Hakon. Sigrid was the kind who needed proof before she believed anything. And that was why they had to find out more about Hakon and Steinar.

'You could talk to the Abbot,' Sigrid was suggesting.

'The Abbot! Do you think he would help?'

'Sure to,' said Sigrid, as confident as anyone who was not actually going to do the task at hand. 'How's your Latin?'

'Maybe Father Tosti would translate for me.' He tried to picture it, found the idea strange. 'There's no one else, really, is there?'

'Not yet, no. Later, when the dust has settled, perhaps - but if you want to make progress today, it's back up to the Brough with you and see if the Abbot's in a chatty mood.' She spoke brightly, but he could tell she was trying to cheer him out of his gloomy memories. The annoying thing was that she was probably right.

'But you're going back down to Asmund's house now?'

'I shall, and I shall see what I can find out. It's getting late, Olvor will be wondering if I'm coming back for supper, and I don't want to miss it. And you'd better have your dish out and ready in Thorfinn's hall, too. If nothing else, no doubt Ingibjorg will miss you.' She grinned. 'I'll see you tomorrow!'

She turned and walked down the hill, towards Einar's place and the harbour. It was still full light and would be for hours yet: there was no need to feel anxious for her, but he watched her go, following the little figure with the white headcloth until she disappeared around the corner of Einar's longhouse. Then he sighed, and began the windy walk back along the headland to the Brough.

Around the hall on the Brough, there was the sense of work winding down for the day, though there would be an hour or so left before supper. The blacksmith at the smithy had leaned back from his fires for a gossip with a customer, and you could smell the water heating at the bath houses. Ketil skirted the hall and the church, climbing the gentle slope to the monastic quarters behind them, hoping as he went that any gossip was not about him. Then a thought occurred to him, and he returned to the hall, his spine shuddering a little as he entered it again. There was no sign of Hakon inside, however, nor of Thorfinn. It was busier than it had been earlier, with Ingibjorg's women making preparations for the evening, wiping tables, sweeping the floor. In the midst of them Lambi dozed on his bench, a beatific smile spread across his features. He reminded Ketil of all the worst parts of cats.

'Right, wake up,' he said, shaking Lambi's shoulder without warning. Lambi leapt, mouth agape.

'Ketil! I was just waiting for instructions. Do you want me to go and see that man Steinar's family?'

Ketil was a little surprised to find Lambi quite so ready with an appropriate suggestion. It was not what he had been going to tell him to do: he was not quite sure that Lambi had the intelligence to ask the right questions, and by his record so far he was more likely to find a comfortable ditch to sleep in for a couple of hours instead. In fact he had no immediate use for Lambi, but he wanted the man awake and at least training to be alert.

'Yes, that's exactly what I want you to do,' he said. 'Be respectful. Be careful. And straighten your shirt. And when you get there, remember to take your cap off.'

Ketil watched Lambi disappear down towards the gate of the Brough, making sure he was at least setting off in the right direction, before he himself returned to his route around the church and up to the monastic quarters. He knocked on the door.

It was a moment or two before Otto opened it, and when he did, Ketil almost did not recognise him without his usual multiple onion layers of shawls. He was still wrapped in two or three, though, which was a wonder, for the building was toasty warm, too warm for the day outside. Ketil blinked as the inside air hit him, and hoped that he would not doze through any conversation in this place.

'I've come to see the Abbot, if I may,' said Ketil, speaking fairly slowly. Otto still looked blank, but waved him inside, his gaze flickering from Ketil to something uncertain behind him and back like a sparrow's wing in flight. Ketil remembered how he himself had felt in countries where little Norse was spoken: you found yourself always watching for clues, hoping for a familiar word to appear, interpreting gestures. He smiled reassuringly at Otto, and in a moment he was brought in to a central room on the ground floor with a large fireplace, laden with blazing peat. The Abbot sat in a high-backed chair at a middle distance from the fire, while Father Tosti, for the sight of whom Ketil gave quiet thanks, perched at a kind of table as far from the flames as he could be and still be in the room. There were papers and pens in front of him, and Ketil realised that he must be acting as the Abbot's clerk, as well as his interpreter. He was a busy man.

The Abbot raised his eyebrows as Ketil was shown in, and raised his hand in what Ketil knew well to be a blessing. He bowed his head. Tosti slid off his seat and came over, with a smile for Ketil and a word to the Abbot, who said something. Tosti interpreted.

'My lord Abbot welcomes you to his quarters, and offers you refreshment.' Tosti nodded behind Ketil. Otto was a magician, or had left and returned very quickly: he had in his hands a tray made of polished soapstone on which he carried a jug and two cups. He poured wine for Ketil and the Abbot, set the tray down on Tosti's table, and slipped back to the door again. He returned a moment later with a carved stool which he set behind Ketil. Ketil nodded his thanks, and sat, looking about him at the room. He had not been in the monastic quarters before.

He had seen monasteries, old ones, over in the Western Isles – Thorfinn's territory – and in Ireland, on raids. Something about the little huts, separate, individual, like beehives for a single bee, had appealed to him. He could have seen himself long ago in that solitary existence, truly apart from the world. Hwitebi, where he had been before Thorfinn's summons had hauled him back to Orkney, had seen to the end of that kind of monastic life here, or so he had heard. After the great church meeting there, so many years ago, long before the Danes came, everyone followed the Roman pattern, and Thorfinn's new quarters were no exception. This chamber, stone-built, stuffy, smelling faintly of apples, would be the chapter house, for daily meetings: there would be a dormitory for all the monks to use together, a washing house, an eating room, a general kitchen, probably, and no monk was likely to be on his own for more than a few seconds during the day or night. One might as well be a soldier, for all the solitary time there was to think or to pray or to remember. Yet perhaps, one day, when he had had his fill of fighting …

Abbot Konrad was speaking again, and Tosti had his mouth open to translate.

'My lord Abbot asks what he can do to be of assistance to my lord Thorfinn's man,' he said.

'Please ask my lord Abbot to forgive me for disturbing him, but I am trying to find out a little more about what Steinar

Valison did in Colonia, and about his life there. I know that Steinar was not in the same exalted station in the world as my lord Abbot, but no doubt my lord Abbot has many sources of useful information concerning the people about him, and any fragments of that knowledge that he would be generous enough to bestow on us would be very much appreciated and would no doubt expedite our investigation of Steinar's death, which would be most pleasing to Steinar's family, and would of course be in no small way of practical value both to my lord Abbot and to my lord Thorfinn, whom I serve.'

Tosti's eyes widened, and he looked away to gather his thoughts. He launched into a lengthy speech in Latin, while Ketil watched the Abbot closely, trusting Tosti's translation.

Abbot Konrad listened attentively to Tosti, his gaze fixed somewhere past Ketil's ear, but Ketil had the impression that the Abbot was able to focus on several things at once. A small, thoughtful smile played across his lips, and once or twice he gave a little nod, though whether he was acknowledging a point or approving Tosti's Latin style Ketil could not tell. At last Tosti drew to a halt, and the Abbot pursed his lips, pressing the pads of his thumbs together while his fingers lay interlaced on his lap. Then he freed his fingers, and began to enumerate points on them, as if to do so enabled him to give a clear account. Tosti, too, was able to translate point by point, which must have made his work easier.

'One,' he said,'- though actually, he's not counting, but I know his style – my lord Abbot first met Steinar Valison in Colonia with my lord Thorfinn's party, on their way to Rome. My lord Abbot says that he would have been just another courtier, only that he was notable for his Christian fervour and piety. He was seen on several occasions visiting the various churches of the city, more often than a passing traveller merely seeing the sights.'

'He was seen? Not by my lord Abbot himself, I assume?'

'I think,' said Tosti, his own gaze on the floor, 'that my lord Abbot has many eyes at his disposal.'

'I'm sure he has,' said Ketil.

'Steinar attended services in several of the churches, more than his companions did.'

'All right, a pious man,' Ketil noted.

'My lord Abbot had no personal contact with him on that occasion.' Tosti cast an eye back to the Abbot, who smiled and spoke again. Soon Tosti was able to continue. 'My lord Abbot says that when my lord Thorfinn's party returned through Saxony, they stayed a little while in Colonia, because Thorfinn wanted advice on setting up his new church and monastery here. He also asked for donations of relics and sacred objects to bless the new buildings. Steinar Valison made himself both to my lord Thorfinn and to the Colonia authorities useful at this time, being respectful and knowledgeable concerning the sacred gifts. But, my lord Abbot notes, it seemed clear that Steinar also managed to be liked by his fellows, too. He has observed on many occasions that too strict an adherence to the laws of the church can cause animosity between the adherents and their more ignorant, less disciplined fellows. This did not happen in Steinar's case, for he had a true Christian charity in his heart that even the most unregenerate soldier might recognise and value, and that was clear even to someone like my lord Abbot who was not, by reason of his office, directly concerned with the selection of sacred gifts for the new Birsay church.'

'Indeed it seems impossible to find anyone who had a bad word to say about the man,' Ketil acknowledged. Who kills a man that everyone likes? Could Sigrid be wrong, and the whole thing be robbery with violence?

'And then my lord Abbot says that Steinar returned to Colonia a matter of months ago, early in the spring. He had come this time at my lord Thorfinn's behest again, to find out about the coinage – you know it's a good one, very accurate,' Tosti added, 'and about how they value land to arrange fair rents. It's the Abbot that oversees the administration, you see. So this time he had more to do with Steinar, and he thought Steinar a very fine man, godly and intelligent. The two things the Abbot values most,' Tosti said.

'Does he know if Steinar made any enemies this time in Colonia? Or was there anything he was involved in where he might, perhaps, have ... well, got in someone's way?'

A concerned frown twisted Tosti's amiable face, and he gave Ketil a puzzled look before turning back to the Abbot. It was a moment before he had the answer.

'My lord Abbot cannot at least at present call to mind any

incident or circumstance of the kind to which Ketil refers, nor can he think of any reason why Steinar Valison should have made contact with anyone in this way. He spent most of his time working with and observing the clerks in the Abbot's scriptorium, and occasionally travelling with them to see how land was assessed for valuation. Only if he were travelling in a party with my lord Abbot himself would he be staying in a place with people of any quality or influence – my lord Abbot himself personally oversees the valuations of the lands of major landholders – and even then he would be staying where the clerks stayed, not with the family of the landholder with my lord Abbot. It's how things are organised,' Tosti finished, and Ketil was not sure if that was something the Abbot himself had said, or something Tosti had tacked on in a kind of apology. He nodded, wondering what to ask next, while the Abbot was co-operative. It was hard to think in the thick warmth of the room, and just as he noticed that the fire was dying down a little, the servant Otto scurried forward and heaped two more peats on to it, causing its glow to spark and flare for a second. Ketil watched Otto, then said,

'Tosti, does Otto speak Latin?'

It seemed unlikely, but Ketil wondered. Who knew what useful talents the servant of an Abbot might have? But Tosti was shaking his head.

'No, only Saxon,' he was saying, when there was a noise at the door.

'Father Tosti!'

One of Thorfinn's men, red from running, burst in. Tosti put out a hand to steady him, and the man stopped and gave the Abbot an uncertain bow of the head.

'Father Tosti, it's the wife's mother – remember? It looks as if she's going.'

'Oh!' Tosti spun and explained himself to the Abbot, who nodded at once and waved Tosti to the door. 'I'm sorry, I have to go,' he said to Ketil in Norse. 'I promised.'

And that left Ketil standing uselessly, head low to receive once again the Abbot's blessing, and no way of asking him or Otto anything else that day.

They were about to leave when the Abbot himself stood, and said something to Otto in what Ketil supposed was indeed

Saxon. Then he turned to Ketil, and pronounced with great care,
  '*Cena sine dubio nunc parata est!*'
  'Of course,' said Ketil, and bowed again as the Abbot left the room before them, escorting him in person to the door of the monastic quarters.
  Ketil was visited with a sudden alarm that the Abbot was making sure Ketil did not abscond with any of his valuables, but then he realised something of what the Abbot must have been saying. The Abbot was hurrying to the door because it was supper time in Thorfinn's hall.

  The Abbot, by whatever divine revelation he knew it, was right: when Ketil slipped in through the hall doors, supper was hovering in the hands of Ingibjorg's women at the back of the hall, and the Abbot was rising to say grace. Lambi, Ketil observed, had already found himself a prime position on the right-hand side, not far from Hakon. Ketil slid on to the end of the left-hand bench, hoping not to be noticed. When they had all seated themselves, the women came forward with broth, bread and cheese, and some began to slice thick rounds from a roasting pig over the central fire. Someone's tax well paid, no doubt. The pork, rich and juicy, found its way on to broad platters on the tables, along with parts of a number of chickens. Ketil wondered exactly how Abbot Konrad would distinguish the value of the scrawny individual whose elderly limbs had been deposited in front of him, and that of the plump and lovely specimen whose breasts reclined before the Abbot himself. No doubt he had a method. Ketil took a sip of ale, and a movement across the hall caught his eye. Hakon raised a cup in toast to him. He could do nothing but raise his own cup back, though he could not return that smile.
  'Hello,' came a light voice from behind him. He turned. 'Ketil, isn't it? The warrior who told me he sold cups for a living.'
  'A misunderstanding,' said Ketil. Thorfinn's daughter, Asgerdr, with the white-blonde hair: always to be treated with extreme caution. 'How's your mother this evening?'
  'Very fat,' said Asgerdr, nodding to where Ingibjorg was trying to disguise her swollen belly under her bear fur. She must have been roasted. Asgerdr sighed. 'But nothing stops her flirting.'
  'How very embarrassing that must be for you,' Ketil said

politely.

'You can't imagine.' She topped up Ketil's cup from the jug she was holding, then balanced it again on her hip, staring about the room. 'More women than men here, anyway. And at least she's stuck in one place.'

'Allowing you to roam freely?' Ketil asked.

Asgerdr raised her eyebrows. He suspected she coloured them somehow, or they would have been invisible even on her pale skin.

'I have my duties to do, in her place,' she said. 'Though honestly, with half the men away raiding, if that's what they do these days, it's very dull here. Very dull indeed.'

'Surely there's someone left. What about Otto there?' The Saxon was standing attentively behind the Abbot's chair. He almost looked as if he were listening to something. 'He has a nice exotic flavour to him. And he would never understand a word you said.'

'The Abbot's servant? How desperate for company do you think I am? Oh!' She slammed her jug down on the table, and flopped on to the bench beside him. 'Entertain me, Ketil.'

'Now I know how desperate you are. I thought you and Hakon were getting along well.'

'Hakon?' He found it interesting that she did not, as would be natural, look around to see where Hakon was at the mention of his name. 'He's married, didn't you know?'

'I did,' said Ketil. 'I didn't know if you did. Anyway, you can get on well with someone without necessarily seeing them as a potential husband, can't you?'

Her eyes slid sideways towards him, and away again.

'Perhaps.'

'Did you know Steinar Valison, then?' he asked, before the conversation turned dangerous.

'Steinar? He was married to Svanhild, wasn't he? She's lovely. He wasn't around that much, I thought, and they live down beyond the harbour, anyway. Had I even met him?' She considered. 'Yes, I did. I saw him when he came up to tell my father how wonderful everything was in Colonia. It was a bit boring, to tell the truth. A good-looking man, though. Oh, look: Father's seen me sitting here. I'd better move, before he starts asking you what you're up to. Which, of course, isn't anything.'

Before he could decide whether she was instructing him, or making her disappointment clear, she had hefted the jug once more on to her slim hip and moved on around the hall. Aware of both Thorfinn and Hakon looking over at him, he deliberately turned his gaze somewhere, anywhere, else.

The Abbot was finishing a piece of bread, delicately dipped in the juices of the pork. The bones of that well-developed chicken lay neatly on the side of his plate, and he wiped his fingers on a cloth, addressing a few words to Tosti by his side. It must have been some kind of appreciative remark, for Tosti immediately passed it on to Thorfinn and Ingibjorg, who both nodded and smiled. Otto had leaned away. Ketil wondered for a moment where he had gone, then saw he was bent over taking a glug from a wine cup of his own behind the Abbot's chair. No doubt he had to grab his meal while he could between episodes of attending to his master. Lambi had moved round to chat with him, pouring more wine into Otto's cup. Could Lambi speak Saxon? Ketil had not thought to ask him. That would make him a useful commodity at present.

Thorfinn was gesturing to three lads at the back of the hall, near him, and they went forward to stand near the high chairs. One had a board pipe, and the other two long pipes made from sheep bone. They began to play a cheerful tune, and the company began to relax and enjoy themselves.

TÓLF

XII

SIGRID'S HEAD WAS whirling as she made her way past Einar's place at Buckquoy and down to the settlement past the harbour. Foremost in her mind was a picture of a figure, small with black hair, lying broken in a midden in the snowbound forest, but a close second was the image of Ketil's bared face as he told the story. It may have happened years ago, but his pain was still clear.

But Hakon had had every right to dispose of what had been, however loved by someone else, still his property. It meant nothing in the current matter, and nothing in law – no doubt Abbot Konrad would tell him so. It did make you wonder, though: had Ketil been right to have loved a slave? What had he said earlier about animals? Or, looking at it another way, was someone who could be loved and love in return really only a piece of property? The thoughts muddled her head, and she was glad when she had passed through the rest of the village, finally reaching Olvor's longhouse and the sweet scent of supper cooking.

'Sigrid! You're back,' said Olvor. 'Asmund is just washing outside, and supper will be ready soon.'

'Thank you. How did you get on with the nailbinding today?'

'Oh! A little better, I think,' said Olvor, though she still looked deeply anxious. 'See? It's just there by the door.'

Sigrid picked up a woollen object of indefinable shape, in the textures of which some traces of nailbinding were almost identifiable, tilted to the right light.

'Well done!' she said. 'That's really coming on. You'll be turning out hats in no time.' She tucked it back into its basket quickly when she heard footsteps near the door: Asmund knew what nailbinding should look like, and would not consider telling his wife even an encouraging lie. 'Good evening, Asmund.'

'Sigrid,' he acknowledged, going straight to his high chair and sitting expectantly. She slipped off her cloak and short dress, not wanting to spill anything on it, and went outside to wash quickly. By the time she returned to the fire, Olvor had served Asmund and was filling Sigrid's own plate with fragrant stuffed bread and stew. Sigrid found that she was famished, and set to, postponing any conversation about Steinar and Colonia until her stomach could no longer distract her with its demands.

'I wanted to ask you about Steinar and what he did in Colonia,' she said at last, sitting back and seeing that Asmund, too, had finished eating. Olvor, a little frown on her pale face, topped up their ale cups and took their dishes to the water butt.

'He told me a good deal about Colonia,' said Asmund. 'He had been there three times. Once with Thorfinn going to Rome, once with Thorfinn coming back from Rome, and once because Thorfinn sent him there again for information.'

'And every time he brought you more information, too?'

'Not after the first time,' said Asmund ponderously. 'Because between the first time and the second time he was in Rome, and I didn't see him.'

'Oh, of course, silly of me.' Sigrid sipped her ale, feeling almost as if she had wasted a question. 'Did he talk about the people he met there? In Colonia?'

'He talked about Archbishop Herman and Abbot Konrad and other church men,' said Asmund. 'He told me what they did and how they ran the place with laws and taxes.'

Sigrid was beginning to feel that Steinar's whole existence had been taken up with laws and taxes, and that the phenomenon was threatening to spread to Birsay.

'And what about other people he met? People he made friends with? He was there for a long time.'

Asmund frowned.

'I don't think he mentioned any friends.'

'Are you sure? Steinar was a very nice man, and lots of people here liked him. I'd be surprised if he hadn't made friends in Colonia, too.'

'He didn't talk about friends,' Asmund repeated.

'What about people he didn't like? Or people who didn't like him?'

'Steinar was a very good man.'

'I know, that's what everyone says. But even very good men can make enemies, sometimes.'

'Asmund often says that,' Olvor said suddenly. 'Don't you, Asmund? You tell me that Steinar was a very good man when he was in Colonia.'

'He was,' said Asmund. Sigrid had jumped when Olvor spoke, not realising she was back from washing the plates. She did not often butt into conversations. Sigrid hoped there had been some purpose to this interruption.

'Wasn't he always a good man?'

'No, I mean something that Steinar said – he had done something good while he was in Colonia.'

'Something for Thorfinn?'

'I don't think so,' said Olvor. 'I thought it was something more like stopping a thief, maybe? I'm not sure.'

'What, in the street?'

'No,' Olvor frowned. 'It was more complicated than that, wasn't it, Asmund?'

Asmund nodded solemnly.

'Steinar caught a thief that was stealing from lots of rich houses, and told … I think he told the Archbishop, or maybe the Abbot. I have forgotten which he said.' His mouth turned down at the corners. He seemed genuinely distressed at having forgotten something so trivial, or at least unimportant in his own life.

'Clever Steinar,' said Sigrid, trying to distract him. 'He did a good job.'

'He was a good man in Colonia,' Asmund repeated. 'The Abbot told him so. Everyone knew Steinar was a good man.'

Sigrid was beginning to feel she was going round in circles. Steinar was a good man, and his work was to do with laws and taxes. Sigrid wondered what the law in Colonia said about thieves at rich houses. But there was something about that titbit of information that niggled at her – could this be the key? After all, someone had stolen from Steinar's body, and he had caught a thief

– it looked like a kind of link. She had gone outside for a breath of air after supper, and almost despite herself stared across at the place where Steinar's body had been found, and beyond to his home. She scowled at the thought of disturbing his family again, but at that thought she heard a sound behind her, from the direction of the path, and Steinar's dog Freya trotted up, followed by Thorgunna. Sigrid wondered for a moment if they were the grieving household's only link to the outside world, but in a moment Ubbi appeared, too, one foot wet from the river crossing, and the pair linked hands. Sigrid might have hesitated to intrude, but just then they saw her, and Ubbi waved.

'Sigrid! Good evening,' he called, and she waited for them to join her on their way to their longhouse. The dog, a little brighter than earlier, loped gently ahead, but never went far before looking back for reassurance. Ubbi made a rueful grin at her, and lifted his wet foot. 'Look at me,' he said, 'clumsy as ever! I've been crossing that river all my life and I can still put a foot in the wrong place. Did your friend find the man he was looking for? Does he really think he knows who the killer is?'

'He found one man, anyway,' said Sigrid, 'and I don't think he's sure yet, I'm afraid. He's looking into the idea that Steinar's death was connected with Colonia.'

'With Colonia? But I thought it was robbery?' said Thorgunna, distracted from the dog. Sigrid shrugged, not wanting to make them committed to any particular theory.

'It could still be, or it could even have been a robbery that was somehow linked with Colonia,' she said, half-thinking aloud. That, in effect, would match what Asmund had just been telling her. Wouldn't it be strange if a robbery Steinar had thwarted in Saxony had been the cause of his death in Orkney? She was playing with the idea when she caught a look pass between Ubbi and Thorgunna, as they paused at the wall of Olvor and Asmund's infield.

'A robbery linked with Colonia! Do you really think it could be?' asked Ubbi. 'That would be … well, that might just make sense – in a way.'

'How do you mean?'

'Well,' said Thorgunna. 'No, actually, you tell it, Ubbi. You know more about it than I do.'

'I'm not sure I do: my brother-in-law was not really a talkative man, Sigrid, or not about his own deeds, anyway.'

Sigrid waited only a moment before prompting him to go on. She was not in a patient mood.

'Ketil needs to consider all the possibilities before he can come to a decision.'

'Is he the Ketil who found out what had happened to that stranger last year? The one whose body was found on the Brough?'

'Not quite on the Brough,' said Sigrid quickly, 'but yes, Ketil … yes, Ketil found out all about it.' With some help from her, she added to herself. Some considerable help from her. But she did not want to diminish Ketil's authority here just yet.

'So he's used to finding out about this kind of thing, then,' Ubbi said, half to himself, as though he were justifying telling Steinar's story. 'But honestly, Svanhild could probably tell it better than me. And he probably gave her more details, because she's only his wife – oh! You know what I mean. It's not boasting if you're only telling your wife something that happened, and Steinar wouldn't boast.'

Sigrid nodded, thinking she understood. Or understood that it could happen that way, in some marriages, anyway.

'Come on to the house, and we'll ask her,' Ubbi went on.

'No, I couldn't disturb her again …' Sigrid was remembering Svanhild collapsed on Ubbi's shoulder.

'Not at all! When you came earlier she was just having a bad moment. She was much better at supper – not that she'll really get over it until after the funeral, of course.'

'She'll not get over it then,' Thorgunna put in. 'It'll be a long time for Svanhild. For all of us.'

Her shoulders hunched, and she took the dog's collar, steering the animal the last few steps towards their door. Ubbi met Sigrid's eye.

'We'll really miss him,' he said.

'Of course,' said Sigrid, but she still walked on with him, hoping he would not change his mind about inviting her in, yet dreading asking more questions if Svanhild were as lost as she had been earlier.

But Svanhild was up and about, cleaning dishes after their supper, and when she saw Sigrid she gave a slight smile before hurrying to bring her a cup of wine. Steinar's body had been wrapped in its shroud, head covered, perhaps to avoid the doing of such work on a Sunday, perhaps because it had been expedient. Sigrid noticed the scent of herbs was considerably stronger than it had been earlier in the day, masking what must have been the increasing smell of decay. They would be glad to have the funeral over in more ways than one, in this warm weather.

'Have you news?' Svanhild asked, as soon as they had sat down. Her fingers were twisted around her own cup.

'I have none, really,' Sigrid said apologetically. 'Ketil has an idea but he hasn't really any firm information.'

'Is it an idea you agree with?' asked Svanhild, the least glint in her eye. Sigrid smiled.

'Not entirely, I'm afraid. I want more information, too.'

'Does he listen to you?'

'Sometimes. Not often enough!'

Svanhild gave a light laugh.

'I saw the look on your face earlier. He's a bit like a brother to you, isn't he?'

'Hey!' said Ubbi, recognising that this was not altogether a compliment.

'We've known each other a long time,' said Sigrid, trying to be diplomatic. It was clear that Ubbi and Svanhild were fond of each other, anyway.

'How can we help you this time?' asked Svanhild, sobering from her moment of levity. 'And will it help us?'

'As to that, I'm not sure,' Sigrid admitted. 'I'm trying to find out more about what Steinar did in Colonia, who befriended him, who was admired by him, who was distrusted by him, anyone he might have made an enemy of.'

'You believe the answer to his death lies in Colonia?' Svanhild seemed to be considering, one hand fiddling with the contents of a broad soapstone dish beside her. Sigrid's gaze fell on it, too: it seemed to be one of those dishes so many houses had, where the oddities ended up, small things for mending, keys to long-lost boxes, an old pair of scissors not quite ready to be thrown away.

'I think it's worth investigating further, yes. Did he name any friends? Or enemies?'

'Friends, yes, I believe so. They were mostly clerks in Abbot Konrad's scriptorium. He admired the Abbot, but he would not have called him a friend. Society was not structured that way in Colonia, I believe. The Abbot would have made his friends amongst important people.'

Her fingers continued to play in the bowl, but her gaze was elsewhere, somewhere in her memories of Steinar's stories. Sigrid chanced another look at the contents of the dish, and caught a glimpse of silver – Steinar's bangles, the ones not stolen by his killer, she thought. They would be removed for burial, Christian burial, not the way it was done in the past. Just as well, no doubt, Sigrid thought practically. The family could certainly use the silver. Though there was no hint that this family was in immediate need of money – not until Thorfinn started demanding taxes, anyway. Her mind was wandering. It had been a long day. She deliberately focussed on the bangles and the dish, pulling her thoughts together. There was a comb there, too – broken? No, it looked new, the antler fresh and white. In fact, it looked like the high-quality work of her own comb maker on the Brough.

'So he mostly associated with the clerks? The Abbot's clerks?' she asked.

'That's what it was, I think.'

'Do you think he hoped that Thorfinn might have him do the same thing here in Orkney? Do the work the clerks were doing, valuations and things?'

'Oh! I'm not sure.' It was clearly a new thought to Svanhild, and she turned back to Sigrid with a silver bangle between her fingers, working slowly round it. 'I don't know if he wanted to or not. He enjoyed learning about it, but Steinar always enjoyed learning about new things. I think … I think he would have preferred Thorfinn to have sent him off somewhere else, or back to Colonia, to learn something else.'

The bangle had been lying on the comb, and Sigrid now had a better sight of it. Her heart skipped. She had seen it before. Those runes across the brace bar … How could that have ended up here? It had only been bought this morning.

'Is something wrong?' Ubbi asked, nudging her.

'Oh! No, nothing at all. I was thinking about Steinar. And my eyes fell on that comb – is it from the comb maker up on the

Brough?'

'I don't know,' said Svanhild, fishing it out of the dish. 'Someone brought it this morning.'

'Did they? Who was that?' Ubbi asked it, saving Sigrid from looking too curious.

'It was ... I can't remember. You know everyone came this morning to pay their respects. Some of them brought food and wine.'

'But a comb?' Ubbi had his finger on the very point. Who brings a comb to a grieving widow? He picked it up, turning it back and forth. 'It has your name on it. Svanhild?'

'Has it?' Svanhild took it from her brother, and looked at it more closely. 'So it has. That's odd. Oh, I know who brought it – it was that man who – well, he said he was here with the Abbot's party, when – when we were with Steinar, outside.'

'A foreigner? Ah, well, maybe they have different customs in Saxony.'

'Maybe so. It was kind of him, anyway. Kind to visit.'

Sigrid blinked, wondering, but she thought she had better bring the conversation back to Steinar while she had the chance.

'Anyway,' she said, '- oh, did he say anything about knowing Steinar in Colonia?'

'No,' said Svanhild simply. 'He didn't say anything about Colonia, as far as I remember.'

'Oh, well. Anyway, did Steinar mention any enemies he might have made? I know he was a good man, and a popular one, but even popular men can ... well, they can find themselves in difficult situations, can't they? And sometimes it's the good men who find them even more difficult.'

But already Svanhild was shaking her head.

'He didn't say anything about not liking anyone. He might have mentioned someone not being as efficient as another clerk, but that would have been all, and it would not have been his place to complain or even point it out, I would think.'

'There was that thing about the robberies, Svanni. What was all that again?'

'The robberies?' Svanhild blinked. 'Oh, that! He helped to bring a thief to justice, that was all.'

'Can you tell me what happened?' Sigrid asked.

'I was going to tell her, but I thought you might know more about it than I did,' Ubbi explained. 'He would have told you more than me, I thought.'

'I don't know that he did, Ubbi. He told us all around the fire that night, didn't he? I think that was the only time he spoke of it.'

There was a pause, where everyone seemed to be waiting for someone else to tell the story. Sigrid tried to suppress an impatient sigh.

'I thought it might be connected,' she explained, to encourage them. 'A theft, a robbery ...'

'More than one theft,' said Thorgunna, who had been seeing that the children were settled in their bedspace. She refilled all their cups before sitting with them at the fire. 'Wasn't it, Svanhild?'

'Yes, I believe so. Well, if it hadn't been, then he wouldn't have noticed, I suppose – or that's how I understood it.'

'You'd better tell her,' said Ubbi. 'You're just tantalising her now!'

'Oh, no, you tell her,' said Svanhild. 'I don't want to start crying again.' She gave a slight smile at her own weakness.

Somebody had better tell me soon, Sigrid thought to herself, or I don't know what I'll do. She held her breath, and at last Ubbi shrugged and settled back, stretching his legs out, ready to tell his story.

'Well, then,' he began at last. 'The last time Steinar was in Colonia, he was finding out about –'

'Laws and taxes, yes, I know,' Sigrid said, without thinking. 'Oh, sorry! Someone else mentioned that, too. Asmund, in fact. You know how much he admired Steinar. He's been going on about the laws and the taxes. But maybe you intended to say something else?'

'No,' said Ubbi, his eyebrows high, 'no, it was laws and taxes he was there for. And he travelled about a good deal, seeing how they valued land and so on. Most of the time he travelled with the clerks in Abbot Konrad's scriptorium, but sometimes he was lucky enough – blessed enough, he would say – to travel with the Abbot himself, and see him carrying out some of the larger valuations of lands belonging to some of the chief people in the country. And once or twice – well, more, I think – he and the clerks travelled to places the Abbot had already been, delivering tax assessments, or asking any extra questions that were needed, or ... well, I don't know what. It was complicated stuff, you know?'

'Not something I'd fancy doing myself,' Sigrid agreed.

'Best left to the men, eh?' Thorgunna suggested, and they grinned at each other. The ways men found to occupy themselves were often a mystery to Sigrid, and no doubt Thorgunna felt the same way.

'But what has this to do with robberies?'

'Theft, actually,' said Ubbi, nodding with a serious air. 'There had been thefts at several of the big halls, not while the Abbot was there, fortunately, but afterwards. And the thing was, Steinar, before he had heard about the thefts, had noticed someone – the same man, sometimes on the road, sometimes actually staying at a hall, or just leaving, when a theft took place or when it was discovered. He pointed the man out to one of the Abbot's officers, and it wasn't long before the man was found guilty.'

'Goodness! They must have been pleased with Steinar!'

'I gather they were,' said Ubbi, clearly rather proud of his brother-in-law. 'He didn't say much about it himself, but you could tell that things had gone particularly well for him in Colonia after that episode.'

'And what of the man? The thief?' Sigrid asked. 'What do they do with thieves in Colonia, with its Christian laws?' She had heard things about Saxony, and was quite ready to hear about hands being chopped off, or even heads, if they took a fancy to the notion.

'Oh, exile,' said Ubbi, with a shrug. 'No doubt the man is off thieving somewhere else now. Once you start that kind of thing, I should think, earning an honest living loses its appeal.'

Exile, thought Sigrid. So in all likelihood the man was not still in Saxony, but he could be pretty much anywhere else. What if he had come to Orkney? Seen the man who had had him arrested and sentenced? How would he react then? And worse, perhaps, if he had had family, or a life well-established in Saxony: she had had reason, from time to time, to dwell on the sentence of exile, and imagine what it might do to a person, banished from their community, their trade, their kin.

'Do you know anything about the man?' she asked. 'I suppose he was Saxon.'

'I suppose – wait, though,' said Ubbi. 'He wasn't, you know. I've hardly thought of this since Steinar told me, but no, he wasn't Saxon at all. He was Icelandic.'

Icelandic, thought Sigrid. Like the man who had bought that comb this morning.

THRETTÁN

XIII

PERHAPS THE INSTRUMENTS were a little basic and lacking in variety – well, they both needed to be blown down – but the quality of the playing was very good. For a while the two boys entertained with tunes both lively and wistful, then they played a few that people would know the words to. One man stood and sang a song of his own devising to the hall, which Ketil had not heard before and enjoyed. Another couple recited verse, giving the players a rest. Then, dangerously, a few of the women declared that dancing was what was required, and before anyone could escape a circle had formed in the middle of the hall, the women outnumbering the men, hands clamped together, elbows pressed hard, and the dance began. Ketil, who being at the back of the hall had managed not to be caught, watched with some amusement: some of the dancers sang along with the tune, while others called out encouragement, and a significant number simply counted with ferocious concentration to try to keep step.

The dance drew to an untidy halt with much hilarity, and the circle resorted itself for another to start. One of the players objected to something and a minor quarrel started, while others urged settlement and a new tune. Thorfinn laughed and pointed something out to Ingibjorg – he was never much of a dancer himself – as Lambi, panting, escaped and staggered past Ketil for the door. He had a greenish tinge. Ketil slipped off his bench and followed him outside. Lambi had staggered round the corner to the wall of the smithy, well away from the hall door, fortunately. Ketil waited while Lambi leaned over, a hand against the wall, clutching his stomach, but eventually his breathing settled and he managed to retain his supper.

'All right, there, Lambi?' Ketil asked, and the Icelander jumped. When he saw Ketil, he groaned, and leaned back against the wall.

'Strong ale,' he muttered, 'then there's a lassie in there and nothing would do her but she would have me up on the floor and dancing. Ugh,' he added, with feeling.

'Good evening, though, eh? A fair number there, for the summer time.'

'Aye, not bad. And the food's grand. I'd have hated to have lost it.' Lambi managed a grin.

'Oh, Thorfinn always manages good food,' Ketil agreed. 'And the company has been interesting, too. I –'

'I didn't see you speaking with that Hakon, though, eh?' said Lambi. Ketil's mouth snapped shut. Lambi really was not the brightest man. The sooner Ketil could dispose of him somewhere – preferably outside Thorfinn's lands – find him some alternative employment, the happier he would be. But for the moment, Lambi seemed likely to have a use.

'Did I hear that you speak Saxon?'

There was a pause, two breaths long.

'I speak a kind of Saxon, yes. From the north of the place, up nearly Denmark. See, I was around there for a year or two, but it was a long time ago and I've forgotten most of it.'

'Up near Denmark? Whereabouts?'

'Near,' Lambi seemed to squirm a little, 'near Heithabyr.'

'Oh? Interesting.' Ketil was from Heithabyr, but on the Danish side of the border any contacts with the Saxons were not, at that time, much encouraged. He wondered what Lambi had been doing there, over the border. 'Been anywhere near Colonia?'

Lambi considered, puffing out his lips.

'I don't think so. I've been trying to remember, see, with all this talk of Colonia, but nothing I've heard is making me think "Oh, aye, I remember that!" But it was all a fair while ago.'

It couldn't have been that long ago, Ketil thought: Lambi was a young man.

'But you do speak a form of Saxon, then?'

'Yes, a bit,' Lambi admitted at last.

'I might have to ask you to help me speak to that man Otto – the Abbot's manservant, you know? I'm trying to find out who knew Steinar in Colonia, and if he made any enemies.'

'Ha,' said Lambi, 'I'd doubt that. Everyone seems to have thought he was the grand man. I mean, they all liked him. Kind, and all that.'

'That's what I keep hearing,' said Ketil. 'Which makes me wonder why he was killed. He might have found out something that no one wanted him to know, for example.'

'Oh, aye?' Lambi turned the idea over in his head for a moment. 'Aye, that would work. So he wasn't doing anything bad that someone wanted revenge for.'

'That's right. Shall we go and see if we can have a chat with Otto now, if he's not too busy?'

But even as Ketil turned to go back to the hall, he saw Thorfinn at the door with Ingibjorg on his arm, bidding goodnight to Abbot Konrad. With Otto in close attendance, the Abbot headed off in the opposite direction from them, towards his monastic quarters.

'Looks like it'll be tomorrow,' said Lambi, philosophically. 'We'll just have to go back for another dance, eh?' He wiped his mouth on the back of his hand, and made his stoical way back to the hall. Ketil waited a moment, and then followed, his mind already darting off to the questions he might ask Otto. It would be a good opportunity: Steinar had not moved in Abbot Konrad's circles, and he would have been as far above Otto as he was below the Abbot, but servants often saw much more than their masters. And Otto may well have had friends around the Abbot's scriptorium, too, from whom he might have heard things. Even if Abbot Konrad might have been willing to interpret for his servant, for the sake of the investigation, Otto would be less likely to speak freely in front of his master. There would be no reason for him not to tell all he knew when the interpreter was Lambi.

By the time Ketil entered the hall again, Lambi had been sucked back into a new dance, giving every appearance of slightly desperate enjoyment. Ketil smiled and took his place at the back of the hall again. He had no wish to speak to anyone, particularly Thorfinn or Hakon, and this position seemed safe. He would happily have retired to bed except that this hall was the place he was sleeping, and there would be no peace here for a good while yet.

When he looked around, anyway, Thorfinn was heading off towards the back of the hall, Ingibjorg still tenderly weighty on his arm. He must be seeing her off to bed, but he would probably be back. Ketil accepted another helping of wine in his cup from a broad-faced woman who appeared at his elbow, and thanked her. She smiled, meeting his eye for just a second more than was necessary. He smiled back but turned away: his mind was too much on Mara that night to want anything to do with other women. He felt her move off. The dancing had changed again, a more complicated figure requiring more thought and ability, and only a small circle had formed. Ketil watched with interest until he felt again that someone was standing behind him. Anxious that the woman might have mistaken him and come back, he spun hurriedly in his seat and found Hakon standing there, a wide, friendly grin on his face. As soon as Ketil had seen him, he took a seat on the bench next to him.

'That's some grand dancing!' said Hakon. 'I saw your man had to go out. Too much spinning around, eh? Good of you to go and see that he was all right, though.'

'He was fine. He only needed a breath of air.'

Hakon's grin broadened, as though he thought Ketil were hiding something, and nodded. Ketil found his jaw was clenched, and tried to ease it. He should apologise to Hakon, probably, for what had happened earlier. But it was difficult: he knew he would not mean it, and the words were not even close to forming in his mind, as if they had no wish to. He could feel Hakon watch him for a moment, then look back to the dancing.

'It's hard, isn't it, when you were so sure?'

Ketil did not trust himself to agree or disagree, or even to acknowledge that he knew what Hakon was talking about. He stayed silent.

'But I'm sure Thorfinn understands. Anyone can make a mistake, can't they? And in the end it didn't matter very much.'

No, because Thorfinn believed you and not me, Ketil thought bitterly. And maybe, just maybe, because you didn't kill Steinar. But did you have him killed? That's the question.

Ketil cleared his throat.

'You could be very useful, though,' he said, 'telling me what you knew of Steinar. We're investigating the possibility that he died because of something that happened, or someone he met, in Colonia, so we're talking to everyone who knew him there - to see if anyone saw anything happen, or heard any rumours.' Or fell out with him and came here to kill him, Ketil added to himself. But he had to make it sound as if he no longer believed Hakon had anything to do with it.

'Who's "we", then, eh? You and that poor little widow woman?'

Ketil opened his mouth to reply but stopped. It was another point he was not going to win, whatever he said. He managed to change back.

'How well did you know him?'

'Actually I barely knew him at all,' said Hakon, seriously. 'He had already left Colonia by the time I turned up to give the Abbot Thorfinn's message, asking him to come here.'

'And did you hear any rumours?' Ketil's voice still sounded stiff, to him. He hoped Hakon had not noticed.

'Or see anything happen?' Hakon grinned. 'No, I don't believe his name was ever mentioned. That may, though,' he said, 'have been a mercy.' Ketil watched in surprise as Hakon's posture changed completely. He leaned his elbows on the table so that his head was closer to Ketil's, his face suddenly concerned, all frivolity gone. Ketil said nothing, waiting, trying to assess this odd change. He had seen it before, years ago, when there was fighting to be done: Hakon took his fighting seriously.

'The thing is,' Hakon said, his voice low, 'I didn't see Steinar this time, but I went to Rome with Thorfinn, and of course Steinar was in the party.' He pronounced Steinar's name with great caution, clearly not wanting to be overheard. 'And there may not have been rumours this last time, but there certainly were then, you know?' He met Ketil's eye, and nodded significantly. Ketil raised his eyebrows, still saying nothing. 'He was a younger man, then, of course – very pretty. And very interested in visiting churches. And, well, you see, Abbot Konrad has always had his … favourites.'

'Oh, really?' Ketil had to admit he was surprised. Such things happened, of course, but still, the Abbot had not struck him as that kind of man. He thought back to that stuffy little room, the Abbot in the high-backed chair by the fire, Tosti at the desk as far from him as possible. Was Tosti trying to avoid close contact with his superior? Would Tosti say if it were so?

'I'm not saying it has the remotest thing to do with anything that has happened here,' said Hakon, his voice still low, 'but I'd imagine it's the kind of thing you need to know about. I mean, I'm sure you've noticed, or your widow lady has pointed out, that it's a bit of a coincidence that the Abbot arrived and a couple of days later Steinar was dead. I haven't said anything to Thorfinn, of course: I'll leave that up to you. And it doesn't answer all the questions, of course: I mean, I'm sure Abbot Konrad would be more than capable of facing any rumours or accusations without going to – well, extremes – but there could be jealousy, somewhere? Something like that?

Ketil considered. His questioning of Otto was now going to take another form, and a much more delicate one. He hoped that Lambi would be up to it tomorrow.

'Ah, I see Thorfinn's back. I wanted to go and ask if Ingibjorg is well – it's not like her to leave a feast early, don't you think?'

'Perhaps not,' said Ketil. He should have thought to go and enquire after Ingibjorg himself, though he disliked the woman. Hakon rose and patted him on the shoulder, and went off back to the top of the hall, weaving his way between the drinkers. The dancing had pretty much come to a halt, and the two musicians were arguing again. One group were singing, but whether they intended their own entertainment or a wider audience it was hard to say: they seemed to be singing two rival songs simultaneously. Ketil drained his cup, felt over heated, and went outside.

It was late, but no one could call it dark. To look up at the sky was, he thought, suddenly fanciful, to imagine oneself encased in a piece of amber, the world outside coloured by the warm, mysterious glow. There were one or two others outside the hall, recovering from their consumption, and he stepped a little away from them, down towards the bath houses to the ledge overlooking the gate, staring back along the spit of land towards the mainland, the bays on each side, the dim shadows of the settlement near the harbour where Steinar had met his end. This information about

Abbot Konrad was unexpected, he thought, but it might well be the key – and linked to Colonia, too, which would keep Sigrid happy. His mouth twisted into a smile, then he heard voices below him. The gate guards had stopped someone.

He listened. He could tell from their voices already that they did not perceive much threat from whoever had arrived, but he strained his ears to hear more over the sighing of the night wind and the constant rhythm of the sea below.

'Need to see Ketil Gunnarson,' he caught almost at once. Sigrid? He moved closer to the edge and looked over, catching the white of a headcloth down below him. 'It's urgent.'

Yes, it was Sigrid. He hurried back to where the gate path led down, and almost bumped into her striding up the hill.

'You were looking for me?' he asked, pleased at her expression of surprise.

'I was, yes. I found something out about Steinar! I thought you ought to know at once, particularly since he's probably up here.'

'Steinar?' he asked, deliberately misunderstanding.

'No, no, let me tell it properly! Is there somewhere we could go where no one's likely to overhear?'

'The church,' Ketil suggested. 'There shouldn't be anyone there just now. The Abbot's gone to bed, and Tosti is still in the hall.'

'Late night,' Sigrid remarked, following him towards the church.

'Good feast,' Ketil agreed. They reached the door, and he held it open for her. The church was indeed empty, a little darker than outside, though that may have been because the eye focussed on pools of light where lamps burned here and there. There was a low bench to one side, seating for the old and infirm during long services. Sigrid went to sit on it, leaning back against the pale new stone wall. She sighed.

'I have information, too,' said Ketil, sitting beside her.

'To do with Colonia?'

'Yes.'

'Maybe it's the same thing. Listen, how much do you know about your man Lambi? Has he been with you for long?'

'Not long at all. I'd be pleased enough to be rid of him,'

Ketil said.

'And he's Icelandic, isn't he?'

'So he tells me. But apparently he speaks Saxon, or a northern form of it, so he might be useful to keep around for a little while.'

'No wonder he speaks Saxon,' she said in satisfaction. 'He lived in Colonia.'

'He did? He said he lived in the north, near the Danish border.'

'Maybe he did. And actually,' she said a little sadly, 'I might be wrong about him. But here, Steinar did something in Colonia. He worked out who had been carrying out a series of thefts, important ones from important houses. And the man he identified was an Icelander.'

Ketil sat back and considered. There were many Icelanders in the world, even outside Iceland. But Lambi was a thief, or so it seemed – so his men thought, anyway. Was he jumping to conclusions?

'What happened to the Icelander in Colonia?'

'He was exiled.'

'Hm.'

'And I might not have made any connexion – well, I probably would have,' she said, 'because he's the only Icelander I've met recently, but the thing is, do you remember this morning he was at the combmaker's? He was in front of me, so I saw the comb he had made. Or the two combs.'

'So?'

'Well, I saw one of them again this evening. It was in Ubbi's house – Svanhild said someone had given it to her today. Lambi. Isn't that his name?'

'That's an odd gift to give a grieving household,' Ketil said, though he suddenly remembered Lambi arriving at the scene of Steinar's murder. 'She's beautiful,' he had exclaimed, on his first sight of Svanhild. Would Lambi really move so fast?

'It wasn't a gift to the household,' said Sigrid wrily. 'It was to Svanhild.'

'How do you know?'

'It had her name on it.'

'Really?' He turned and stared at her.

'So you have a choice,' said Sigrid, with some satisfaction. 'You have the jealous lover, or you have the thief taking revenge on the man who had him exiled. How do those sound?'

'I have a third, then,' said Ketil. He drew breath, and explained what Hakon had just told him. Sigrid sat in silence for a long moment, frowning.

'Do you think that's possible?' she said at last.

'I'm not sure how I think about it,' said Ketil. 'If it's true, it still doesn't explain what happened, or who killed him. It just opens up a new range of possibilities. Doesn't it?'

'Hm,' said Sigrid.

'And certainly, the Abbot – ' he found himself glancing around, as if mentioning the man in the church was particularly unsafe, 'has enough power to have Steinar killed, if he wanted it to happen.'

'That would mean his grumpy servant, wouldn't it? What's his name? He has no other following here, does he?'

'Everyone has a price …'

'He would still need to know who to ask. At home, perhaps, the grumpy servant could help him, make some kind of contact. But here, when the servant doesn't even speak the local language, how would he find a willing killer? It would be very dangerous. And if he doesn't go through the servant, what other options does he have? "Father Tosti, do you happen to know a handy killer who could help me out with a little problem I have?"'

'Lambi is going to help me question the grumpy servant – Otto – tomorrow.' It was Ketil's turn to sigh. There were almost too many possibilities here. 'I was just going to ask him about anything he had heard of Steinar in Colonia, but now, of course … The trouble is, I don't much fancy asking Otto about his master's possible associations through Lambi. He doesn't strike me as particularly discreet. Or clever, indeed.'

'And if Lambi had something to do with it, you don't even know if you can trust what he's telling you that Otto is saying, can you?' said Sigrid. 'He could tell you that Otto's admitting to the whole thing, and you'd have no proof he wasn't.'

'I think I could probably tell something from Otto's face,' Ketil said, defensively. 'I can tell the difference between someone saying they're throwing themselves on my mercy and they're sorry they killed him, and someone saying they barely knew the fellow at all.'

'Well, it might not be as obvious as all that ...'

'We should go and talk to Lambi now, anyway,' Ketil decided. 'If he seems innocent, we can use him as an interpreter. If he doesn't, then we might not even need one.'

'Sensible,' Sigrid admitted, allowing Ketil a moment's satisfaction. 'Do you think it would be all right if I came too?'

'I've rarely been able to stop you,' said Ketil, straight-faced. Sigrid scowled at him, and stood up.

'Come on, then. Best get it done.'

But no one in the hall knew where Lambi was.

'Didn't he go outside with you? A while ago?' Tosti asked, looking weary.

'Yes, he did,' said Ketil. 'He thought he was going to be sick, but he recovered and we came back inside.'

'Well, I haven't seen him. Sorry,' said Tosti. He drained his cup, and stood. 'Ah, well, better be alert for the morning. See you in church.'

'He's nowhere to be seen,' announced Sigrid, coming back from asking the women in the hall. 'Can we take our chance and have a look at his pack? There might be something in it to help.'

Ketil hesitated. After his experience earlier, he was uneasy about checking another pack. But if Lambi was out, this might be the moment to try it. He led the way, slowly, giving Lambi a chance to reappear, to the back of the hall where the packs had been pushed to make room for the feast. Lambi's, untidy and ragged-looking, was easy to identify. Sigrid poked it gently with her foot, and looked up at Ketil.

'Go on, then.'

Ketil cast a glance behind him, but no one was looking their way. He crouched, and pulled the top of the pack a little wider. Inside were a number of separate little bags, all pulled tight at the neck. He picked one up, and felt coins shift inside it.

'He's not a poor man, then,' Sigrid remarked, hearing the chink of metal.

'Evidently not.' He picked out another bag, and found it full of hose, rolled just as it had been pulled from Lambi's sweating feet. He swallowed hard, and pulled the strings quickly shut. 'I don't see that we're going to get far here,' he said, poking a third bag. It, too, gave a metallic clink, but not quite as coins did. He considered. Was it worth opening it? Should he try a different one?

'Get on, will you?' Sigrid muttered. 'He might just have gone out to the privy, you know.'

'I know,' said Ketil, who had had that possibility in his mind. At last he found himself, against his better judgment, pulling open the bag. He tipped the contents gently out on to his palm. It was jewellery, rings mostly, including one formed of a sturdy twist of silver, the twist itself adorned with two very fine lines running its length. He picked it out, and held it up to Sigrid.

'Steinar's ring?' he asked, and she nodded.

FJÓRTÁN

XIV

SIGRID SAW KETIL hand over the ring to Thorfinn, telling him where it had been found. She had been inclined to take it away, herself, but she could see the sense in Ketil's decision: Lambi might notice it was missing, perhaps, and if Ketil were accused of theft, after this afternoon, things would not go well for him. Ketil said nothing about the ring to Thorfinn beyond where he had found it and that it was probably Steinar's: Sigrid was pleased that he did not make any wild accusations as he had earlier. He seemed relatively calm about Hakon now, too. Sigrid hoped that all the other possibilities concerning Steinar's death had distracted him, perhaps even pushed the awful memory of the slave girl to the back of his mind again. Thorfinn suggested Sigrid should stay for the rest of the night at his hall with Ingibjorg and the other women, but she was happy enough to walk back to the settlement on her own. It was a beautiful night, and Olvor and Asmund might possibly be wondering where she was.

On Sunday morning, however, the mist had descended, and it seemed a silly notion to walk up to the Brough to go to church, rather than staying in the settlement and going to the chapel there. Yet curiosity, which she told herself was concern for Ketil and whether or not he would do the job properly, made her leave early and take the longer walk, around the quiet Sunday harbour and up the path to the church in which she had sat with Ketil last night. The mist was the kind that feels like tiny spits of rain hovering in

149

the air, and she felt very damp by the time she squeezed in through the fine wooden doors Thorfinn had ordered for his new church. Inside it was busy, the air heavy with the scent of candles, incense and wet wool, but the service had not yet started: there was a little conversation in hushed tones. The women stood mainly at the back – Thorfinn had of course arranged seats for himself and Ingibjorg at the front and they were just settling themselves there – and Sigrid had a chance to see, as much as a short person can, everyone in front of her.

Ingibjorg looked terribly tired, she thought, and bearing in mind where she was, Sigrid offered up a short prayer for her, though she had never liked the woman. Even Ingibjorg's usual smug expression, as she glanced around to see who was available to admire her, seemed to be sliding down as if her features were too weary to sustain it. Her rather pretty daughter, Asgerdr, stood in attendance on her. Sigrid, considering what she knew of Asgerdr, also thought it was wise to keep her in full view of her parents, or she would spend the service flirting.

There was another seat empty at the front of the church, and in a moment the Abbot arrived. His Sunday robes were only slightly more elaborate than his workaday ones, to Sigrid's disappointment – she had been hoping for some fine decoration to admire and perhaps copy - but his manner of arrival implied that he was much more used to being the highlight of a grand procession. Having only the shawl-beswathed Otto in front, making sure the way was clear, and Tosti pacing in modest solemnity behind him, had little effect on the Abbot's own poise. Sigrid looked closely at him. Was he the kind of man who could do what Hakon had said he had done, and seen to it that Steinar Valison was killed? There was power in his face, certainly, authority and self-assurance. But there was something else, too, that Sigrid found more surprising: there was a humanity there. For a moment she stared, taken aback, and the Abbot caught her eye. She looked away quickly, found Ketil and then Hakon in the crowd, and glanced around for the plump Icelander Lambi. But there was, as far as she could see, no sign of him.

'Where's Lambi, then?' she asked Ketil when they managed to meet outside the church after the service. The congregation were dispersing slowly, stopping in small groups for a gossip, exchanging news in twos and threes.

'No idea. He didn't come back to the hall last night, anyway.'

'What does Thorfinn say?'

Ketil sighed.

'Lambi's my man. If he's missing it's my job to bring him back or dismiss him. And he hasn't been gone long. I can't imagine he went far without his pack, either. He strikes me as the kind of man to hold his possessions as important.'

'And the ring?'

'I'll have to confirm with Svanhild that it's the right one. There are plenty of rings with twists.'

'The two lines engraved along the twist would be a bit of a coincidence,' said Sigrid, but she knew it was safer to make sure. Ketil seemed tired today, she thought. Perhaps he had stayed awake all night, just to watch for Lambi. She hoped he was not running out of interest in Steinar's murder, but to be fair the matter was growing very complicated. Robbery? Revenge? Jealousy? Fear of betrayal? Even if you narrowed it down to one murderer, you would still have to narrow down the motive, too – and perhaps even the other way about. She shook her head, absently watching as Thorfinn guided Ingibjorg out of the church. Usually the pair of them would have been the first of the congregation, the leading laity, to leave after the service, but Ingibjorg had remained seated and Thorfinn had gestured to some of his men to go on without him. Ingibjorg leaned heavily on Thorfinn's arm, moving very slowly, as if she were afraid to take too long a step. Her long sheep-face was even paler than usual. Sigrid, seated on a low wall next to the monastery, felt herself tense in sympathy, willing the pair of them to get back to their longhouse without mishap. Ketil, too, watched them in silence.

'There'll be little from Thorfinn until that resolves itself,' he remarked when they had vanished from sight.

'He's worried – you can see it. And she's not well. I know Ingibjorg loves to be the centre of attention, but not like this.' Again she prayed for the woman, remembering the losses she had suffered, the pains, physical and deep in her heart. Ingibjorg had lost children before: Sigrid knew how frightened she must feel now. Being the wife of Earl Thorfinn would not protect her.

'So,' said Ketil, breaking into her thoughts, 'what next?'

'We need to ask Svanhild about the ring – show it to her, in fact.'

'Except that Thorfinn has the ring and I don't want to disturb him just now.'

'Right. We want to talk to Otto about Colonia and the Abbot and Steinar.'

'Except that we can't, because he only speaks Saxon and Lambi has disappeared.'

'Yes.' He was not being very encouraging, she thought. She began to list in her head the various people who were connected with the matter – who else had been there when they were standing about Steinar's body?

'Do you think,' she asked tentatively, 'that Father Tosti might be able to tell us anything useful?'

'Do you think he would tell us if he could?'

'I don't know. We could ask,' she said, trying not to sound impatient. 'I think he's still in the church. And I'm not sure that anyone else is just now.'

Ketil looked over at the church door, then reluctantly pushed himself to his feet.

'Come on, then.'

When they pushed open the church door, Father Tosti leapt to his feet. He had evidently been sitting on the bench Ketil and Sigrid had perched on last night, but when he saw them a look of profound relief passed across his youthful face.

'Oh, I'm sorry,' said Sigrid, 'were you at prayer?'

'Yes – sort of,' said Tosti, then gave a rueful grin. 'Well, not quite. Though I was giving thanks for a few minutes' peace.'

'Oh!' Sigrid did not want to go, but she was about to leave when Tosti waved a hand at her.

'I don't mean … I mean all this interpreting is quite … a great privilege, you know. And a joy to use Latin in everyday language, and not lose that skill. And to spend time with the Abbot – such a very clever man. I'm honoured.'

'But you could do with a break?' asked Sigrid. Ketil gave a little snort, clearly sympathetic.

'I wouldn't put it quite ... just a very short moment of peace, when I don't have to find answers to all his questions, all the details he wants, all the ... A very great privilege, of course, but I fear my poor head is not up to his level. It's spinning!'

'And here we come with more questions,' said Ketil. Tosti glanced up at him, anxious.

'Oh, no. Is this to do with poor Steinar Valison? It's his funeral tomorrow, isn't it?'

'I believe so.'

Tosti sank back on to the bench, folding his hands into his sleeves as if he could form a barrier to protect himself from unwelcome thoughts.

'What is it you need to know?'

'Well, first, I suppose, what did you know about him? I suppose you knew him.'

'I did, yes. I married him to Svanhild, and I married Thorgunna and Ubbi, too, and baptised both of the children.'

'He and Svanhild were married first, weren't they?'

'Oh, yes, by quite a few years. But the children are the same age, roughly. Svanhild lost one or two before her boy was born, but this is Thorgunna's first, I believe.'

'A big christening, then? Lots of family there?' Sigrid asked. It was a pleasure asking easy questions for a change, and she had realised that she knew little of Steinar's family outside the longhouse where he had lived.

'Well, two christenings,' Tosti corrected. 'Thorgunna and Ubbi had some of her family at theirs – she's from Skaill direction and some of them walked along for the day. I don't think Steinar has any family near here, and Ubbi and Svanhild are the only ones left of theirs.'

'Was Steinar home for the christenings? For the births?'

'No, he wasn't. That was when he was off in Colonia.'

'So what do you think of him?' Sigrid ignored Ketil's scowl: presumably he wanted to get on to the more dramatic subjects.

'He was a good man. A bit – well, a bit severe, sometimes. He was one for following rules, regardless of their effect on people. You know the kind.'

'I heard he was a gentle man.'

'Oh, yes, I believe he was. And I'd say he was devoted to his wife, and cared for his family very deeply. He was just a bit – strict, maybe. Ha!' he said suddenly, 'what a good priest I sound, don't I? Criticising someone for being strict in their behaviour? A good priest would be grateful for such a worthy person in their flock.' But he smiled, and Sigrid knew that there were other things that mattered to Tosti in his flock, too.

'If he followed rules,' she said carefully, struck by a thought, 'would that mean obeying rules about morality? His personal behaviour?'

'Well, yes, that's what I meant. The very letter of the law.'

'So ... would he allow himself to be, um, attracted to another man?'

'Gracious, no!' Tosti's eyes were wide with shock. 'He would never do anything like that – he would not allow himself to do that! Never!'

'Not even if he was approached by a man he considered his superior? I don't mean his chief,' Sigrid added hurriedly, 'I mean someone in the church.'

'In the church?' Tosti's face was contorted with horror. 'Why do you ask? Has someone told you ... no, I cannot believe it. I mean, I know there are some churchmen with a bad reputation. I don't like it, particularly where power is misused, but everyone is human. Things happen. But I still cannot believe that Steinar Valison would go with a man even if that man were high in the church.' He frowned, trying to find words to explain himself. 'Steinar would denounce him. Steinar would have denounced the Holy Father himself, if he thought that he had gone against the rules of the church.'

Sigrid met Ketil's eye. Ketil was frowning, too, clearly wondering who to believe. She gathered her skirts and sat quietly on the bench beside Tosti, partly because he seemed to need comfort, partly to signal to Ketil that he could ask some questions now. Could Tosti be right? He was a lovely man, Sigrid had always thought, gentle with his erring parishioners. Was he too gentle to see a sin like that in Steinar?

'We're trying to find out more about what Steinar did in Colonia,' Ketil was saying. His left hand rested on his belt, where his sword would usually be if he had not been in church. Sigrid

154

wondered what it was like for men to have to leave their swords outside, a limb relinquished for a couple of hours. Tosti had probably held a sword once, too – most men did. How had it felt to relinquish it for good? Tosti, she realised belatedly, was mentioning the usual tax and valuation business.

'We've heard that he helped apprehend a thief, though,' Ketil said.

'Ah, yes. Abbot Konrad mentioned that, when we came back here after Steinar's death. Someone Steinar had seen around a number of grand halls that were later raided, wasn't that it? Abbot Konrad had been impressed with his observation, and with the calm way Steinar reported it.'

'That's what we've heard,' said Ketil, nodding. 'The thief, we've also learned, was from Iceland, and was exiled when he was found guilty.'

'Oh!' Tosti was not slow. 'Then he could be here?'

'He could. There's a possibility,' Ketil's voice grew stiff, 'that it's my man, Lambi.'

'Oh? That's awkward.'

'He had only joined my men recently,' said Ketil, defending himself. 'But I brought him here, hoping to keep an eye on him. If I have been the cause of this ...'

'You wouldn't be,' said Tosti after a moment. 'You might have brought him here, in all innocence, but you did not place the axe in his hand, or help him to bring it down on Steinar's head, did you?'

'Of course not.'

'Well, then, there you are.' Tosti smiled. 'God does not hold us responsible for the deeds of others.'

Ketil bowed his head, somewhere between acknowledging Tosti's words and, Sigrid thought, making some kind of prayer. For forgiveness? She had not realised that he might hold himself partly responsible for the death of Steinar, who had been a stranger to him.

'So what is your thinking?' Tosti asked. 'That your man Lambi killed Steinar in revenge for causing him to be exiled?'

'That's one possibility,' said Ketil. 'There could be something else left over from Steinar's time in Colonia that has in some way pursued him here. I was told about Steinar and Abbot

Konrad – you say that is impossible, but you'll realise I need to ask other people, too, to see if there was anything in the story. If there was, then someone could have killed Steinar from jealousy, or to keep him quiet about the matter.'

'I cannot believe it,' said Tosti again, simply.

'Then there is robbery,' said Sigrid quickly, to take Tosti's mind off what was so abhorrent to him. 'A ring and a couple of bangles were stolen. And it is possible that someone killed him because they were in love with Svanhild – Svanhild need not have known anything about it, of course.'

'Goodness!' Tosti sat back, leaning against the wall. 'You have a complex puzzle to unravel! What is your next step, then?'

'Well,' said Sigrid, 'we wanted – Ketil wanted – to question Otto, but apparently he only speaks Saxon.'

'He does,' Tosti said, nodding.

'Lambi can communicate with him, but he's missing this morning,' Sigrid explained. 'And the only other person who can speak Saxon here is Abbot Konrad. That might make it all very difficult, as you can imagine.'

'I speak Saxon,' said Tosti.

'What?'

'I speak Saxon,' Tosti repeated diffidently.

Ketil looked at her.

'Why didn't we know this?'

'I imagine we never thought to ask,' Sigrid replied, tart with annoyance at herself as much as at Ketil.

'It would certainly be difficult to manage over in the monastic quarters if I had to ask the Abbot to interpret every time I wanted to ask Otto something,' said Tosti mildly.

'Is it – sorry, Father, but is it good Saxon? I mean, is it just 'Please fetch me a cup of wine' or could you carry on a conversation?'

'I lived in part of Saxony for a year or so,' said Tosti, 'and I've always been quite lucky with languages. They stick, you know?'

'Then would you mind,' said Sigrid, 'coming with us to talk to Otto now?'

'I'll need to bring him out,' said Tosti.

'Away from the Abbot?'

'Well,' Tosti looked awkward, 'you're not really allowed in the monastic quarters, if you'll forgive me, Sigrid. Seeing that you're ... well, not a man.'

'Oh!' The monastic quarters were new. Sigrid had not even thought.

'But I'll fetch him,' said Tosti, and rose from the bench without apparent weariness.

They followed him back across to the entrance, but lingered to one side as Tosti went to the door. They heard an exchange in presumably Saxon – odd language, Sigrid thought, full of angles – and in a moment Father Tosti led Otto round to where they were waiting. Beside them was yet another of Thorfinn's building sites, the low stone walls of who knew what, and as it was Sunday the place was deserted, and sheltered a little from the wind. They gestured Otto to follow, and found a corner to perch on stones, their feet sliding in loose and dusty earth. Ketil glanced at Sigrid, but she suddenly had no desire to lead the questions. She shook her head a little, knowing she could push her way in later if she wanted to. Ketil shrugged, and turned to Otto. The man had swathed himself in shawls again, presumably against the haar. What would he do if they had to stay for the winter, Sigrid thought? He would disappear completely.

Ketil cleared his throat.

'Can you explain to Otto, please, Father, that we are trying to find out more about Steinar's time in Colonia – friends or enemies that he made, significant things he might have done?'

Tosti nodded and turned to Otto. In a moment he was translating Otto's words back to them.

'He says that Steinar had a reputation in Colonia as a very good man and very hard-working. He did not see much of him, only when he had to go with the Abbot to the scriptorium to talk to the clerks.'

Sigrid watched as Otto seemed to relax a little, the shawls sagging slightly. Why had he been tense? No one suspected him of anything – unless he had been the one to kill Steinar on the Abbot's instruction. Then she saw his fingers, wrapped tight around each other between his knees. Cold? Or waiting to make a fatal mistake? She watched with more interest.

'Did he hear anything about Steinar catching a thief?'

Still the easy questions, Sigrid thought. Then we'll get on to whether or not Steinar and Konrad could have met more intimately. Tosti translated, and Otto's head tipped back.

'He says he knows nothing about that. Steinar was very clever to have caught the man. It was the right thing to do. But he knows nothing about it.'

'Didn't he accompany his master on these visits to the great estates?'

'He did, but he only works indoors. He has nothing to do with going outdoors. He would not have seen any thief around any of the halls.'

That's odd, thought Sigrid. I can't tell: is he nervous, or is he really sure of himself? There was a kind of bravado about his shoulders. Sigrid wished he would take off his shawls so that she could see him better.

'All right,' said Ketil. 'Does he attend his master all the time when they are in Colonia? Does he live in his … they don't have longhouses, do they? Some kind of hall?'

Tosti blinked at Ketil, and translated again. Sigrid caught some word that sounded like 'house'. Otto was already nodding his head and starting to explain.

'He does, yes. Abbot Konrad keeps a modest household for his status. There are only a few servants – there's a cook, and a man to do some heavy work inside and out and the gardening, and Otto does the rest. The Abbot trusts him, he says, even though he is quite young.'

He is, too, thought Sigrid, peering at the shawls again. A bright, unblemished face, when one could see it, with dark hair and not much sign of a beard yet. From the way he huddled himself together, she had thought him a much older man.

'So Otto would see any visitors to the Abbot's … house, whether day or night?'

'He certainly would,' Tosti replied, having consulted Otto.

'When the Abbot goes from home, does Otto always attend him?'

'Yes, he does.'

'And did Steinar ever visit the Abbot, or visit the Abbot's quarters when they were staying from home?'

Sigrid tried to observe Otto without emphasis, in case he

realised that this was a significant question. Otto did not seem to think it anything important at all, though his eyes became a little bleak at the memory.

'Only the once,' Tosti reported, after a moment. 'That was the time he came to say he thought he had identified the thief. As he was there on the Abbot's behalf, or with the Abbot's clerks, he felt he should report it to the Abbot first. Which, says Otto, was quite right. If it's any help,' Tosti added, on his own behalf, 'Otto is very loyal to the Abbot. But I don't think he's lying, here, do you?'

Ketil sighed, staring hard at Otto. Otto shrank briefly, then stared back, as if he had remembered something about himself or about Ketil that made him unafraid. Sigrid frowned. What could it be?

'No,' Ketil said, answering Tosti. 'I think we can take it that if Steinar and the Abbot ever met for anything other than business, Otto knew nothing about it. And that seems to mean, as far as I can see, that it never happened.'

FIMTÁN

XV

'OTTO SAYS HE needs to go back inside,' Tosti said. 'He says the Abbot should be finishing his prayers by now and he'll need some food.'

'Fine,' said Ketil. He watched as Tosti led the servant back to the monastic quarters.

'He's very young, isn't he?' Sigrid remarked.

'Yes ... I suppose he's been in the Abbot's household since he was small. You know the way.' He was not really thinking about it. He had been standing during the questioning of Otto, but now he settled on the stone Otto had used, his long legs at awkward angles. There never seemed to be a seat quite high enough for comfort.

'Well, where are we now?' Sigrid was impatient, as always. Ketil considered before replying.

'It doesn't look as if the gossip I heard from Hakon had any foundation. There was nothing between the Abbot and Steinar. I don't see, then, that the Abbot or Otto had any reason to kill Steinar, do you?'

'Unless there is something else we have not yet discovered ...'

'Show me some way of finding out and I'll do it,' he said, feeling suddenly weary. 'We've talked to everyone here who knew him in Colonia, and to those who knew him here around his visits to Colonia, the people he told about Saxony. Apart from Thorfinn, I suppose: he must have talked to him. But he won't have been invited to sit by the fire and tell him his traveller's tales: it will have been the information he had to report, and that would have been all.'

'So what are we left with, then?' Sigrid seemed tired, too. She stretched her arms out in front of her, clasping her hands, easing her shoulders. He wondered how her braid-making business was going. Would she be able to afford Thorfinn's new taxes? 'I thought we had revenge, theft, jealousy or fear of betrayal,' she said, unwinding her fingers to count on them. 'Theft is still possible – but we found the ring in Lambi's pack and the bangle in Hakon's pack, and there's still one bangle missing.'

'Hakon and Lambi could be working together,' said Ketil, trying to make it sound convincing. Sigrid gave him a look.

'They could,' she admitted, kindly. 'Jealousy … someone who wanted Svanhild, and decided to get Steinar out of the way? Do we have any sense that Svanhild has been unfaithful to Steinar?'

'I haven't seen any sign of that at all,' Ketil said, thinking back. Svanhild had seemed the most devoted wife, and there had been no hint at all that it might have been an act. 'And killing Steinar simply in the hope that Svanhild might then take notice of him, whoever he was – that's an act of desperation. Or madness, possibly.'

'And no one around here is showing any more signs of madness than usual,' said Sigrid. 'Jealousy of Steinar's position with Thorfinn, his responsibilities abroad? That seems unlikely, too. Steinar was home, and there was no talk of him being sent anywhere else, or even back to Colonia, now the Abbot himself had appeared.'

'Revenge, then,' Ketil said. 'Is there anything we've heard of for which someone might have taken revenge on Steinar?'

'The thefts, of course,' said Sigrid.

'Of course – but apart from that?'

Sigrid's fingers were twisting again as she thought.

'Unless someone just didn't like how pious he was. That's sort of revenge, isn't it? I mean, maybe he told someone they were not acting according to religious law. It sounds as if he was very strict about that, with himself. What if he was strict with other people, too? That would not make him very popular.'

'But he was popular,' Ketil objected. 'Everyone we meet seems to have liked him, to have found him kind and generous. I agree, people who go round reminding others of their sins are not good at making friends, unless they are priests, but he cannot have been like that and still be so much liked.'

'I suppose you're right,' said Sigrid with reluctance. 'And I suppose, too, it's not the kind of thing you put an axe through a man's head for, not unless he had really driven you beyond the bounds of patience.'

Ketil looked at her.

'I must remember to keep away from any axes when you're looking impatient,' he said.

'So.' She seemed to ignore him, but he caught the look she gave him. 'The only revenge we can think of is for helping to catch that thief. Now, what about fear of betrayal?'

'He was not going to betray the Abbot, not if we're right and there was nothing to betray.'

'Yes … could there have been anything else? Anyone else?'

Ketil bit his lips together and frowned.

'I think this could be where his being strict comes in,' he said, after some thought. 'He might not have gone round instructing people in their behaviour, but what if he found out something about someone and threatened to tell their priest? Or the Abbot? Or perhaps even Thorfinn, if he's bringing in new laws, too.'

'And perhaps they wanted to stop Steinar speaking before the new laws came in? That's possible: it would explain the timing, of course.'

'But how could we find out about someone like that?' Ketil pulled in his knees, and glanced around again to see that no one was listening to their strange conversation. It was a good place to talk, on a Sunday, anyway. He was not comfortable on building sites – he winced at one particularly bad memory - but when they were quiet and daylit they were not so bad. You could already see the outline of the new building – another longhouse, perhaps? With room for a craftsman to work and trade? Soon the Brough would be another Heithabyr, or Kaupang. Overhead the bonxies, no longer the aggressive blood-hawks they would have been a couple of months ago, soared and circled, fading in and out of the haar, while smaller, busier gulls sliced white lines through it. He rubbed his eyes, watery from staring up into the bright mist, tired from no sleep last night. Lambi: theft and revenge and perhaps even fear of betrayal all pointed to Lambi, and if Sigrid was right about the comb then perhaps even jealousy pointed his way.

'I need to find Lambi,' he said at last.

'Yes, I should think so,' said Sigrid, sitting up suddenly. He thought she might have nodded off. 'We need to know if he is really the Icelander that Steinar had convicted of theft in Colonia. We need to know why he had Steinar's ring, even if he isn't the right Icelander.'

'I think,' said Ketil slowly, 'that whatever Lambi has or has not done, he has never really been the right Icelander.' He propped his elbows on his knees for a moment, then stood up. 'I'd better make a start,' he said. 'I'll go back to the hall and see if anyone there saw him leave last night, or knows which direction he took. He could still be on the Brough.'

'He could have been drunk and fallen into the sea,' said Sigrid cheerfully. 'But yes, we'd better go and ask.'

'We?'

'I want to enquire after Ingibjorg,' said Sigrid innocently. Ketil, who knew exactly how Sigrid felt about Ingibjorg, chose not to comment.

The hall was quiet, as befitted a Sunday afternoon. No one had slept late that morning even after the feast, as missing church was not something that these days endeared you to Thorfinn, not without a good reason. But some of those who had managed to struggle through the service had retreated here afterwards, where the fire was lit against the chill of the haar and some food had been served, under Asgerdr's supervision. Ingibjorg was nowhere to be seen, unsurprisingly. She had no doubt retreated to the relative privacy of her own longhouse next door. More unexpected was Thorfinn's absence – was he braving no doubt a small battalion of women, just to be near his wife?

He looked around, and recognised a couple of sleeping faces that did not belong to any of the feastgoers. He stepped across, and shook one of the men by the shoulder. He woke sharply, already sitting up.

'I'm sorry to waken you. You were on guard duty last night, weren't you? All night?'

'Yes …' the man looked at him warily. Guards could be accused of all kinds of mistakes and misdemeanours.

'Did you see the man Lambi at all? Icelander, wears a woollen cap?'

The guard blinked, then remembered.

'Oh, aye, the one with the hair? Aye, he was out and about a fair bit in the course of the night.'

'During the feast, or once things had settled down?'

'Both! Aye. Aye, well, he was out and in maybe twa-three times, and then after the lights went out he came down to the gate and asked to go through.'

'He left the Brough?'

'He did, aye. Well, we let him. It's mostly our job to make sure no one comes in. Oh, well, we let her in, aye,' he said suddenly, catching a glimpse of Sigrid round Ketil's elbow, 'but she said she wanted to speak to you and we knew she was … we knew who she was, so on she went. But ken, strange men and that, we don't let them in. Not at night.'

'Good man. And did Lambi go out after she arrived? Just to give me a sense of time.'

'Oh, aye, after. When the feast was over, like I said, and things were quiet.'

'I see. I take it he was on his own?'

'Oh, aye, he was.'

'Which way did he head?'

'Out along the way, ken, out towards Buckquoy.'

'Not down to the harbour?'

'No. No, 'cause we watched him for a bit, as far as we could see, and the night was clear. There was nothing else much to look at.'

'Fair point. Did you let anyone else out?'

'No, just him. See, we don't often let folks out at night, unless they're feast guests that live nearby, Buckquoy, maybe, or down by the harbour. Like we let her out again later, ken? Heading back to the harbour.' He jerked his head again at Sigrid. 'But there was no one else.'

'Not even anyone who just nipped out for a moment, and came back in?'

The man considered, and yawned.

'You can ask Aud over there.' He indicated an enormous man, lying flat on his back and snoring delicately. 'He was on with me. But if I was you,' he added, slumping back down on to his bedding, 'I wouldna wake him till supper.'

Ketil straightened, and glanced back at Sigrid. She was grinning.

'I think I'd agree. He seemed reliable enough, without tackling his pal. Oh! How is your mother?'

Ketil looked round. Asgerdr, her hair like braided barley silk, had appeared beside them, eyes mostly directed at Ketil. He looked away, and Asgerdr replied to Sigrid.

'Oh, she thinks she's dying,' she said. 'She's been like this before. She's taken to her bed, and is adorning herself with her best clothes and jewels like some ancient princess about to be buried in a boat.' She smiled. 'I'm not calling Father Tosti just yet, though.'

Then she winced suddenly. A muffled scream could be heard, coming from somewhere outside the hall. Asgerdr dropped the jug she was holding and ran to the back of the hall, while everyone else fell silent. Then, with a look, Sigrid and Ketil raced after her.

The back door opened on to a narrow laneway, opposite Thorfinn's own large longhouse. Its door stood open, and even as they reached it Thorfinn pushed back the inner curtain and stood on the doorstep. Asgerdr had vanished.

'Is everything all right?' Sigrid demanded. 'Is Ingibjorg all right, my lord?'

'She's ... it's not her time yet,' said Thorfinn, scowling. Asgerdr appeared behind him.

'She's fine,' Asgerdr snapped. 'It's her jewellery.'

'What about it?' Ketil felt a chill on his spine.

'It's missing. All except the things she wears most days. All her grand stuff – it's gone.'

'Lambi,' was all Ketil could say.

'We need to see his pack again. Will you come, my lord?' Sigrid asked Thorfinn, reaching out a hand. Ketil was not sure whether she was trying to distract him from worries about his wife, or making sure they had a witness to whatever they might find. In any case, he was pleased enough that Thorfinn allowed himself to be led back into his own hall, and over to the back corner where the packs were that had not been used last night, or had already been stored for tonight. Lambi's, as before, was notable for its untidiness. This time Ketil tugged at the bottom of it and emptied the entire contents out on to the stone floor, then set about emptying the smaller bags that were inside it. The worn hose came out again, and was examined. The bag of coins was tipped with care into a bowl, and fingered through. Spare shirts and breeches were checked for anything that might have been wrapped in them. A pair of winter boots was shaken and explored with caution. There was nothing else.

'He'll have his knife and sword with him, I suppose,' said Thorfinn, 'wherever he is.'

'Apparently he left the Brough after the feast last night,' Ketil explained.

'And his bowl and spoon and cup – they'll all be with him, too,' added Sigrid. 'I suppose he was wearing his cloak. We didn't ask.'

'No one would have stolen it, anyway,' said Ketil. 'It looked as if it had been through more battles than he had.'

Thorfinn touched the bowl of coins.

'He must be intending to come back, anyway.'

'Yes ... I wonder if he was carrying anything when he left?'

Thorfinn met his eye with an intelligent look.

'You mean he might have taken Ingibjorg's jewellery away, and have hidden it somewhere off the Brough?'

'Exactly, my lord.' Ketil looked around at the sleeping guard. Should he risk waking him again?

'We should try to find out where he went,' said Thorfinn. 'Ingibjorg is upset enough as it is – too upset for her condition. If she loses this child I don't know what she'll do.'

'He set off in the direction of Buckquoy, not of the harbour,' said Ketil, having no wish to imagine what Ingibjorg might or might not do, whatever the circumstances.

'Interesting.' Thorfinn fingered the hilt of his knife, in a way that was not comforting.

'We'll go and see what we can find out, shall we?' Sigrid evidently found the gesture just as disconcerting. She began to heap Lambi's belongings back into his pack, no more tidily than they had emerged from it. It did not take long, then she stood up. 'Come on.'

Ketil glanced at Thorfinn. He had an amused look on his dark face. Well, thought Ketil, at least someone was happy.

Cloaked against wind and haar – anywhere else he knew, the wind would be good enough to blow the mist away, he thought – he and Sigrid strode down to the gate and out across the headland's path to Buckquoy, where Sigrid's own longhouse was. He struggled to think where Lambi might have gone. As far as Ketil knew, Lambi had no friends in Orkney, no relatives. Could he have gone to Kirkuvagr to take ship somewhere? But surely he would never leave his money behind, not Lambi. It would have been the matter of a moment or two to tie up his pack and take it with him, and in the confusion at the end of the feast no one was likely to have noticed. And then there was Ingibjorg's jewellery. Would he just have taken that and run with it, or would he have left the Brough to hide it somewhere? Where would he know well enough to think it a safe hiding place? Where had he been on the island? He had only, as far as Ketil knew, been on the mainland: he would not have had time to travel to any of the smaller islands. That was something, he supposed, but it did not mean that Lambi could not have borrowed a boat – with or without the owner's permission - and have happily rowed himself to, say, Rousay, hidden the jewellery somewhere and already be on his way back, taking his chances. After all, Lambi never seemed like the kind of man who made a plan.

'Where could he have gone?' Sigrid's voice broke into his thoughts. 'Who does he know, apart from Svanhild, presumably?'

Svanhild. Why had he not thought of her?

'We'll start there, anyway,' he said, as if it had been his intention all along. 'Though if he did go there, it's surprising he didn't go along the harbour, rather than this longer way around.'

'He maybe changed his mind, or thought he would like a walk after his supper,' said Sigrid lightly. 'Here's the path.'

They were fairly close to Einar's hall, but there was no one in sight there, and as far as he knew Lambi had never visited Einar's household. They skirted it, and headed for the path down to the sea, the one that would lead along the farthest part of the harbour and directly to the settlement where Steinar had died. It was an easy enough route: Lambi might just have preferred the smoother ground inland, rather than tripping over boats and ropes and barrels down by the shore.

Everything was Sunday-quiet, letting the sounds of sea and seabirds take over. There was hardly anyone about. It was a short walk to Steinar's – or Ubbi's – longhouse, though Ketil made it reluctantly. He had disturbed this family so much since their loss. But Sigrid was forging ahead, reaching the longhouse door before him and knocking gently on the wood, not allowing him any choice but to follow.

'That Icelander? Aye, he was here,' said Ubbi at once when they asked. 'Arrived late last night. I can tell you, I don't like to say it with my brother-in-law lying there and any mourner welcome, but I'm a bit tired of seeing him here. You know he gave Svanhild a comb? With her name on it in runes? That's not right, not for a new widow, not from a stranger.'

'He is a stranger, then? I thought perhaps he had met at least Steinar before,' said Sigrid chattily. Ketil knew he could not ask that way: his questions always came out portentously, he feared. Sigrid made everything a gossip.

'He's a stranger to me, and I don't mind if he stays that way,' said Ubbi. Thorgunna nodded.

'He's been here more than any of our friends and neighbours, and they haven't neglected us,' she agreed.

'He's being kind.' Svanhild sat as usual by her husband's body, one hand on it still. She managed also to be feeding her child. Thorgunna was the same. Without the body, it would have been a peaceful family scene, with the soft sound of suckling babies. Even Ubbi was unable to be hostile for long.

'Well, I suppose it was kindly meant,' he said. 'And if he comes to the funeral I'll take it as a sign of respect to Steinar. But he's your man, isn't he, Ketil? Could you not send him off somewhere tomorrow or the next day, take him away from here? He just eats, and gazes at Svanhild, and pulls his hat down over that hair of his.'

'Did he have anything with him when he arrived here last night? A bundle, or anything like that?'

'No,' Thorgunna sighed. She pushed a curl gently off her son's forehead and he gurgled. 'I thought he might have brought some food, but he was empty-handed, completely.'

'When did he leave? Did he say he was coming back for the funeral?'

'I can't remember,' said Thorgunna. 'He might have. It wouldn't have surprised me.'

'He left – when? Oh, I know,' said Ubbi, grinning a little. 'I said he'd be doing us a great favour by going to the chapel and praying for us during the service this morning, since we couldn't go.'

'That's right! Well done, Ubbi!' said Thorgunna, smiling back at him. 'And I went to take Freya for her walk, and he was definitely heading off that way. He saw me watching him and gave me a wave – he looked as if he knew I was making sure he was going. You can't see the chapel door from here, but he was certainly going in the right direction.'

'Was he alone?' Ketil asked.

'Well, there were others going the same way, of course. Olvor and Asmund, other neighbours going to church. You left earlier, Sigrid, they said.'

'I did – I went up to the Brough,' Sigrid told her.

'But I didn't think – I don't know if I would have noticed, but I don't think there was anyone really walking with him. He doesn't know anyone down here, does he? Apart from us.' She made a face, then turned it into a funny expression to amuse her son. He giggled.

'He's lovely!' said Sigrid. 'I mean, both the babies are lovely, of course. I'm not just saying that: they have lovely faces.' Ketil glanced over. The children looked like small blobs, well-wrapped in shawls. 'May I hold him?' Sigrid went on.

'Oh, I wouldn't recommend it just now!' Thorgunna smiled. 'He's dreadful for puking just after his meal! Some other time, if you're still keen.'

'I'll hold you to that,' said Sigrid. 'Handsome babies: a good future, I hope.'

She blushed a little, Ketil noticed, as if she felt she were stumbling through an awkward conversation.

'Shall we go and ask at the chapel?' he suggested, coming to her rescue in case she needed it. She turned gratefully.

'Yes, we'd better. We need to find Lambi,' she said, excusing them from the longhouse. 'We think he might know something useful.'

'He hides it well, then,' said Ubbi with a laugh, and escorted them to the door.

They met the priest long before they had reached the chapel.

'I'm going to see Svanhild – the funeral's tomorrow,' he explained to Sigrid, with a nod to Ketil. 'An Icelander? No, there were no strangers in the chapel this morning. I'd have noticed.'

They walked on.

'He headed this way, at least to start with,' said Sigrid.

'He might have doubled back.'

'What about the harbour? It'll be quiet on a Sunday: a stranger would have been notice there, too.'

Ketil nodded. They passed through the settlement without meeting anyone else: only a cat walked across the path, stopped and regarded them, and darted on as if they had shouted something offensive.

'There's Asmund,' said Sigrid, and Ketil saw the big man standing halfway along the harbour, his head bowed.

'Does he count boats on a Sunday, too?'

'Oh, yes. Never a day goes by. Asmund, good day to you!' she called.

Asmund turned and looked for the voice, then bowed his head again. He called something, but it was hard to hear.

'Look who's here,' he said again, realising that they were closer now. He was standing between two prows, staring down at the sand in between the boats. Ketil rounded the boat, and looked.

On the ground, with two arrows sticking out of his back like a pointer to show where he was, lay Lambi.

SEXTÁN

XVI

'OH!' SIGRID'S CRY came out indistinctly as she slapped her hand over her mouth. She wanted to look away, but somehow her gaze seemed stuck to Lambi's body, like a fly on honey.

His woolly cap had slid off and his terrible hair was free, rambling in all directions. He lay almost face down, as if he had fallen and then his head had turned at the last moment, trying to see what had happened, or the muscles in his neck had sagged at death. His wind-chapped face was layered with sand, even his lips and eyes, and his hands and clothes were full of it. She swallowed. She had seen dead bodies before, of course, and ones in a worse state than this, so why did this one affect her so? Was it that Lambi, hovering behind them as they talked to Thorfinn, waiting cheerfully at the combmaker's, annoying Ubbi and Thorgunna, had seemed, for all his size, to tread so lightly, so unconcernedly, on the earth that it was wrong for him to be lying so heavily on it now?

She swallowed again, tasting salt in her mouth, and prayed she was not going to be sick, not in front of Ketil. She realised that one of her hands was on the gunwale of the boat next to her, nails digging into the wood, and for a moment she turned her head to examine it closely, the grain, the wear, the salt, a tiny picture to concentrate on until her heart and head and stomach had calmed. Then she made herself look back at the corpse on the sand.

Ketil was kneeling beside it, somehow neatly slotted into the narrow space between the boats.

'He's been dead for an hour or so,' he said, brushing salt from the fingers that had touched the dead man's throat and hands. Unable to shut the salty eyes, he arranged Lambi's woolly cap to cover his face. 'Two arrows. I wonder …' He angled himself to look more closely. 'Hm. What do you think, Asmund?'

'What?' Asmund was still as a hound marking his master's kill, his Sunday cloak flapping about him. Whatever the weather, Asmund wrapped up sensibly.

'The arrows are at two different angles, yet they have hit the same spot. And … yes, they look the same – but we'll think about that in a moment.'

Sigrid could see what the problem was there. The two arrows had been broken off, near the top of the shaft. Anything that would tell them whose arrows they were would most likely have been in the fletching, the three feathers at the tail. These must somehow have been distinctive enough that someone had come and broken them off, even at the risk of being seen with a dead body, in the middle of a Sunday afternoon. Sigrid shivered. This was a bold killer, or a desperate one.

Ketil and Asmund were still examining the wound. Sigrid, despite her nausea, tried to see, but the rumpled wool of Lambi's cloak obscured her view until Ketil's deft fingers flattened it, and he nodded.

'Yes,' he said, 'the two arrows came from the same angle, but whoever came down here afterwards – presumably the killer – tried to pull the shafts out, and they had to do that from an awkward position because of the way he is lying here, between the two boats. They must have hauled to one side – look, you can see the way the flesh is torn and the shirt pushed back – but it wouldn't work, so they broke off the fletching.' He sat back into a crouch. 'Oh, Lambi,' he said, 'you must really have annoyed someone this time. I wonder what you stole?' Then he looked cross with himself, and Sigrid glanced away as Ketil bent his head, praying for his not much regretted soldier. She would say her prayers later, she thought, when she had recovered a bit – and not just for Lambi, but for all of them. Who knew where a killer like this might strike next? Shivering again, she did what she thought she should have done in the first place, and stared up to the hillside above the harbour, the top of the headland that stretched out to the Brough.

There was, of course, no sign of life up there apart from kittiwakes and other seabirds for whom Sundays meant nothing. She considered. Presumably the killer had been up on the top, on the edge. The cliff itself was friable like the other side of the headland, and no one could rely on standing steadily on most parts of it, or climbing it without sliding down again. Or could they have shot from the base of the cliff? She made herself look again at the arrow stumps. They were close to being upright, and they were, she thought, a long way in. Didn't that mean they had been fired from quite close by? And then, that would have made it easier for the killer to stroll across and break off the ends. To stand on the top of the cliff, where people passed by so frequently, would have been extraordinarily bold. But to stand at the base, even on a Sunday when the harbour was quiet – even to carry a bow on a Sunday, when many men would have left all but their knives behind to go to church – that would take, as she had thought before, courage or desperation.

'Shot in the back,' Ketil was saying now, returning to his task. 'What was he doing?' Looking for a boat to take?'

'He might just have stopped and been looking out to sea,' Sigrid suggested. 'There could have been a seal, or something – you know, you glimpse the head out of the corner of your eye, and maybe think it's a person in the water.' She was not even sure she was making sense, but Ketil raised his eyebrows and seemed to acknowledge the possibility.

'Asmund, can you help me turn him over? Just on to his side, because of the arrows.' Ketil took Lambi's shoulders, and Asmund, blank-faced, grabbed the dead man's legs by the ankles. Ketil paused to see which way Asmund was turning the corpse before he went the same way. In a moment Lambi's face was exposed again, eyes half-open, mouth agape, and his cloak slipped down to show his shirt, belt, and pouch. Nothing he owned seemed to be out of the ordinary, Sigrid thought, knowing what the cloak would feel like without having to touch it. If he was such a prolific thief, why did he not dress and equip himself better? Was he just trying to hide his success?

Ketil pulled open the pouch on Lambi's belt, fingers fastidious on the rough linen.

'Spoon,' he said, '- horn, a good one – wooden dish, fire

lighter, and comb. Is this the comb he bought on the Brough, Sigrid?'

'Yes.' She could see it clearly, and recognised the Brough combmaker's work.

'His usual cloak brooch. His knife ... much good it did him, in the end. A few bangles under his shirt sleeve – all his money is up in the hall, of course.'

'That must be his best shirt,' said Sigrid. 'It's a good deal better than the one in his pack.'

'He would have worn it for the feast, and it would have been the one he wanted to wear visiting Svanhild and going to the chapel, too,' said Ketil. He waved at the sweat stains under the arms. 'A shame he hadn't another one, and time to launder this one.' He lifted the woollen cap again and tried to arrange it over Lambi's face, knocking sand off in a pattern of tiny trickles.

'We should tell Einar,' said Asmund suddenly.

'Well,' said Ketil, 'Thorfinn, I think.'

'No, Einar,' said Asmund, firmly. 'When something has happened, we tell Einar Einarson.'

'Hm, but in this case, because I work for Thorfinn,' said Ketil, 'and because Einar would tell Thorfinn anyway, I think I'd better go straight to Thorfinn.'

'No, you need to go to Einar. That's the proper thing to do.'

'Look, Asmund,' said Sigrid, trying to keep her voice reasonable, 'this man – this dead man – was visiting to pay his respects to Steinar today. Would you be very good and come with me to tell Svanhild and Ubbi that he's had an accident? I don't want to go on my own.'

'Why not?'

'I'd just rather have someone with me.'

'And it wasn't an accident,' said Asmund, dealing with the details one by one. 'How can a man have an accident where there are two arrows in his back?'

'You're quite right, but it might be kinder to start by telling them it was an accident.'

'But it's not true ... I think you need to tell Einar what has happened.'

'I tell you what, then,' said Ketil. 'If you go with Sigrid to tell Svanhild and the family, I'll go up the hill and tell anyone who needs to be told. Einar, Thorfinn, the Abbot – anyone. Is that all right?'

Asmund thought about it for so long that Sigrid began to think he had forgotten what the question was. But Asmund was not stupid. Eventually he frowned, and nodded his agreement.

'But Einar is the right person to tell.' He began to stamp off along the harbour, and Ketil watched him go.

'I'll stay here till someone comes back,' he said quietly to Sigrid. 'We can't leave Lambi alone.'

'No. I'll be as quick as I can.'

'And I'm not telling Einar,' Ketil added. Sigrid gave him a little smile, and hurried after Asmund.

'Were you at the harbour after the chapel service, Asmund?' she asked when she caught up with him.

'Yes, I was,' he said, solemn. 'I came to count the boats and see if there were any new ones, but it's a Sunday and there weren't. Sometimes there are, even on a Sunday.'

'Do you think you would have found Lambi then, if he had been there then?'

'Yes. He wasn't there when I went after church. But then I came back when I had eaten some food, and he was there then.'

'Do you think you saw anybody who might have been the person who shot him?' asked Sigrid, wondering if Asmund would understand such an idea. She modified the question. 'Was there anyone else about when you came back to the harbour, just before you found Lambi?'

'I didn't see anyone,' said Asmund. 'I was looking at the boats.'

'Oh, of course. Of course you were.' Unless one of his friends had greeted him, Asmund would quite likely not have noticed anyone. Or he would have seen them, and asked them all about their name and age and reasons for being there, and then likely he would be lying, too, with an arrow or two in his back, dead on the shore. She knew she should be thankful for small mercies. Olvor certainly would be.

Asmund walked fast, not looking to either side, and Sigrid needed all her breath to keep up before they reached the last houses in the settlement, his and Ubbi's. Focussed on his task he strode to Ubbi's door and rapped hard on the doorpost. It had an ominous sound, and Sigrid darted in under his arm to reassure Ubbi and his family that they were not come to tell them any bad news that affected them directly, or so she supposed. Freya the dog, after one monumental bark, decided it was not worth it and came across instead to sniff her and declare her harmless. Ubbi and Thorgunna watched and smiled: they were playing with their child who lay half-on, half-under a blanket, while Svanhild held her own son by the hands, encouraging him to take a few steps while she stayed close still to Steinar's corpse. There must have been a draught from the door: Thorgunna flipped more of the blanket over her boy, keeping him cosy, as Svanhild looked up to see which mourner had come to keep company with them now. The dog returned to lie at Steinar's feet, with a sigh. Sigrid was pleased to see the welcome Ubbi gave Asmund, bringing him forward to the fire.

'We have some odd news for you, I'm afraid,' Sigrid began, raising her eyebrows at them. But Asmund was less subtle.

'That Icelander Lambi is dead. We have to tell Einar.'

'Dead? The man with the woollen cap?' Svanhild asked, as if there were several Icelanders going about the islands in different headgear. 'The one who was here?'

'Yes, that one.'

'How dead?' Svanhild asked, utterly bewildered. Ubbi, watched by Sigrid, exchanged a worried look with his wife.

'Shot: two arrows in his back. Some time after the church service, down at the harbour.'

'But ... why? Who?' asked Ubbi. 'I mean, he was annoying enough, but not so that you would shoot him, I would have thought. Has anyone confessed? Said it was an accident?'

'It wasn't an accident,' said Asmund. 'He was shot in the back. Two arrows. It wasn't an accident. We have to tell Einar.'

'Oh, Einar won't be interested. Better tell Thorfinn,' said Ubbi, unaware of Sigrid's warning look.

'We'll make sure everyone knows who needs to know. Ketil's going up the hill to do it,' she said hurriedly. 'I just thought you should know, as you saw him this morning.'

'Well, I didn't much like the man, but that's not what I would have had in mind for him,' Ubbi said again. 'Was he generally not liked?'

'I'm not sure that he had made many friends here, certainly

– but then he had only been here a few days. Did he mention anyone else he was visiting? Or anyone he knew here?'

'No, not at all,' said Svanhild, and the others shook their heads.

'I'm sure he didn't,' added Thorgunna. 'He didn't really say much at all. He just ate, and drank, and hung around getting in the way. Even the dog didn't like him much.'

'Really?' Sigrid thought for a moment. 'Did Freya go with Steinar on his travels? To Colonia?'

'Yes, of course! He would hardly have left her behind!' Svanhild gave a slight laugh, and touched the shoulder of her husband's corpse. 'They were inseparable. Weren't you, Freya?'

At the sound of her name, in Svanhild's voice, the dog twitched and gave another great sigh. Sighing was all very well, Sigrid thought, but she wished the dog could talk. Had she disliked Lambi because she recognised him from Colonia? Was that more evidence that Lambi was really the Icelander who had been convicted of theft? Unless Abbot Konrad recognised his corpse, they were never going to be able to prove it one way or the other now. She bent and rubbed the dog's ears, imagining she could read thoughts through that hairy skull.

'Did you recognise Lambi, then, old girl?' she whispered, but Freya seemed reluctant to co-operate. It was Sigrid's turn to sigh.

'Come on, then, Asmund, we'd better tell Olvor there's been another killing,' she said.

'Why?' Asmund asked. 'She didn't know the man on the shore.'

'No …' Sigrid paused, wondering why she had said she should tell Olvor. She had said it without thinking. 'I suppose because it's news? Because there will be people coming from Thorfinn – I mean from Einar – to ask questions, and it would be nice to warn her? Something like that. Come on, anyway.'

If nothing else, she had to get back to Ketil to allow him to go up and report the death to Thorfinn. She managed somehow to edge the reluctant Asmund to the door and outside, and back over to his own longhouse. Feeling slightly guilty, she prodded him through the door, waved to Olvor, and promised she would be back for supper.

'Asmund has some news, too,' she said, and waved a curt farewell. Poor Olvor: even with the attraction of being paid to teach nailbinding and tablet-weaving, it was hard for Sigrid to find her own position in the household attractive. It said a good deal, she thought to herself as she trotted quickly back to the harbour, that she wanted to spend a while with a corpse rather than spend Sunday afternoon by Olvor's fire.

Ketil was waiting, leaning against the gunwale of one of the boats that half-hid Lambi's body. It was a position of repose, but he was alert to any approach. He pushed himself upright as he saw Sigrid.

'He didn't mention knowing anyone else, or visiting anyone else, according to Ubbi and his household,' said Sigrid, without preamble. 'But the dog didn't like him. And the dog went with Steinar to Colonia.'

'Did she? A shame she can't talk, then.'

'My very thoughts.'

Ketil had turned Lambi back on to his face. He would need help to move the corpse out from between the two boats, and until there was more space around it it would be difficult to remove the arrows, as the murderer had proved.

'I'll go and see Thorfinn, then, if you're happy to stay here.'

'Well … it's the best offer I've had so far this afternoon.' She grinned, but Ketil looked solemn.

'I'll be back as soon as I can. If you see anyone behaving strangely, hide between the boats. I don't think anyone would hear you, if you shouted for help from here.'

'On a Sunday, with the wind and the water, probably not,' she agreed, suddenly nervy. 'I'll be fine.'

He looked at her oddly for a moment, then turned away, long legs carrying him quickly along the shore to where the broad path led straight up to the gate of the Brough. She watched him go, unexpectedly desolate, then took a good look about her for wandering bowmen. Seeing no one about, she sank down until she was crouching comfortably on the sand, an arm's length or so from Lambi's head. He would give her no trouble, anyway. She hoped no one else would.

Time passed slowly. Waving flies away from Lambi's

corpse was not particularly engaging work. She began to feel hungry: it was all very well telling Olvor she would be in for supper, but she had eaten nothing at midday. She thought about poor Lambi eating his fill at Svanhild's fire, making himself unpopular. Had he been hoping to court Svanhild? So soon after Steinar's death? There were some wives, she knew, who would be more than happy for the attention, but Svanhild had been so much in love with Steinar, for all Sigrid had seen and heard, that there seemed little hope she would even consider marrying again for a year or more. She herself was still a widow, nearly a year and a half after her husband's death – but in her case that was relief, the joy of freedom and pleasing herself – and not that many offers, either, she reminded herself with a grin. While she had just enough food and wool to scrape by, she was happy. She could look after herself.

The soft sound of a boot on damp sand made her jump. Ketil, back so soon? She listened. Something brushed against the boat she was leaning on, the least pressure change, the least noise. She was on the point of calling out, but something stopped her. Ketil on his own? Walking so softly? She found she was holding her breath. Ketil would be coming from the other direction, anyway.

She moved very slightly, and tried to peer under the boat without being heard. But she was leaning against it: it meant bending double, while doing her best not to shift her weight. She pressed the fingers of one hand into the damp sand, trying to find her balance. At last she was able to squint, almost upside down, under the sweep of the prow. A boot! Someone was there! At that exact moment, she lost her balance and fell forward with a squawk, almost landing on Lambi's head.

'What are you doing?' Ketil, rounding the boat in front of her, had appeared more soundlessly than whoever had been behind her.

'Someone's there! Someone – over – back there!' She gesticulated, and Ketil vanished at once. Sigrid struggled to her knees, then rose unsteadily as she realised Thorfinn had been behind Ketil. 'My lord,' she said.

'This is the fellow, then,' said Thorfinn. 'I can't say I took much notice of him. I remember the hair, though.'

'Are you sure someone was here?' Ketil had returned. 'There's no sign of anyone. He could be in one of the boats, though, I suppose, but I couldn't search all of them on my own.'

'He was there, on the other side of this boat.' She slapped its wooden side. 'I saw his boot.'

Ketil gave her a look, and went to the other side of the boat.

'There are footprints here, certainly – and they look fresh.'

'I told you so,' Sigrid muttered.

'The Abbot is just coming,' said Thorfinn, ignoring them. 'I tried to dissuade him, but he insisted. He wants to see if it's the man Ketil mentioned – the one Steinar apparently accused of theft in Colonia.'

'He won't be able to tell under here,' said Ketil. 'I'd hoped there might be someone around to help me shift the body.'

'It's not beyond me,' said Thorfinn, with a shrug. He let Ketil slip between the two boats, though, where his heavy shoulders would not have fitted, and between them they had Lambi's body out on to the bare sand just as a small procession wound its way towards them: Abbot Konrad, Father Tosti, and as well-wrapped as usual Otto the manservant. The Abbot paused, stately, and raised a hand in blessing. Tosti scuttled forward and began to translate.

'My lord Abbot, with the kind permission of my lord Thorfinn, is desirous of seeing the body of the dead man, believing there to be a suspicion that this was the man indicated by the late Steinar Valison as suspect in a series of thefts, and therefore likely to be connected in some way, though this way is not at present clear, and with his own death is likely to be more, and not less, obscured. Nevertheless if this point at least can be made plain it may be of some moderate assistance in the discovery of the overall solution to the deaths of both Steinar Valison and of this poor man, may he however sinful rest in peace.'

The Abbot nodded with satisfaction, a little smile on his well-bred face.

'Right,' said Thorfinn. 'Aye. Well, the corpse is here. He'd need to come forward a bit to see him better.'

However Tosti expressed this to the Abbot, the Abbot did indeed move forward, the focal point of a little knot of Tosti and Otto. The Abbot looked down, and Ketil, at a nod from Thorfinn, shifted the woollen cap which he had used again to cover Lambi's face. The Abbot leaned down. He reached out a fine hand, as if to touch the face, but pulled back, glanced at Thorfinn, and nodded solemnly. Then he turned away.

His view suddenly unimpeded, Otto had his first glimpse of the corpse.

He screamed.

SJAUTÁN

XVII

THEY ALL LEAPT at the sound, but Abbot Konrad was the first to recover. He took one long stride over to Otto, and slapped him on the face. Then he laid a hand on each shoulder and gave his manservant a little shake, not unkindly meant, Ketil thought: almost reassuring, reminding him he could be strong. For the first time, Ketil considered that the Abbot might actually be a man to be liked, rather than just admired. When the Abbot moved out of the way again, Otto stood, gasping, staring down at Lambi's corpse as if he could not believe it. Was it the first dead body he had seen? Surely not.

The Abbot now drew Otto a little further away from the corpse, turning him to face away from it. All the time he spoke, gently, but with a firm edge that was not going to allow room for disagreement. Ketil glanced at Tosti.

'Saxon,' Tosti murmured. 'Um … the Abbot doesn't know I understand it.'

Ketil raised his eyebrows.

'But you do,' he replied, his voice low enough that even Thorfinn, who still stood nearby, would not hear. 'What's he saying?'

'He's asking Otto about Lambi. Asking if he knew him.' Tosti stopped again to listen. 'And Otto says he did.'

'You mean he recognised him here? From when he was charged with theft?'

'Shh!' Tosti waved at Ketil, and stepped a little to one side, staring deliberately out to sea, presumably trying to look as if he were not listening to the Abbot's conversation. But Ketil's mind ran on. Steinar had spotted Lambi and suggested him as a thief because Lambi had been at several places from which things had been stolen. Steinar had been there because he was with the Abbot's party. What if Lambi had had a man on the inside, telling him where the valuables were? It would make perfect sense, he thought. Lambi had never looked that systematic and organised: a sneak thief, a picker-up of things not quite watched carefully enough – that was Lambi. To undertake a series of thefts from wealthy places would indeed have required someone with more organisational skill, a man, for example, who, however young, managed to keep the Abbot straight in all his travels and ran his household mostly on his own. Ketil watched the Abbot and Otto closely as they continued their conversation in a language he could not understand. Otto was in tears, his right hand expressive though his left, for some reason, he kept clutched under his shawls. Ketil tensed a little – some kind of weapon, hidden there? But the abbot showed no such suspicion: his expression was still kindly, as if the kindness had been set on a shelf and half-forgotten, for it was obscured now by bafflement, and pain. His servant had betrayed him.

They paused, heads both bowed. The Abbot raised his hands, as if to rest them once again on Otto's shoulders, but they hesitated, hovering in the air like birds uneasy about settling.

'You know that I cannot protect you,' Tosti murmured, coming back to Ketil. 'That's what he said. 'Or keep you? *Servare* … could mean either, really. Perhaps he means he cannot keep Otto as his servant. He's talking in Latin now, as if he's … well, as if he's an Abbot again, someone superior.'

'Does Otto understand Latin?' Ketil was surprised.

'A bit, I think, not much.' Tosti shrugged. 'Maybe the Abbot doesn't even realise he's changed language. Happens to me sometimes – I see someone I usually speak Frankish with and I just talk Frankish, never think about where I am or who else is there.'

Frankish, too, thought Ketil, faintly envious. One of these days maybe I should learn to speak another tongue. Irish, maybe.

'So what's happened, then? Otto knew Lambi, but why has that made the Abbot so … wretched?' Sigrid asked. She had been quiet for so long, Ketil had almost forgotten she was there. Tosti drew breath to reply, but at that moment the Abbot, pulling his shoulders back, signalled to Tosti that he needed an interpreter. Tosti trotted over, bowing.

'My lord Abbot says,' he began, 'that he must needs apologise with the utmost humility to my lord Thorfinn –'

'Never mind all the braid,' said Thorfinn abruptly. 'Just tell us what he's saying.'

'My lord,' Tosti blinked, and cast the least anxious glance back at the Abbot. 'Um, well. He says that Otto knew Lambi – the Icelander there – when Lambi was in Saxony. He remembers him – the Abbot remembers Lambi as the man Steinar accused of thefts from houses the Abbot was visiting. What both the Abbot and Steinar were unaware of, he says, is that Otto was giving Lambi information about where the valuables were hidden in each house they stayed at.' Ketil gave a tiny sigh of satisfaction. 'He says – the Abbot says – that Otto was completely innocent in this, and he was tricked by Lambi into giving more detail than he realised.' Tosti glanced down at the ground, then over to Ketil, meeting his eye with a tiny shake of his head. 'Nevertheless, he says his servant has acted with some degree of stupidity, and must receive a like degree of punishment – at the hands of my lord Abbot.'

'I see,' said Thorfinn. He propped his fists on his hips, and considered Lambi's corpse with a frown. 'So if he knew this Lambi,' he went on after a while, 'and perhaps resented having been used by him in this way, could he perhaps,' he looked up abruptly at the Abbot, 'have murdered him?'

The Abbot seemed to be bringing his features under control. His dark arched eyebrows twitched, then settled.

'Is there any chance,' Tosti translated, 'that this man was killed in any way other than by those two arrows in his back, fired from a bow?'

Thorfinn looked to Ketil. Ketil shook his head. There was no other wound, and the arrow gash had bled as much as he would have expected a death wound to bleed.

'No,' said Thorfinn. 'He was shot.'

'Then no,' Tosti translated back and forth. 'Otto would not be able to kill in that way, even did the Abbot believe him capable of killing at all. He is at heart a gentle man, if a foolish and gullible one.'

Thorfinn gave a sharp sigh, and rubbed his forehead with the heel of his hand.

'Then he'd better – my lord Abbot had better – do with his servant as he wishes. He has broken no laws here – though I should be interested to see how the Abbot might suggest I judge him if he had,' he added. 'That's not for translation, Father Tosti.'

'No, my lord,' said Tosti, and reverted to Latin again in the same breath.

'He's kind to his servants, isn't he?' said Sigrid. 'I mean, there are plenty of masters who, finding their servants had been that stupid, or involved in that kind of crime – and it can't have looked good for the Abbot, either, if thefts were following him about the countryside – they wouldn't be patting him on the shoulder and trying to comfort him, would they?'

'No ...' Ketil agreed, only half listening. Tosti had not translated quite what the Abbot had said – no, that was not it, Ketil realised. The Abbot had not said in Latin, to Tosti, what Otto had told the Abbot in Saxon. Where had the change crept in? Had Otto confessed to more than the Abbot had admitted? He needed to know, but he could not tell Thorfinn here how he might have been deceived. For one thing, he wanted to check with Tosti. For another, Thorfinn's feelings could always be charted on his face: if he were displeased with the Abbot, it would require no translator to let the Abbot know. If Ketil wanted to work discreetly, he could only tell Thorfinn later, well away from Abbot Konrad.

'Oh, look,' said Sigrid suddenly, her voice flat, 'here comes Hakon.'

Ketil spun to see. Sigrid was watching him, but he stared off towards the settlement to the south, where a familiar figure was picking his way along the shore. It was indeed Hakon.

'Come to give us the benefit of his kindly advice,' Ketil found himself muttering. He felt Sigrid's hand briefly on his arm, and was annoyed with himself. Hakon always seemed to make him reveal his weaknesses, even when he was still some distance away.

'Ah, Hakon,' said Thorfinn, seeing him too. 'Tosti, tell the Abbot we'll wait a moment: if the manservant gives any trouble on the way back up to the Brough, it mightn't be a bad idea to have another helping hand with him.'

Tosti began a low explanation in Latin, and the others stood about until Hakon saw them and greeted them.

'What's this, then, my lord: are we looking for a boat to somewhere?' he asked cheerfully. Then he rounded the last sheltering boat. 'Oh! What's happened?'

'Ketil's man, Lambi, the Icelander. He's been shot,' said Thorfinn briefly. 'There's wood here, if you and Ketil could carry him up to the Brough. And keep an eye on the Abbot's manservant, as we go.'

'Has he claimed manslaughter?' asked Hakon, already comparing pieces of wood to borrow. Ketil thought absently that they would have to make sure it was returned later: he was well aware how valuable wood was here in Orkney.

'No, he has not,' Thorfinn was saying. 'But he did know the man, and helped him carry out some thefts in Saxony. The Abbot will deal with it, but it's possible the man will try to flee on the way back to the monastic quarters. Are you ready?'

Ketil found a couple of long poles and matched them, wordlessly, to Hakon's. They spread their own cloaks across them, then laid Lambi, covered neatly in his own cloak, on top. He had been a heavy man: he made an unwieldy corpse, trickling sand as he went. The Abbot murmured prayers, Tosti joining in at moments, Thorfinn and Sigrid bowing their heads. Ketil and Hakon lifted the makeshift stretcher, and began the awkward walk back up to the Brough. The Abbot with Otto, Tosti and Thorfinn led the way, and Sigrid followed. Ketil could hear her trying to keep up while dusting sand from her Sunday boots. He almost smiled.

They took the corpse into Thorfinn's hall. Thorfinn vanished towards his longhouse, saying he would fetch the women to lay out the body, though presumably he also wanted to see how Ingibjorg was. In a few minutes he returned with the women and a slightly less concerned frown.

'She's still waiting,' he said, to Sigrid's enquiry. 'They say she's comfortable at the moment.'

'Then there's probably a while to go yet,' said Sigrid, and Thorfinn shrugged. There was an awkward moment as they stood about, prayers lapsed, the women assessing their task. Then Thorfinn looked at Otto, who seemed to be doing his best to be invisible.

'Let's take him over to the monastic quarters, then,' he said.

Ketil glanced at Sigrid. She raised her eyebrows, but she would know she would have to wait here if she wanted to hear any more. Ketil was fairly sure she would still be here when he came back. She laid aside her cloak and pushed up her sleeves, ready to help with the laying out. He nodded, and followed the others back out of the hall.

They walked, slowly, as if they were all suddenly weary, up past the church to the Abbot's quarters. Ketil watched Hakon's back ahead of him. If only, he thought. If only he had plucked up the courage to say to him earlier – I have some money, I hope it's enough, can I buy your slave? Can I buy Mara? Then if she had broken her leg – and she might not even have done that, for she had done that working for Hakon – but if she had still broken it, he could have nursed her, looked after her. If only he had been quicker, braver, but he had been nervous about approaching someone like Hakon, someone that bit senior to him, someone who had already been so generous that Christmas. And Ketil himself had been so young. That was his excuse, if he looked for one, but it was a poor one, really. He had known what had to be done. He had – almost – enough money. All he had needed to do was to speak – even if they had come to some kind of accommodation, it would surely have meant that Hakon would not have disposed of Mara when she was injured, or not without consulting Ketil first, as an interested party. Why had he not spoken up? The pain, the regret, so long buried, was surging up again, almost as bad as when they were fresh.

And there, Hakon had been down at the settlement. What had he been doing there? Had he stopped along the way to shoot Lambi, and had he killed Steinar? Hakon was more than competent with a bow, as he knew very well. But why? Why would he kill Steinar? Why Lambi? Sigrid was right: it made very little sense. Neither Lambi nor Steinar was a broken slave, more expensive to let mend than to replace. There was no pattern there, however much he might long for one. He had to focus on the facts. He had to find out all he could from Otto, too. It really began to look as if the answer to all of this lay in those thefts in Saxony, far away from Orkney, but quite capable of ruining lives here, too. He sighed. He should never have brought Lambi here, either, but in the end that was not a death to be laid at his door. He could not have known what Lambi had been up to in Colonia, and if Ketil had left him at Hwitebi who knew who else Lambi might have annoyed and driven to kill him. Certainly Ketil's own men had looked murderous enough.

They were at the door of the monastic quarters before he noticed, and filing inside. The Abbot led them to the same small parlour in which they had sat before, and Otto, unbidden, scuttled to build up the fire. Ketil, noticing him more than usual, saw that he still used his right arm much more than his left. Was he hiding something under all those shawls? The Abbot signalled to everyone to sit where they could, and then waved to Tosti. Ketil stood by the door.

'My lord Abbot says that he will keep Otto here, in the quarters, until they are ready to leave for Colonia again. That way he can do no harm and if you need to ask him any questions concerning the death of the Icelander Lambi, the Abbot will be happy to assist.'

'That's very generous of him,' said Thorfinn. 'It would be difficult to ask him anything otherwise. Ketil, have you any questions?'

'Not just now, my lord,' said Ketil quickly, knowing that he wanted to think about it, 'but I should like to see Otto's belongings, if my lord Abbot would permit.'

Tosti passed on the request, and the Abbot nodded at once, obviously thinking it was a sensible idea. He drew breath, then stopped: Ketil was sure he had been about to send Otto to fetch the things, just as he would usually have him do any task like that. Instead, he rose from his chair, gestured to Otto to accompany them, and led the men out of the parlour and off to a tiny room near the door, probably intended, when the monastery was complete, to be some kind of porter's lodge.

'This is where Otto sleeps,' Tosti explained.

Otto kept it tidy, Ketil thought, standing in the doorway. There was a roll of bedding against a wall, a small stool which seemed to be used as a low table with a lamp on it, and a wooden kist, an arm's length long but only a handspan wide, a good shape for tying on to the back of a pack horse. Ketil looked at it with interest. Surely a servant like Otto would more usually just travel with a pack?

The Abbot saw the direction of his gaze.

'Otto looks after my lord Abbot's more valuable items when they are travelling, of course,' Tosti translated. 'A chalice and patten, a pectoral cross for formal occasions, and some rings.'

'May I look?' Ketil asked politely, one hand already gesturing. Otto, just behind him in the narrow space, gave a little squeak. Hakon laid a hand on Otto's shoulder, less kindly than the Abbot earlier. The Abbot, paler than usual, nodded. Ketil turned and held out a hand to Otto, who immediately scrabbled in his pouch. He produced a key, and Ketil crouched at the padlock. The key turned smoothly, the bolt it secured glided back, and Ketil opened the chest.

'Ingibjorg's beads!' cried Thorfinn at once. 'And her cross – and that's a ring I gave her!'

Otto's breathing turned to gasps. Looking up, Ketil saw that he had turned a nasty greenish-grey. He fell to the floor.

The Abbot was on his knees beside him in a second, calling his name, rubbing his face. Tosti, too, squatted down and took one of Otto's hands. Gradually, Otto returned to consciousness, and Ketil slammed the kist shut, locking it again and handing the key to Thorfinn. Thorfinn looked as if he had no idea what to do, between stolen jewellery and fainting servants. The Abbot looked up, and waved at Tosti.

'My lord Abbot says,' Tosti began hurriedly, 'take the kist, please. He trusts my lord Thorfinn, of course, with the chalice and other things. Later, he will come to the hall or the longhouse, as will be most convenient for my lord Thorfinn –'

'Yes, yes,' said Thorfinn impatiently, already lifting the kist.

'– and they can examine the contents between them and determine ownership. In the mean time, my lord Abbot is delighted to see that my lady Ingibjorg's jewels will be so quickly restored to her.' Tosti finished breathlessly. The Abbot began again, and Tosti almost rolled his eyes. 'My lord Abbot asks that as the man Otto is not at present in a fit state to be questioned, that he be left in the Abbot's charge to recover for now, and my lord Thorfinn and the others might please allow the man Otto to lie down in his own chamber, that is, here, in peace.'

'Oh!' Thorfinn glanced around, as if he had forgotten where they were. 'Yes, of course: that makes sense. Never seen a man look so ill. Clearly not fit to be questioned.' He stepped back into the entrance hall, and as best they could Hakon and Ketil squeezed out of the tiny room. Tosti knelt and unrolled Otto's bedding, and between him and the Abbot they laid Otto amongst his blankets, tucking him in almost solicitously. Ketil frowned. This was a close-knit little household. Would the Abbot really hold Otto safe for questions, or would he see him safely away out of Orkney, somehow? Could they be sure that he had not killed Lambi? After all, it made most sense: the two men who had died had been the ones most able to accuse Otto of complicity in the Saxon thefts. Yet once Otto saw the body, he seemed to confess anyway. Why did the Abbot say he could not have done it?

Thorfinn and Hakon were making their way out through the main door of the quarters, but at the last moment Ketil glanced back into Otto's room. They had unwound his shawls from his chest, for once. He could at last see the shape of the man. And there was something very wrong with his left shoulder.

Outside, the haar was at last lifting, and the early evening sun was still high in the sky, amber gold. Gulls flew far up, distant specks against a blue still too bright to stare into. Frowning at the thought of what he had just seen, Ketil followed a little after Thorfinn as he carried Otto's kist back to the longhouse and Ingibjorg. Hakon hesitated, and Ketil stopped.

'So, do you think that little creature could have killed your man Lambi?' Hakon asked, smiling.

'No, I don't,' said Ketil. 'I've just seen his shoulder – his left shoulder. He's deformed. The Abbot was right: he could never manage a bow.'

'That must be disappointing for you,' said Hakon kindly. 'Another potential killer proved innocent!'

'Yes, very sad,' said Ketil, trying to match the tone. Thorfinn must have reached his longhouse: Ketil could see Sigrid, cloakless, flying up the path wearing a shocked expression, exactly as he would have expected. He did not want to discuss anything with her in front of Hakon, though. His head was whirling with complexities. A deformed man – deformed from birth? Yet under the church law that the Abbot was promoting, a deformed child should be exposed and left to die, could not be baptised – was that not part of Ingibjorg's fear, that she would give birth to another child who was not perfect enough to be considered … what, a real person? But Otto attended church, partook of Communion, was servant to an Abbot – he must be baptised, surely. Baptism was only for real people, not for cripples, nor indeed for slaves. Cripples and broken slaves could be disposed of like sick animals, tossed aside, of no consequence to anyone. But some slaves were important.

'Ingibjorg's jewels!' Sigrid cried, reaching them. 'You found them in Otto's room?'

'Yes,' he said. 'He seems to have been helping Lambi with the thefts.' Hakon had walked on a few paces, to the building site where they had questioned Otto earlier. He stepped over the low walls and took a seat on a stone, much as they had. Ketil found he was following.

'Could he have killed Lambi, then?'

'No,' said Ketil. 'He could not have.'

His words seemed to echo in his head, as he settled his shoulders against a higher section of wall in the quarter-finished building. Hakon was close by. Sigrid, her face puzzled, sat on the lower part of the wall, watching them both. Ketil stared up at the sky. It seemed to be waiting for him to speak.

'Hakon,' he said at last, more loudly than he had meant.

'Yes? How can I help, Ketil?'

'Hakon, when I stayed at your farm that Christmas …'

'Yes, Ketil?'

'Do you remember a slave girl of yours – she broke her leg.'

Hakon's brow wrinkled lightly, then he smiled.

'Mara, was that it?'

'That's the one. Do you know, I was going to offer to buy her from you?'

'I know.'

Ketil's gaze fell from the sky and on to Hakon. Hakon was smiling.

'You know?'

'Of course I know. You had your eye on her, didn't you?'

'I –' He did not quite trust his own voice.

'Oh, yes – and she was fond of you, too. My slave, though, Ketil: my slave. I wasn't having that. That was why I killed her.'

ÁTJÁN

XVIII

'YOU KILLED MARA – because I liked her?'

Sigrid stared from one to the other. Ketil had pushed away from the wall, and now he stood like stone. His hands had not even gone to where his sword should be, but had frozen by his sides.

'Oh, not just because you liked her, Ketil,' said Hakon, with a casual shrug. 'Because she liked you, too. You mean you didn't realise that we all knew? Mother was particularly keen to put an end to the problem. You can't go encouraging slaves, you know. They start to think that they might have feelings, and then you can't do anything with them.'

He smiled: an amused, satisfied, nasty little smile that Sigrid wanted very much to slap. But this was Ketil's battle, wasn't it?

'I thought it was because she broke her leg,' said Ketil, his voice – not his own.

'Did she? Oh, she fell when she was trying to run away – perhaps that was it. But of course I caught her then, quite easily. Dear me, broken, was it?'

'I was going to offer you a fair price for her,' Ketil said, and now she saw his fists were clenched. Was he going to strike Hakon?

'I daresay you were going to try. We did discuss it, Mother and I. But we knew you wouldn't have that kind of money. It was much simpler just to dispose of the whole thing.' He gave a laugh. 'She always was an odd one, that Mara: I had it in mind we might have to get rid of her one day. Do you know she claimed to be a Christian? Said she was baptised and everything! Of course, Mother never believed her.'

Sigrid looked at Ketil. As far as she could tell, he had stopped breathing. His battle? Yes, but she had had enough.

'Right,' she snapped, swinging over the part-built wall and standing in front of Hakon, 'you can go now.'

Hakon laughed again, a surprised, breathless chuckle.

'What?'

'Go. Now. Go fast. I don't care where, but if you are still here by the time I count down from ten, you'll regret it.'

'I'll regret it?' Hakon stood, slowly. 'Why should I regret anything you might do to me, little widow woman?'

Sigrid snatched her knife from its sheath at her shoulder.

'Ten,' she said. Hakon looked at the little blade. His lips curled, very slightly. Then he looked at her face, and the curl dropped.

'Nine,' she said, her voice low. Hakon drew breath.

'Eight …'

'All right, then,' he said. 'I'll go, but only because I don't want to cause Thorfinn any more trouble than Ketil has already caused him.'

'Did I say talk? I don't think so. Seven.'

'Glad to go anyway,' said Hakon. 'Axes and arrows and now you. These islands are full of nutters.'

'It'll be better when you've gone, believe me. Six.'

'I'm gone!'

And, to her surprise, he was. He skipped elegantly over the wall she had just climbed, and strode away, down the hill. For the moment she did not care where he was going. She turned in triumph to Ketil, and saw him drop to the ground.

She was too shocked to stop him or save him. He fell to his knees, curled over on himself, his linen shirt tight over his curved back so that he reminded her of the hard shell of her own shoulder brooches. His hands clenched under his skull, and the tendons in the back of his neck were as tense as bowstrings. He was shaking.

He was cloakless – the day had been mild, and he must have left it somewhere – oh, yes, under Lambi's body. Her own cloak was in Thorfinn's longhouse, which she had left so hurriedly when she heard about Otto and the stolen jewellery. Giving an exasperated sigh, she crouched by Ketil and flung her arm around him, trying to warm him. There was no response. She laid her cheek against his shoulder blade, and closed her eyes, willing him to be strong, to say something, to breathe properly. They stayed there, unmoving, for a long time.

At last Sigrid heard people, the movement of a number of people, footsteps on dusty earth, chattering. Frowning, she sat up cautiously, not wishing to draw any attention. She peeped over the low wall. Of course: it was time for the evening service. The inhabitants of the Brough were making for the door of the church.

She prodded Ketil, gently, and was relieved when he groaned a little. He let himself fall sideways a little, and his eyes opened, though he did not look directly at her.

'People going to church,' she said in a low voice. 'Do you want to join them?'

He groaned again, and shook his head.

'I am not fit for church,' he said.

'And presumably you don't want to be seen, then. Lie low.'

Ketil rolled on to his back, rubbing his eyes as though trying to scrape them from his skull. Then he blinked.

'Someone will see us over the wall.'

'Then come this way.'

Keeping down, she led the way, not even glancing back to see if he was following. The building works here stretched up the hill a little, but where they stopped it was open ground, grazed only by sheep, easing up to the smooth summit of the Brough. Once they were over the last bit of wall she straightened, sure no one would bother to look up the hill as they went into church. Ketil stepped long-legged from the last unfinished wall, and joined her. Without looking back, they began to walk on up the hill.

Here the wind was steady, a wall at their side. They said nothing, walking in a straight line as if they had somewhere to be, until at last they came over the brow of the hill and reached the cliff edge. Beyond them now was nothing, until you reached the Faroes or Iceland. After a moment gazing out at the glaring clouds, slices of grey and salmon and gold and blue across the sunlight, Sigrid sat down on the close-cropped grass. It was dry enough, this summer, and she was suddenly weary. She wished she had brought her cloak. Ketil remained standing, staring out to sea, wishing, no doubt, to be free of these islands again. He had said before that he thought islands were unlucky, neither land nor sea but an in between place, full of mists and strangeness. Maybe he was right. Maybe Hakon was right, too – were the islands full of nutters? No worse than he was, anyway, keeping a Christian woman as a slave then killing her when she inconvenienced him. And his mother. Sigrid would have liked a word or two with Hakon's mother.

She glanced up at Ketil. The cold wind did not seem to affect him, standing there in his shirt sleeves with no cloak. She had pulled it herself from under Lambi's body as they had turned the corpse, and folded it neatly to take back to him, but then the whole matter of Ingibjorg's jewellery had come up. Ingibjorg had been so excited to see her jewels back that Sigrid had half-thought she would go into labour on the spot. Thorfinn had said that the Abbot had said – through Tosti, so who knew what had been lost along the way? – that Otto had innocently helped Lambi with his thefts in Saxony. How innocent could Otto be if he were hiding the stolen goods in his own kist with his master's Communion chalice and pectoral cross? Could Lambi really have spun him a good enough tale to persuade him to hide the stuff without Otto realising what he was up to? That might be hard to find out, now.

Ketil sat down at last, propping his elbows on his knees, eyes still on the horizon. She said nothing, waiting.

'Do you know,' he said, his voice mild, 'I believe I hate Hakon now more than I ever loved Mara?'

'Hm.'

'I don't like it,' he added. 'I don't like hating someone.'

'No. It's not good for you.' Her own husband, after the injury that had stopped him raiding, had become a twisted ball of resentment and jealousy, consumed by it from within like a cancer. She was convinced that his anger had weakened him, that he could have fought off the illness that had killed him if he had been as strong in his heart and mind as he had been before. She swallowed hard at the thought of Ketil going the same way.

She thought of Ketil as strong, she realised. When she had first met him last year, the first time since they had parted in Heithabyr as children, she had thought of him as her little brother –

he was only a couple of years older, and boys always matured more slowly than girls, didn't they? – somewhat incompetent, a bit foolish, needing to be looked after. He was always being injured in some fight or other. Yet Thorfinn, despite Ketil's rashness over accusing Hakon, still seemed to trust him. When the Abbot had arrived, Ketil was the man Thorfinn had sent for. Ketil must be quite good at what he did, whatever that was. It seemed to involve a bit of fighting, a bit of representing Thorfinn at the Norwegian court, a bit of … whatever required courage and, she was forced to admit, intelligence. Either Thorfinn was desperate for good men, or Ketil fitted the part.

She watched him out of the corner of her eye. His short blond hair was almost white in the light of the sinking sun, his angular face expressionless, well-muscled limbs apparently relaxed. She could not quite, from where she sat, see his eyes. In a way she was glad: she knew there would be hurt there, there would be tension that whatever training he had had did not allow him to show. The boy she remembered had been her friend: the man here, too, she cared about. She could not allow him to let hatred break him.

She drew a long breath.

'Ketil,' she began.

'What's that?'

For an instant she thought he was responding to her, but no: he was pointing out to sea, not far from the cliffs they sat on. Sigrid scrambled to her feet to see better.

'It's a boat … not too sure what's going on there, though.'

The little boat, with one man seated in it, was not making much headway. It looked rather as if the man wanted to go one way and the boat another, and the result was a track that curved first to one side and then to the other.

'He only seems to have one oar,' Ketil commented, frowning. 'I wonder what he thinks he's doing?'

'He can't be fishing, surely. Not on a Sunday.' Sigrid watched. She could almost feel the man's frustration.

'He could be drunk,' said Ketil. 'He doesn't seem to be in trouble, though. Apart from going very slowly in not quite the right direction.'

'As long as it's not Hakon making a bid for escape,' sighed

Sigrid, flopping down on the grass again, a little further from Ketil than she had been.

'Hakon is a very competent oarsman. Of course,' said Ketil, tight-lipped.

'Oh, of course. Wonderful at everything, I suppose,' said Sigrid, with a grin. 'As long as his mother approves.'

'His mother?'

'Didn't you notice? It all came down to what his mother thought was right or wrong. No wonder he ran away when a little widow woman waved a toy knife at him. He's probably gone off somewhere to greet.'

Ketil gave a dismissive grunt.

'I've never seen Hakon cry.'

'That's because he runs away and hides in his mother's skirts,' said Sigrid firmly. She saw him allow himself a tiny smile, and mentally gave herself a pat on the back. Progress. 'But he still didn't kill Steinar, I'm convinced of it.'

'No ... all right, I believe you're right.'

'Good! Now, who did? It sounds as if we have an interesting candidate in Otto, don't we? He killed Steinar because Steinar was the one who found out about the thefts and presumably might identify him as being involved in them. And then perhaps Lambi ... Lambi, his friend in all of this, maybe objected because killing someone was a step too far. Lambi was only in it for the thefts, but when Otto killed Steinar Lambi said no, he was going to tell Thorfinn, or you, or someone in authority. So Otto killed Lambi, too.'

Ketil sighed, and rubbed a hand over his face.

'It's so tempting. It fits so beautifully.'

'Doesn't it?' she said, pleased.

'But it doesn't work. For one thing, why would he wait so long to kill Lambi? Presumably Lambi would have known pretty much straightaway who had killed Steinar. He could have told Thorfinn or me at any time.'

'Perhaps he wanted to try to persuade Otto to give himself up. Or – oh! or maybe Lambi killed Steinar, in case Steinar recognised him, and Otto was worried that Lambi would say something about it to someone!'

'The main trouble,' said Ketil, 'is that Otto could not have killed Lambi.'

'Why not? If the Abbot is saying Otto was somewhere else, I'm not sure I'd believe him.'

'I think the Abbot is an honourable man.'

'I agree. But I think he's too loyal to his servant to give him up that easily. Did you see his face when he was questioning Otto? He was nearly in tears!'

'Yes, well, again, maybe. But Otto could not have killed Lambi because Lambi was killed by someone using a bow and arrows. And Otto only had one working arm.'

Sigrid stopped and stared at him.

'Really? How do you know?'

'I saw it. Otto collapsed when Thorfinn took the chest of jewels away. He couldn't seem to breathe properly. The Abbot and Tosti were attending to him, and I happened to glance back into the room – a tiny room – when they had pulled his shawls away from his chest. His left arm is withered – I think has probably been withered from birth. He could not possibly use a bow.'

'Well,' said Sigrid, after a moment, 'that probably explains all those shawls.'

'Indeed.'

She thought back to the few times she had really noticed Otto. Had she ever seen him use his left arm much? She could not say she had.

'That's very annoying,' she said at last. 'It was just perfect, wasn't it?'

'Maybe not perfect,' said Ketil, 'but good enough.'

She kicked his foot.

'Well, who do you think did it, then?'

'We know Otto can't have killed Lambi. I'm not even sure Otto killed Steinar. It seemed to me to be a two-handed blow, which, as I say, Otto could not have done. Also, Otto is quite short: to get the right angle he would have needed to be not only two-handed, but also standing on a rock, or something.'

'All right. Otto didn't kill either of them. I'll accept that.'

Ketil's mouth twitched, but he carried on.

'Lambi might have killed Steinar, and he certainly had a reason to do so. I think Steinar was the kind of man who would have been enough of an adherent to the law to feel that he had no reason to see Lambi punished here: the thefts that Steinar knew about had happened in Saxony, under Saxon law, and Lambi had paid the penalty by going into exile. But I could also see Steinar feeling it necessary to warn Thorfinn or the Abbot that there was a known thief around. And he would have been right to do so: Lambi and Otto were at it again, taking Ingibjorg's jewels.'

'Yes, that's fair enough,' Sigrid agreed, 'though Lambi did not seem like much of a killer to me.'

'Nor to me. He had not been in my service long enough for me to see him kill anyone, but he certainly did not strike me as a killer. Or not ... I could perhaps see him knife someone from behind to rob him, but to drive an axe into his head while looking him in the face? That does not strike me as something Lambi might do, except in a panic in case he was discovered doing something.'

'Could that be it? Could Steinar suddenly have come upon him that morning when he was up to something?'

Ketil shrugged.

'Maybe – but that still doesn't tell us who killed Lambi, does it?'

'No.' She stretched, her neck stiff, and hugged herself against the wind. 'The nearest men were Ubbi, his brother-in-law, and Asmund, Olvor's husband.'

'Ubbi seems to have been devoted to him,' Ketil remarked. Sigrid thought back to when she had first met the family, only a few days ago. They had all been close, and yes, Ubbi seemed to regard Steinar as his beloved older brother.

'And what possible reason could he have, anyway?'

'It's Ubbi's house, isn't it? Perhaps Steinar had some claim to it?'

'Only, surely, if Ubbi was childless and died, and the farm went back to Svanhild. That wouldn't be likely.'

'Einar wasn't threatening to take the farm away for any reason?'

'Well,' said Sigrid, 'I never heard anything about it, nor anything that might be a reason for it. And if Einar took the farm from Ubbi, why would he give it to Steinar, who would probably let Ubbi stay anyway, and maybe even let him farm the place while he travelled about for Thorfinn? And anyway again, Einar's not really up to threatening anyone at the moment.'

'Of course.' Ketil paused, presumably digesting that information. 'Asmund, then?'

'Asmund is undoubtedly odd. He liked Steinar very much: admired him, I think, enjoyed his company. Steinar represented all that Asmund aspired to, in a way: order, law, the right way of doing things. And he gave Asmund information that Asmund found interesting. Would Asmund ever kill Steinar? Hm. He would be upset, I think, if he thought Steinar was doing something that went against the right way. But I'm sure Asmund wouldn't kill him, because that wouldn't be the right way of doing things, either. I think. Does that make sense?'

'Sort of,' said Ketil. 'But Asmund was there with Lambi's body. He could have killed Lambi, then come down to retrieve the fletches from the arrows, just before we found him.'

'That was just Asmund doing the right thing again. If he had killed Lambi, he would have waited by the body but then as soon as someone else arrived he would have confessed everything. And he would probably still have been holding the bow. And I don't think he would have broken the arrows. And I don't think I've ever seen him with a bow, anyway.'

Ketil sighed.

'And you still won't let me have Hakon.'

'I'd let you have Hakon in a fair fight, unless I kill him myself first,' said Sigrid.

'Why would you kill him?'

'Nasty piece of work, world would be a better place without him,' said Sigrid. 'And anyway, it would save you the bother. I'm half joking,' she said. 'Hakon's poking you because he knows which bit hurts. Don't let him.'

'That's easily said.' She saw his face tighten again, but she had to draw the poison out of his wounds.

'Think about his awful mother,' she said. 'He's probably spoilt. Or his sister got all the attention and he's been trying to get his mother to look at him, look at what he's achieved, ever since. Poor little Hakon!'

'Shut up, Sigrid,' said Ketil, standing up.

'Hm, well, looks that way to me,' she said, scrambling to her feet. 'I'm frozen, are you?'

'The wind's chilly.' He reached out and rubbed warmth

into her arms for a moment, as he might have when they were children, then stopped awkwardly, turning away. 'Come on, let's go back.'

'Will you do something for me, though?' said Sigrid, skipping to catch up with him as he set off back up the hill.

'What?'

She took a deep breath.

'Will you pray for Hakon? A man that nasty – he needs a prayer or two.'

He stopped and stared at her. Then he swallowed, and gave a brief nod, before starting back along their path again.

The evening service was a shorter one than the morning gathering, usually. Sigrid was surprised to see that people were still milling about the church door as they approached: she had hoped to slip back between the buildings of the Brough unseen, but it might work just as well to join the crowd unobserved, as long as Hakon was not among them. She surveyed the open area between the church and the monastic quarters quickly, as she thought Ketil probably would as well, and could not see the loathsome man. She could, however, see the Abbot, tall and stately, in the midst of everyone. Actually, though, as she looked, she realised he was not quite as stately as he usually looked. His hands were not folded in front of him but waved, pointing back to the monastic quarters, gesturing towards the church, and Father Tosti in front of him, presumably trying to interpret, had the look of a man battling into a strong wind. Thorfinn stood to one side, fists on his hips, a look of thunder on his dark face. Sigrid and Ketil exchanged glances, and she let Ketil stride forward into the fray, glad to see him drawing energy from somewhere. But she was not far behind.

'Ketil, where have you been?' Thorfinn demanded, as soon as he saw Ketil. 'Neither you nor Hakon at evening service. I thought you must be off somewhere investigating.'

'Talking over the case, my lord,' said Ketil briskly, 'and lost track of time. What's happened?'

'It's Otto,' said Tosti. Now Sigrid could see his face more clearly she noted how worried he looked.

'What about him? Is he still in a bad way?' Ketil demanded. The Abbot poured out a jumble of incomprehensible words, and Tosti blinked rapidly, nodding.

'We don't know. He seemed better, and the Abbot locked him in while we went to church. And when we went back just now, he had vanished.'

NÍTJÁN

XIX

'BUT I THOUGHT he hadn't done anything,' said Sigrid. 'I mean – he couldn't have killed Lambi or Steinar. Why has he run away?'

'He's a thief,' said Thorfinn.

'My lord, my lord Abbot says he was used by Lambi, an innocent victim,' said Father Tosti, breaking off briefly from his rapid exchange with the Abbot.

'Nevertheless, he was guilty of hiding stolen items, and probably of telling that Icelander where the items were to steal. That doesn't sound like innocence to me.' Thorfinn appeared to have left his patience at home this evening.

'Do we know what he might have taken with him, my lord?' Ketil asked, having no wish to waste time with a debate. It would be immaterial if they could not find the man and bring him back.

'Nothing, that I've heard,' said Thorfinn, though he turned to look at Ketil as if some common sense would be refreshing. 'I took the kist.'

'No, nothing,' said Tosti, interrupted again. 'Not even his bedding roll. Only his cloak.'

'And did anyone see him go? Or see which direction he might have taken?'

'Well, the Abbot says off the Brough, obviously,' said Tosti.

'Not that obvious,' said Ketil mildly. 'He might be hiding. He might, indeed, have thrown himself off the cliff edge.'

Tosti turned pale, and swallowed before he relayed that to the Abbot. The Abbot did not seem to have thought of either possibility, and fell silent for a moment, eyes darting about as if to discover Otto's hiding place.

'No one saw him go,' said Thorfinn. 'It must have happened while we were all in the chapel. Where were you?'

'Over the other side of the Brough. I think we would have noticed if he had walked around there.' He glanced at Sigrid, and she nodded.

'The harbour, then, do you think?' asked Thorfinn.

Ketil was about to agree, when he considered.

'Only if he could find someone to take him. He would not have been able to row, I should have thought.' Thorfinn raised his eyebrows, and Ketil remembered that he had not reported what he had seen at the monastic quarters. 'Otto is a cripple. His shoulder is deformed. He would not have been able to use a bow this afternoon, or to row in a straight line.'

'Oh!' said Sigrid. 'Ketil, that odd boatman!'

Ketil looked at her, his mind blank for a second, then remembered.

'Of course: that may well have been him. Listen, my lord, we did see a man having trouble with a small boat, heading north around the Brough. He was making slow progress – he can't have planned to go far.'

'Right,' said Thorfinn, and spun to find some of his men. 'You two, off along the north coast, keep an eye open for a small boat in difficulties. You, down to the harbour, see if you can find out whose boat he has taken, what it looks like, whether or not he had permission.'

'It's Sunday, my lord –'

'Still? It's been a long one,' Thorfinn grumbled.

'There's barely anyone down by the harbour,' Ketil explained. 'It will take a while to account for all the boats.'

'Then go on with him,' said Thorfinn, gesturing to the first man he had sent. 'Report back to me, then if you find out anything useful catch up with those two so that they know what they're looking for.'

Ketil nodded. Sigrid was already beside him.

'Your cloak is in the hall,' she said. 'Mine's in the

longhouse – I'll just fetch it.'

'Where are you going?'

'Back to Olvor's, of course. If there's a man who knows about boats in the harbour, even on a Sunday, it's Asmund.'

She scurried off to fetch her cloak, and Ketil strode briskly to the back door of the hall. It was open, and inside he found that the women had already laid out Lambi's body on a table, his cloak covering him. Ketil's own cloak was folded at the foot. He picked it up, grateful suddenly for its warmth, and stood by the body, bowing his head. He had not liked Lambi much, it was true, but Lambi had still been Ketil's man: Ketil had not taken the responsibility for him that he should. He made an apologetic prayer, and stepped back to swing his cloak around his shoulders, fastening the brooch, then fetched his sword from the pack where he had left it before the church service that morning, an age ago. It was a comfort. He cast a last glance at Lambi and the women watching him, and left the hall. Sigrid was waiting outside.

The other man Thorfinn had despatched to the harbour had not waited for them, eager to obey Thorfinn's commands. They could see him in the distance already, striding out, parallel with the men detailed to watch from the north coast of the headland. Ketil peered in that direction before they descended the path through the gate, but he could see no sign of Otto's dismal progress. Would he manage to find a safe landing place, and reach it? He found that he was more worried about Otto's safety than concerned he might escape justice. There was something pathetic about him, with his withered arm. Ketil surprised himself hoping that the men who caught him would not be too rough with him.

Sigrid was already veering off towards the harbour path, and Ketil followed, slithering a little on loose stones. He was tired: the day had been, for him, dreadful. He longed to find somewhere to sleep, away from Thorfinn's hall with its possibilities of Hakon's return, with its memories of Lambi. Maybe Olvor and Asmund would offer him a bed for the night – but then he remembered he was supposed to be reporting to Thorfinn about missing or borrowed boats. He sighed, more deeply than he had intended. The thought of Hakon made his stomach clench. Why had Sigrid asked him to pray for Hakon? Could she possibly feel sympathy for the man? Surely not: anyone who had heard what he had confessed must, must recognise him for the monster that he was. What was Sigrid up to, then? He watched her straight back in front of him for a moment, then stumbled and kept his eyes on the path. He wanted to look about and see if any boat was obviously gone that had been there earlier, but in the dimming light he was not sure he would know. Sigrid was right: Asmund would be the person most likely to be able to tell them.

But all Asmund could say was that a small boat was missing from the far end of the harbour, nearest the Brough; that the man who owned it had not been down to the harbour for a while, having broken his leg in the spring; and that it had still been there when they were discussing Lambi's body, but was not there at dusk, such as dusk was.

'I don't know who took it,' he said, sadly, completing his list of facts. 'I didn't see. But I don't know that it had been very well looked after, the last few months. I'm not sure I would have liked to row in it myself.'

'Do you have a boat, Asmund?' Ketil asked.

'Oh yes!' Asmund's face lit up, so abruptly that Ketil almost jumped. 'Afi built her. She's fast, very fast, but you can get four sheep in her if they settle.'

'Sounds like a good boat,' said Ketil with a grin. 'I'd like to see her some time, if you'll show me.'

'I can show her to you tomorrow,' said Asmund at once. Ketil caught some kind of look passing between Sigrid and Olvor at the fire, and smiled quietly to himself. He had made a connexion with Asmund that Sigrid could not, or at least had not. Whether it would be of any use to them he had no idea, but he relished the feeling, nevertheless.

Olvor, who seemed concerned that Sigrid had been out for so many meals, had been determined to make up for it by serving supper to both her and Ketil tonight, even though Ketil had insisted he had to return to Thorfinn's hall afterwards. The smell of the fishcakes she was toasting over the fire was a strong argument for staying, never mind the chicken stew bubbling next to them. If he had been a guest here, Ketil thought, he would not have been absent for any meals.

The evening was strangely companionable: he and Asmund

discussed boats they had known, their finer points and their problems and in some cases their unfortunate ends, and Sigrid worked on a braid that she said was so familiar to her she did not need particularly good light to work on it. Olvor watched Sigrid's fingers and asked her questions about, as far as Ketil could hear, dye colours and patterns. Asmund gave every sign of enjoying himself. When Ketil at last stood to leave, Asmund walked with him to the door.

'Come again,' he said. 'Come and talk about boats. I like talking about them, and I miss Steinar. And you don't have a dog!'

'I'll see you tomorrow, anyway,' said Ketil, the sad thought striking him. 'I'll be here for Steinar's funeral.'

Asmund's face fell, but he still patted Ketil on the arm, in mutual consolation, before waving him off into the bright evening.

The skies stayed cloudless for Steinar.

Ketil had returned to the hall as quietly as possible, and found himself a corner to sleep in. Lambi's body had been removed to the chapel, but Hakon was presumably still around and Ketil had no desire whatsoever to meet him just now. Before he slept, though, offering up his usual silent prayers for his brothers and for Thorfinn, he screwed up his eyes and made himself add 'And for Hakon – whose needs are greater than most. Amen.' It was not, perhaps, the most gracious prayer that the Lord had ever received, but it had been said.

Thorfinn led the men of the Brough who had known Steinar down to the settlement by the harbour as soon as they had broken their fast. Steinar's home, familiar now to Ketil, was already full, the people of the settlement squeezed in around Steinar's corpse, cocooning his family in their midst. Olvor and Sigrid were helping to serve ale and bread to the mourners as they arrived. Thorgunna was attending to the children, tucked down at the far end of the longhouse and already restless, sensing the unusual crowds, the tension in the air. Svanhild sat, as she seemed to have done since the day of his death, by Steinar's shrouded head, and Freya the dog sat at his feet, watching each mourner arrive with an expression of resignation. Ubbi had a hand on her collar.

When everyone was gathered, the moment finally arrived. Svanhild stood, as did the dog, claws scratching uncertainly on the stone floor. The bearers came forward, at a nod from Ubbi: Asmund took his part, and two men from the settlement. They would not need more: it was only a short distance to the chapel near the harbour. They carried the bier to the door and paused outside, making sure it was steady on their shoulders as the men of the party filed out of the longhouse behind them, silent and sombre. Ketil was near the end. He glanced back: Sigrid met his eye, her face pale. Thorgunna looked up from the children's bed. Svanhild stood, a beautiful wraith, staring off after her husband. And the dog, the embodiment of all the misery in the house, sat back on her haunches, and howled.

Ketil left, to follow the body of Steinar to his resting place.

The little chapel was even more new than Thorfinn's building on the Brough, and had also been organised by the Earl, determined as he was that none of his people on the islands should have an excuse not to attend church. There were perhaps five graves already in the ground about it. The hole cut for Steinar seemed a bright gash in the green earth, as the bearers jostled with their own sharp shadows to lower the corpse into the grave. The priest, an older man, seemed a little nervous at the presence of Abbot Konrad, Tosti by his side, but he carried out the funeral with precision. He admitted to Ketil afterwards, though, that he had barely known Steinar.

'I only came here at the end of the winter,' he explained in a low voice, when Ketil asked him. His accent was perhaps something Frankish. Thorfinn was collecting his churchmen from all over the place. 'I met Steinar for the first time when he returned from Colonia. He seemed a good man, very devout. And I suppose my lord Thorfinn must have valued him, coming down here for the funeral.'

'I believe he did,' Ketil agreed. 'You didn't hear of anyone with any particular grudge against him, then?'

'Not at all! I've heard only good things about him. And that was before he died, too, not just the kind of thing men say about the recently dead. Strict, but good, and kind. That's what I've always heard.'

They walked in silence for a pace or two, following the crowd back to the longhouse.

'I think I heard,' said the priest uncertainly, 'that his death was somehow connected with whatever he was doing in Colonia? Is that right?'

'That's what we think. He seemed universally popular here.'

'I suppose so. And better for the community,' the priest added pragmatically, 'if the killer is found to be someone from outside.'

He seemed a little alone here, and they had already separated slightly from the rest, slipping backwards.

'Father,' said Ketil, 'I have a question. Should we pray for the people who hurt us?'

'You mean should Svanhild pray for Steinar's killer? Yes, of course she should.' Ketil did not bother to redirect him. 'For one thing, everyone needs prayers. For another, a killer needs them more than most. I have met men who have killed, of course, in the line of a battle or other – difficulty, and they certainly need prayers. Theirs is not always a light mind, or an easy sleep.'

'Of course,' Ketil said. There had been times when he himself had killed, and had not rested easy. He would have appreciated prayers then. How much more when someone had committed murder?

'And then, of course,' the priest went on, 'it's better for Svanhild herself.'

'For Svanhild? To pray for her husband's killer?'

'Yes, of course, son. It's better for her soul, and for her heart. You cannot let anger and hatred bind you, and if you pray for someone you hate, hard though it might be at first, insincere, even,' he added, and as he stopped and looked into Ketil's eyes suddenly, Ketil blinked, 'if you pray for someone you hate, that hatred begins to unwind, bit by bit, from your heart. Tell her that, if you can, or I shall. Hatred more often kills the hater than the hated, and it's a much nastier death.' He gave a little shivery nod and crossed himself, making his point, remembering, Ketil suddenly saw, some instances he had seen in his past. A man of experience, then. Perhaps he should pay attention.

The longhouse had filled again but the fine day made it possible, indeed desirable, for the many funeral guests to overflow and linger outside, drinking ale and reminiscing. Svanhild must have borrowed extra tables from her neighbours for the food, too, was laid outside, arranged so that people could perch on a low wall and eat from the table on one side, or stand or use stools on the other. Chairs were found for Thorfinn and the Abbot, who seemed more gloomy than even a funeral demanded. Ketil knew that there had been no sightings of Otto since he and Sigrid had probably seen him the previous evening, and it was clear the Abbot feared the worst.

Aside from their fixed seats, there was much milling about as the guests fetched food, and retreated from the table, and went to speak to friends and acquaintances. Thorgunna and Svanhild each held a child on their lap, but the women in general moved amongst the guests, topping up dishes, taking away empty ones, filling cups with ale. Olvor in particular, Ketil noted, seemed to enjoy the anonymity of serving, avoiding conversation. Sigrid was brisk but stopped now and again to exchange words with various people, none of the chats lasting very long. Asmund was eating steadily at the table, but even as Ketil noticed him he stopped, cleaned off his knife with a piece of bread, and began a conversation with his neighbour, as if he had flipped from one to the other like a dab fish, and could not do both at once. Ketil strained to hear, but Asmund seemed to be repeateing some of Steinar's stories of life in Colonia, nothing Ketil had not heard before.

Thorfinn stayed as long as politeness dictated – he really was an Earl, Ketil thought, not just a warrior – but was clearly eager to be away back to the Brough and to Ingibjorg, still stubbornly pregnant. The Abbot rose with him, and gracefully expressed his thanks and his sympathies to his hostess through the medium of Tosti, who had eaten hardly anything and looked as if he had not slept, either. Once they had gone, inevitably, the funeral guests relaxed, had their cups refilled, and turned to more general conversation.

Ketil watched Thorfinn and the Abbot leave, a few of Thorfinn's men following, attentive to their duties. The Abbot contrived to glide, even though his shoulders were hunched in anxiety. Thorfinn's usual steady, swift stride was just about enough to keep up with the taller man, and Tosti had to trot behind them to stay within hearing distance. They passed the point at the harbour where Lambi's body had been found, and evidently stopped for a moment to discuss, from their arm actions, angles of arrow flight and possible hiding places for a killer. Then they passed on, towards the path up to the Brough's gate, and Ketil turned away. For a moment he scanned the sea, half-hoping to see a little boat, badly directed, but the waters were busy with trading vessels today, merchants transferring their goods by smaller boat to the harbour, men on shore ready to trade. Asmund's gaze, too, occasionally drifted that way, Ketil noticed as he turned back to the tables. He would be off and counting boats as soon as the feast was over.

'Right,' said a voice, and a jug appeared at his elbow. Sigrid filled his ale cup, filled one of her own and stood at ease beside him. 'Where is he?'

'Where is who?' he asked innocently, though he knew exactly what she meant. Hakon had not appeared. Ketil had not seen him all day.

'What have you done with him?' she demanded, keeping her voice low.

'I haven't done anything with him! I haven't even seen him since – since yesterday evening,' he finished. Sigrid fixed her eyes on his, examining him closely.

'Then where is he?' she asked, still sounding cross, though he could tell, he thought, that she believed him.

'I don't know. I expected to see him here. He's always very … attentive to the idea of doing the right thing.'

'You here again?'

The voice was just on the point of being aggressive. Ketil spun, hands ready, to find Ubbi standing next to them.

'Ubbi,' said Ketil, 'a hard day for you.'

Ubbi nodded, wordless for a moment. His handsome face was streaked with tears, blotchy and drawn. He wiped the back of his hand over his mouth.

'Any … any progress?' he struggled to get the words out.

'Otto, the Abbot's manservant, has fled, and there are parties out searching for him. We don't think he killed Steinar, but we think he might know who did. He was working with Lambi, thieving from big houses in Saxony, then stealing from Thorfinn here.'

'Lambi was?' Ubbi looked bewildered, not in a fit state to take in new stories. 'Then did the servant – what was his name? – did he kill Lambi? What's going on?'

Ketil resisted the urge to tell Ubbi he had no idea, that nothing was making any sense.

'The servant has a withered shoulder. Lambi was shot with a bow, and Otto could not have wielded a bow.'

'A withered shoulder? The Abbot's servant?' Ubbi blinked rapidly, his face contorted. He swallowed hard. 'Could he have managed an axe?'

'It doesn't look like it, Ubbi,' said Sigrid, her voice gentle. 'We're still not sure – I mean, Ketil's still not sure who might have killed Steinar, but it does look as if it's all linked with these thefts that Steinar was involved with in Saxony. I mean, where he worked out that Lambi was responsible.'

'So Lambi could have killed Steinar,' said Ubbi, sounding slightly steadier. 'Lambi would have had the reason to do it, wouldn't he? He might have wanted revenge on him for telling the Abbot he was the thief.'

'He might indeed,' said Sigrid. 'Or Lambi might have wanted to go on with his thieving here – in fact, he did – and not want Steinar to recognise him and have him stopped again.'

'Then whoever killed him has done what I would have done,' said Ubbi. 'That man killed my brother, and then came and sat in our house, paying court to my sister when Steinar was lying there, dead.' Ubbi was growing more focussed, his anger rising almost as if he were trying to cultivate it. 'Lambi deserved to die.'

'Lambi deserved to be brought to justice before Thorfinn,' said Ketil, putting to the back of his mind what he thought Hakon deserved. 'He did not deserve to be shot on the shore without warning.'

'Ubbi, I know how you feel,' said Sigrid, a hand on Ubbi's arm, 'but you have to remember that whoever killed Lambi probably wasn't just doing it for you. Whoever it was might kill again. We still need to find out who it was.'

'Well, you'll get no help from me,' said Ubbi, his face closing. 'I've had enough of this. Steinar is avenged, and I have a family to protect. I don't care about anything else.'

He turned his back on them, and strode, only slightly

unevenly, back to his longhouse door, and did not even glance back before he marched inside.

TUTTUGU

XX

THE LIGHT THAT seeped through the smoke holes in the roof of
Asmund's longhouse was too bright for night time. Sigrid lay on
her back, staring up at it. The longhouse was as silent as
longhouses ever are: hens murmured to themselves at the animals'
end, and a cat went about its business keeping mice under
supervision. Olvor snored softly, on the other side of the house,
and every now and again Asmund gave a long, squeaky sigh,
perhaps his version of a snore. Outside she could hear gulls, never
tiring even through the long bright night, and tiny creatures tiptoed
along the cracks in the stone wall beside her head. And as far as
restfulness in her head was concerned, the tiny creatures might
well have been tiptoeing along the cracks in her thoughts, too, and
mice might have scurried. Her head was busy, and had been since
the middle of the night.

The funeral feast had meandered along for a little after
Ubbi had disappeared into the longhouse. But the neighbours had
boats to see to, and sheep to inspect, and the children grew restless,
and eventually everyone melted away and Olvor and Sigrid were
left to tidy up the last of the leftover food and ale, to wipe down
the tables and fold them ready to return to wherever they had
arrived from, to feed Freya and pat her sharp head. Svanhild and
Thorgunna, settling the children, had dazed looks, pale and washed
out. Sigrid knew how Svanhild was feeling. From the moment of
her husband's death, no doubt, she had been in a tunnel, leaving
her old life behind, venturing into new territory but still wrapped,

safe and dark, in that in between world. Now the funeral was over and Svanhild was at the end of the tunnel, staring out at her new world, a world without Steinar. No wonder she was hesitant. Even Sigrid, with less reason to miss her dead husband, had paused at that threshold. Svanhild would step out eventually – she had to – but it would take courage, and even more courage the longer she left it.

Sigrid wondered if they had found Otto yet. She had not seen his withered shoulder, but she had observed his mishandling of that little boat. He might be a thief, but he was a pathetic creature. She did not like to think of him out there in the night somewhere, struggling still with the boat, or drifting and exhausted, or even perhaps clinging to the boat's wreckage, frozen in the water. She wondered if she might have felt different if Otto had helped to steal her own jewellery, rather than Ingibjorg's. Possibly, she admitted, allowing herself a rueful grin. Ingibjorg had some nice jewellery, and Sigrid had often thought it deserved a better home. And there was some ostentatious beadwork, too, and Sigrid felt that anyone who stole that probably deserved it. Poor Otto. But at the same time, lucky Otto. His master seemed willing to support him, and was clearly distraught by his absence. Not everyone had a master that understanding.

And Otto was not a slave, but a free man.

In her mind's eye, she could see Hakon, imagine Mara. She must have realised what he was going to do. Had he told her? Taunted her? And she had run, and fallen, and while she was lying there in agony he had killed her, and tossed her broken body into the midden – or more likely ordered a couple of other slaves to throw her away. After all, why should he be expected to clear up the rubbish? Slave or not, it took a monster to treat someone like that. Hakon was more unpleasant than she could have imagined. And his mother sounded even worse.

But where was Hakon? Was Ketil lying when he said he did not know, or had he met Hakon somewhere and - but was Ketil capable of that? A cold-blooded killing? On the other hand, would it have been cold-blooded? She remembered Ketil huddled on the ground, sensed his helpless rage. Ketil might look cold on the surface, but underneath … she shuddered. No, it would not have been a cold-blooded killing, and Ketil, she realised, would be more than capable. But would he then have lied to her? She liked to think that he could not.

But if he had not, then where had Hakon gone? No one seemed to know. Had he gone hunting for Otto? But why should he bother, on his own, going after an insignificant thief? Just to please Thorfinn?

And had Ingibjorg had her baby yet? If anything happened to her, Thorfinn would be in a bad way. How would that affect the islands? His plans for laws – and more importantly, for taxes? Would he lose all interest and send the Abbot home to Colonia? Sigrid had no idea how she would pay more taxes on her little bit of land. Existence was perilous enough as it was.

And she should go and see that little bit of land again soon, she thought, her grasshopper mind leaping on to the next topic. How was Gnup doing? She hoped he would have the sense to come down and see her if there was a problem, but he could be a proud boy: he might not want to ask for help. And if something went wrong, if she lost one of her two cows, or some of her sheep, then how could she afford to replace them? And pay more tax? And she should be up there now gathering wool, and not down here wasting her time trying to teach a woman with more thumbs than fingers how to nailbind, and wondering how her neighbour died. She should be getting on. And if she was lying here wide awake, she would be better up and about. It was past dawn anyway, though maybe not past the time people usually rose in the summer. These bright nights were just confusing.

It was even as she considered rising and pressing on with the day that she fell sound asleep, only to be woken what felt like moments later by Olvor, sorting out the fire for breakfast.

'I thought I might go up this morning and take a look around my own place,' Sigrid announced, bleary-eyed. 'Just in case Gnup needs any help.'

'I'm not progressing well, am I?' Olvor said sadly. 'You're tiring of teaching me.'

'You'll make a nailbinder yet, Olvor,' said Sigrid stoutly, privately wondering just how long it would take. 'But you've reached the stage where you're much better off without me keeking over your shoulder all the time. I'll only be away till midday, and then when I come back I'll expect at least the makings of a woolly cap. All right?'

She managed a smile, and so did Olvor, reluctantly settling down with nail and wool in the doorway. Then Sigrid marched off to spend the morning blissfully alone, in her own domain.

They had made an early start, despite her restless night, and after a brief conversation with Gnup, who seemed in control of everything, Sigrid worked hard gathering wool in one sack, and in the other dried-out thistles and other useful kindling for the winter, before the weather grew damp again. She would come another day for bags of bog myrtle against midges and pests, and for rushes for lamps: they could take a soaking better than the wool or the kindling. The wool looked good: it would need cleaning and carding, of course, but then the fun would begin – the fun that would perhaps enable her to pay her taxes, too.

With a sigh she bade farewell again to Gnup and the cat and the valiant old cow Kari, and made her way back down the hill to the settlement past the harbour. Olvor met her at the door with a smile, hiding something behind her back like a little girl.

'What is it?' Sigrid asked warily. She hoped it was food: it had been a long morning.

'Look!' Olvor produced a broad ring of really quite evenly worked nailbinding, wide enough to form the base of a cap, about halfway finished. Sigrid felt her jaw drop, and Olvor's face lit with delight in a way Sigrid had never seen before.

'You did all this?' Sigrid asked, trying not to sound too disbelieving.

'I did! It suddenly all started to go right! It is right, isn't it?' asked Olvor, suddenly not sure.

'It is, my dear, it really is. Well done! See, I told you it would come!'

Olvor positively giggled. Sigrid was beginning to wonder if she had accidentally strayed into the wrong longhouse, but the smell of cooking was as good as ever.

'Asmund is eating at a friend's house,' Olvor explained, laying slices of stuffed bread on Sigrid's plate. 'It gave me a chance really to concentrate, you know?'

She did not meet Sigrid's eye, but Sigrid thought she did indeed know. Asmund was never, as far as she had seen, hostile to his wife, but his silent expectations, when he was the one who had asked that Olvor be able to nailbind and weave, were devastating. A little break from his attentions would no doubt be welcome.

'Has there been any sign of Ketil this morning?' Sigrid asked.

'I haven't seen him. Were you expecting him?'

'No, but he has a habit of turning up when least expected.' She smiled. 'He could just have turned up at the farm, actually.'

'What did you do this morning? Was everything all right on your farm?'

Sigrid reassured her and described her hours gathering and organising, the satisfying piles of kindling stacked inside the longhouse near the animal place ready for the cooler nights. Olvor looked thoughtful.

'You're right, you know, this dry weather is a blessing. Would you mind helping me do some here after our meal? I had been concentrating so hard on the nailbinding ... and then with Steinar, too, I had forgotten how much needs to be done.'

Sigrid agreed readily enough: it was good to be out in the fresh air and though she was delighted with Olvor's sudden progress, she was not that keen to sit over her again while she finished the cap. After they had cleaned their plates, they gathered sacks and headed off over the river, knives at their shoulders and leather gloves tucked into their belts, ideal for dealing with thistles.

The sun was warm and they worked slowly but steadily, feeling sweat prickle and trickle down their faces and under their shifts. The gloves made Sigrid's hands sticky, too, but she filled two sacks with dead thistles, dry and crisp, along with other kindling, while Olvor teased wool from shrubs and plants.

'Want to change over?' Olvor asked at last. 'We could take a rest first.'

Gratefully, Sigrid tugged off the gloves and they gathered the sacks together, propped against each other, before sitting on a flat stone. Olvor had a flask of water with her, and Sigrid had brought a couple of bits of bread and cheese. She poked at the blaeberry plants at her feet optimistically, but it was a month or so too early for those: the berries were still green pips hiding in the leaves. A few sheep, clearly offended by their presence, moved off to find more congenial grazing. The women sat for a moment in Olvor's accustomed silence, munching, resting, and listening to the larks above them. But then Olvor spoke.

'Were you really expecting Ketil to visit this morning?'

Sigrid shrugged.

'I don't know. He's not done with investigating what happened to Steinar and Lambi, but he could be helping to look for Otto, the Abbot's manservant.'

'And you – you're helping him?'

'Well, he needs it,' said Sigrid. 'I mean, he's not a local. Nor am I, really, not like you,' she acknowledged Olvor's Orcadian roots, 'but at least I live here. He's only been here a few weeks, all in all, over the years.'

'Then why does Thorfinn ask him to do things like this?'

'I'm not sure what he does for Thorfinn, as a rule. Thorfinn seems to trust him, anyway.'

'And you? You knew him when you were children, isn't that right?'

'I did: Norwegian trading families in Heithabyr. We stuck together. But then we both left for Norway, at different times, and I ended up here.' Sigrid wondered where this conversation was going. She had never known Olvor ask so many questions before – or indeed hold so long a conversation. And even now she thought Olvor had stopped again, exhausted by the effort, but she was wrong.

'And do you think Ketil thinks that Steinar's death and – was it Lambi? – the Icelander's death and the servant running away – does he think that they are all connected?'

'Yes, we think so. You see, Lambi and Otto – the servant – they were conniving to steal things from places the Abbot was visiting in Saxony, and Steinar found out. Well, he found out about Lambi, and Lambi was exiled, but he turned up here. And they had already stolen jewellery from Ingibjorg before Lambi was killed. So it looks as if Lambi killed Steinar to stop him telling the Abbot he was here and likely to steal again. But we don't know who killed Lambi.'

'Not the servant?'

'No, not the servant. He has a withered arm, and could not have used a bow.'

'Then why are they trying to find him?'

'Well,' said Sigrid, feeling again as though she were going

round in circles, 'because he ran away, I suppose. It looks as if he has something to hide, maybe something to tell us – I mean to tell Ketil. And he is a thief.' And the Abbot is worried about him, she added to herself, but somehow did not want to say.

'And what is the connexion with the harbour, then?' Olvor asked, a little stiffly. Sigrid's eyes were drawn down the hill to the shore where the boats were busy. No doubt Asmund was there, counting as usual, before going back to his farm work.

'The harbour? Well, um ... Otto seems to have taken a boat from there, though Asmund says it wasn't a very good one, and anyway, he can't really row. That's why they're a bit worried about him. He can't have gone very far, and he may be in danger.'

'Is that all?'

'Well, Lambi's body was found there.'

'By Asmund?'

'Yes, by Asmund, who quite rightly stayed by it until somebody else turned up. In this case, Ketil and I.'

'You say he was shot?' Olvor really was working on her questions today. Sigrid wondered again if she had been exchanged for someone who could actually nailbind and talk.

'He was, but we don't know who the bowman was, because whoever it was came down and broke the fletches off the arrows before the body was found.'

'So you could even have met the bowman down by the harbour. He would have been there, anyway.'

'I don't think he would have lingered after taking the fletches, though. He probably snapped them off and ran.'

'So you don't think that someone standing near the body necessarily had anything to do with it?'

'Not necessarily ... No, Olvor, I don't think Asmund killed the Icelander. I really don't.'

Olvor burst into tears.

Sigrid patted her on the arm, then with a sigh put an arm around her, and hugged her close. The sobbing went on for a while.

'Oh, Olvor, did you think we thought Asmund had killed them both?'

'No, no,' Olvor spluttered. 'I thought you thought Asmund had killed the Icelander, because Steinar was his friend. I know

Asmund's … a bit odd. Ketil seemed to want to talk to him a lot. Boats and things. I thought maybe he was trying to trap him.'

Sigrid blinked.

'I think he was just a man talking about boats. Nothing suspicious about that.'

A giggle whooshed out of Olvor, and she pulled away from Sigrid.

'You really think so? You don't think he thinks Asmund is a killer? I can't lose Asmund, and I don't think I could bear exile.'

'I really don't think Ketil thinks Asmund is a killer,' Sigrid assured her.

'Because you know he gets up really early in the morning. He would have seen Steinar that morning, maybe …' The tears threatened again. Sigrid shook her head firmly.

'I really don't think Ketil has even considered the possibility.' But even as she said it, she began to wonder why. Why had Ketil not even asked Asmund what he was doing early on the morning of Steinar's death? Why had she herself not asked him?

'Olvor,' she began, 'is it possible that you think Asmund might have killed Steinar and Lambi?'

Olvor stood abruptly, scrambling off the flat rock. She turned to look at Sigrid, but before she could speak, a dull voice came from behind Sigrid.

'Oh, hallo. Gathering wool, then?'

Sigrid turned, then also stood.

'Hallo, Ubbi. How are things today?' She tried not to look as if she wished he had arrived three heartbeats later.

'Oh, as you see,' said Ubbi, waving a hand around. 'Trying to catch up. Checking the sheep. I let a few things slip. You know what it's like.'

'Of course. You'll miss Steinar's help, too, at this time of year.'

'I just miss him,' said Ubbi.

'And Svanhild - has she left the longhouse yet?' Sigrid asked, remembering her thoughts about thresholds and new worlds. Ubbi jerked his head.

'Over there,' he said. 'I told her to wait, there was no need, we would manage, but she said she needed to work.'

'She's right, you know,' said Sigrid. 'The longer she waits, the harder it is.'

'Oh, yes,' said Ubbi. 'You're a widow. I forgot. Sorry.'

Grief came out in waves, Sigrid knew, sometimes long after you thought it had gone to hide for ever far inside you. But Ubbi seemed more distressed now than he had done at any time Sigrid had seen him before the funeral. Perhaps reality had finally struck him. She looked beyond him, and saw the slim, straight figure of Svanhild and beside her the stockier shape of Thorgunna, Svanhild holding a sack and Thorgunna squatting to pull wool from low blaeberry plants. They were almost out of earshot, but something about the way they had angled themselves to each other suggested to Sigrid that the women had been quarrelling, the first evidence she had seen for dissent in that household. Ubbi did not look round. He had his fingers in Freya's collar, holding her absently, though the great dog clearly wanted to greet both Sigrid and Olvor with her usual curiosity. She gave a gruff bark in protest.

Thorgunna must have heard voices, or missed her husband for a moment, for she glanced up from her blaeberries and wool, and rose to go over to Olvor and Sigrid.

'Hallo,' she said. 'Good weather for it, isn't it?' Both she and Svanhild had their babies in baskets on their backs. 'Nice to be out in the fresh air again.'

But she, too, seemed dulled. As for Svanhild, when she eventually finished folding over the neck of the sack, an elaborate, unnecessary process, she turned away from all of them for a moment. Sigrid suspected she was wiping her eyes. But straightening her shoulders again, she came over, mouth twisted into a mockery of a smile. If she had stepped into her new world, it was clear to see it was a nightmare one. In defiance of the sunshine her skin was almost grey, and though she made a half-hearted attempt to hide it Sigrid could see that her hands were shaking. Could she have drunk too much wine last night, perhaps seeking help to sleep soundly? It was possible – likely, even – but somehow there seemed to be more to this than a hangover, and neither Thorgunna nor Ubbi showed any sign of overindulgence, just misery. They were all tired and short-tempered with each other, and no wonder. It had been far from an easy time, and until they discovered the whole story behind Steinar's death, that time would not be over.

Thorgunna's baby began to snuffle, and before she could swing the basket round to the ground and lift the child out, the boy's snuffles had given way to a full-blown wail. Thorgunna swore, jiggling the child angrily on her hip, glaring at the bawling face. Ubbi, one hand on the dog's collar, did nothing – not that most husbands would, but Sigrid had seen him before tender and caring with both child and wife. Thorgunna reddened, embarrassed at the child's noise. Sigrid recognised the tension, and so, apparently, did Olvor. She stepped forward, arms out.

'Let me take him for a minute, and you can sort things out,' she said. Any mother was well used to rearranging the loose neck of her shift with one hand while holding a hungry child with the other, but sometimes it was good to be helped. Clearly, however, Thorgunna did not think so. She stepped back sharply, snatching the boy from Olvor's reach. Olvor backed off, now as embarrassed as Thorgunna, her newfound confidence knocked. Thorgunna burned an even brighter red, and Ubbi, now cross, pushed with the dog between Thorgunna and Olvor, as if to protect his wife. But he snapped,

'Thorgunna, can't you feed him? Look, there's a rock over there.' He almost shoved Thorgunna off towards another flat rock, when, Sigrid thought, she could as easily have sat on the one she and Olvor had just vacated. Thorgunna stamped off and sat with her back to them all, wrapping the child in luxurious folds of blanket, arranging it to feed as if she had never been angry with it at all. Ubbi watched her for a moment.

'We're all very upset,' he said slowly, as if it somehow came as a surprise to him. 'Very upset.'

Svanhild bowed her head, and the tears poured, dripping to her feet, smearing the front of her dress as they passed. Sigrid took Olvor's hand in hers, and grabbed their sacks of wool and thistles, and the two women crept quietly away.

TUTTUGU OK EIN

XXI

IT WAS EARLY when Ketil awoke the day after Steinar's funeral. He was already aware of the bright morning light, but according to his habit he assessed what he could hear around him before he opened his eyes. Snoring, mostly: Thorfinn's hall was half full of men without longhouses of their own to go to, or with longhouses that no longer appealed to them, but who had for various reasons not disappeared to the western isles, to Ireland or to the east coast of Fife and further south. Some were injured, some had been selected by Thorfinn to remain, some perhaps were just lazy or old. There had still been plenty of room for extra men, visitors like himself, like Lambi. Ketil remembered Lambi's untidy pack, now his responsibility, and wondered what he was to do with it. Was there a wife somewhere, Saxony perhaps, or Iceland, to whom it should be returned? Otto might know, if they ever found him.

He sensed that no one was particularly close to him, in his corner near the hall's main door. The barrel of water next to him cooled the air and made it pleasant on these warm nights, but he had not wanted to find himself anywhere near Hakon, either.

Slowly he opened his eyes, and moved his head slightly. Where was Hakon? He had not appeared after Steinar's funeral, not even for supper in Thorfinn's hall. Thorfinn himself had barely put in an appearance either, slipping in to start proceedings then vanishing back to his longhouse to be near Ingibjorg, in case anything happened. From all Ketil had heard amongst the women, nothing was likely to happen for a while but Ingibjorg was thoroughly relishing the attention. Even Asgerdr, her daughter, was paying her service, and not available for flirtation in the hall except, like her father, for a few minutes here and there to see that all was well. But it was unlikely that Hakon was helping there: that was not a man's job.

From his position, he still could not see Hakon, though he knew where the man's pack was, about halfway up his side of the hall. Could he have sneaked in late and just slept where he could find space without disturbing anyone? That was not Hakon's style, but he might have done it for once.

Ketil eased himself further upright, pulling his knees up and sitting against the barrel. He scanned the hall in the bright early morning light, counting the men he remembered being at supper. There were no more now. He studied the huddled sleepers one by one, in case one had left and Hakon replaced them. But no: he was sure he recognised each man, and none of them was Hakon.

He stood silently, dropping his bedding about him and pulling out breeches and a clean shirt before he opened the hall door and headed out to privy and bath house. It was too early for water to have been heated: the fires would still be warm from yesterday but no attendant would yet have stoked them up for the day. Ketil bathed quickly in cold water, shaved, combed his cropped hair, and tugged on his clean shirt over half-dried skin. Tucking it in he stared out through the bath house's opening over the sea, examining the grey surface for any little boat that might still be adrift. Thorfinn's man who had been sent down to the harbour had returned to report on the Brough before he himself had come back last night, both of them with the news that Otto seemed to have taken a badly-maintained small boat from an obscure corner, without permission. The men who had been dispatched along the north coast had not returned before dark, and were assumed to have found nothing and still to be hunting. Thorfinn, his face grim, had directed another few men to take out a couple of boats at first light to look for wreckage, but Ketil did not know the coast well enough to make a detailed search by boat. In any case, the men had not yet woken, never mind set off, and he wanted to be doing something. He thought he would walk in the wake of last night's hunters, along the coast, and see what he could see. He returned to the hall and tidied his bedding away, and quietly made his way to the back quarters to find himself some of yesterday's bread and a hunk of cheese to take with him in his pouch. The gate guards, when he approached the Brough gate, were dozy, stretching and nodding a greeting as he passed, then rubbing their eyes and reminding each other that it was morning. Ketil smiled at their confusion, and set off along the long tongue of the headland, as near as he could to the crumbling cliff edge on the north side. Ahead of him the sun was already dazzling, unimpeded by haar and low enough to sear his eyes. He kept his focus on the sea to his left and on his feet on the damp earth, and paced slowly, determined to miss nothing that might be useful.

It would be hard for anyone on their own, unfamiliar with the coast, to land along here anyway, and still harder for a man with only one reliable arm: at the foot of the crumbly cliffs, low but hard to scramble up in most places, were long clawlike rocks, stretching out like the teeth of a dark brown comb into the snipping waves. In some places a small boat could wedge itself between them, but it required experience and dexterity, or a remarkable helping of luck. The tide was almost at its lowest point, and the claws were exposed. Wreckage, here, might be the more likely sign of Otto's passing, but Ketil could see nothing of interest. Further ahead, past a couple of longhouses that were familiar to him, he remembered a bay where there were boat nousts and a reasonable beach – Skipi Geo, he thought it was called. If Otto had been eager to go for the first available easy landing place, that would be it. And from the way Otto's voyage had been going, such a decision would have been a wise one.

Ketil walked on, glancing now and again at the nearer longhouse. Set on the side of the hill, its door was still firmly shut: no doubt Gnup was still asleep. Sigrid's sheep wandered about it, a couple of them regarding him with interest as he passed. He was tempted to wave. The next longhouse was Helga's, again with a closed door. He had no wish to disturb that one, and made sure he was even quieter than usual as he slipped along the cliff and past the building. No smoke came from the smoke holes. He hoped all was well, despite everything.

The bay with the boat nousts, Skipi Geo, opened up as he climbed the hill. A few more longhouses, inhabitants unknown to him, took advantage of the bay's shelter, too. Here doors were already open, and smoke trickled over the turf roofs, carrying with it the first hints of breakfast. At the nearest one, a woman in a brown overdress was chasing chickens out of their night time roosts indoors, scattering grain on the ground as a temptation. When she noticed him approach, she glanced back at the doorway, as though making sure it was still there, then raised a hand in slow greeting.

'Good morning!' said Ketil. 'I'm from the Brough, Thorfinn's man. I'm looking for two of my fellows, would probably have passed through here early yesterday evening. Have you seen them?'

'They would have been looking for wreckage?' asked the woman, friendly enough but keeping her distance. He held back, having no desire to make her nervous. She seemed certain that someone would emerge from the longhouse to protect her if necessary, and he did not wish to provoke whoever it might be.

'Wreckage, yes,' he said, 'or a man with a withered arm, fleeing from the Brough. Have you seen them, or have you seen the man?'

'I've not seen the man,' said the woman, curiosity alive in her voice now. If she did see the man now, she would undoubtedly give him a good look over. 'But I saw Thorfinn's men last night. They came here and looked in all the nousts, and asked us if we had seen anyone.'

'And had you? Were you able to help?'

'Well, aye, sort of,' said the woman. 'Wait there. Svart?' she called.

There was a grunt from within the longhouse, and a shuffle as if of someone rising reluctantly from a comfortable seat. Or bed, as it turned out, thought Ketil, as a man appeared in the doorway with his black hair on end, dressed only in a long shirt. Breeches dangled from his hand, and at the sight of Ketil he began to pull them on, not in any great hurry.

'Aye? What's to do?' he asked. Breeches fastened, he began running his fingers back through his hair, trying to smooth it out.

'Yon man they were looking for last night, mind?' said the woman, and the man nodded, raising his eyebrows.

'Oh, aye. Are you from the Brough and all?'

'I am.'

'Then you'll hear the same story when you catch up with

the others. But I've no objection to telling it twice.' He settled his shoulders back against the doorpost, and folded his arms comfortably, quite at his ease. 'I was out here yesterday, early evening, I'd say it was and I said the same to them, and I saw a boat cut across the outside of the bay there.' He pointed, sweeping his arm to describe a route from left to right. 'Well, he looked as if he might have wanted to come right into the bay, but he wasna altogether in charge of the boat, if you see what I mean. In a fair fight, the boat would have won, any day.'

Ketil nodded.

'Uneven rowing?'

'Round in circles, half the time,' the man agreed. 'Anyway, he didn't look fit to be left on his own with it, and I had my own boat handy enough in here, so I hopped in and rowed out to him. When I came in hailing distance I called out and asked him if he needed help. He said no, he was fine, and it crossed my mind then to wonder if he might be drunk. But he spoke clearly enough. I asked if he wanted to come into the bay – it was evening, ken, and I told him it was good and sheltered. But he said no, he was for heading on to the east. I asked him how far he was planning to go, and he said he was for Kirkuvagr. Well, then I knew fine he was mad, not drunk. The way he was rowing he'd have been lucky to be in Kirkuvagr by the end of the summer, never mind by night. So I asked him if he knew the way, and he said yes, he just had to keep on going round. Well, I thought about Eynhallow Sound, and getting across Wide Firth, and I asked him if he'd done the trip before. And he said aye, he had, many times. Which is either a lie or madness, for he looked young enough to be my own son and I've been watching these waters and those on them for thirty years or more, and I've never seen him before in my life.'

'Madness, maybe, as you say,' said Ketil. 'Tell me, did he speak to you in Norse? In your own tongue?'

'Well, now you come to ask it, no, he didn't. He spoke a kind of Saxon, for I learned it when I was with Thorfinn travelling through to Rome.'

'You did?' Ketil bit his lip. 'Did you know Steinar Valison?'

'Steinar? Of course I did. I was at his funeral yesterday – did you no see me?'

'Sorry,' said Ketil. 'Too many strangers to me.'

'Aye well, he'll be a sorry miss. A good man, ken? A kind man.'

'Any idea who might have killed him?

Svart shrugged.

'Probably a thief. They say his ring was taken, was it not? Here, you're no after that wee man with the boat for it, are you? He didn't look as if he could wring the neck of a hen, never mind take an axe to a man's head.'

'No, we don't think he murdered Steinar. Are there many others around here who travelled to Rome with Thorfinn?'

'Aye, a few, but they're mostly still at the Brough. They'll be raiding now, or whatever it is Thorfinn sends men to do these days in the summer.'

Ketil smiled at that. What Thorfinn sent you to do was fine, as long as he left you alone to do it and didn't interrupt it to summon you to Orkney to solve another puzzle that made no sense.

'And did you see him carry on, then? Round the next headland?' He jerked his head towards the sea.

The man gave a brief laugh.

'Aye, I did. As much for entertainment as anything, but I did wonder about the wee man, ken? And off he went, right enough, three strokes left and two right, and whiles round in circles altogether, and at last that was him off out of sight, and I rowed home. I told your friends the same.'

'I'm sure. And my friends, where did they go?

'On over there,' said the woman, happy to contribute again. 'I gave them a cup of ale each and I said they could stay for supper, but on they went. Aye, even going slowly I'd say they'd have caught him soon enough.'

The woman seemed keen to offer Ketil ale as well, and food besides, but he shook his head politely and thanked Svart for his help. The couple walked with him a little way, passing the other houses in the bay and greeting the families there with a few words: everyone seemed to know the story of the incompetent boatman crossing the mouth of their little shelter, and wished Ketil luck in finding the man, though whether they wanted him taken back to face Thorfinn's justice or just rescued from the consequences of his own foolishness was not entirely clear.

Ketil avoided the main path towards Kirkuvagr and Toun o' Firth, keeping by the coast as the cliffs rose again. The view was a fine one on this bright morning, the sky dazzling bright, the northward isles laid out green and startling against a glittering blue sea. There were plenty of boats already out and about, moving between islands or pausing to fish, but they all seemed to be moving predictably and he could see none that resembled the one he and Sigrid had spotted from the end of the Brough. It would have been a perfect day to be out in a boat himself, he thought as he walked, and half-wished that he had borrowed one. It was a while since he had taken a boat out on his own somewhere. He wondered if Hakon could have done something like that – he was, needless to say, an excellent sailor – and gone off somewhere. Perhaps he had fallen in and drowned ... Lord, protect Hakon from his own follies, he forced himself to think. And protect me from anger and hatred. And help me to think of something else.

He wondered where he would catch up with Thorfinn's men ahead of him: they must have spent the night somewhere, but had they discovered anything more than he had done on the way?

The answer came when he reached Tingwall. He did not remember being here before, though he had heard of the low harbour, spread down below twin brochs that marked a meeting site for those who lived round about here. The place had been important long before the Norse had come to Orkney, he realised, when the old people were here, and you could see why: the harbour pointed the way to a whole cluster of the northward islands, Rousay, Egilsay, Wyre, even as far as Westray, the sea laid out invitingly before it as smooth as a flag floor, looking as if it were never anything but calm and sheltered. Kittiwakes croaked from the low rock walls around the harbour's entrance, and a selection of boats was coming and going all the time while others lay stranded by the low tide, waiting their turn. As Ketil watched them, he became aware of a couple of familiar figures emerging from a longhouse near the old brochs, blinking in the bright sunlight. He had found Thorfinn's two men.

'Oh! Ketil,' said one, Skafti by name. 'Message from

Thorfinn?'

'I came to see how you were getting on. I heard Svart's story, down by Skipi Geo.'

'Aye,' said the other man, a heavily bandaged arm explaining why he had not set off on any summer expeditions this year. 'I think our man kept the whole place entertained last night, rowing past there.'

'Was either of you with Thorfinn on the way to Rome? Or on the way back?' Ketil asked. He was annoyed with himself that he had missed this possible source of information for so long.

'Oh, aye,' said Skafti, blinking at the unexpected question. 'But if you mean did we know Steinar well, well, we didn't really, did we?' He turned to his injured companion.

'No,' said the other. 'See, we were like the scouts? We went ahead to make sure there was somewhere for everyone to stay, and that the local high heidyins knew the Earl of Orkney was coming through so they could welcome him, you know the kind of thing. Steinar was further back, though we knew him to see, of course.'

'Did he have a particular task on that journey?'

'Aye, inspecting the churches!' The man with the broken arm laughed, and Skafti joined in. 'Never out of a church, was Steinar. Still, nobody minded. He was a nice man, see? And if he was ever – well, you know, pointing out people were sinning, that kind of thing, well, he was always harder on himself than on anyone else.'

It was always the same story, Ketil thought. Pious, a little strict, ultimately kind. He sighed. It must be true.

'Well, what news of our boatman?' he asked. 'Did he get this far?'

'He did, and further,' said Skafti, looking as if he did not quite believe it himself. 'You'd have thought we could walk more quickly than he was rowing, with his birling about, but he passed here late in the evening.'

'He passed here?'

'Aye, and worked his way on all the way to the Toun o' Firth. He must have got a good current, or something. Otherwise he'd never have made it all that way, not the right way up and still breathing, anyway.'

232

'And did you catch him?'

Skafti made a face.

'No, he was long gone when we got there.'

'Gone again?' Ketil could not believe it. The man must have been determined on self-destruction – and at the same time blessed with extraordinary good luck.

'Aye,' said the man with the broken arm, 'but with help this time!'

'Who helped him?' It made some kind of sense, but who would have helped Otto?

'They were seen at the Toun o' Firth,' said Skafti, 'near the river. Your man Otto was close to the shore but from what they say the river water was pushing him out again, but a man waded in and pulled the boat ashore. There was some kind of conversation – no one was close enough to hear it – and then the other man, the stranger, he hopped into the boat and the pair of them set off back out round the coast again. And this man could row, they said – you know, in straight lines and everything.' He grinned, but Ketil was baffled.

'So this man just offered to help?'

'You mean like a chance met man? No, that's not what they said. They said the two men seemed to know each other.'

But who, who on earth did Otto know in Orkney? When he didn't even speak Norse? Ketil scowled, running over possibilities in his head.

'Thing is,' said Skafti, 'we don't even think they went to Kirkuvagr in the end. We found the boat dumped round the headland.'

'Then where did they go?'

'We don't know. Inland, maybe? There's no trace further along the coast, sea or land.'

Ketil's fingers drummed on his sword hilt.

'What did the man look like? Was there any description?'

'Oh, aye, they could see him all right, though it was late: the light was still good last night. They didn't know him,' said Skafti, 'but they said he was well-built, very good with the oars, with brown hair and a reddish beard, kept short. A fine looking fellow – it was one of the women said that.'

Hakon. For heaven's sake, Otto was in league with Hakon.

TUTTUGU OK TVEIR

XXII

BUT SIGRID AND Olvor were not to escape from Steinar's mourning relatives that easily. Sigrid did not want to look around when she heard hurrying footsteps following them, but in the end she really had to. Still clutching Olvor's arm she stopped, and turned. Svanhild, her child still on her back, was right behind them.

'Please, please forgive us!' she gasped, breathless and bright-eyed from crying. 'I cannot imagine – my poor brother is so short-tempered today, but it is grief, so much grief! He always looked up to my husband.' She choked again on the word, but recovered herself again, refusing to give way to another wave of weeping. Olvor patted her on her damp sleeve. Sigrid looked beyond her for the short-tempered Ubbi but he seemed to have disappeared, off to take his feelings out on the sheep, perhaps. Thorgunna, with Freya the dog perched by her side, was still feeding her little boy on the rock that Ubbi had sent her to. Her expression was bleak as winter. The strain of the last week was telling on all of them.

'It takes time,' she said to Svanhild at last, trying to find something to say.

'But does it?' Svanhild snatched at the words. 'I mean, does time really help? You two, you have both lost husbands, yet now you seem to manage to live and laugh – and even love again,' she added, her eyes on Olvor. 'How can it be?'

Olvor and Sigrid exchanged glances in which there was perhaps a little guilt. Sigrid had always had the impression that Olvor's first husband had not been much missed, and her own …

well, he had certainly been a mixed blessing. Were they wrong to live and laugh and love again after their husbands had died? No, she could not accept that. But for Svanhild, who had definitely loved … perhaps it was different?

'Yes,' said Olvor unexpectedly, 'time does help, it really does. It won't make you love him any less, but it helps with the missing.'

Sigrid stared at her in surprise, startled at her sudden confidence, but quickly nodded agreement. Svanhild blinked at each of them in turn, searching for reassurance. She was caught, it was clear, between a desire to believe, to have that hope of recovery, and a conviction in her heart that it could not possibly be true – perhaps even a need to know that the love she and Steinar had had was much stronger than the ordinary.

A sharp bark distracted her, and she looked around. Thorgunna had quickly tucked up her child and already had a hand on Freya's collar. An old man was approaching, unsteady steps supported by a stick, wincing at Freya's continued barking. He stopped at a sensible distance from Thorgunna, and seemed to be asking for directions.

'Did Steinar have Freya with him the morning he died?' Sigrid asked absently.

'He always had Freya with him,' said Svanhild, also watching to see what the old man wanted. Thorgunna, a tight grip on Freya's collar, shook her head at whatever the man had asked, and gestured to Svanhild, Olvor and Sigrid. Thorgunna stood and they all walked towards each other.

'This man is looking for, um – who was it, sorry?'

'For my cousin, Ingvar Karlson,' said the man. His voice creaked. Close to, he was ancient, his face as wrinkled as fine leather washed. He would have benefited from washing, too, Sigrid thought: there was a distinct old-man smell about him, clothes worn too long, a privy visited too late or too carelessly. But she knew Ingvar Karlson, and gave directions up the hill and along past Einar's place to the east, all the while with something tickling the back of her mind. What was it? The smell of the man reminded her of sitting with Lambi's sagging corpse in that cramped space between the boats, the relentless lapping of the waves, the threatening footsteps … She shivered, then, as the old man left and went on his way, and Thorgunna bundled her baby on to her back and took the eager dog back towards their longhouse, Sigrid remembered something else.

That smell of piss … it had been blown to her on the wind – the wind that had come from the east, along the shore. It was not the fresh smell that poor Lambi was giving off, but a warm, stale, solid slice of aroma, deliberate and steady. It could only have been coming from the dye works.

But Lambi had died on Sunday. What were people doing working at the dye works on a Sunday?

She glanced back at Thorgunna, now disappearing around the corner of their longhouse, and at Svanhild. For a moment she paused.

'Svanhild? Are you all right?'

Svanhild blinked, and shook her shoulders, lovely even in her confusion and misery. Even her headcloth sat perfectly.

'Yes, yes, I think so. I mean … yes. Tired, I suppose,' she added, half-managing a smile. 'But I don't want to go home just yet. It's a beautiful day, despite everything … yes. I'll go for a bit more of a walk, I think. The baby will sleep better afterwards, too. Maybe I'll find some more wool.'

'If you're sure you're all right,' said Sigrid, hesitantly. She was eager to go at once to the dye works and ask her questions. She did not really want to be delayed by looking after Svanhild: Svanhild had her family, after all, and she was just going to have to face up to that new world of hers. Sigrid had done it: anyone could.

'I'll be fine.' Svanhild smiled again, slightly more convincingly this time, shifted the baby on her back and took a few steps away, heading round the end of her own longhouse towards open country. Sigrid watched her go for a moment, making herself count to ten to see that Svanhild did not actually collapse or fall sobbing to her knees. Then making her excuses to Olvor she scuttled off towards the shore, impatient to try out her theory.

The dye works stank as much as it did on any working day. She knew that Ketil had seen to it that everyone around the shore and the harbour had been asked what they had seen around the time of Lambi's death, but it was just possible that either he had not asked the dye workers, assuming that they had not been there, or that the dye workers had chosen to deny that they had been working on a Sunday, something upon which the church, and Thorfinn, did not look at all favourably. But if they had hidden the fact from Ketil, how was she to find out the truth?

Well, obviously by using local knowledge and intelligent persuasion, she answered herself. Ketil would have gone in all stern-faced and grim, hand on his sword, and of course they wouldn't have told him the truth. They might even have lied just to spite him. There were times when she felt like that herself.

But when she approached the door of the dye works and saw again the broad, bald man stirring the pots inside, she felt less sure of herself. He really was quite forbidding, she thought. Though to be honest, he didn't look as if any edict of either Thorfinn or the church would deter him from doing what he pleased. Before she was quite ready, he looked up and noticed her standing at the doorway, and came forward, wiping his hands on a rag and smiling. The smile, if anything, made him less reassuring.

'Aye, what can I do for you, then, eh?'

'I was wondering,' said Sigrid, her mouth suddenly dry, 'what you had in the way of greens today?'

'Greens?' He glanced back at the pots behind him. 'Aye, we have a couple of greens. Was it a yellowy green you fancied, or a bluey green?'

'Bluey,' said Sigrid at once. Just because she made her own dyes did not mean that she might not like the look of one here, and it was worth knowing what the dye makers thought might be popular. She might even pick up a few tips – there was always more to learn.

'Here.' The man led her further into the recesses of the stinking shop, and her eyes began to water. She wondered how anyone could see the colours they had come to choose, and peered at a length of rough woollen cloth he passed her. It was still wet and steaming. 'That's this one on wool. Comes out a bit different on linen, with a different mordant, ken?'

'Oh, that's very fine.' Sigrid took the cloth in her fingertips, tilting it towards the light at the front of the dye shop. The colour was lovely, really neither blue nor green but somewhere in between. 'What is it goes into that, then?'

The man winked heavily.

'Aye, that would be telling! It's our own secret recipe,

ken?'

He laughed, gusting more stench around her, and she tried not to grimace. Could this man be married, she wondered? Could a wife take that kind of smell every night? Or did she get used to it, maybe even start smelling that way herself, not realise the children smelled worse than their friends – if they had friends at all? Or did dyers just marry other dyers, so that it didn't matter?

'You could give me an idea of how long it takes to stew, though,' she said, trying to assume a charming smile. It was not really her best skill – it wanted practice. 'I mean, was it just on this morning or does it take a few days? It would be useful to know, in case I might need some in a hurry.'

'Oh, aye, working for Ingibjorg, are you?' asked the man, with another wink. 'Aye, she's the one always wants it yesterday, is that not so? And it's a colour she would love, and all.' He gazed, eyes soft, at the blue-green cloth, not just proud of his workmanship but clearly appreciating the results. And he was right, it was just the kind of thing Ingibjorg would fancy. 'I believe she has her eyes on it already, though. That's why I thought it would be good to get a few pots on the go, for it takes a few days and you need to keep your eye on it, ken? Don't want it boiling dry, or the roof going on fire.'

'No, indeed. So when would you have put this lot on?'

'Oh, um, Saturday,' he said, watching her.

'Then you've been watching it ever since?'

'Aye,' said the man, carefully.

'I'm not running to the priest,' said Sigrid, equally cautious, 'but you'd have been here over Sunday, then?'

'As you say,' said the man, without expression.

'Well, if we accept that,' said Sigrid, 'can we maybe say that you might have been here, and you might maybe have seen the Icelander who was killed along here on Sunday?'

The man looked at her assessingly for a moment, then led the way slowly back to the front of the shop, to fresh air and daylight. He leaned against his doorpost, and folded his arms, staring out to sea. It was still fine, the fluttering waves glittering. The sunlight glinted on his bald head.

'It's no that thrilling,' he said, 'watching pots boil all day and trying not to draw attention to yourself. So I sat here, and I saw a few people up and down to the harbour or to the settlement that day. You'd think folks would sit at home on a Sunday, and only go out to the chapel, eh?' His eyes twinkled, and Sigrid smiled.

'You would,' she agreed.

'Let me see,' he said, thinking back. 'My wife brought me stuffed bread the middle of the day –' (so he was married, Sigrid thought, and could maybe still taste things, too) '- and it would have been after that I was looking outside now and again, for the pots were on the simmer. I seen your Icelander – was he not the one with the hair? And the woolly cap?'

'That's the one,' Sigrid nodded.

'That's what I thought. I seen him going past. Not a care in the world, you'd have said: if you tried to think what a man might look like that was going to be murdered, it wasn't him.'

Sigrid called the living Lambi to mind: he had had that carefree look to him, as if he just wandered through the world without letting its concerns affect him.

'He was the first. Let me think, now. He was heading towards the harbour from the settlement, and I suppose I thought he was away back up to the Brough. He wouldn't have been taking a boat out on a Sunday, would he? So that was him. Then later on I saw Asmund. You know him – oh, of course you do. That's where you've been staying, is it not? Well, he's past here twa-three times a day, maybe more, to go and look at the boats. A nice enough man,' he added, as if daring her to argue. She did not. 'He went past, just his usual self, looking ahead at the boats so he would never have noticed me standing here.'

'And you wouldn't have been standing right at the door anyway, I should think?' Sigrid put in, with a meaningful look at him. He would not have wanted to be so obvious. It was bad enough that smoke would have been whipping out through his roof's smoke holes.

'I was a wee bit further back, true,' the man agreed affably.

'Who else did you see, then?'

'I saw you and that long Norwegian fellow, the one with the short hair. And not long after that you and Asmund came back, did you not?'

'We did indeed.'

'And then you came back again. Oh, it was a busy

afternoon!' He seemed pleased, as if they had performed all this action just to save him from boredom.

'Nobody else?' This seemed to be the end of the story: the body had been found, and by that stage Ketil had been heading up to the Brough to fetch Thorfinn. She herself had been squatting by Lambi's body, between the boats, waiting for Ketil's return. The murderer would have been long gone ... except for those footsteps, those feet, beyond the boat beside her. She shuddered suddenly.

'Something wrong?' the man asked, concerned.

'Oh, just remembering Lambi's body. The Icelander,' she replied. 'Did you see anyone else that afternoon?'

'Oh, aye, after you'd gone past I saw another man heading back this way.' He released one hand to wave at a route from right to left, from the harbour to the settlement.

'Someone you knew?'

'I'd seen him around,' the man said easily. 'Fine looking, strong man. Norwegian too, I think. Brown hair, reddish beard, curly like, you ken?'

Sigrid swallowed hard.

'You saw him – just let me make sure I've grasped what you're saying – you saw him walking along here, on Sunday, from the harbour direction towards the settlement?' She tried to hide her excitement. 'After I'd gone back that way? How long after?'

The dyer shrugged.

'More than a minute, less than an hour,' he said. 'The pots needed stirring. After I saw you go past I stirred them, then I came back out here and sat on that stool.' He pointed. The stool allowed him a view of the doorway. 'A wee bit after I sat down again, I saw him going past. Another one looking easy with the world, eh? I don't know his name, though.'

'Never mind, I think I do,' said Sigrid. It had to be Hakon. Hakon, looking pleased with himself, heading away from the place where she had seen boots beyond the boat beside her. She could not remember him coming down from the Brough with Thorfinn – in fact she was sure he had not been of that party. Then where could he have come from? Down the hill from Einar's place, at the near end of the shore? But then he would not have been walking past the front of the dye shop: he would have been behind it. She swallowed again. How was she going to explain this to Ketil? She

dreaded setting off his anger again, his despair. She might need to
find out more before that could happen. For example, wherever
Hakon had been, where had he been going? Was he heading for the
settlement? For Steinar's house, the night before the funeral? And
that was a funeral at which he had been expected, but which he had
not attended. Her head was beginning to spin.

'Here,' said the dyer, 'keep that bit of cloth. See what you
think of it when it's dried off properly. And mind you might be
seeing a lot of it, if Ingibjorg really wants it.'

'Oh, yes,' said Sigrid, glad to return to something she really
understood. 'That's very true. Thanks for that,' she said, and
holding the wet cloth carefully away from her skirts she waved
goodbye to the man, and turned back to the settlement, her mind
working.

When she reached Olvor's longhouse, she saw that
Thorgunna had again emerged with Freya and was seated outside
in the sunshine, chopping vegetables. Both children were at her
feet, tussling amiably amidst their swaddling clothes on a blanket.
Thorgunna looked up as Sigrid approached.

'I suppose we'll still eat,' she said. 'I don't think any of us
feels hungry.'

'Is Svanhild back, then?' Sigrid nodded at the child. 'I'm
glad to see it. I was worried about her.'

'She loved Steinar more than I've seen any woman love her
husband,' Thorgunna said. 'And I love mine well enough. Most of
the time!'

'Aye, well,' said Sigrid. 'But speaking of men, do you
remember the man Hakon? He was here when we found Steinar's
body: he came along in the party with Ketil. And the Abbot.'

'Hakon? Is he the manservant that's missing?'

'No, that's Otto.'

'Oh, aye, a Saxon name, right enough. Hakon … was he
the good looking one? Well set up, with a curly red beard? Brown
hair?'

'That's the one.'

'I saw him that day, true enough.'

'Have you seen him since, at all?'

'Well, he wasn't at Steinar's funeral, I'm fairly sure. But I think I maybe saw him in between … when would that have been?'

'Sunday?' Sigrid was impatient, and bit her lip. It was no good putting ideas in the minds of people you were asking. She had told Ketil that. But Thorgunna was already nodding, as though she had been about to say that anyway.

'That's right, Sunday. I saw him in the evening, I think it would have been, or a bit earlier. He came to see if there was anything we needed – said Thorfinn had sent him, which was good of them both. I'd half-forgotten that was him.'

'And since? Any time after the funeral?'

Thorgunna squeezed her eyes shut, as if that might help her picture him.

'Today … I think I saw him today. But where? It was in the distance, anyway. Somewhere around here, for I've not been far, yesterday or today.'

Freya nudged her nose into Sigrid's hand, and Sigrid stroked her head.

'You gave that old man a good fright earlier!' she told the dog. 'Do you always bark at strangers, then?'

'She does, mostly,' Thorgunna answered for the dog with a fond smile. 'She's a good guard dog, though it's all talk!'

'Have you remembered yet where you saw Hakon?' Sigrid asked.

'No, I can't call it to mind. Maybe later it'll come.'

'I'll ask Svanhild, then, if I may,' said Sigrid, giving the dog a final pat.

'Ah, she might be resting … But go and see, by all means,' said Thorgunna. 'I'd better get on with these, though, before Ubbi gets home. Let's hope a good dinner will help him recover his temper, eh?' Her look was apologetic: Sigrid remembered doing that herself, when her husband had offended or insulted someone. It hurt her heart to see it in someone else, though she was convinced Ubbi and Thorgunna were usually much closer than she and Thorsten had been. And they both seemed devoted to their little boy – Thorsten had never tended to her Saebjorn that way. She glanced down at the two children playing. They were very alike, she thought, the same tousled fair heads, but one seemed much further on than the other, for two boys of the same age: one was pushing himself along happily, while the other lay a little awkwardly, curled in his blankets, watching his cousin's every move. She smiled and turned away, and stepped over to the longhouse door, calling out to Svanhild as she knocked on the doorpost.

'Svanhild? Can I come in?' If Svanhild could confirm that Hakon had been in the settlement on Sunday, or even today, then she would have to go and tell Ketil, wherever he was. She found she was tapping her feet, impatient at the thought, and glanced back apologetically at Thorgunna. There was no answer from inside, though. Thorgunna raised her eyebrows and shrugged. Sigrid was not sure if she meant 'There, she must be resting, so sorry, come back later,' or 'Odd, never mind, go in anyway.' Sigrid chose to take it as the latter, and poked her head into the longhouse.

Taller and more ethereal than ever, Svanhild was standing in the centre of the room, hands by her sides, her back turned on Sigrid. Her hair was loose, a fine silver-fair river, and her head was tilted, curiously. Had she seen something that had distracted her? Alarmed her, even? Sigrid moved forward to see past Svanhild's slim frame, and something must have disturbed the air. Svanhild swung a little, side to side, then spun slowly around to face Sigrid. Her beautiful face was grey-black, her lovely eyes bulged, her tongue lolled. Only then, her head spinning, did Sigrid see the rope that led from a beam to Svanhild's pale throat. She screamed.

TUTTUGU OK THRÍR

XXIII

KETIL STOPPED ON the threshold of the longhouse, one hand on the doorpost, and prayed.

Behind him, Sigrid was sobbing quietly. She had somehow known his step on the path, or she had come to the door at every sound from outside, but however she had known she had emerged to greet him, hollow-faced. The local boy she had found to run fast up to the Brough and seek him out and fetch him, seeing his exciting quest end in some unknown tragedy, faded back into the small huddle of neighbours at the wall of the infield. They had gathered there nearly a week ago to discuss Steinar's corpse, and now they waited again, held off by Sigrid, to hear what awful thing had now happened in Steinar's household. Near the door Ubbi and Thorgunna sat, each with a child on their lap, watching Ketil intensely. Did they want answers? Had Sigrid barred them from their house, or had they chosen to wait out here? In the soft evening sunlight, they had the look of many a couple, taking a moment's rest after the day's labours, if only you didn't look at their faces, at the tension in their shoulders, at the tight way they clung together and to the children. The dog Freya huddled at their feet, smaller than usual, giving only a token bark at Ketil's appearance.

Ketil himself had no idea what awaited him, though he could guess. Where was the beautiful Svanhild?

He stepped into the longhouse, and knew.

Sigrid had not been able to cut her down, alone. Between them they managed it, and laid Svanhild out on the bed platform, her hair pale in the golden light. He reached a finger out to touch it, to make a connexion with all that loveliness, before he allowed himself to look at her face. It was no longer beautiful.

'You sat with her?' he asked Sigrid, finding his throat was dry.

'I didn't want anyone … I mean, I wanted to make sure that no one disturbed anything, before you saw it. I knew the moment I let Thorgunna or Ubbi in the whole thing would change.'

'That can't have been easy.'

She shrugged, and wiped her eyes with the heel of her hand.

'It's done.'

He stared at Svanhild's face, and at the rope around her neck. The fine skin under it was bruised a little, rubbed by the fibres.

'Nettle rope?'

'Yes – every household has some. It would have been easy to find.'

'And how did she reach the beam?'

Sigrid glanced around – she had already considered this, in her time waiting there alone.

'There's a stool, look.'

'Did you straighten it?'

'No.' She met his eye.

'Do you think Thorgunna or Ubbi was in here before you?'

'If they were, they're not admitting it. But Thorgunna walked away for a while with the children and the dog, after Svanhild had come in to rest. Anyone could have come in, I suppose.'

Ketil, his hands gentle, prised open Svanhild's clinging fingers.

'Her hands are empty … and her nails are clean.'

'What does that mean?'

'I've seen men who have hanged themselves,' said Ketil, bleakly. 'They scratch at the rope, however eager they are to go. Their spirit clings on. There would be scratches on her neck, blood under her fingernails. There isn't.'

'So someone – ugh – someone killed her and then, just, arranged her there?'

'To make it look as if she had hanged herself, yes.'

'That would have to have been quick. I mean, they must have killed her and then used the rope quickly. Otherwise she would have been stiff.'

'Yes, I agree, or beginning to be,' said Ketil. 'So we are probably looking at just one person here, not a killer and then some other person who came in and found her dead, and arranged her, as you call it, but someone who killed her and tried to hide it.'

'Strangled her?' Sigrid swallowed audibly, as if she could feel hands around her own throat.

'Probably.'

But Sigrid was peering at Svanhild's open mouth, the tip of her blackened tongue.

'Look,' she said. 'There are little threads there – fluff, almost. And between her teeth.'

Ketil looked more closely. It had taken someone used to fibres to see them, but yes, there were tiny unbleached threads on Svanhild's lips, tongue and teeth.

'Suffocated, then.'

'Just an ordinary cloth, if I'm seeing them right,' Sigrid agreed. She turned to Ketil, and for a moment they looked into each other's eyes, frowning, wondering.

'We need to talk to Ubbi and Thorgunna,' said Ketil at last. 'How much have you asked them?'

'Not much. Ubbi not at all. I didn't know he was back until I came out to meet you.'

'Back?'

'Olvor and I met them earlier. He was off to see to the sheep. He was in a bad temper – the worst I've seen him, in the short time I've known him.' She met his eye again. 'I don't know if that's significant. But he seemed more cross with Thorgunna than with his sister.'

'We'll have to see.' He folded Svanhild's hands across her chest, delicately, and closed her eyes. They both stood then, and bowed their heads. He felt immensely sad, and horribly helpless.

Outside, the evening light was rich and fine, when it should have been grey. He rubbed a hand over his short hair, and turned to face Ubbi and Thorgunna, aware of a raised murmur from the crowd of neighbours. He had better make this quick, and quiet.

'Svanhild had gone out for a walk, I gather?' he began.

246

Thorgunna nodded, her eyes begging for answers. 'Did you see her when you came back?'

'Yes,' she said at once. 'I did. She said she wanted to lie down for a little while, and asked if I would look after her boy. She went inside. The dog was restless, and after a few minutes I took her and the babies down to the burn so she could drink and have a quick run. Then I came back – I wasn't long, really – and there was no sign of Svanhild. I didn't want to disturb her, so I stayed outside, just down there.' She pointed to the infield wall where the neighbours waited. 'The little ones were happy and the dog had settled, and I was in no hurry to start cooking: I had the vegetables to prepare and I did that and played with the children, really, until Sigrid here turned up.' She cast a glance at Sigrid, a hint of hostility in it. Sigrid was going to be blamed, at the very least for being the bearer of bad tidings. 'And then I heard her scream.'

'Did you see anyone else about?' Ketil asked, trying to keep his voice light. He would make no suggestions, he promised himself.

Thorgunna thought.

'I don't know, really,' she said at last. 'I wasn't thinking much about anything, just looking down at the vegetables and the children. I saw Olvor, I think, and maybe Asmund? But I see them every day: I know I'd already seen them today. I might be mistaken about when I saw them or if I saw them. Ketil,' she said suddenly, and her voice was agonising, 'what has happened? What has happened to Svanhild?'

Ubbi clutched her arm, and the children at once began to cry, hearing her pain.

'I'm sorry,' said Ketil, 'but Svanhild is dead.'

She nodded: she had known, of course. What else could it be?

'Then why can we not see her?'

'You can, now. Ubbi, a moment though, please.' Thorgunna half-rose, then heard his words and sat down again. She was not going to abandon her husband. 'Where were you?'

'Up on the pastures, checking on the sheep,' said Ubbi, though Ketil thought he was not even listening to himself. 'I came down to find Thorgunna out here, and she said Sigrid had found something and she thought it was Svanhild. Ketil, tell me: did my sister kill herself?' His words faded away at the end. Ketil glanced at Sigrid.

'It looks like that,' he said. Ubbi made an indistinct noise, and buried his face in his hand for a long moment.

'I should have known,' he muttered. 'I should have protected her. Even from herself ...' His hand returned to the child on his lap, embracing him as he cried. 'Oh, my wee one, we'll look after you!'

'You'd better go inside,' said Ketil, an encouraging hand on Ubbi's shoulder. 'Thorgunna, she'll need your attention, of course.'

'Of course,' said Thorgunna, though she was shaking as she stood. 'Come on, my love,' she added softly to Ubbi. Bound together, the children borne between them, they disappeared through the doorway of the longhouse. Ketil watched them go, something twisting in his heart at the sight of such closeness. He added to his prayers for Svanhild with one for Thorgunna and Ubbi and their family. They needed no more distress for now.

He jerked his head at Sigrid, drawing her away from the longhouse and away from the watching neighbours. They walked towards the burn at the settlement's edge, and found the rock they had leaned on – when? It seemed like weeks ago. They sat there again, as if accustomed to it. No one else was about: most were at home by now, ready for their supper. Ketil was hungry, but there were more urgent things to consider.

'How was your day?' he asked, while his mind sorted out all he had learned, all he needed to tell her.

'Not great,' Sigrid admitted. 'But I think I found out a few things.'

'Oh, yes?'

'Did you talk to the man at the dye works?'

He frowned.

'No. Why?'

'Because he was there on Sunday, working when he shouldn't have been, and he saw Lambi go past. And Asmund, and me.'

'And?' There was nothing new in that.

'Remember when you came back with Thorfinn and the Abbot, and I said I was sure someone had been standing nearby, on the other side of one of the boats?'

Ketil thought back. It had been a detail, in the midst of everything, and a detail that had come up just before Otto had admitted knowing Lambi, but he did remember – the footmarks in the sand, a little scuffed, as though someone had quickly tried to hide them before making their escape. Had it been the murderer, arrow fletches in his hand?

'Yes, of course I remember. Why, who did the dyer see?'

'Well,' said Sigrid, hesitant, 'it sounded, from his description, very like Hakon.'

Ketil realised he had been holding his breath. He breathed out slowly, almost until his chest ached.

'I still don't see that he could have killed Steinar,' Sigrid was saying, from somewhere far away. 'But I asked Thorgunna and she thinks she saw him in the settlement on Sunday – and today.'

'Today?' Ketil snatched at the word.

'Yes – she's not sure, though. I was going to go and ask Svanhild as well when I found ... her.'

Ketil frowned. Could it work?

'What's wrong?' Sigrid asked. 'I thought you would have been dancing with joy.'

'When was he seen today?'

'Later. Not long ago. I think. Thorgunna thinks.'

'Listen,' said Ketil, 'I've been along the north coast today, trying to find Otto. The men Thorfinn sent out there last night, they'd done well. Otto made it as far as the Toun o' Firth –'

'Really?' Sigrid interrupted, shocked. 'Rowing like that?'

'Yes, but listen. He was met by a man at the Toun o' Firth who seemed to know him. People who saw them didn't hear what they said, but reported that the two men looked as if they knew each other. The other man boarded the boat, and the two of them rowed away – or rather, the new man rowed away. Properly. Otto had told someone he was heading for Kirkuvagr.'

'For Kirkuvagr? For a ship somewhere?'

'I suppose so, but listen. I don't think they went there.'

'No?'

'No. Thorfinn's men found the boat on the next headland.'

'Wrecked?'

'No, pulled up, but in a place that it wouldn't have been found quickly. There was no trace of either man beyond there by land or by sea, according to Thorfinn's men.'

'Has he gone into hiding?'

'I don't think so. I came back here along the road by Harray and Dounby. Several people had seen them: a small man, huddled in a shawl, black hair, not saying much, and another man.'

'And the other man?' Sigrid looked away, an expression on her face as though she were preparing herself to hear the worst.

'By the description – but I've no proof – it was Hakon.'

'Of course.' He felt her hand take his, and squeeze it hard. He was not quite sure which of them she was trying to comfort. Or was it an apology? She had nearly had him believing that Hakon could not have murdered anyone.

Whatever she intended, she let go, leaned her head back against the rock, and rubbed her face with both hands.

'Thorgunna didn't mention seeing Otto.'

'Otto's the kind of man that people don't notice.'

'True.' She sighed. 'It's nearly dark, or as dark as it'll get. We'll not find them tonight.'

'Unless they do something else. I should have told Ubbi to be careful.'

'But why, Ketil?' Sigrid demanded. 'Why kill Svanhild? It makes no sense!'

'It does, if Steinar had perhaps spoken to her about Otto before he was killed. Hakon must somehow have been involved in these thefts, too. Could that be right?'

'Yes,' said Sigrid slowly. 'It must be, mustn't it?' She swallowed. 'Someone held a cloth over Svanhild's mouth, so that she couldn't speak, couldn't tell.'

'Maybe,' said Ketil, though he could picture it. It would be a while before he could forget that image.

'So the only person who could have killed Steinar – because Hakon was with Thorfinn, and Otto couldn't – was Lambi. And presumably Hakon killed Svanhild, maybe with Otto's help.'

'The only question then,' said Ketil, 'is why they didn't just flee to Kirkuvagr and away, while they had the chance? What was the point of coming back and killing again? If they had fled out of Thorfinn's lands, no one was going to pursue them.'

'Oh,' said Sigrid, 'maybe we'll catch them and find out. Maybe Otto was seasick and refused to go any further. Maybe Olvor has the supper on and has made enough for you, too.'

To Ketil's deep satisfaction, Olvor had indeed made enough and welcomed Ketil to the fire. Asmund nodded, too, and sat up in his seat. Ketil smiled at him, and tried to put the killings out of his mind while he thought of boat stories to share. It was not usually difficult.

In fact, despite everything he found the evening was a pleasant one. Olvor seemed to find him less intimidating, and though she spoke mostly with Sigrid she addressed a few words to Ketil, interesting enough, talking of journeys she had made around the islands in the company of her first husband. Sigrid smiled, happy to let the conversation flow, it seemed. Ketil was not much used to socialising in small groups where the members were not just fighting men, but he enjoyed the talk, and the food, and was beginning to regret having to return to the Brough for the night when they heard a noise outside.

Asmund sat up, alert, but Ketil was already on his feet. There seemed to be some kind of scuffle near the door, and a low gasp. Ketil had his knife out and was at the door before he had time to think about it. He glanced back, and put out a hand to still the others while he listened. Then he opened the door a crack, reached out a hand, and caught something weighty and woollen. He pulled.

In through the door, about as impressive as a half-drowned rat pulled from a barrel of ale, came Otto.

Olvor gave a little yelp, and ran behind Asmund. He stood, forming a protective wall, but Sigrid was still. Ketil knocked the door closed with his elbow, and held Otto tight by a curl of his shawl, the knife adjacent to useful parts of the manservant's throat. Otto was shaking so hard Ketil thought he might even lose his grip.

'What are you doing here?' he snapped.

Otto looked blankly at him, and shrugged, eyes wide.

'Oh, stupid!' cried Ketil. 'Hakon. Where is Hakon?' He spoke slowly. Saxon sounded a bit like Norse, so perhaps if he was clear Otto might grasp his meaning. But then, would he understand Otto's answer? He hissed in frustration, and half-turned to the others. 'I'll have to take him up to the Brough. The Abbot will sort it out.'

'He might,' said Sigrid, considering. 'But I did wonder if it was the Abbot who helped him to his freedom in the first place? He was very good to the man, when he was so upset over Lambi, wasn't he?'

'For those encouraging words, Sigrid, you can come too. No doubt you'll think of the right questions to ask.'

He expected her to refuse, but instead she grinned, and pinned her cloak over her back before he could change his mind.

'Are you sure he won't escape?' asked Olvor, trembling behind her husband.

'We could do with a bit of rope,' said Sigrid, and Ketil could see in her face the very moment she connected that with finding Svanhild's body. But she took the rope from Olvor's unsteady grasp, and tied some efficient-looking knots around Otto's wrists. 'Come on, then,' she said.

Once outside, blinking to readjust to the light, Ketil issued instructions in a low voice, his cheek almost brushing Sigrid's.

'And keep your ears open. No idle chatter. We don't want the other one sneaking up on us – this may be a trap.'

She nodded, and wound her hands into the free end of the rope. If she guided Otto, Ketil would have both hands ready for any attack. He drew his sword, but kept his knife handy, too. He jerked his head in the direction of the path, and they set off. Part of him longed for Hakon to spring out from behind a wall and attack them: he was ready. If Hakon gave him an excuse to kill, then kill he would.

But the walk to the Brough was without incident. The gate guards, already assuming comfortable positions that would prop them up through the night, regarded their arrival as the best entertainment they were likely to find, and gave Otto a few unnecessary pokes and prods before Ketil called them off. They took their prisoner to the hall, a relatively quiet place tonight. Thorfinn sat in his high chair, with Ingibjorg's chair empty beside him and a look of distraction on his face. The Abbot, with Tosti slumped, uncharacteristically dull, by his side, seemed anxious also. Ketil's entry followed by a woman with a prisoner caused a mild sensation, and certainly drew the attention of the two great men.

'Otto!' cried the Abbot, not, for the moment, needing a translation. He sprang to his feet, with a strength unexpected in one of his age. Breaking free of Sigrid's grip, Otto flung himself under the table in front of the Abbot, and as far as Ketil could see clutched at the cleric's feet. Sigrid cried out and rubbed her hands, burned by the rope. Ketil darted around the table so that he could see what Otto was doing. The manservant was indeed kneeling, abject, at the Abbot's feet, sobbing with hard, miserable jerks, face invisible under folds of his fallen shawl. With his back bare of all but his shirt, the misshapenness of his arm was clear.

The Abbot, his mouth agape, fumbled a hand out from his long sleeve and raised it in blessing as if to any penitent asking for grace. But halfway through the words, familiar to all there even if they had no Latin, he stumbled on a phrase, came to a halt, and suddenly fell back to his seat. From there, like an icicle melting in spring, he slid down to the floor in front of Otto, and embraced him. Otto began to speak, urgently, the words rattling out like stones in a flood, the Abbot nodding and hushing him. Both spoke in Saxon, though the hall was silent and the men stared, confused. Father Tosti, unobtrusively, rose from his place by the Abbot's kneeling form, and tiptoed round to where Ketil was standing, unsure what to do next.

'Here's a thing,' said Tosti, nodding at the Abbot.

'Yes,' said Ketil. 'But what is it?'

'Otto's asking for forgiveness for running away,' said Tosti. 'The Abbot is saying it's all right, he's back now. But Otto is upset, because he didn't want to cause his master any trouble or annoyance. And the Abbot says no, he didn't, it's all right, and everything will be sorted out. And Otto is saying yes, my father, but he doesn't understand everything that has been happening. And the Abbot is saying it doesn't matter, you're my son, I will do all I can for you.'

'Father,' said Ketil. 'Son. Do you mean in the religious sense? The way we call you Father Tosti, even though – well, you're a little younger than me, I think?'

Tosti blushed.

'Yes, a bit odd, isn't it? But no, I don't think so. I mean: well, it looks to me as if Otto is actually the Abbot's natural son.'

Ketil took a moment, noting that Sigrid had caught up with them and was standing listening.

'Did he baptise Otto?' Sigrid asked. Ketil frowned.

'What?'

'The church won't baptise people with that kind of defect, will it, Father Tosti?'

'Ah … no,' said Tosti, warily.

'Then how was Otto admitted to Mass? He was, you know: I saw him,' said Sigrid briskly. 'Has the Abbot given special preference to his own son?'

'And if so,' said Ketil slowly, working his way through this new turn of the labyrinth, 'what else would he do for him?'

TUTTUGU OK FJÓRIR

XIV

SIGRID STARED DOWN at Otto as he surrendered himself to the Abbot's all-enveloping arms. She had glimpsed, before he was hidden, the shape of his back, his shoulder and arm. No wonder he wrapped himself in concealing shawls. He was lucky to have kept it hidden for so long, lucky to have had the Abbot's protection.

She rubbed her eyes and wondered what was bothering her. Was it something to do with the whole story they had worked out about Steinar's death and Lambi's death and Svanhild's death? Did it all make sense? Otto could have done very little: his part had been to tell Lambi and Hakon where the things were that were worth stealing, and then, perhaps, to hide the stolen goods. But why had he done it? Surely he was endangering his peaceful, fortunate existence, possibly drawing attention to himself? The only reason that Sigrid could think of was that Hakon or Lambi had found out about Otto's deformity and threatened to tell someone, the Archbishop, perhaps, in Colonia, about it, which would not do the Abbot any good at all. And Hakon – why was he in this, anyway? Did he just like to live dangerously? It could happen to men, she had seen it: the ones who couldn't raid any more but who threw themselves into mad games and competitions, scaled ridiculous cliffs or rowed out to sea during storms, as if some animal, some demon inside them drove them on. It made no sense to her. Why could they not be grateful for a peaceful life?

She glanced at Thorfinn, wondering how well he was taking his life after raiding. It was enough for him at the moment to worry about murders on his lands and his wife's confinement, she thought. Tosti was by Thorfinn's side, presumably explaining some of the things he had just told her and Ketil. Ketil appeared to be rounding out the story. He would be so pleased if they found that Hakon really had done something actually wrong, for which he could be punished. All the more if they could find Hakon and see the punishment applied. Would that help him shed his burning resentment of Hakon, lay to rest his memories of Mara, broken and dead? She was not sure. She hoped he was taking her advice to pray, however he might do it. But not now, while he was explaining the whole thing to Thorfinn. Thorfinn had the look of a man who had enough information in his mind for now, and no space for any more. She knew how he felt.

So, she thought, leaning against a table. They had been galloping along with this, and she needed to take it in properly. Lambi must have killed Steinar, because Steinar could tell the Abbot that Lambi was around and warn Thorfinn and anyone else to watch their valuables. That was the first stage. Then Hakon had killed Lambi, possibly because he thought Lambi was going to betray the comrades. Then Hakon and Otto had killed Svanhild because they found that Steinar had told Svanhild about the gang before he died.

Well, she thought, there were a few things there that she was not altogether happy about. For one thing Lambi had not seemed like a killer. Dishonest, yes, ready to do the easiest thing for Lambi, without regard for anyone else, to pick up anything that might be valuable, yes. But she had trouble even imagining him in a battle, never mind killing a man in cold blood.

Then why had Hakon killed Lambi? Surely that just drew attention to them all the more. If he had killed Lambi somewhere where the body would not be found, that would have made more sense. A disappearing Lambi could have been thought a guilty Lambi, whereas a dead Lambi raised a lot more questions. But perhaps Lambi had not been happy about killing Steinar, and had threatened to tell, and Hakon had had no chance to do it any other way? That sort of fitted.

Thoughtfully, she picked at some cheese left on the table beside her. She was eating well at Olvor's house: if she had been living at home she would have been more grateful for any crumbs left on the table. She was looking forward to going home soon, though, once she was sure that Olvor really had sorted out her nailbinding – the tablet weaving was perhaps more of a challenge, but even Olvor understood the basics now. She would go back to her farm, to Gnup and the animals, to a quiet house at night and a solitary waking in the morning. She sighed. But there would be less food. There was always a drawback.

She had the longhouse in her mind, thinking about the view from the doorway over the north coast. Otto had rowed – if you could call it rowing – past there yesterday, struggling so hard to escape, making, if you believed it, for Kirkuvagr. Had he known there would be help meeting him at the Toun o' Firth? If not, how could he even have hoped to reach Kirkuvagr safely? And if he had been so determined, how had he felt when they ditched the boat and turned back inland, walking back all the way to Birsay again to help kill Svanhild? And why had Hakon suddenly decided that Svanhild had to be killed, too? Why was it suddenly worth leaving that useful boat and turning back from the clear path to Kirkuvagr's harbour and a ship and freedom, even if they had left their stolen goods behind?

Well, she thought, there must be answers to all of these. But one thing she really found hard to picture. Could it really be that the handsome, charming, Hakon, so dismissive of life in the lowliest of characters, had really allied himself with a miserable cripple like Otto? That was where something jarred. Whatever was going on, Hakon must still think that Otto was useful to him. But how?

While her thoughts wandered, she had been paying less attention to what was actually going on in the hall. Thorfinn had stood up from his high chair, in slow state, leaving the furs that covered it crushed by his weight. He moved to the back of the hall where conversations could be held in relative privacy: the body of the hall still housed his men, who, not able to see much of what was going on at the Abbot's feet, had given up hope of a gossip and returned to drinking and singing. Otto and the Abbot made one heap, masked by the Abbot's robes, until Thorfinn tapped Abbot Konrad on the shoulder and pointed to where he wanted their conversation to be. Ketil helped Otto up to follow, and Tosti and Sigrid, exchanging a worried, intrigued, glance, went along with the party.

In the dimness of the back of the hall, Thorfinn pointed the Abbot to a stool, and took one himself. He drew in a deep breath, and sighed heavily. Clearly he wanted this whole business cleared up and forgotten about.

'Ask him,' he said to Tosti, through gritted teeth, 'ask my lord Abbot what in God's name is going on?'

Tosti may have rephrased the question a little, but the Abbot would have heard the tone.

'My lord Abbot begs the forgiveness of his generous host my lord Thorfinn, and asks to give some explanation.'

'Can the man Otto speak for himself?' Thorfinn asked, drumming fingers on his knee.

'The problem is he only speaks Saxon, my lord,' said Tosti disingenuously. Thorfinn regarded him coldly.

'As do you, I believe,' he said.

'Well, yes, my lord,' said Tosti, squirming a little, 'but you see, the Abbot doesn't know that.'

'Never mind. I've had enough with subterfuge. Ask Otto what he was up to. From the time we left him – locked up,' he added with considerable emphasis, 'to the moment Ketil found him down past the harbour. Right?'

'Of course, my lord,' said Tosti nervously. He turned to the Abbot and seemed briefly to explain something in Latin, then, as the Abbot's face froze, he turned to Otto and changed languages once again. Sigrid almost grinned. Tosti, alarmed as he was, was in control of the situation and the rest of them simply had to wait.

'He says,' said Tosti eventually, after a little toing and froing, 'that a man came and unlocked the door of his room, and told him to make a run for it. He said there would be a boat down at the harbour, that he had left a sign on it to show which one Otto should take. When Otto said he could not manage a boat, the man encouraged him and said if Otto took the boat around the Brough and along the coast on the other side, in the second big bay the man would be waiting for him and would help him on to Kirkuvagr, where he could take a ship anywhere he wanted, away from Orkney.'

'And he went?' Thorfinn could not quite keep the disparagement from his tone. In his book, no one ran away while they still had any chance of fighting.

'He said the man was very ... um ... strong? I think he means domineering, maybe bullying?'

The Abbot, who had been following the conversation closely, raised a hand, and broke in. He spoke in Saxon, presumably so that Otto could also understand. Tosti listened, nodding, and turned back to Thorfinn.

'My lord Abbot says that the man must have been forceful. Otto would never have dreamed of taking a boat anywhere, and the Abbot has been his protection from when he was a small child. He would have nowhere to go even if he had made it to Kirkuvagr.'

'From what you say, the Abbot is his father, anyway. No doubt he would do anything to protect him,' Thorfinn growled. 'And say anything.'

'Otto is not a strong man, my lord, that much is true,' said Tosti. 'Nor a courageous one, that I've ever seen.'

'Well, never mind,' said Thorfinn. 'Go on with his story.'

'Otto left the monastic quarters and went down to the harbour, where he found the sign just as the man had told him, on top of a small boat. The oars were under it – I think here he half-hoped he would not be able to find the oars and could just go back to his room, but it was not to be.'

'What was the sign?' Ketil asked suddenly.

'What?' Tosti blinked.

'What was the sign that had been left on the boat?'

'Oh,' said Tosti, a little pale, 'the fletch off an arrow, broken, you know?'

'I know,' said Ketil. Sigrid thought he looked grim.

'So Otto took the boat and, well, you know, rowed as best he could around the Brough and along the coast, and he saw some men on the shore in one bay but they weren't the right ones, so he carried on and saw his man by a stream. He managed to row near the shore and the man helped him, then hopped into the boat himself and Otto was relieved as the man began to row on around the next headland, towards where Otto believed Kirkuvagr lay. But then for some reason they turned inland, and the man said they would have to walk from there. Otto was happy enough and did what he could to help haul the boat up out of the water, but then he was surprised when the man led them inland. He said it was a shortcut, taking off the long path round the headland, and Otto's sense of direction seems a little poor for he allowed himself to led along a road that seemed a lengthy one, back towards the west again. And before he knew where he was, he found himself back near the settlement where that man Steinar had been killed, last week, with, he says, that awful axe in his head. I don't suppose Otto has seen much violence in his life, actually,' Tosti added thoughtfully. 'The Abbot does seem to have protected him quite a bit.'

'What time did he reach the settlement? Does he know?' Ketil asked.

Tosti checked.

'He says it was maybe late afternoon, or even further into the evening. He says he can't tell with this funny northern light.'

'Hm,' muttered Thorfinn. 'He should try Trondheim some time. What happened then? I want to know about Steinar's wife Svanhild.'

Sigrid's hands tightened into one another behind her. She wanted to know about Svanhild too, but on the other hand she had no wish to hear all the details. She felt sick. Poor, beautiful, unhappy Svanhild.

Tosti was exchanging more words with Otto. The more the little servant was listened to, the more clearly he spoke out, glancing now and then to the Abbot for reassurance. The Abbot's hands were tense on his lap, perhaps wanting to touch his son to support him, but he stayed seated, only using his eyes to send strength to Otto.

'When they reached the settlement, the man stopped and seemed to watch from a distance for a while. They kept well clear of any paths, he says. Then the man showed Otto a curve in the river – that one just south of the settlement, I suppose – where the water had cut out a kind of ... not sure how he's describing it ...' Tosti paused, and they all watched as Otto carved a kind of shallow cave with his hand, a small one, his fingers said, showing for a moment how he had curled up in the shelter of the bank. 'Yes?' Tosti glanced around, making sure they had all understood. 'The man told him to stay there. He said now that Otto was a fugitive, Thorfinn would kill him if anyone found him, so he would have to stay still and quiet until the man came back.'

'And where did the man go?' asked Thorfinn, scowling. Otto looked scared.

'He doesn't know. The man went off, and Otto hid.'

'How long was the man away for?' Ketil asked.

'He says that the man never came back,' said Tosti after a moment. 'Otto lay there, and after a while he began to think that he had been stupid. He would have been safer staying with the Abbot, his beloved master. The man seemed more frightening than anyone else he had met. So when it grew darker, and the man had still not reappeared, he crept out of his hiding place and tried to remember how to get back to the Brough and the monastic quarters. He was outside someone's longhouse, smelling the scent of dinner and thinking how long it had been since he had eaten anything, when he fell over something and you,' he nodded at Ketil, 'came out and caught him and nearly, apparently, made him die of fright.'

A slight smile twitched the corner of Ketil's mouth, then he frowned again.

'Well, that all makes some kind of sense,' he said. 'My lord?'

'What about Svanhild?' Thorfinn demanded.

'I think,' said Ketil, 'that if this fellow had had anything to do with that, he would be in a worse state than he is.'

'Even if he had already had something to do with the death of your man Lambi?' Thorfinn asked, dubiously. 'I know he doesn't look like a killer – if I had him on my side in a battle I'd put him behind the lines and tell him to mind something unimportant – but he could have been there and helped, at least.'

'If I were intending to kill someone quickly and discreetly in their own longhouse,' said Ketil in return, 'with their family almost on the doorstep, I wouldn't take him with me.'

Thorfinn nodded.

'You're right. I'd leave him hidden somewhere, too.'

Sigrid swallowed. They were right, she thought, but they both sounded so heartless. Poor Svanhild. Poor Otto, too.

'Well, then, my lord,' said Ketil, 'it only remains to find out about this man who rescued Otto. Tosti, can you ask Otto about him? His name, or his description?'

There was hardly any need for translation this time. When Tosti put the question, they all made out Otto's clear response:

'Hakon'.

'How long had he known him? We need to find out about this conspiracy to steal, Otto and Lambi and Hakon. How was it organised? Why was Lambi killed?'

Tosti raised his eyebrows in mild desperation, running through possible questions in his mind. He began tentatively. Otto looked puzzled, then shook his head. Tosti tried something else. Sigrid found her fingers digging into one another again. It was so frustrating, having all this at second hand, but it really made you look at Otto's face, undistracted by the words. The man was clearly baffled.

'He says,' said Tosti, 'that the first time he saw Hakon was in this hall, and Hakon had never said more than two words together to him before yesterday evening.'

'Does he know if Lambi knew him?' Ketil asked, his voice suddenly urgent.

'Lambi had never met him, either. He doesn't think Lambi and Hakon said much to each other. Hakon was ... well, a bit above Lambi.'

'Hakon was a bit above most people,' Ketil murmured, frowning. Sigrid knew what he was thinking. The conspiracy they thought they had detected was falling apart before them. If Otto was telling the truth, Hakon was clearly up to something – but what? And if he had no enmity with Steinar – whom he could not have killed in any case – then why would he have murdered Svanhild?

'Nothing is making any sense.' She could not help saying it out loud, and though Ketil caught her eye, he nodded. 'We're missing something important in all of this.'

'Father Tosti,' said Thorfinn, also acknowledging her, 'do you firmly believe that this man Otto is telling the truth?'

'I do,' said Tosti, after a moment's consideration. 'I really do.'

'Then yes,' said Thorfinn to Sigrid. 'You are missing something. You have your thief, but do you have your murderer? And if it is Hakon, then where is he?'

At that, Thorfinn rose sharply from his stool, bowed a good night to the Abbot, and marched off to the rear door and his longhouse. The Abbot watched him go, then asked Tosti a rapid question, gesturing to Otto. Tosti shrugged.

'Do you want Otto to be kept locked up, now that he's back? The Abbot says he will if need be.'

Ketil looked at Sigrid.

'Keep him in the monastic quarters, yes – but as much for his own safety as for anything else. Yes, he connived with a thief, and his sentence is up to Thorfinn, but I don't think he's going to run again. But if Hakon is still around, and Otto can point to him as the man who encouraged him to run away – then I don't see that Hakon would stop at killing Otto, do you?'

'No,' said Sigrid, 'not if he has done everything else we think he has done.' But had he?

Tosti looked pleased, and relayed the information to the Abbot. He rose, too, from his stool, and bowed to Ketil, relieved gratitude on his long face. Sigrid thought again that she rather liked the man. He was not as stern as he had at first appeared. The Abbot, Tosti and Otto left the hall by the main door, heading back to the monastic quarters for the night. Sigrid found herself praying that they would all be safe.

The hall was quieter now, the drinkers too far gone to sing much, or already asleep across the tables. One or two had decided to curl up in their bed rolls already, while the women were still tidying up, settling the central fires, gathering dishes and leftovers.

'Let's talk outside,' said Ketil, nodding towards the main door.

It was still light enough to see anyone who might overhear their discussion. Sigrid felt a chill in the air, and wondered if the fine weather was finally on the turn. The pastures would benefit from some rain anyway. They walked uphill, past the church and the works behind it, and out again on to the broad green back of the Brough, only going slowly, not intending to put a great distance between them and their beds. Sigrid considered the walk back to Olvor's, and for once felt unsure of herself. She did not like the thought of going on her own, not with Hakon somewhere around. She might beg a space in Thorfinn's longhouse, even though the prospect of sharing with Ingibjorg did not appeal.

'What do you think?' Ketil's voice interrupted her thoughts.

'I can believe that Hakon would not have allied himself

with Otto. Could he have used Otto as a distraction, though? Maybe even left us to think that Otto had something to do with Svanhild's death?'

'He could,' agreed Ketil. 'But Otto couldn't possibly have killed Svanhild, I'm sure of it. He would have been distraught, and anyway, he couldn't have hauled her up on that rope – even if he had been strong enough to kill her in the first place. That shoulder of his ...'

'Yet the Abbot must have had him baptised, or baptised him. He took Communion,' said Sigrid. Even as she said it, she knew there was something else in her mind – something she had seen, or thought she had seen, today. What was it? It was not as if the day had not been a full one. Ketil was speaking about Hakon, what he might have done, where he might be hiding, but in her mind she was skipping through the day, trying to place what it was. It had been at the settlement, she was sure. Something to do with children ... the lad she had dispatched to look for Ketil? No: he had made very little impression on her at all. Then the children at Steinar's house? The two little boys, playing on the blanket. Only that really, only one of them was playing. The other was lying and watching. Lying and watching ... she could picture him at last. There was something wrong with him. He was the wrong shape. She remembered suddenly Ubbi's deformed hand, a shape not brought on by injury, but born that way. Often a parent could pass such things on to a child, could they not? And in some places, she had heard, such children were not only unfit for baptism, but were ordered to be exposed, put out of society and left to die.

But Tosti said he had baptised both the babies. So who was hiding what?

TUTTUGU OK FIMM

XXV

HE WALKED WITH her in the shadows of the midnight glow, their voices only whispers as they hurried back once again to the settlement by the harbour.

Ketil was not yet convinced that she was right, and he walked with her partly because he would not have encouraged anyone to take that path in the dark with Hakon still unaccounted for, but he listened nevertheless as she explained what she had seen, and what she had not heard.

'Think how Thorgunna is always clinging to her child. She wouldn't let me hold him. She swathes him in blankets as soon as anyone goes near. She and Ubbi cosset him.'

'I've seen other new parents act in much the same way,' said Ketil mildly. 'A firstborn is precious.'

'Yes, indeed, a firstborn is precious. But that means the parents usually want you to see them, not protect them from you.' She stopped when he laid a hand on her arm, and froze. He had his knife ready in the other hand, but in a moment relaxed again. Somewhere near them a sheep cropped the grass steadily: he had briefly thought it was footsteps.

'But Tosti baptised the baby, didn't he?' he asked. 'Surely he would have noticed if something was wrong?'

'I'm sure he would, normally. But the children are quite alike. I think they somehow tricked him, showing him Steinar and Svanhild's child but letting him baptise Ubbi and Thorgunna's boy.'

'But that makes no sense. Surely they would be found out?' A child had to grow, after all. As with Otto, the deformity would be discovered sooner or later.

'I think they were playing for the short term,' said Sigrid after a moment's thought. 'Look, a deformed child, a badly deformed one, is not supposed to be baptised. No parent wants their child left like that. And then, if it really is badly deformed, there are plenty who would say the child should be exposed, left out somewhere for the wild animals to eat. Again – well, you're not a parent, or not that you've said, but could you imagine your brother and his wife wanting to abandon any of their children?'

He tried to picture it. There were certainly times when his brother Njal, a woodworker back in Heithabyr, would happily see one or other of his rowdy sons quietly taken away, but he would always want them brought back again. Njal would never allow harm to come to any of them. And if someone had threatened that, when he and his wife were cosseting their newborn, he could imagine Njal might have turned violent.

'So you think Ubbi killed Steinar? And then Svanhild? Steinar whom he looked up to, and his own beloved sister? Anyway, why?'

'Well,' said Sigrid, 'I've been trying to think this through. Steinar was away when the babies were born and christened, wasn't he? He was off in Colonia doing all he did in Colonia. Svanhild loved her brother, I'm sure of it, and so I think she was part of the trick – it would have been hard to do it otherwise. She lent her baby, her well-formed child, to Ubbi to show Father Tosti. She might have known that her husband would not have approved – how often have people told us that though he was kind, he was strict about church law? He would have been the one taking Ubbi's son out and exposing him, I'm sure. But Svanhild's loyalty to her brother was still strong. She helped, and the baptisms took place as if everything was all right. But then,' and he could hear her voice grow grim, 'Steinar came home.'

'But even if he hadn't, they would have been found out, don't you think?'

'Well,' said Sigrid, 'the thing is, lots of children with deformities die young anyway. Maybe … they sort of thought that might happen. Before Steinar came back, even. But before anyone else would notice. And I think Steinar noticed that night in Asmund's longhouse – he went to help Ubbi with the child, and the child must just have felt wrong. And they couldn't let Steinar spoil everything. They just ... they just wanted to give their child that chance, the gift of baptism, the few years of life it might manage to snatch.' She broke off, and he did not speak. She had lost a child, he knew, though from illness. What would she have done to give that boy a few more years?

They walked in silence for a while, not uncomfortably, though he stayed alert for anyone approaching them. The light was awkward now, reaching that stage where pale things loomed, and colours were deceptive. What would they do when they reached the settlement? They were already at the harbour, the smell of fish mingling with the stench of the dye works, the place where Lambi's body had lain not so clear now, as boats had been shifted, taken out and brought back to slightly different places. His fingers played with his knife, as he wondered. What reason would there have been for Ubbi to kill Lambi? Had he seen something, hanging around the longhouse before Steinar's funeral, and threatened to tell someone? But if it were Ubbi who had killed Lambi, what had Hakon been doing down here that afternoon? And would Ubbi, in mourning, have risked being seen out along the harbour? It was different to be seen tending to your animals, but if there was death in the household people expected you to stay and watch with the body. Ubbi might have had some excuse to be out, but he would certainly have been noticed, and noted. Why would he have risked it, unless it was urgent? Could Lambi have headed off specifically saying he was going to see the Abbot, for example, or Father Tosti? But then why run up on to the hill to shoot him? Wouldn't it have been quicker to run after him and hit him from behind, perhaps with an axe again?

How long were they going to be running up and down this path before anything really made sense?

'The dog, of course,' murmured Sigrid. 'And that makes it partly my fault.'

'What?' He was taken by surprise.

'That dog, Freya. She went everywhere with Steinar, so she was almost certainly with him the morning he was killed. And she barks at strangers. I asked Svanhild. Well, I was awake that morning, and I was out at the privy, and I never heard Freya bark, I'm sure of it.'

'So it was definitely not a stranger. Yes, I see.'

'I asked Svanhild about the dog, and I think she realised then what must have happened to Steinar. And that was more than she could take. Deceiving him was one thing, but killing him – that was obviously a step far too far, killing the man she loved.'

'And she challenged her brother.'

'And he killed her, to protect his child. I think so, yes.' He heard her clear her throat. 'Perhaps if I hadn't said anything, she wouldn't have realised, and then …'

'She would have realised soon enough,' said Ketil quickly, his tone harder than he had intended. He knew what it was like to live with self-inflicted blame. 'Look, we're nearly there. What are we going to do? Presumably they're in bed by now. Do we want to disturb them?'

Sigrid stopped to consider, leaving him to wonder briefly why he had asked her. He did not normally consult before acting. But he waited to hear what she would say.

'The other thing is Hakon,' she said, though he knew she did not want to mention him. 'What has he done, and what is he doing now?'

'Could he have killed Lambi?' He hoped he did not sound as if he were clutching at straws.

'But why?'

'Why did he release Otto?'

'It doesn't make sense.'

'But we know he did it.'

'But there's a difference between letting a prisoner out and shooting someone. I don't know … if he really didn't know Otto, and I'm inclined to believe Otto, then it looks almost as if he's just making mischief.'

'I know,' Ketil agreed. 'And that bothers me. Because I don't think I would put it past Hakon to kill Lambi just for the sake of making mischief, too.'

'To distract us, you mean? To draw you off from the hunt for Steinar's murderer?'

'It worked, didn't it? We invented a long chain of events, so neatly lashed together, though all the time something or other would not quite fit. And we went chasing after Otto, with Hakon leading us by the nose. If we assume that Hakon is up to mischief, and separate out the killing of Steinar and Svanhild – if you're right about the baby – then things start to make sense, don't they?'

Sigrid nodded slowly.

'They do, I suppose. And I will admit,' she said, 'that Hakon certainly seems like a man who would like to be up to mischief, whenever he sees a chance.' She crossed her arms and rubbed her shoulders, as if she were feeling the cold. 'But where should we go now? As you say, everyone will be asleep – except maybe Olvor, if she's waiting up to let me in.'

'Then maybe we should go there. Would she have space to put me up? I can sleep on the bare floor happily enough.'

'I'm sure she'd rather do more for you than that,' Sigrid laughed softly, patting him on the arm. 'But are you sure? You don't think Ubbi, if he thinks it through, might realise that someone roused Svanhild's suspicions, and try to flee?'

Ketil was growing tired of the whole business, a niggling feeling in his mind that they would never sort it all out, particularly the Hakon part.

'So what if he does?' he sighed. 'He'll have to live with it. I don't think he's a dangerous man, generally. If he fled, where would he go? He'd have no land, and he'd still run the risk of people seeing his child was deformed. Punishment enough, I'd say, whether he flees of his own accord or goes at Thorfinn's instruction. If he's there in the morning, we'll take him up to the Brough. If not, then I'll answer to Thorfinn.'

'There! A decision,' said Sigrid. She straightened and stretched her back. 'Let's see if Olvor is waiting up for me.'

They passed in silence through the little settlement, seeing the last two longhouses loom out of the dusky light. They could smell smoke light on the breeze: if Ubbi had not run, then presumably he and Thorgunna were sitting up with Svanhild's body. He would not abandon her unburied, surely, Ketil suddenly thought. He would be there in the morning.

He was considering the distance between the two longhouses, wondering if Ubbi knew that it was Sigrid who had warned Svanhild, if Ubbi would murder again, if Sigrid would really be safe down here, when he saw a shadow near Olvor's longhouse. He stopped, silent, and put out an arm to halt Sigrid. They drew into the shadow of a wall, crouching low. Who was it?

From this distance, it looked tall and strong. Asmund, using the privy? Not Ubbi: he was more slightly built. Neither of the women, certainly. He squinted, trying to make out any details in the poor light. The figure seemed to be wearing a cloak.

Ketil swore under his breath. It was Hakon.

Now what?

He thought quickly. Hakon was standing out between the longhouses, not hiding. Did he expect to be seen? If so, why? Well, there could be only one reason: he wanted Ketil to see him and attack him. Therefore he had the advantage somehow, if he wanted to be attacked. So Ketil should not attack him. But then where could they go? They would not be able to reach either longhouse from here, with Hakon standing between the two.

Sigrid had turned to watch him, waiting for instructions. He was fairly sure she had seen what was stopping them from going on. Could they go back and round? No: they would almost certainly trip over a cat, or set off a dog, or step on a straying hen. He had attacked enough settlements in his time to know the risks. To their right there was a little bit of shoreline, not much else, and no shelter. Ahead was the river, and the road to the south. Would Hakon be able to see the crossing from where he was? Ketil tried to remember, but he thought not. And if they crossed the burn, what then? Was there anywhere they could shelter for what remained of the night? He remembered rocks and heath, but nothing large enough to block the wind.

Then something brought to his mind Otto's miserable account of his hours at the settlement, hiding on Hakon's instructions. A curve in the riverbank, a curling shelter – Hakon knew about it, obviously, but he would not know that they had heard of it. He would not look for them there, particularly if he expected them simply to walk into him by the longhouses. And they could reach it if they went to the river crossing and worked their way upstream: their feet might be wet, but the rest of them would be out of the wind and warm. He nudged Sigrid, and murmured,

'Follow me close.'

It seemed to take an age to reach the burn. For a little of the way, Olvor's longhouse would block them from Hakon's sight, but after that for a few tens of paces they would be exposed. They kept low and moved very slowly, their pale faces averted, trying to hide anything else that was light-coloured. When they were sure they were out of sight again, down by the river, they sagged against the wall that had sheltered them, trying not to breathe out as heavily as they wanted to. For a moment Ketil was half-tempted to stay there – Hakon could not stand outside the longhouses forever, waiting for them – but there was nowhere that the wind would not catch them, and Hakon had only to walk a few paces forward and they would be in his line of sight, even if the light was still poor. They took a moment and then he nudged Sigrid again, leading the way up by the edge of the river. It was not more than a burn, really, and the banks quickly began to rise from the crossing place and curl up over the water, but the riverbed was wider now than the stream itself, in this unusually dry weather. They crouched low, Sigrid holding her skirts as clear of the water as she could, and in a few minutes they had reached what Ketil was sure was Otto's hiding place, a half-cave scooped sideways by old floodwaters at the curve of the river, but now dry and sandy, with a jutting-out edge that made a token roof over their heads. Anyone standing above them – carefully, for the roof would bear little weight – would see them, but from a distance they were well hidden. It was easy to see how Otto could have spent a few anxious hours in this spot and not been found.

Ketil turned and sat down, feet braced on the sandy slope, gesturing to Sigrid to sit beside him. He held up his hand for her to keep silent, and listened for a long moment, but he could hear no movement behind them, above the soft murmur of the stream.

'All right,' he said, 'let's not say too much or too loudly.'

'It was Hakon, wasn't it?' she demanded. He nodded.

'Waiting for us, I think.'

'How long should we stay here?'

'Till light. Comfortable?'

'I suppose.' She made a fuss of wrapping her cloak around her shoulders and huddling into it. Ketil was already at his ease, his sword angled to be accessible, knife to hand.

'Sleep if you want,' he said. 'I'll watch.'

'You'll nod off,' she grumbled, rearranging her headcloth to support her neck. But in a few minutes, she herself was asleep, slumping rounded into the hollow of the bank. He smiled, and looked up at the stars, picking them out of the still-light sky as best he could, naming their arrangements as old friends.

His mind drifted to other times and places where he had watched the stars like this, by winter or by summer. And Hakon's farm came to mind, as it had so often in recent days ... standing in the clearing among the trees, staring up at the black sky sprinkled with stars, waiting for Mara to meet him. It must only have happened a few times and yet it felt to him as if he had waited for her there on countless nights, a thing of happy custom, the memory of that anticipation still a delight even beyond the shadow of all that had happened since. If it had been her there with him, instead of Sigrid – well, what? He considered. Honestly, he didn't know. He realised he had barely known Mara, knew better the image of her perfection he had lived with in all the years between. As for Sigrid: that was a different matter altogether. They might have lost track of each other as children, but he felt he knew her, sometimes far too well. He glanced at her, curled up beside him, sleep wiping that determined grumpiness from her face to leave it calmer than he had seen it for a long time. Or perhaps it was just the dim light.

The light was already brightening, though. As he watched, the stars grew even more difficult to discern. Soon people would be up and about, tending to animals, taking their boats out for fish. Hakon would have to make his business clear, or leave. And if he decided to attack Ketil, there would be witnesses.

Ketil stretched his legs, and poked Sigrid's shoulder.

'I'm awake,' she grunted. 'Shove off.'

'Dawn,' he said, keeping his voice low still. 'Time to shift.' He acknowledged the other tension that had kept him awake all night. 'Time to go and see Ubbi.'

She shook out her cloak and opened her eyes wide enough to glare at him, then led the way, still crouching, back down the stream to the crossing point. There they stood straight and took stock in the sharp morning breeze.

'I don't see your friend Hakon,' said Sigrid, 'and I'm not hanging around here forever. Olvor has a very well built privy, and I intend to make use of it.'

'Just a moment longer ... All right, but I'm going first. I mean I'm walking ahead of you,' he added quickly, seeing her scowl. He kept his hand on his knife, not wanting to draw his sword here. He gave the longhouses a close scrutiny, then sent Sigrid round the lower end of Olvor's, telling her to make plenty of noise. If Hakon were round the back, he would most likely come round the upper end of the longhouse to avoid her, and then Ketil would see him.

But what, he thought to himself suddenly as Sigrid marched off to find the privy, what if Hakon thinks it's a good idea to do something to Sigrid? Your pretty little widow woman, he had called her. If he could kill Lambi, how much more could he harm Sigrid? He watched closely till she was out of sight, then ran, checking behind every obstacle as he went, across the infields and around the longhouse, just in time to see Sigrid's skirts catch the wind as she closed the privy door. Clear.

He glanced up along the back of Ubbi's longhouse, and more cautiously advanced to see if Hakon was hiding himself near it. But he found no trace of the man. Had they spent the night in hiding for nothing? Despite himself, he grinned. His men would approve: his caution was why they were all still alive.

He strolled back to the other longhouse and waited a discreet distance from the privy until Sigrid was ready, then went with her to Olvor's door. To his relief, Olvor and Asmund were both unharmed, too, and though Asmund already wanted another conversation about boats, he had to explain that they were there on Thorfinn's business. Sigrid only wanted to reassure Olvor that she was alive, and to wash her face and hands, before they faced what they had to do. And there was still a chance that Hakon was in Ubbi's longhouse, or had done his damage there. What would they find? At the thought of the possibilities, Ketil's heart skipped, and not with joy.

The whole thing felt unreal, the way it sometimes does when you spend the night in an unexpected place, he thought to himself. He half-listened to Sigrid's talk with Olvor, and splashed water over his face and scalp, rubbing his hands as if they needed life rubbed into them. They were going to talk to the man they thought had killed Steinar, at last, yet he felt no great sense of urgency. They had avoided Hakon, yet he felt no sense of relief. If nothing else, Hakon was still around, waiting, somewhere, even if not here.

'Ready?' Sigrid asked.

'Yes, I – yes.'

The door was opening as they approached Ubbi's longhouse, and as soon as Freya saw them she shoved herself outside, barking happily. Thorgunna, pale face blinking in the light, saw them and gave a half-smile of recognition.

'She's laid out, if you want to see her,' she said, pushing the door wide.

'We'd like to see the children, please, Thorgunna,' said Ketil.

'The children?' She jerked backwards, as if to slam the door shut again.

'Please,' Sigrid said. 'Both of them at once.'

Thorgunna stared at her for what seemed a very long time, propped between the door and the doorpost. Then, slowly, she leaned against the door and opened it fully, letting them pass her. Sigrid went in first, and Ketil, remembering all they thought had happened here, followed with his knife drawn discreetly by his side.

Sigrid went to the bed where the two children were still cocooned, awaiting their breakfast. Thorgunna came silently to join her husband. Ubbi, sitting by the fire, already dressed, greeted them with sorrow in his eyes. Svanhild's body lay where Steinar's had, wrapped with reverence and care. But Sigrid only glanced at it with a slight nod. The children were her focus.

Ketil, keeping an eye on Ubbi and Thorgunna, was only able to cast a glance or two at what Sigrid was doing. It was clear, though, that one child was bright and alert, already pushing himself up to see over the edge of the bed, while the other lay awkwardly, watching his companion. Sigrid picked up the lively one first, with encouraging words and gentle hands, and unfolded the blankets from around him, holding him up to check his limbs and his joints. He seemed a perfectly normal child, interested in what she was doing but not overly concerned. Sigrid sat him back in the bed again, and turned to the other. As she lifted him, Thorgunna gave a little gasp, and Ketil saw Ubbi's arm slip around her waist, holding her close. He had done this for her. Both of them watched Sigrid's every move.

Sigrid settled the boy on her lap, and gave him a moment to grow used to her, smiling and playing delicately with his little nose. He smiled back, gurgling. Ketil, surprised at this new side to Sigrid, allowed himself a moment longer to watch, then turned back to Thorgunna and Ubbi. Their faces were appalled.

Sigrid slipped the linen cloth from the boy on her lap, holding him firmly with her other hand. Then she lifted him high so that Ketil could see.

One half of the boy's little body was as perfect as his cousin's. The other was withered, arm and leg half the size they should be, fingers and toes oddly formed. No priest who wanted to obey the church's law would have baptised this boy.

Carefully, Sigrid wrapped him again in his linen, and held him close.

TUTTUGU OK SEX

XXVI

KETIL DIDN'T EVEN look tired.

In all the tension of Thorfinn's hall, Sigrid found this quite annoying. He had been running around possibly even more than she had, and she felt like a bundle of sheep's wool torn off a bush, while he stood there looking all alert and relaxed at the same time, a hand on his sword, the other calm at his side, face expressionless. Sometimes she had to admit he had grown up quite well. She managed to drag her tired gaze away from him, and on to try to assess what was happening.

The tables and benches were untidy, and littered with crumbs. The women who had been tidying had been sent out abruptly, though a couple of the men had lingered to witness events and deal with anything Thorfinn required. Likewise the Abbot had stayed, Tosti by his side, to see how Thorfinn carried out such business in his earldom. Both the churchmen were intent, concentrating. There was no sign of Otto. In the centre of the hall the fire was still burning from breakfast, and the smell of fresh flatbreads was sweet in the air. Sigrid's stomach began to rumble, and she crossed her hands over it, pretending nothing had happened. Thorfinn ignored it, anyway. Now he *did* look tired: there were inky circles under his eyes, and his mouth was grim.

In front of him, observed by Ketil standing to one side, were Ubbi and Thorgunna.

Thorgunna's face was set, but her eyes glowed desperate. Ubbi was biting his lip. There were tracks of tears on his face – for his sister, perhaps, whose cold body they had left in the charge of a neighbour in their longhouse. Or for his own situation, for his child, for his broken world. To complete the family, as they now existed, the dog Freya sat directly behind them, patient as long as she could see where they were and be near them. Thorfinn's lapdog, lounging at his feet, did not regard Freya as any kind of threat, and Freya appeared not to have noticed the lapdog at all.

And the child was here too. Sigrid, perched on one of the benches, held him, lulled to sleep after his breakfast and the fresh air of the rapid walk up to the Brough. He seemed happy enough with Sigrid, to her surprise: she cradled his contorted form in her arms with ease. His cousin, who was not the issue here, had stayed with the same kindly neighbour. There was nothing to disturb the child's rest except for the beating of Sigrid's heart. The hall had been silent for some time.

Thorfinn made a frustrated sound between his teeth.

'Have you nothing more to say for yourselves?' he demanded.

'Nothing, my lord. I did not kill either Steinar Valison or my sister Svanhild,' said Ubbi. His voice trembled and he looked very young, not yet ready to live without Steinar or Svanhild to guide him.

'I swear to you he did not,' added Thorgunna, extremely white but steady. 'He did not leave his bed that early on the morning that Steinar was killed. And he was on the hill after the sheep when Svanhild died.'

'Have you anyone else who can confirm any of this?'

Thorgunna's lips twisted.

'There was no one else in bed with us, if that's what you mean, my lord.'

Thorfinn struck the side of his chair angrily, glaring at her. She flinched. He lifted his hand in half-apology.

'I think,' Sigrid foun herself saying, 'that Steinar had only realised there was something wrong with the child the night before. He took the boy from Ubbi when they werer leaving Asmund's longhouse. I saw his face – Ubbi must have seen it, too.'

Thorfinn scowled, nodded, and turned.

'Ketil?'

Ketil's gaze flicked so briefly to meet Sigrid's, then away.

'I have no proof, my lord. But the child is deformed, and Father Tosti was tricked into baptising him.'

'That's for the church and Father Tosti to sort out,' said Thorfinn, 'though I'm beginning to realise there's more than that wretch Otto who has passed by their rules.' For a moment his tone was bitter, and Sigrid remembered that he and Ingibjorg had had children die not long after birth, perhaps rejected for baptism. She looked across at the Abbot and Tosti. The Abbot had his hands folded in front of his face, as if in prayer, while Tosti, head lowered, murmured a translation. For a moment she wondered. Could God, who sent these children, really want them turned away by His church? Seeing the Abbot weeping over his son, seeing the devotion of Ubbi and Thorgunna to theirs, she could not see that God would love them any less. Could Steinar have condemned his nephew so easily?

'And there's the question of the dog, my lord,' Ketil had continued. 'The dog went everywhere with Steinar. And she barks at strangers on her land.'

Thorfinn regarded the dog with slightly more interest than he had shown for a little while.

'And did she bark?'

'I believe not, my lord.'

Thorfinn snorted.

'So his killer was not a stranger. Could it not have been some acquaintance in the neighbourhood? Not part of his family?'

Ketil's face remained expressionless, but his eyes glinted.

'The dog appears to be quite selective, my lord.'

'Ubbi did not leave his bed that morning until after Steinar was dead,' said Thorgunna, stubbornly. 'Anyone who says he did is a liar. That man,' she gestured to Ketil, 'has been in and out of our longhouse every minute since Steinar died, and if not him then his man Lambi, paying court to Svanhild before Steinar was even buried, pretending to be interested in us. I see now what he was up to: instead of looking for the real killer he was trying to find anything he could to pin the blame on us. We loved Steinar and Svanhild. They were our family,' she declared, her voice rising defiantly. 'Anything more ridiculous would be hard to find.'

Thorfinn regarded her for a moment.

'Ubbi,' he said at last, 'have you anything else to say?'

Ubbi was shivering, and there were fresh tears on his face.

'I'm sorry we tricked Father Tosti,' he said. 'But Svanhild knew all about it – I mean, we asked her, and she was so kind-hearted she agreed. And Steinar was away. I can't see how my son being – like that – has anything to do with my sister's death, or her husband's. My wife's right: we loved them both. The house is empty without them.'

'Ketil,' said Thorfinn, and gestured to him. Ketil stepped up to Thorfinn's seat, and the two men began a low-voiced conversation. Ubbi and Thorgunna exchange glances, and Sigrid could see that they were holding hands, fingers entwined tight around each other until it was impossible to work out whose fingers were whose. She felt an odd pang, and cuddled the child close on her lap.

Thorfinn was frowning now and Ketil had apparently fallen silent. Was Thorfinn angry with him? But Thorfinn was looking towards the door of the hall at the outline of a man just appearing there. Ketil turned too, and even as Sigrid turned to see where they were looking, she caught a glimpse of his eyes. They were the steel blue of ice.

'Ah, Hakon – where have you been?' Thorfinn called out.

Hakon moved up the hall towards them, his gaze lightly curious as he took in Ubbi, Thorgunna and the dog, and then Sigrid sitting with the child. He smiled.

'Oh, dear. Who has Ketil brought in for accusation this time? Is it the dog or the child he says wielded the axe?' He stood by the fire, pulling something dark from his pouch and flinging it into the flames.

Sigrid half-closed her eyes, silently begging Ketil not to react. Instead there was a flash of movement, a ring of metal, and in three long strides Ketil had Hakon pinned back against the fire, almost touching it.

'Ketil!' Thorfinn snapped, but for once Ketil paid no attention. Nor did Sigrid. Hakon had his back to her, and she thought she could smell his fine cloak begin to smoulder. Ketil must have smelled it too, for he tilted back just a little, and Hakon slid away and around to Sigrid's side of the fire. Ketil followed, and again trapped Hakon, this time with his back firmly against a table.

'Ketil, what is this about?' Thorfinn asked, but his voice was not insistent. If Sigrid didn't know better, she might have thought that Thorfinn wanted the two men to play out their argument and get it over with. She glanced down at the fire, and gasped.

She leaped to her feet, tucking the sleeping child over her hip, and found a pair of tongs to pull out from the flames the objects that Hakon had tossed in there.

'Look!' she said. 'Not you, Ketil. Arrow fletches. Remember, my lord?' she turned quickly to Thorfinn. 'The arrows in Lambi's back had the fletches broken off.'

'Are these the remains of your arrows, Hakon?' Thorfinn demanded. He rose from his seat to inspect them at closer quarters, leaving Ubbi and Thorgunna confused at the way their trial was now going.

'I suppose there's little point denying it,' said Hakon, with a shrug.

'Why?' Ketil asked him. 'Why kill Lambi?'

'Well, he was your man ... oh, poor Ketil!' Hakon exclaimed, all mock concern. 'Have I done it again? Were you all lovey dovey over Lambi, too?'

'Don't let him, Ketil!' Sigrid muttered, and Hakon, annoyingly, heard. He turned, despite Ketil's sword point at his throat, and gave her a grin.

'Maybe it's the little widow woman I should have dealt with,' he said. 'But I haven't had the chance - yet.'

'Hakon,' said Ketil, and Sigrid was pleased to hear ice, not fire, in his voice. 'You killed Lambi and you released Otto from his prison, helping him to escape before bringing him back. What were you doing?'

Hakon laughed.

'Isn't it obvious?' he asked.

'Not to me, it isn't,' growled Thorfinn, leaving the arrow fletches by the fire. 'Now get on with it. Explain.'

'I shall if young Ketil here takes his sword off my throat. It's not conducive to good conversation.'

'Back, Ketil,' said Thorfinn, '- by the width of your little finger.'

Ketil bit back a smile, Sigrid could see, and brought his

sword a fraction backwards. Hakon grinned.

'So much better,' he said.

'Well?'

'I'm just thinking where to start. Many years ago, when Ketil was a very young lad under my command, I took pity upon the miserable orphan and invited him to join my family on my farm for Christmas. There he abused my hospitality by making himself free with my slave girl.'

'Is this the case, Ketil?' asked Thorfinn.

'It's a matter of perspective, my lord. His on one side, mine and the slave girl's – her name was Mara – on the other.'

Thorfinn nodded.

'Now, I was very fond of this slave girl,' Hakon went on, confident, 'but she broke her leg and so she was of no further use to me, so I disposed of her as it was my right to do. And Ketil has held a really quite irrational hatred for me ever since.'

Thorfinn looked at Ketil.

'He murdered her, my lord, purely because she loved me. Or because I loved her. It irritated him.'

'Still he was, as he says, within his rights.'

'He was not within his rights when he shot Lambi.'

'That much is true.' Thorfinn turned to walk back to his chair. Hakon leaned forward, as close to Ketil as he could go, and spoke. Sigrid strained to hear: Hakon's voice was not its usual light tone, but harsh and low.

'*I loved her, Ketil.* And she was mine. You had no rights in her, no rights at all.'

At that there was a metallic sound, and suddenly Hakon had his own sword in his hand and tried to swipe Ketil's blade away, pushing Ketil back towards the fire. Ketil staggered a little and righted himself, and in that moment Hakon made his attack.

Round the fire they fought, striking blow for blow, two good swordsmen. And Ketil was good, Sigrid saw: she had often teased him about his abilities, but she could see now just how skilled he was. Ubbi shielded Thorgunna in the corner, the dog Freya tight at their feet, the Abbot and Tosti kept low behind their table, and Sigrid backed away too, sheltering the child she was carrying behind Thorfinn's chair. Thorfinn himself sat, watching intently, just as Sigrid thought. He was going to let them finish it.

'There's very little point in even trying, Ketil,' Hakon called out. 'I taught you everything you know! What hope do you have of beating me?'

'What happens if you win, though?' Ketil asked. 'Do you think my lord Thorfinn will treat you more kindly if you've defeated one of his men first?'

Hakon laughed, and managed to throw in a swift bow in Thorfinn's direction before driving forward, pushing Ketil backwards towards the fire. Sigrid held her breath.

'Who's going to miss Lambi, anyway? A thief, a lazy lump of no value to anyone.'

'But my man, nevertheless.' Ketil shoved Hakon back towards the open door.

'You always did take on too much responsibility for your men. What credit was he to you? Or was he a devout Christian, so you had to look after him?' Hakon taunted him. That one would not go down well with Thorfinn, though, Sigrid thought. A misstep on Hakon's part.

They were fighting across the doorway now, the light outside making shadows of them for those watching. It would not be the first swordfight Thorfinn's hall had seen, of course. A wary man would hear the clatter of swords and hesitate before stepping inside.

Hakon was backing now, giving ground, and for a moment Sigrid allowed herself to hope that Ketil might be on the point of winning. Then she saw Hakon's face, eyes bright – too bright - and knew it for a tactic. She prayed Ketil would see it, too, but Ketil drove on, pushing Hakon backwards towards the tables on that side of the hall. Had he decided to try to use it against Hakon? If Hakon took three steps more, he would be pinned against the table. One step ... the blades still crashed with all their vigour. Two steps ... please, Sigrid thought, prayed. Please keep Ketil safe. Three steps ... Hakon stepped backwards, twisted like an eel, and suddenly Ketil was lying backwards against the table. Hakon raised his sword arm and brought it down at a strange angle, but straight into Ketil's stomach. Sigrid trapped a scream in her mouth, as Hakon nodded, cackling and breathless, to Thorfinn, and leapt for the door. Somehow Sigrid caught the look on his face before he vanished: he's insane, she thought. Then Ketil sagged on to the floor, without a sound.

'Skafti! After him, you two. Bring him back, bound.' Thorfinn's voice rang out, as Sigrid flung the child she was carrying back into Thorgunna's arms and ran to Ketil. As she reached him, he took a shuddering breath.

'Winded,' he gasped. 'S'all.'

'Oh, heavens, I thought he'd stabbed you!' Sigrid sat back, embarrassed, as Ketil struggled to a sitting position. Her throat hurt as if she held back tears. She shook her head, and found Tosti was behind her.

'No need for any final prayers, then? Just yet?' he asked, but there was relief in his smile. Ketil shook his head briefly. His hand still clutched his sword, and he looked at it as if wondering why it was there. Then Tosti scrambled to his feet, and Sigrid looked up to find Thorfinn, fists on hips, staring down at them.

'You've made a bad enemy there, Ketil.'

'I know, my lord,' Ketil wheezed, but grabbed the side of the table and managed to stand.

'He fought to humiliate, not to win. Well, we'll not have him back here, anyway, not after I've spoken to him. Exile for murder – though in his case it'll just mean Norway and his farm, I suppose. He won't be there on my behalf, and I'll make sure the King knows it.'

Ketil nodded. He opened his mouth to reply, but at that moment there came a cry from the back doorway.

'Father!' Asgerdr, Thorfinn's daughter appeared, her face wide with alarm. 'Definitely soon now! We need help!'

'What?' demanded Thorfinn, but at their two ends of the hall Thorgunna and Sigrid both knew. Thorgunna passed their child to Ubbi as Sigrid rose from the floor beside Ketil, and the two women hurried to the back door, and out and across the flagged yard between the hall and Thorfinn's longhouse. Inside, Ingibjorg was near her time.

Not as near, though, as Ingibjorg and everyone around her might have liked. The women in the longhouse were experienced – even Asgerdr had already seen a few births though she was not a mother herself – but none of them could speed this baby's entry into the world. Proper labour had certainly begun, but Thorfinn's child was not going to rush into anything.

From urgency, the atmosphere in the longhouse lapsed into something else, a place where time was different from outside the doors. It was measured in contractions, in heartbeats, in boiling pots and cooling cloths, in periods of rest and moments of intensity and hope. Ingibjorg even slept a little, her long sheep face pink with fatigue, while the women around her tidied and then slumped with their heads in their hands, or on one another's shoulders. Outside the day dwindled to twilight, and as the first stars became visible the most learned woman amongst them, feeling Ingibjorg's stomach delicately, announced the news that there was more than one baby in there, debating precedence. Ingibjorg's eyes widened in shock and alarm. Sometimes twins were both born alive, but more usually at least one died. The women around exchanged glances, no doubt reliving memories, but as another contraction seized Ingibjorg they set to work again with determined cheeriness, trying their best to take the bite from this time of double trial.

And in the end it worked.

As dawn distinguished itself tentatively from the bright night, the first child slipped at last into the air, and drawing breath howled. A boy, with the cord cut he was swiftly passed into linen cloths and warmth and soothing arms, and Ingibjorg concentrated on the next, final surge. And once again the miracle happened: new lungs filled with life and bawled it out again, and Asgerdr, tears streaming down her exhausted face, ran to tell her father that he had not one, but two, perfectly formed sons, and that there was nothing wrong with their voices, at least.

Exchanging grins, like all the other women in the room, Sigrid and Thorgunna helped to tidy up for the first visit of the father, and made sure Ingibjorg was arranged to her satisfaction, hair combed and shift fresh, for her husband to admire. Thorfinn was not long in coming, striding across from the hall with a face full of anxiety, as if Asgerdr might be hiding the horrible truth from him. When he saw the boys, though, he knelt by his wife's bed and kissed her, touching both the children in delight. It was enough for Sigrid. She made her way to the door, and outside.

The air was like a bucket of water in the face after the heat of the longhouse. Sigrid leaned back against the doorpost, breathing it in, strangely content but exhausted. From inside the longhouse came chatter and laughter, and Thorfinn's low voice murmuring his satisfaction. At a movement near her feet she glanced down. Freya the dog had been lying against the longhouse wall, waiting, and now had raised her head to listen. There were footsteps behind Sigrid, and she turned to see Thorgunna, a tired smile on her face, approach the door. The dog scrambled to her feet and went at once to nose Thorgunna's hand, asking for her ears to be fondled, panting delight at Thorgunna's return. Thorgunna crouched to greet her. And Sigrid, looking down at them, knew at last who had murdered Steinar.

TUTTUGU OK SJAU

XXVII

'IT HAD TO be Thorgunna, not Ubbi,' Sigrid explained. She was speaking quite slowly and carefully. Ketil had already heard her conclusion, but Thorfinn had a dazed look on his face and Ketil was still not sure that the information was going in.

'A woman?' Thorfinn said, puzzled. 'With an axe?'

'Yes. You see, Thorgunna was really the only one that the dog Freya trusted enough not to bark at her, particularly when she attacked the dog's master. Freya was upset, but she still didn't bark. Thorgunna is the only one who could have stopped her barking.'

'Well ...' said Thorfinn. They waited. Ketil, standing very straight, contemplated the pain in his stomach. It ached, but he was not too worried. He had had worse: it was just infuriating. Skafti and his friend, the two men who had tracked Otto to the Toun o' Firth, had not yet returned with or without Hakon, and the longer they were gone the more Ketil was convinced that Hakon had escaped for good.

'And the thing is,' said Sigrid, persistent, 'she really was the only person around when Svanhild was killed. She says she went off to the river with the dog, but the children were very settled there in the sun. It would have been awkward to pack them both up and take them down the river just for a few minutes, just because the dog was restless. Going into the house and killing Svanhild wouldn't have taken so long. She probably left Freya to guard the babies, and moved fast.'

Thorfinn blinked at her. Behind Ketil he heard the ebbing murmur of Tosti's translation to the Abbot. Thorfinn stirred on his chair.

'Where are they?'

Ketil cleared his throat.

'They're waiting outside. They've given their word not to run – and anyway, Asgerdr is looking after their son.' He nodded to the back of the hall, where Thorfinn's daughter held the uneasy child on her lap. She had not wanted the job, but all the other women were cooing over Thorfinn's new sons, and Ketil had somehow persuaded her, at Sigrid's suggestion.

Thorfinn glanced round at them, a flash of tenderness in his eyes. Then he seemed to shake himself.

'They said that Svanhild knew about the deception,' he said, his voice gruff. 'Why did she kill her?'

'Oh,' said Sigrid, 'because Svanhild realised that she had killed Steinar. That it hadn't been a stranger at all, but someone under her own roof.'

Thorfinn nodded, and drummed his fingers on the table in front of him, staring off into the distance. Ketil knew that look: Thorfinn was trying to decide what to do with them. Deception and murder, double murder. Exile was the only possible sentence. And what would that do to them? For Hakon, who farmed but whose livelihood was in his sword and his service, exile was bad enough. But Ubbi was a farmer: his life was here. Would he stay and let Thorgunna go alone, off into the world with only their child for company? Surely not. They were too close.

'Bring them in,' said Thorfinn suddenly. Ketil met Sigrid's eyes, and went to the door. Outside, Thorgunna and Ubbi were locked together in a tight embrace, as if they were saying their farewells already. Freya the dog, as ever, stood by them. Ketil coughed gently, and they broke apart, but kept hold of each other's hand. Silent, they exchanged another long look, then preceded him into the hall.

Head high, Thorgunna led her husband up to face Thorfinn.

'Thorgunna, you admit to the murder of your brother-in-law Steinar, and of your sister-in-law Svanhild?'

'I do, my lord.' Her voice was clear. 'I'm not proud of what I've done – and I told you the truth, my lord, I loved them both. But I loved my son more.'

Thorfinn sighed.

'I have no choice but to send you into exile, Thorgunna.' But he broke off, as Tosti leapt to his feet, followed closely by Abbot Konrad.

'My lord! My lord, forgive me, but my lord Abbot has a suggestion which he would place humbly before you at this juncture.'

Thorfinn sighed again.

'All right,' he said, 'but try to keep it short, eh?'

Tosti nodded quickly.

'My lord, my lord Abbot begs leave to take this family back with him to Colonia.'

'What, all of them? Man, wife, and child?'

'And dog, he says,' said Tosti, with a smile.

'Why?'

Tosti cleared his throat.

'My lord Abbot says that he knows well that this woman has sinned grievously against her family, and has sinned against the law of the Church. But he can see too that she had reasons for what she did, and that she did it for the sake of her child. He says that if it will serve my lord Thorfinn's purpose he proposes to give the man Ubbi a livelihood of some kind in Colonia and to see to it that the woman serves a penance for all she has done, but then that being done she and her family may live in peace there, with their child.'

Thorfinn frowned, staring at the Abbot as if to determine whether or not the man was serious. But Ketil could see the Abbot's reasoning – or at least how his mind was working. Apart from baptism, who knew what else he himself had done and served penance for, to protect his own deformed son?

The Abbot kept his face expressionless, waiting for Thorfinn's decision. Thorgunna and Ubbi, shocked to find help offered from such an unexpected quarter, stood close together, eyes flicking between the Abbot and Thorfinn. Ketil glanced at Sigrid. Lips parted, she seemed to be holding her breath, eyes fixed on Thorfinn.

It seemed to take him an age to speak.

'My lord Abbot has offered a tempting solution,' he said at last. 'Do you understand what is suggested?' He looked at Thorgunna and Ubbi.

'That we are to be exiled,' said Ubbi slowly, 'but that there will be a kind of welcome for us in Colonia. Where Steinar liked it so much.'

'True,' said Thorfinn. 'It is, I think, a good offer. As I must exile you anyway, is this an offer you wish to accept?'

Thorgunna and Ubbi looked at each other. They would have little idea what would be there for them in Colonia, but it was likely to be better than starting without friends, in a land completely strange. Ubbi looked at the Abbot, then at Thorfinn, and nodded, still wary. But he did not know about Otto.

'Thank you, my lord,' said Thorgunna. The Abbot was speaking, too, and after a moment Tosti translated.

'My lord Abbot says he wishes to leave for Colonia at the beginning of next week. His work here has been made difficult through no fault of my lord Thorfinn, and he wishes to return to his home to recuperate his strength.'

Thorfinn looked at the Abbot.

'After the baptisms?' he said. Tosti smiled.

'Yes, my lord Abbot will, as agreed, baptise my lord Thorfinn's sons on Sunday. But the man Ubbi and his family must be ready to leave the next day.'

Ubbi nodded again, this time with more enthusiasm.

'My lord,' he said to Thorfinn, 'there is much to prepare. May we take our child and go?'

'Yes, yes,' said Thorfinn, his mind already back on his sons, if it had ever left them. 'Go and prepare.'

Thorgunna hurried to reclaim her boy from Asgerdr, and the couple, with their dog, left the hall. Thorfinn bowed to the Abbot.

'My lord Abbot is most gracious,' he said, then turned as his men Skafti and his companion arrived breathless at the door. 'Can a man have no peace with his wife and children?' he snapped.

'We lost him, my lord,' Skafti announced.

'You lost Hakon?' Ketil could not help it. Skafti cast him an apologetic look.

'Aye, he took ship at the harbour. A kvarr heading for Lervik.'

'Not far enough,' Ketil muttered. Sigrid caught his eye.

'We'll find him,' said Thorfinn, standing and clapping

Ketil on the shoulder. 'In the mean time, I think it best that I don't send you back to Trondheim. I have no powers there to stop him or help you.'

'My lord.' It was good of Thorfinn, but he should not need such protection. And Trondheim was as close to a home as he had, wasn't it?

'For now,' Thorfinn went on, 'I want you back down south to finish the job in Hwitebi.'

'Very good, my lord.' That was a relief. He needed to get back to his men, see how they were doing, tell them about Lambi. He did not think that they would weep for him.

'And then,' said Thorfinn, 'I want you back here.'

'Back to Orkney?' Ketil asked. He would have expected to feel dismay. Where was it?

'Yes, this is where I am now. You should be, too. Bring your men. There will be room.' Thorfinn nodded sharply, and at last headed off where he wanted to go, back to his longhouse and his new children. Asgerdr cast Ketil a look he could not interpret, and followed her father.

Sigrid was watching.

'Thorfinn has plans for you, by the look of it!' she said lightly.

'Plans?' he asked, not sure what he was asking.

'Asgerdr. Now he has sons, he needs to sort out a husband for that little madam. Watch out, Ketil!' She laughed, but he was not sure that she was entirely amused. 'You'll stay until after the baptisms?'

'I think I'll have to,' he said.

'Poor Ketil! I know how much you dislike Orkney. Maybe he'll grant you some land in Caithness, when you marry.'

'I don't know,' he said, rallying from the surprise of Thorfinn's instructions. 'I think I'm growing used to this place, at least when the sun shines. It's the people I find hard to take.'

She jabbed him in the ribs, and walked away, laughing.

Outlandish words in *A Wolf at the Gate*:

Aback of	reluctant to
Birl	spin
Bygg	barley, the kind known in Orkney as bere
Claik	gossip
Greet	cry
Hamnavoe	Stromness
Heithabyr	Hedeby
Hwitebi	Whitby
Kirkuvagr	Kirkwall
Kvarr	broad merchant vessel
Lervig	Lerwick
Newsan	gossipy
Noust	boat shelter
Rackvig	Rackwick
Smero	Tormentil (potentilla erecta)
Toun o'Firth	Finnstown – yes, I know this sounds more Scots than Viking, but it is an older name than Finnstown, anyway!

About the Author

LEXIE CONYNGHAM IS a historian living in the shadow of the Highlands. Her historical crime novels are born of a life amidst Scotland's old cities, ancient universities and hidden-away aristocratic estates, but she has written since the day she found out that people were allowed to do such a thing. Beyond teaching and research, her days are spent with wool, wild allotments and a wee bit of whisky.

We hope you've enjoyed this instalment. Reviews are important to authors, so it would be lovely if you could post a review where you bought it!

Visit our website at www.lexieconyngham.co.uk. There are several free Murray of Letho short stories, Murray's World Tour of Edinburgh, and the chance to follow Lexie Conyngham's meandering thoughts on writing, gardening and knitting, at www.murrayofletho.blogspot.co.uk. You can also follow Lexie, should such a thing appeal, on Facebook, Pinterest or Instagram.

Finally! If you'd like to be kept up to date with Lexie and her writing, please join our mailing list and claim your free copy of three novellas here:

Murray of Letho

WE FIRST MEET Charles Murray when he's a student at St. Andrews University in Fife in 1802, resisting his father's attempts to force him home to the family estate to learn how it's run. Pushed into involvement in the investigation of a professor's death, he solves his first murder before taking up a post as tutor to Lord Scoggie. This series takes us around Georgian Scotland as well as India, Italy and Norway (so far!), in the company of Murray, his manservant Robbins, his father's old friend Blair, the enigmatic Mary, and other members of his occasionally shambolic household.

Death in a Scarlet Gown

The Status of Murder (a novella)

Knowledge of Sins Past

Service of the Heir: An Edinburgh Murder

An Abandoned Woman

Fellowship with Demons

The Tender Herb: A Murder in Mughal India

Death of an Officer's Lady

Out of a Dark Reflection

A Dark Night at Midsummer (a novella)

Slow Death by Quicksilver

Thicker than Water

A Deficit of Bones

The Dead Chase

Shroud for a Sinner

Hippolyta Napier

HIPPOLYTA NAPIER IS only nineteen when she arrives in Ballater, on Deeside, in 1829, the new wife of the local doctor. Blessed with a love of animals, a talent for painting, a helpless instinct for hospitality, and insatiable curiosity, Hippolyta finds her feet in her new home and role in society, making friends and enemies as she goes. Ballater may be small but it attracts great numbers of visitors, so the issues of the time, politics, slavery, medical advances, all affect the locals. Hippolyta, despite her loving husband and their friend Durris, the sheriff's officer, manages to involve herself in all kinds of dangerous adventures in her efforts to solve every mystery that presents itself.

A Knife in Darkness

Death of a False Physician

A Murderous Game

The Thankless Child

A Lochgorm Lament

The Corrupted Blood

A Day for Death

Orkneyinga Murders

ORKNEY, C.1050 A.D.: THORFINN Sigurdarson, Earl of Orkney, rules from the Brough of Birsay on the western edges of these islands. Ketil Gunnarson is his man, representing his interests in any part of his extended realm. When Sigrid, a childhood friend of Ketil's, finds a dead man on her land, Ketil, despite his distrust of islands, is commissioned to investigate. Sigrid, though she has quite enough to do, decides he cannot manage on his own, and insists on helping – which Ketil might or might not appreciate.

Tomb for an Eagle

A Wolf at the Gate

Dragon in the Snow

The Bear at Midnight

The Fate of the Sea Stag

Alec Cattanach

HITLER MAY HAVE declared war, but police work continues in Aberdeen. Detective Inspector Alec Cattanach, torn between his work in the city and his love of the countryside beyond, has to deal with new crimes and old, regardless of the bombs and the blackout.

A Vengeful Harvest

The Gowden Wifie

The Journals of Dr. Robert Wilson

After Waterloo, and his service with the Honourable East India Company, Dr. Robert Wilson decides to travel east. He is accompanied by his secretary, Gil Archibald, who has his own reasons for the journey. With neither able to tell the truth to the other, how will they cope when faced with murder?

The Business in Blandyce

LEXIE CONYNGHAM

Other books by Lexie Conyngham:

Windhorse Burning

'I'm not mad, for a start, and I'm about as far from violent as you can get.'
When Toby's mother, Tibet activist Susan Hepplewhite, dies, he is determined to honour her memory. He finds her diaries and decides to have them translated into English. But his mother had a secret, and she was not the only one: Toby's decision will lead to obsession and murder.

The War, The Bones, and Dr. Cowie

Far from the London Blitz, Marian Cowie is reluctantly resting in rural Aberdeenshire when a German 'plane crashes nearby. An airman goes missing, and old bones are revealed. Marian is sure she could solve the mystery if only the villagers would stop telling her useless stories – but then the crisis comes, and Marian finds the stories may have a use after all.

Jail Fever

It's the year 2000, and millennium paranoia is everywhere.
Eliot is a bad-tempered merchant with a shady past, feeling under the weather.
Catriona is an archaeologist at a student dig, when she finds something unexpected.
Tom is a microbiologist, investigating a new and terrible disease with a stigma.
Together, they and their knowledge could save thousands of lives – but someone does not want them to …

The Slaughter of Leith Hall and The Contentious Business of Samuel Seabury

'See, Charlie, it might be near twenty years since Culloden, but there's plenty hard feelings still amongst the Jacobites, and no so far under the skin, ken?'
Charlie Rob has never thought of politics, nor strayed far from his Aberdeenshire birthplace. But when John Leith of Leith Hall takes him under his wing, his life changes completely. Soon he is far from home, dealing with conspiracy and murder, and lost in a desperate hunt for justice.

Thrawn Thoughts and Blithe Bits and Quite Useful in Minor Emergencies

Two collections of short stories, some featuring characters from the series, some not; some seen before, some not; some long, some very short. Find a whole new dimension to car theft, the life history of an unfortunate Victorian rebel, a problem with dragons and a problem with draugens, and what happens when you advertise that you've found somebody's leg.

Printed in Dunstable, United Kingdom